THE ENEMY WITHIN

THE ENEMY WITHIN

A Faith Clarke Mystery

Julie Bates

First published by Level Best Books/Historia 2025

This novel is entirely a work of fiction. The names, characters and incidents portrayed in it are the work of the author's imagination. Any resemblance to actual persons, living or dead, events or localities is entirely coincidental.

Julie Bates asserts the moral right to be identified as the author of this work.

Author Photo Credit: Julie Bates

First edition

ISBN: 979-8-89820-121-0

Cover art by Level Best Designs

This book was professionally typeset on Reedsy.
Find out more at reedsy.com

To my family. Nothing would get done without you.

Foreword

Ten patriots all in a row
Ten faithful followers, where did they go?

To wash his head, one arose
Slipped into a creek, and so he froze.

Nine officers walking without care
One caught a branch, now he's dancing on air.

Eight recruits marching straight from bed
One little misfire took off a man's head.

Seven camp followers nursing the sick,
Until a fine horse delivered a kick.

Six men at the ovens baking bread.
One played with fire, now he's dead

Five soldiers out on a drill
One found a rock useful to kill.

Four men drinking rum.
One had too much. Now he's numb.

Three young officers in their cloaks
One's scarf got caught, now he's choked.

Chapter One

Fresh snow covered the winter encampment of Washington's army. It provided an illusion of peace and serenity, belied by the shivering man unfortunate enough to draw sentry duty. Will McKay nodded at the man as he passed by. "Take care, Jonah, stay out of the wind." The man shivered as he made his way to his picket post. His bare black head frosted with snow as he walked out, gun on his shoulder. He had come up with a group of freedmen from the Rhode Island Colony. Valley Forge was many things, but it was not a land flowing with milk and honey. Washington had retreated here with his army to lick his wounds after a sound thrashing from the British.

McKay felt sorry for the poor devil. He had no coat and only a ragged blanket to shield him from the cold. No stockings covered his legs, but rags swathed them down to shoes that looked ready to disintegrate. Will had worn his jacket thin in places. The elbows had long since developed holes. At least he had boots. They stayed on his feet, even at night, lest someone slip away with them. The path between the rows of cabins, the soldiers lived in was rough and slippery, and not a little foul. McKay stuck to the middle, knowing only too well that there were patches of ice from where men had barely left their doorway to relieve themselves. It disgusted him, the lack of order or even basic sanitation. It was as if, in the wake of defeat, the Continental Army had become savages. Some nights, he wondered if they would survive.

The cabin he shared with five other men stood amid his brigade. Will tolerated the temperatures in his mid-row bunk, but no one was really comfortable in the cabins. They provided minimal protection from the elements. His recently gained sergeant's rank entitled him to sleep closer in, but Will knew he handled the cold better than some of the other men. Keeping his head under British threat at Brandywine earned him the promotion. There was that, and the man who had been sergeant before him had not survived the battle. McKay tried not to think about it. If he had learned nothing else, it was that life could end in an instant. It was a thought that did not go away and made him pray more than he ever had. Just as he was about to enter his cabin, an officer hailed him. McKay recognized him as being from one of the Pennsylvania regiments. He'd seen him around General Conway's encampment. He had no business over here where General Muhlenberg's men stayed.

"McKay! Report to the Lifeguards headquarters immediately!" Captain Lombard barked. He was too loud for the short proximity between them. Will bet he got teased for that high squeaky voice. He looked him up and down quietly, without moving. Soldiers from his unit had talked about him during card games played to pass the time. None of the comments had been flattering.

Lombard's uniform looked remarkably clean for a resident of the camp. Rumor had it he'd taken up with one of the camp women who took care of it for him. The staff sergeant under him claimed he had gotten his rank because of an influential family member. He'd also heard that he was a cocky little snot who knew little about how to be a soldier, even if he liked to issue orders. The enlisted men care little for him after the debacle at Germantown. They swore he had been among the first to turn tail and run when the British tried to outflank them. An angry Conway had demoted him and threatened to lash him for cowardice.

Will wondered why he came halfway across the parade grounds to find him. He suspected errand duty was another way to humiliate the man. He looked none too pleased.

"Who asked for me?" McKay's tone was wary. There had been more than a little jostling in the camp. He didn't put it past any of the state militia officers to trick a man from another unit. The only one everyone respected was Washington himself. There was no reason a Pennsylvania Captain was issuing orders to a Virginia sergeant.

Lombard shot him a narrow-eyed look. "I'm just delivering the message. It's your hide if you disobey an order." With that, he stomped off toward his unit's encampment. He cursed when his feet slipped in something nasty, causing him to scramble for his balance.

McKay tried not to smile at the other man's flailing. Once the captain recovered his footing and walked out of sight, McKay considered his choices before choosing the obvious one. It was not a long walk to the quarters of Washington's bodyguards, definitely less painful than a lashing. He turned and headed out toward the cabins, trying not to inhale when he passed a rotting horse's carcass on the way.

Throughout the camp, men worked at various tasks, trying to pass the time. Will McKay had made some good friends since he had enlisted in the Virginia Militia. They had all suffered from the lack of decent food, blankets, and arms while fighting a well-provisioned opponent. Together, they felt the pinch of not being paid. By his own count, it had been four months since he had last received his wages. Sometimes he wondered if the Continental Congress really wanted to win this war. They made brilliant speeches but did little to back up their words.

Crossing the wide meadow that made up the parade ground, he viewed the sweeping meadows that housed the encampment. Conditions had improved since he had marched in with his regiment a few months ago. Ahead of him lay the cabins designated quarters of Washington's personal lifeguard, not that they were any grander than any of the others. A short distance behind the cabins lay the Schuylkill River, winding its icy arm around the northern boundary of Valley Forge. Behind the farmhouse Washington rented were the cabins of the artificers who built and repaired the various items needed for war. To the west were the artillery and the redoubts that guarded the Inner Works of the camp.

The snow rose around his ankles, making him glad for his boots. Despite their wear, they had held together through the weary months of marching and skirmishing with the British. It had been months since Washington's army tasted victory. It was discouraging to both heart and soul. Some nights, he woke in a cold sweat, having dreamed that the enemy had overrun the encampment, bayoneting any unfortunate continental caught unaware.

Will's goal was to gain his personal freedom. He had agreed to serve in place of his mistress's son, and in return, she would cancel the remaining years of his indenture. It seemed like a good bargain, provided he survived. Some days, he worried he would join the fallen. When he had enlisted, he had not contemplated freezing, starving, and trying to work with men not used to obeying orders, much less fight as a unit.

Off in one of the frost-covered fields, a group of about a dozen men stood with their arms on their shoulders. As an officer barked a command, they fired into the woods. After the volley, they stopped to reload. A loud voice rang out, cursing in German.

Will grinned as he listened to the colorful language. Three months at sea with a group of Germans had taught him some rather unfortunate language. One of them had gotten an indenture only a stone's throw away from Will's print shop in Williamsburg. When Peter came to town, they would reconnect in a tavern. He wondered who the officer was. He had to be a recent arrival. Will had not seen him before or heard the resonant language.

Will hopped over a small stream, avoiding the smelly water. Sanitation was not a priority in the camp. The smells of human waste and dead animals permeated the camp. It had rained a few days ago. What had not frozen ran off in the low spots in camp. His eyes glanced uphill at the cabin designated for the sick and injured. He prayed he never had to go there. Sickness, and the vulnerability it caused, frightened him. Will never wanted to be helpless. Being unable to care for himself and his loved ones was the worst fate he could imagine. He would rather be dead.

Washington had hired some women in camp as nurses. While some were conscientious, others appeared more experienced in another profession. He preferred to treat his own injuries rather than go there. While he saw plenty of men carted up there, few had returned.

The lifeguard's cabins loomed ahead. Will picked up his steps, eager to get out of the cold. Mindful of his rank, he knocked and waited to be admitted. Being called out made him uneasy. Will made a point of keeping his head down and following orders, even if he considered some of them daft. More than a few had broken and run once the British turned the full force of their troops upon them. Will watched the debacle at Brandywine in horror. He was thankful General Greene, a man who knew how to keep his head in a fight, led his unit. It was in these battles he had seen the mettle of the commander of the Continental army. Washington had ridden back and forth to the various regiments during the disaster, taking command where needed.

After hearing a voice bidding him enter, Will slipped in. A group of men stood gathered around a table poring over a map. Voices spoke in both English and French as they discussed what they saw. In the back, a large fire roared, taking the edge off the cold. Will headed to the warmth of the fire. As he drew closer, an officer spun around, revealing the face of someone he knew well.

"Will McKay, it is good to see a familiar face, even in these circumstances." Jeremy Butler came around the table, a smile creasing his face. He enveloped the younger man in an enormous bear hug. Like Will, he was considerably thinner than the last time they had met. New lines creased his face, but his eyes were warm with greeting.

"I see you have moved up the ranks," Will observed, taking in the blue uniform and buff breeches. Jeremy Butler wore the insignia of a major. He could see the bars on his uniform and the ease with which Butler interacted with the other officers present.

Butler shrugged. "I'm an aide to Washington. Right now, I'm trying to figure out how to support our newest officer, Baron von Steuben. He has lots of energy and ideas and no English." Butler sighed. "My French is pretty rusty, but I get the gist of what he's saying. My childhood priest would cringe at what use I've put to his teachings."

Will smiled. "Is that the burly fellow cursing in German at the troops?

I hear he's been all over the camp inspecting every nook and cranny. It's doubtful that they know what *Arschloch* means, even if they've probably been called asses before."

Butler shot him a surprised look. "You know German?"

Will shrugged. "A bit. When I came to the colonies, I sailed with a group of them. I also worked with one at the print shop. Henrik had little English, so we spoke in his language. There are some who have come into the shop to place advertisements about their work. They're good folk, excellent artisans."

Jeremy Butler's eyes gleamed. "I may have a new position for you," Butler said. "Follow me." He led Will back out and down the hill toward the stone farmhouse where Washington had established his winter headquarters. "Baron von Steuben comes highly recommended. Only one of his staff has any fluency in English. Washington has been scouring his troops, looking for people who can speak to him. If his background is any indicator, he could be the salvation of the Continental Army. He's been using Hamilton and Laurens as translators, as well as his secretary, but he could use another man to help. Your bit of German should come in handy."

Will shrugged. "If you think so." He followed Butler, half listening to the broken French and German words being bellowed across the fields. Translating anatomically improbable acts was not how he had pictured serving in Washington's army, but if that was the job, so be it. It certainly was better than hanging about camp waiting for the next assignment. If boredom didn't kill him, loneliness might.

His nose picked up the scent of bread baking. What came out of the enormous earthen ovens was nothing like the huge yeasty loaves that he recalled longingly from home. The print shop's cook, Athena, turned basic ingredients into sumptuous feasts. What he wouldn't do for one of her meals. His stomach grumbled. Will liked the bakers well enough, but a steady diet of fire cakes did nothing to fill the emptiness in his belly.

Trees stood north and west of the building. Their long limbs reached upward as if appealing to heaven. The smaller branches looked like the skinny fingers of a starving man begging for food. Will shivered at the image his imagination concocted. He endeavored to focus his mind and eyes elsewhere.

Snow had drifted into piles that lay at the edges of the field surrounding the sturdy house. Within the fence, boot tracks obliterated the smooth whiteness into gray, partially frozen slush mixed with mud. Will followed Butler, watching his steps to avoid ice or kicked-up mud. A horse neighed in the stable, one of the few left in camp. There was little hay for them, so Washington had ordered all the Cavalry units away to where they could find food and forage.

Butler carefully scraped his boots before stepping onto the stoop. Will followed suit. "Lady Washington does not like mud tracked into her residence," he warned softly. "This may be an army camp, but our commander's lady expects good manners. Since she and her ladies have arrived, things have become far more civilized here."

Will had heard of her arrival a few weeks ago, but nothing in his duties brought him near to the farmhouse where Washington had made his winter quarters. Will knew better than to curse in front of a lady, although some women in camp displayed worse language than he had ever uttered. He did his best to avoid that area. While he was grateful that someone did laundry and other tasks, he didn't think either ladies or children belonged in an army camp. It was too dangerous, and there were not enough supplies for all those present.

The door opened smoothly, leading them into the entry. The interior hummed with activity. Voices came from either side of the narrow hall. Butler opened a door to the right, leading him into a hallway with a stairway on one end and a door at the other. One door remained wide open. Men leaned over tables, writing correspondence or poring over maps. The door to the other room was closed. People bustled back and forth, down the hall and up the stairs. Amid the congestion stood a petite woman of middle years, warmly dressed in a blue wool dress and exuding such an air of authority that Will knew who she was.

"Lady Washington," Jeremy Butler bowed before the small woman, one of the few people significantly shorter than him. "Allow me to introduce

Sergeant William McKay. I know him from my travels to Williamsburg. He is a printer by trade and a good and honorable man."

Will blinked. Butler had never described him like that before. Not being a complete idiot, he smiled and bowed to his general's lady. He kept his thoughts to himself.

Sharp blue eyes sized him up and down. "At least he's clean," she said drily. "Many of these men appear to be strangers to soap and water."

Butler rose in head. "These are rough times for us all, milady. The men are far from home and the care of their families. They struggle just to stay warm and find food. I'm sure no one means any disrespect."

Martha Washington nodded. "My husband works day and night to find more food and clothing for his men. The supply line needs repair." Her sharp gaze rested on Will McKay once more. "So you are a printer. What other skills do you have?"

"He speaks German," Butler added helpfully. "I thought he might be of some help to the General's new officer."

Lady Washington blinked. "Indeed. That would be useful. Very few people understand the Baron, and talking through his clerk is tiresome. Come with me." She turned and went to the next room off the hall, a path magically opening before her as aides stepped aside to make room.

Off to the side, her eyes caught a group of three officers in a corner of the room, caught in a game of dice. One had a bottle of rum that he drank from before passing it to another. "I trust you have no assignments that need completing." Her tone was chilly. The man who had drunk from the bottle straightened up. "We were taking a few moments of reprieve, Lady Washington," He said. "I'm sure the General-"

"I'm sure General Washington would expect his men to be following his orders, or those of your commanding officer," she said. "I assume you got the rum from the kitchen. Do not trouble my staff again. There is little enough food and drink without taking a bottle for your personal use."

The man's face flushed. "Yes, Lady Washington."

A man spoke from behind her. "Corporal Hazel, perhaps you and your friends need to check in with your regiment. I believe the 8th Massachusetts is preparing to drill. Why don't you join them?" The officer who had spoken glanced at Lady Washington. "I'm sorry you had to see this."

Lips tight, Martha Washington took the bottle with a look of distaste. "Our men should not be idling in my husband's command center, Lieutenant Commander Silver. See that it does not happen again."

Silver's face went pale. "Yes, my lady."

Lady Washington continued, "I need to speak with my husband. Where may I find him?"

"He is in his office. Follow me." Silver led her to a room with a closed door. Knocking firmly, he waited for an acknowledgement.

"Enter," a faintly raspy voice intoned. Its register was deep enough to identify the speaker as male. Lady Washington entered as soon as an aide opened the door for her.

Washington was busy, swiftly moving papers from a large table. The reason for his hurry was clear. A large puddle covered the center, saturating the books, maps, and correspondence on top. Butler and McKay rushed over to help him.

"Some fool put an ice block amid my papers," Washington fumed. He took a map with dripping edges and tossed it on a chair near the fire. His wife moved swiftly, removing her apron and using it to mop up the liquid before it spread further.

McKay lifted a stack of letters off the table, moving them out of the way to another table. As he picked them up, something clattered on the floor. Once he set General's correspondence on a dry space, his eyes swept the floor. Spotting an object in the corner, he reached for it, puzzled by what he saw. "What is this?" He asked, holding up a crude figure made of sticks, and bound in wool.

Butler looked at it. "It's dressed like a soldier. Where did you find it?"

"It fell off the desk." McKay didn't like it. The crudely carved face stared back at him with a crooked slash for a mouth. Sticks formed rough arms and legs, held together with bits of wool and cloth. A few strands of dark wool clung to the head.

"It looks sort of like a soldier," Silver noted. "The light-colored scraps look like a hunting shirt, and someone wrapped the dark gray around its legs like breeches." He pointed to the floor. "It's dripping wet." He idly scratched the back of his head as he looked down at the thing.

McKay looked down at the puddle. "So it is. It's got pieces of ice in it, too. I think someone froze it before bringing it in here. What do I do with it? "

Washington looked at it in disgust. "Put it in the fire. I have no use for it."

It smoked at first as fire burned away at the wood. The scent of wet wool emanated from the fireplace before the flames consumed the tiny object. McKay was glad it was gone. He had found the crude figure disturbing.

Washington straightened his back and brushed his coat before nodding to the others present. "I assume you have something to share with me."

Martha Washington proceeded forward to her husband, who towered over her. Taking his hand, she brought him to McKay. "I would like you to meet someone. This is Sergeant McKay, currently serving in the 1st Virginia Militia. Among his other talents, he speaks German."

Washington met Will's gaze. "How fluent are you?" The general's gaze made him shiver.

"I understand what's being said to me." Will didn't add he'd had no choice but to learn after being stuck for months in a hold where everyone else spoke it. That he'd been able to keep using what he had learned had been a blessing.

"Let's see how you do," Washington gestured to a man behind him. A stocky man in a red coat with bright brass buttons stepped forward. "This is Baron von Steuben of Prussia, more recently from France. Dr. Franklin sent him over, highly recommended to us if we can overcome the language barrier."

Will stared at the man. "Grüße. Willkommen in den amerikanischen Kolonien."

The Baron froze before staring at Will before asking, „Sprechen Sie Deutsch?"

„Ja, ich spreche etwas Deutsch." Will acknowledged.

The Baron turned to one of the other men in the room, speaking in rapid French. „J'ai besoin de cet homme dans mon équipe immédiatement, s'il vous plaît."

Butler whispered in his ear. "Congratulations, you've just become a staff officer for von Steuben."

Will stared at him. "I'm only a sergeant."

Washington replied. "I will inform General Muhlenberg of your transfer from his militia. I will put in the paperwork to advance your rank to captain, which will line up with your new position. Go pack. You will now bunk with Baron von Steuben and his staff.'

Will stared at Washington, dazed. He watched him speak to the others gathered around the table. "I've assigned Baron von Steuben with training officers who can then train our troops in the techniques they need to become a successful army. Lieutenant Colonel Laurens and Captain McKay will aid him in translating his commands to the men." He looked over at them. "You, along with Lieutenant Colonel Hamilton, will also help him develop a training manual we will use to drill all the men. Divine providence has brought him to us; let us make use of his talents to make an army."

The men broke out in applause. Off to the side, Laurens spoke softly to Von Steuben, translating Washington's words. Once he was done, the sturdy German walked to Washington and bowed his head in respect. "Merci Je suis honoré de votre confiance. Je n'écouterai pas dans cette tâche."

Laurens translated. "He gives his thanks and feels honored by your trust. He will not fail you."

Washington offered a brief smile and nodded at the baron. "May you enjoy outstanding success in this country."

Will's head was spinning from all that was happening around him. He had gone from infantryman to junior officer and aide to camp to a foreign officer in the blink of an eye. He wondered what would happen next. Butler tapped him on the shoulder and gestured toward the door.

"Come with me. Before you pack up, there is someone else you need to meet."

Lieutenant Colonel Silver slapped Will on the back. "Welcome to the officer corps. It's good to have another man to help." He turned to a group of other young men. "Allow me to introduce you to Washington's other aides de camp, John Laurens and Alexander Hamilton."

Will nodded. "I'm Will McKay."

He added, "I'm afraid Lafayette is not with us at present. He's busy invading Canada."

Will's eyes goggled. "We're invading Canada?"

Silver's eyes crinkled. "The irony doesn't escape me either. We can't feed our people. The British have taken Philadelphia, and now our Congress has approved a plan by General Gates to invade Canada. We don't have enough arms here. What are they using to fight the enemy there–sticks?" He took a deep breath. "It's too early to discuss politics. Forgive my rudeness. I haven't even properly introduced myself." The man bowed, "Jonathan Silver, but most everyone calls me Jack." He grinned over at the table of men. "You just missed another one of our many meetings. I'm sure you cannot wait to hear about our dearth of supplies and weaponry." He nodded over at the table. "Some of our esteemed physicians came by to request supplies for the sick and injured." His expression changed. "I wish we could do more for those poor devils. Being ill or injured far from loved ones is a terrible situation. To feel oneself wasting away from disease would be the worst possible fate."

Will nodded. He also feared illness more than a quick death in battle.

Butler tugged his arm. "You will have plenty of time to learn your new position. I doubt we will see any action until spring if we can hang on that long."

Will raised an eyebrow. He needed time to learn about his new position.

The Baron slapped him on the back as he turned to go, before returning to the table. "Doesn't he need my help?"

"One of his staff speaks English," Butler pointed to a handsome young man who looked barely old enough to shave. He heard Butler in his ear. "Most of his staff are handsome men. Get used to it."

Will looked at his friend in surprise. "Are you implying something?"

Butler shrugged. "I don't inquire into anyone's personal habits. We've a war to win, and I'm happy to work with anyone willing to aid our cause." He paused briefly. "That said, there are rumors about his relationship with his secretary."

Will raised his eyebrows.

"du Ponceau." Butler hissed. "The young pretty one."

Will turned to look before Butler pushed him down the hall toward the stairs. "Don't be so obvious, McKay. It's far better not to ask questions you might regret later."

Will followed the other man up to the second story, the murmur of voices from below becoming softer as they continued. "Is it always like this?" He inquired.

Butler half turned. "You mean like a beehive preparing to swarm? Yes. There are constant discussions going on, from planning strategy to planning forays into the countryside in search of more provisions for our people. There is always something to attend to. Before Lady Washington arrived, I doubt our commander slept more than a few hours at a time." He stopped at the entrance to another room. "This is Lady Washington's parlor. Many of the ladies gather here to spin wool and knit stockings for the men. We are grateful for all they provide." He opened the door and held it for the other man. "Shall we proceed?"

Mystified, Will entered the room, which hummed with activity. A group of women sat near the fire, their needles clicking methodically as they worked. Silence ensued when Will and Butler entered the room.

A woman set aside the scripture she had been reading to approach the men. "Can I assist you?" Her deep-set dark eyes looked into theirs.

"Lady Knox," Butler bowed. "We did not mean to disturb the fine work the ladies are doing." He looked about the room. "We had hoped to connect with a member of your party that came up from Virginia."

She shot him a sharp look. "Whom are you seeking?"

Martha Washington spoke from behind her. "It's alright, Lucy. I know why he is here. He is welcome."

The two women's eyes met. Lucy Knox stepped aside, allowing both men into the center of the room. Will nudged him. "Why are we here?"

A gasp came from a corner of the room. Will whirled around, hearing something familiar in the tone. A face framed by chestnut strands escaping from her cap came to him.

"Faith." His throat knotted with so much emotion that he could not utter another word. They faced one another, eye to eye and face to face. It was the closest they had been in months. There were no words to say. Will struggled to breathe as the personification of all his hopes and dreams stood before him.

Chapter Two

Faith stared at Will, wondering if she was dreaming. Since he had left Williamsburg, she had gotten two letters. It had been months since the last one. She had wondered if he was still alive. News of the fighting had been grim. When her mother-in-law had mentioned that Martha Washington was preparing to join her husband's winter encampment, Faith had joined them. Anything was better than the agony of waiting and wondering.

Over tea on a crisp January day, Lady Washington had warned her. "Army camps are rough, brutal places. There will be no luxuries and few pleasantries. We will make it as pleasant as we can for the men there. Whether or not your young man is there, you will have responsibilities to perform. There will be men needing nursing, letters to write families, clothing to mend, and stockings to knit. I cannot guarantee you will have any of the amenities you enjoy in your own home."

"I understand," Faith had replied. "I want to go so that I can do my part to help our men. If I find Will, it will be a blessing. If not, I will pray for his safety as I take care of the men who are there." What she did not share was that there was little to keep her in Williamsburg. The tavern had few guests after the militia had marched north. Her staff could easily manage without her. Then there were the dreams of Will covered in blood, calling her name, or being sick with no one to care for him. But when he had been deathly ill from poison, he had not sent for her. Indeed, he had sent her away. The memory still hurt, even though he had long since apologized. Faith wondered if she was a fool to love a man who had broken her heart once before. But no matter how hard she tried, she couldn't forget him. Too many nights she had woken covered in sweat, frightened that something had happened to him, and she would never know.

The hellish journey north felt like it would never end. The flotilla of wagons and carriages made Faith wonder if they were setting up residence. Stuffed in with a group of women, she struggled to keep from falling into one of them as the carriage jolted over the nightmarish roads. After her journey to Philadelphia, she had sworn she would never journey up the King's Highway again. Now, she found herself crammed among strangers heading to Washington's headquarters.

The weather showed the travelers little mercy. For every mild sunny day, there were days of driving, icy rain coming down in intermittent bands, ruining the roads and covering everything in mud. Even when they stopped to rest, the churned-up ground created an obstacle course no one could escape.

Along the way, they picked up other wives of Washington's commanders; vivacious Caty Greene and sturdy Lucy Knox added to the crowd. Faith used the stops to get away for a few minutes to catch her breath. Her head ached from the constant chatter and heavy perfume. The cold, clear air provided a chance to clear her head before she descended into the madness.

Arriving at Valley Forge had been a shock and a relief. Faith had never been so glad to disembark from a conveyance in her life. Riding in a carriage for hours on end had left her feeling trapped and more than a little desperate to escape. Just being able to walk outside without a gaggle of other women was a blessing.

The encampment itself was unlike anything she had ever seen. Groups of tiny log structures dotted the valley. She could only hope Will was somewhere among all these soldiers. There had been no opportunity to look. Martha Washington put everyone to work unpacking and settling in. In a corner of the attic, Faith shared a bed with three other women. It was close to the chimney, which meant warmth crept in from the constant fires below, although it remained chilly enough for her to see her breath each morning.

Faith learned quickly that her experience running a tavern was very useful in helping manage the early mayhem of their arrival. The number of people housed in the Potts House, Washington's lodging, overwhelmed its size. It required a complex dance of maneuvers to ensure everything and everyone received due attention. Knitting and listening to the women's stories became her afternoon routine in Lady Washington's parlor.

Seeing Will took her breath away. She dropped her needles on the floor in her hurry to greet him. She ignored the faint giggles behind her as the many eyes watched her go to him. Faith wanted to hold him close, but heard the silence as they became the center of attention. She didn't care. Will reached out and grasped both her hands. His palms were rough with calluses. He was here, real and alive, standing before her. That was all that mattered. His deep green eyes looked into hers as she squeezed his hands in return.

"Did you miss me then?" His eyes twinkled as he took in her flushed face and lack of breath.

Faith laughed, the weight of months of worry falling away. "Most every day."

For a moment, they stared at each other. Will was far thinner than she remembered. Hollow cheeks and previously unseen shadows darkened his gaze. A faint scar split the line of one of his eyebrows, giving testimony to a close call of some sort. As he looked at her, his lips curved into a smile.

"You're more beautiful than I remember. I was afraid you had forgotten me in all the months I've been gone."

She shook her head. "No. I've prayed for your safety." Faith didn't add that when they received news of the war, it hadn't been good. The Continental Army had faced some brutal defeats, with only the success of Saratoga to provide any encouragement.

"Perhaps your gentleman would like a hot cup of spiced cider," Caty Greene joined them. The pretty young wife of General Greene's wife put down her needlework to join them. Usually, she had a book in her hands. Her scholarly husband kept her well supplied. She smiled, revealing dimples as her bright blue eyes assessed him. "You can tell us about how you met Mistress Clarke." She indicated an available seat near the fire where Faith had been sitting.

Faith retrieved the stocking she had been knitting. It had gathered a little lint but was otherwise sound. She was grateful she had dropped no stitches; picking up dropped stitches was a dreadful nuisance. She moved over to pour Will a cup of cider. As she handed it to him, she realized Caty had moved to Jeremy Butler, who still stood in the center of the room. "Who might you be?" She asked as she smiled up at him. "Perhaps you could join us and share some news."

Butler looked pleadingly at Faith. "This is my brother-in-law, Jeremy Butler." She moved between him and the diminutive Mistress Greene, causing the latter to remove her hand from Butler's arm. Faith had been around Caty Greene for a few months now, enough to know she knew no stranger. "I'm sure Major Butler would appreciate some cider as well."

"Indeed, and where is your wife?" Caty asked as another woman handed her a cup, which she passed to Butler.

Jeremy stiffened. "She is with her family on a farm outside Philadelphia," he answered slowly. "Or so I pray." No inflection colored his tone, but sadness lurked in the shadows in his eyes. He took the cup politely but didn't drink. His gaze appeared to be far away.

Faith knew that Jeremy and Hannah had argued about her staying in Philadelphia. He had known it was a tempting target for the British months before they laid siege to the city. She had worried about what her stubborn older sister would do. Hannah took great pride in the small business she ran in the city. But being the wife of a patriot would be incredibly dangerous once the town was overrun. They had all heard the reports of British troops looting homes of those not loyal to the crown. She hoped Hannah had gotten away.

Caty Greene stood with Faith and Butler until Lucy Knox interrupted. "Perhaps you would do better to return to your needles, Mistress Greene." Her tone was frosty. "I'm sure our soldiers would appreciate warm feet over gossip." Caty Greene shot an annoyed look at the other woman, but didn't comment as she drifted back to the corner where she had sat with some of the other women.

Faith leaned close to Butler. "Have you heard anything?"

He shook his head. "I met her briefly before the town fell. She promised she was going to your Pa's farm. I hope she did. There have been reports of British brutality towards those they consider supporters of the enemy. I know some people have had their homes and businesses burned to the ground."

Faith nodded. They were both worried. Butler had always been careful to keep a low profile, but that guaranteed nothing. There were eyes everywhere, especially in a city as large as Philadelphia. The Payne farm offered no reprieve from patrols; it was only a day's ride from the city.

Butler set his cup down on a tray. "I best be off. The General will want to hear if there is any news from the countryside." He bowed to her and left. The whispering of ladies' voices rose after he exited the door.

Faith joined Will, who looked embarrassed to be the only man in the room. He sipped his cider and said nothing, but his cheeks flushed as the women in the room watched him with interest.

"I need to collect my kit," He said at last. "They assigned me to von Steuben, so I must move my belongings to where his men are staying, wherever that is."

Caty Greene answered. "My husband, General Greene, tells me they're in a farmhouse nearby. The Baron cannot be too far from young Master Laurens, who is his mouthpiece."

Faith noticed that although he listened to Mistress Greene, he avoided her glance. It was just as well. Caty Greene's vivaciousness had already caused trouble. Lucy Knox had been ready to confront her after witnessing animated discussions with her husband, although her own spouse was only a stone's throw away. Greene didn't seem to mind his wife's boldness. The fact he discussed his responsibilities with her caused a stir around camp. Caty's boldness irritated some of the other wives who preferred to focus on more traditional subjects. The two women avoided each other thereafter and sat on opposite ends of whatever room they occupied. It was solely because of Lady Washington's authority that they shared a workspace.

Now that Will was before her, Faith didn't know what to say. There were too many people about to express their feelings. Even had they been alone, she was unsure of where to begin. Her needles lay in her lap as her mind whirled. She wondered what Will had been through. He was dreadfully thin, dark from exposure to the sun, and with a grim cast to his face that made him look older than his years. He reached out and held her hand in his. Faith squeezed it in return. It was enough to feel him next to her. No matter what he had endured, he was here. That was all that mattered.

Will rose when John Laurens entered the room. "There you are. Let's get your kit. I'll show you where you will be billeted now." Will was halfway across the room before he turned to face Faith. "I'm glad you're here," he stammered before walking out the door. Their boots clattered down the steps leading toward the entrance. Within moments, she heard the outer door slam, letting the men out into the cold.

Faith stared after him for a moment. The shock of finally seeing him had left her breathless. The hum of the women talking resumed behind her. She turned to see Lucy Knox's sympathetic gaze. The young woman patted the empty seat next to her. Faith smiled gratefully. If she knew anything, she knew General Knox's wife would not pry. Lucy Knox was only twenty-two, but seemed wise beyond her years. Joining her, Faith picked up her knitting and attempted to get back into the rhythm of knitting around the leg of the stocking.

From the constant chatter of the women, Faith knew a good bit of what was happening at camp. They were all enduring the shortages despite General Washington's many requests to the Congress now ensconced at York. A heavy thread of fear ran beneath all the chit-chat. They all knew that the outcome of the war was far from clear. What no one dared ask was what would happen should they lose.

Faith couldn't contemplate such an outcome. They had come too far and sacrificed too much to surrender. She looked down to realize she had dropped a stitch. Sighing, she unraveled her way back to pick it up, only to drop another. A dull pounding began behind her eyes. She reached up to rub between her brows. When she opened her eyes, Lucy Know spoke to her.

"Perhaps it would be a good time to run to the kitchen and get some coffee for the men downstairs." Her gaze was sympathetic. "Sometimes we all need a moment to ourselves."

Faith nodded and rose, feeling the ache in her back as she straightened. "I am happy to be of service." She walked out of the room, downstairs, and out the door, across the entryway to where she knew the kitchen lay. Once she opened the door, she could smell a stew of some sort on the fire. A dark-skinned woman stirred the pot before moving to a bowl on a nearby table. She wore a dark-colored dress with a patterned apron. A tidy white cap held back her dark hair. She looked about the same age as Faith. Her dark eyes met hers as she entered.

"Can I help you?" Her cultured voice, with its faint nasal inflection, showed she had spent a good bit of her life in the northern colonies.

Faith nodded. "I was hoping to take some coffee for the men. I can get it ready if you can point me to where everything is."

The other woman nodded and set aside the bowl where she had been adding bits of chopped vegetables. "It's a few hours before dinner, Mistress, but either I or my husband can assist you with that."

A man came in with a load of wood. He set it down by the fireplace. "Hannah, you are busy cooking. Let me help her while you work. I roasted some beans earlier today, so it shouldn't take too long to have a pot ready."

Faith stepped out of the way. "My apologies for disturbing you at such a busy time. My intention was to help. I'm Faith Clarke. I came up from Virginia with Lady Washington."

The man nodded. "Isaac Till, and this is my wife, Hannah. We serve General Washington." He stepped around her neatly and set a plate down on the long wooden worktable. "I'm afraid there is little we can offer besides the coffee. There is no milk and very little sugar. Those folks in Congress don't seem to realize that people need to eat if they are going to fight."

Faith had noticed the lack of food and other supplies. She had been relieved to see Will was not among the nearly naked troops struggling to stay warm and clothed. "What is General Washington doing about it?"

Till scowled fiercely enough that Faith stepped back. "Everything a man can do. He writes letters every day to everyone he knows in that Congress and to the Quartermaster, for all the good it does. He invited members of Congress to come and see. The conditions shocked them. It remains to be seen if anything gets done."

"I did not know," Faith murmured. "General Washington works very hard every day. I hear him and his staff up at all hours." From her attic room, she could hear the murmur of voices and the sound of feet on the floorboards below. Sound carried up the stairwell, and she had never been a heavy sleeper. She watched as Till took the coffee grinder and filled the metal bowl on top with roasted coffee beans. He turned the crank at a steady pace that spoke of long practice. Once the drawer below was full, he emptied the ground coffee into a bowl and continued until he had the amount he wanted. He then poured it into a metal pot, which he topped off with water from a pitcher, and set it over the fire.

"It will take a few minutes to heat, if you want to return then."

Faith nodded. She had no desire to be underfoot in the busy kitchen. Back in the main part of the house, people would be engaged in various tasks, going back and forth from room to room. She had no desire to rejoin the melee just yet. Faith went out of the kitchen and into the breezeway that connected it to the main house. The cold penetrated through her clothes in seconds. Wishing she had thought to grab a shawl, she wrapped her arms around herself to stay warm. She looked out across the field and wondered how the men bore the constant cold.

To the north lay the Schuylkill River, which wound its way through the rich farmland of the Pennsylvania colony on its way to Philadelphia. Before her were the earthworks and redoubts, built to help repel any enemies that might attack. Beyond this lay the heart of the encampment. Faith took in all the men milling about. Seeing all the activity, knowing it was a preparation for inevitable battles, was unnerving. She glanced away. Faith didn't want to think about the bloodshed. The brutality of warfare terrified her. She had heard some officers desiring glory on the battlefield and thought them insane.

Desiring to focus on something else, Faith turned back to the kitchen.

Surely that pot had had time to heat by now. As she entered, the kettle hissed on the fire. Taking a padded cloth, Isaac Till lifted it off the fire and set it on a trivet on the table.

Grabbing a cloth, he folded it many times and laid it over the opening of an enamel pot. "I will need you to hold the cloth in place while I pour. No one wants to drink grit."

Faith nodded, familiar with the procedure. She grasped the ends of the fabric and held it over the pot's opening.

"Watch your hands," He murmured. "This is boiling hot." He poured slowly, watching as grounds and water came out, making sure the liquid had time to go down before pouring more. Before long, it was done. Till put the pot and some cups on a tray. His wife put a plate of what looked like biscuits on the tray as well.

"My thanks," Faith said as she lifted the tray.

Isaac Till held the door for her as she left through the breezeway. Hamilton prevented her from having to juggle opening the main house door. Faith thanked him as they passed. After closing the door, Hamilton followed her back to Washington's office, where the other men had gathered. She wondered where he was going before he saw her. She knew little about the camp's activities.

As she approached the door, raised voices permeated the hallway. "I'm not a clerk!" a deep voice thundered. "I am a general. Men follow me into battle for our cause."

Washington's voice remained resolute. "Without a consistent supply chain, we will have no army come spring. The men are starving, freezing, and desperate. I need a man I can rely on to get the job done. Our cause needs you, General Greene. There will be many battles to fight when the time comes. I promise you that. Becoming Quartermaster may well save the war."

Faith would have waited, but Hamilton passed her and opened the door, saying. "You can bring the tray in here, mistress. There is space on the table."

The conversation hushed as Faith walked in. She didn't look at either of the men, but went to the table and set down the tray. Nodding at the men, she began pouring cups. "I'm afraid there is no milk," she said. "And very little sugar."

"Such amendments are unnecessary," Washington assured her. "The men face far worse circumstances. It is my hope we can endeavor to improve on that situation shortly. Our men will die for this cause; food and shoes are minimal requests." He didn't glance at Greene when he spoke, but his message was clear.

General Greene came over for his cup, thanking Faith in a soft voice. He did not answer Washington directly but took his cup to a nearby window where he stood looking out toward the earthworks. His expression was that of a man torn between his duty and his desires.

Hamilton took the last cup. "None for you, my lady?"

Faith shook her head. "No thanks, Lieutenant Colonel." His green sash identified him as an aide-de-camp; his red cockade showed he was also a lieutenant colonel.

He lowered his voice to an intimate level. "You, dear lady, may call me Hamilton." Dark gray eyes looked into hers. He was an attractive man. Normally, this would have flustered her, but she already knew many soldiers saw women as a source of comfort. While she was sympathetic, her interests lay elsewhere. As her eyes met his, she realized they were almost the same height, although Faith suspected his boots had added an inch. His confident smile revealed his expertise in charming ladies.

Faith nodded politely as she put some distance between them. As a tavern keeper, she had long since learned to distance herself from men seeking temporary solace. "It's time I returned to Lady Washington. She keeps us busy. I assume you have many responsibilities as well."

Sighing, Hamilton gestured towards a pile of letters on a small table by a window. "Indeed. General Washington has put me to work recalling troops that were lent to General Gates."

Faith nodded. "I will not keep you from your duties." She bowed to Washington and Greene. Looking around the room, she paused. "Where is Lieutenant Colonel Laurens?"

Hamilton answered. "He has gone out with the Baron to help translate. I imagine your friend McKay will join them before long. The Baron is training our officers in the ways of organized warfare." He grinned. "Because of their hard work, our soldiers will learn the meaning of curses in two different languages." A sprinkling of freckles dotted his cheeks and nose, adding to his charm.

Faith smiled in return. Hamilton had great charm. He had been in and out of Lady Washington's parlor, helping her settle in and find places for all her staff to sleep. It had been a challenging project, given the crowded conditions. She hoped one day he found a woman who was his equal. Such a restless spirit would struggle to settle down.

Faith left the men to return across the hall to where the women worked. As she entered, she heard Lucy Knox hiss, "Stay away from my husband. He has enough weight on his shoulders without having a shameless woman throw herself at him when her own husband is but a few steps away."

"Maybe you should spend more time with your husband if you mistake a few conversations held during social situations as a threat." Caty Greene's voice was sharp, her following laugh high-pitched and vicious. "Cannot we have some fun in this dark place? There is so much gloom. It's not good for any of us."

Her eyes darted over to Faith. "You need to dance with that young man of yours. These days, it's important to grasp happiness while you can. Before long, the men will be gone into battle. Who knows who will return?" She rubbed tears from her eyes. "I want my children to have a father."

Faith realized that Caty Greene was afraid. She had heard there were two young children back at the Greenes' home in Rhode Island. Her thoughts went to her own son, Andrew, who remained in Williamsburg with his teacher, George Wythe. She missed him terribly. A knot formed in her throat. They were all feeling the strain. The conflict separated too many families. There was no telling when it would end. All she could do was pray it would end before long.

She picked up her knitting and took a seat where there was decent light. Despite all the interruptions, she had made progress. There were now nearly three inches of leg on her needles. There was nothing fancy about them.

They were the most basic of design, churned out to warm the freezing legs of soldiers. Faith was glad to produce a tangible form of help to those she saw suffering within the camp.

Martha Washington encouraged one woman to play the flute while the others stitched. Conversation became a faint murmur that flowed beneath the haunting music. Looking at the faces bent over their work, each contributing toward the greater good. Faith knew that a group of the women had gone to the hospitals to serve the sick. Fevers ran through the camp, which worried her. It took very little for sickness to spread. The men's quarters were a miasma of offal pits and dead animals. It was a disaster waiting to happen. She had avoided the cabins for that very reason.

The front door opened. Boots thudded down the hall, startling her out of her thoughts. Someone pounded on a downstairs door. Someone shouted, "One sentry is dead!"

All the chatter ceased.

Faith heard Jeremy Butler say. "General Washington. You need to come. I've seen nothing like this before." The door slammed shut, leaving the women staring at one another, wondering what else was being said.

Chapter Three

Jeremy Butler closed the door behind him. The solid thump seemed to echo across the room. Washington paused behind his desk, an eyebrow raised in query. Instead of annoyance, his clear gray-blue eyes showed curiosity at the interruption. Like most of them, he was thinner than upon arrival, and the shadows under his eyes spoke volumes of sleepless nights.

Butler wished the soldier who had accompanied him had waited before making his announcement. Lady Washington and her ladies were upstairs, and he knew they heard him.

Washington sounded weary. "I'm assuming the man didn't die of a fever. That has become too commonplace."

Butler shook his head. "No. Private Jonah had been on picket duty last night. I'm not sure what happened afterwards. His sergeant reported him missing, so I sent a group of men to look for him." He gestured to the other man. "Private Simmons came to get me when they found him alongside the creek."

Washington frowned. "I don't recall assigning any pickets over there." He walked around his desk so that he was facing Butler. His expression sharpened as he waited for an explanation.

"There aren't," Butler replied. "He's dead, but I'm not sure what happened to him."

Washington gestured to his aides-de-camp. "Very well, Major. Show me what you have found." He opened the door and strode out, his long legs moving quickly down the hall. He grabbed his greatcoat off a hook and went out the door without waiting for his staff. No one spoke as they hurried across the ground. Butler hurried to keep up. Normally, their difference in height was not a problem, but Washington was in no mood to accommodate anyone.

Within minutes, they were on the banks of the creek that ran a stone's throw away from the back of Washington's headquarters. A lone soldier stood waiting by a dark mound on the ground encrusted in snow. Butler sucked in his breath. It didn't get easier the second time around.

"My God," Washington exclaimed. "What happened to this man?" He turned to the soldier, keeping watch. "Did you find him like this?"

The man nodded. "Simmons spotted him first, and we went together to investigate. Poor bastard. I saw him yesterday playing his harmonica." He looked sick. "Can I go now?"

Washington waved him off. "Return to camp. Say nothing to anyone who asks. We will deal with this." He walked around the body. Ice crusted what the snow didn't cover. A thin layer glazed his face and clothing. His skin had darkened to almost a charcoal gray, although his lips had a bluish-purple tinge to them. "Perhaps he fell in the creek?" Washington mused. "But why didn't he get himself to a fire before he succumbed to the cold?"

Butler leaned down to look closer. "Maybe he slipped and fell in by accident? If he were drunk, he might not have realized the danger." Butler tried to roll his body to the side to get a better look, but the ice held it fast. "I believe he's frozen to the ground, sir."

Washington frowned. "We'll need to free him. We cannot leave the man here. The poor devil deserves a decent burial." He rose. "Butler, get a group of men to get this body away from the creek and out of sight." His voice dropped. "Is there anyone in the camp he was close to? Are there any family members who need to be contacted?"

Butler answered. "I'm not sure, but I will find out." He remained crouched by the body, looking for clues to what had happened. He had seen death many times, but something about this caught his eye. Jonah lay flat on his back, his bare legs straight out, his ragged blanket halfway across his chest, his arms by his side. "It looks like someone laid him out," he finally said.

Washington paused. "Perhaps he sensed death coming." He looked at all the men gathered there. "I don't want this discussed in camp. There is more than enough distressing news as it is." He paused as if he were planning to say something else, then, without a word, turned and walked back to his headquarters. Butler may have imagined it, but despite the General's upright posture, it seemed as if he carried an enormous weight on his shoulders.

Butler turned to the junior officers and enlisted men present. "You heard the General, not a word about the circumstances of Jonah's death."

Captain Silver looked over at him. "Won't his commander want to know what happened?" The young man's face had become ghostly pale as he looked over at the body entombed in ice and embellished with frost.

"I will talk with him," Butler replied. "Washington is right. We can't risk upsetting the troops. We are on a razor's edge of a revolt as it is." He pondered how to move the body to one of the empty barns nearby. "Let's get a few men out here with shovels. Perhaps we can break the ice and get him loose that way." He didn't know what they would do if that did not work.

Silver nodded. "I think there are some near the earthworks. He gestured to a few of the enlisted men. "Come on, men, we've all seen dead bodies. Let's give him the same respect we would want if it was one of us lying there." He walked away with three men in tow.

Butler stayed behind. He rose and walked about, trying to find answers. The creek gurgled behind him; Ice hung off the banks and crusted the snow that remained on the rocks and dead grass. Any other time, he would have appreciated the beauty of it. At this moment, it seemed a macabre setting for the body. A bird cried overhead. Its singular voice added to the isolated feel of the place. He wondered what had led Jonah here. After the long hours out in the cold, he would have headed for a warm fire, not a lonely stretch of creek away from everyone else.

A glint of light from the crotch of a small tree caught Butler's eye. He went over to it and pulled out a partial bottle of whiskey. "Well, well," he murmured. Someone hid the bottle where it wouldn't be easily found. He pulled out the cork and sniffed, surprised at the potency of the contents. The troops had been receiving watered-down alcohol for weeks. Someone had taken this from the supply house and hidden it here, where no one went.

It would be a simple place to sneak a quick drink if you knew about it.

Butler looked down at the body. "You had a secret, didn't you?" He breathed. "I'm betting you slipped down here for a quick nip before heading to your bunk." He closed the bottle and stuck it in the deep pockets of his greatcoat. He wanted Abigence Waldo to examine it. He liked the surgeon, both for his skills and his caustic wit.

Jack Silver returned with a handful of men from the dead man's regiment of freedmen. A couple brought shovels. He looked at Butler. "They want to take care of their friend."

Butler looked at the grim-faced men gathered there. Two had a litter, they lay gently to the side. "Alright, men, let's get him out of the elements."

Surrounding their fallen comrade, they worked to get their shovels underneath him at the head and shoulders. The ice held fast at first, then, with a sharp crack, released its prey. One man kneeled and worked at rolling the body to the side as the ice popped and snapped. Frozen snow and ice stuck to his back as they worked to free him.

Butler stared at the body as it gradually broke free. Even though it was cold, it was not bitter enough for the man to have frozen instantly. No one with any sense of self-preservation would have lain down soaking wet in the bitter cold. He contemplated the partial bottle in his pocket.

"Did Jonah like to drink?" He asked.

The men had gotten the body into the litter. They turned as one to look at him. One finally responded. "No more than any of us, sir. And no one would stand out in the cold to enjoy his ration of rum. Jonah liked to drink by the fire. Sometimes, he would sing or play his harmonica. He was good to share if he got his hands on anything special."

"Like whiskey?"

A man's face closed off. "No one has seen any of that in a while, sir. "

Butler nodded. He knew a lie when he heard it. "So he would not be likely to slip off for a quick drink on his own."

The men stared at him before lifting the ends of the litter and walking away. Butler watched them go. Impugning the dead was not a gentlemanly thing to do, but he was more concerned about how Jonah had died than what the men thought of him. While it was possible that Jonah had fallen into the creek after drinking too hard, the idea didn't sit well with him. The freedmen were cautious, aware of prejudice against them.

Butler despised the attitude. He owed his life to the skilled natives who served as scouts for the army. He considered the freedmen no less valuable, and he had seen their strength and courage in battle. If mischance killed Jonah, it was a tragedy; if someone lured him to his death, he deserved justice. Butler sighed. The war had left him suspicious of anything and everything. Jonah had probably tumbled into the water after drinking too much. It was the most likely explanation. After determining there was nothing else to be found by the creek bed, he walked back toward camp.

People stopped to stare as the litter went past and then returned to their work. There had been plenty of deaths since they had entered the valley of the forge. It saddened Butler that it had become so commonplace. He watched the men enter an empty cabin on the edges of the encampment before he turned to go look for Waldo. The man had his own frequent bouts of illness, but once he recovered, he was both an excellent physician and surgeon. He was one of the few doctors whose opinion Butler respected.

The cabin was quiet, making Butler wonder if Waldo was at a hospital. He knocked, listening to the sound echo inside. After waiting a few moments, he walked inside. Waldo sat by a small fire, writing in a small book.

"I'm busy," Waldo growled. "I'm not due at the hospital for a few hours yet." He blew on the page he had just written, and set it on the hearth to dry.

"I thought you might be interested in this," Butler answered, pulling out the bottle and handing it to the other man.

"You're giving me whiskey now, are you?" Waldo eyed the bottle with interest. Pulling the cork, he sniffed the contents. "Nice! I don't detect any watering down." He went to take a drink before Butler stopped him.

"I found that hidden in the crotch of a tree next to a dead man. I'm wondering if there is more than whiskey in that bottle."

Waldo plugged the bottle hastily before setting it down. "Why didn't you say so? I would prefer not to poison myself."

"I didn't think you would be so quick to imbibe." Butler gestured to the bottle. "I could be wrong, but it looks like Jonah fell in the creek after taking a few swigs."

Waldo shot him a look. "Whiskey can do that, particularly on an empty stomach. None of these men are getting enough to eat. He wouldn't need anything added to the bottle to addle his wits if he drank enough."

"Can you examine that and the body and let me know what you think? I imagine we will bury him as soon as the ground softens."

"I'm not expecting a thaw soon," Waldo responded. "There have been plenty of deaths in this camp, and there will be plenty more before spring. What makes this one more interesting than any of these other poor souls dying of disease and deprivations?"

"I'm not sure, but I feel like something is off."

Waldo listened carefully, without interrupting. "Frozen to the ground." The surgeon looked puzzled. "No one who's fallen into a creek of freezing cold water is going to just lie there waiting to die, not if he's conscious. Did you see any marks on the body–like a blow to the head?"

Butler shook his head. "Nothing, but he was as stiff as a rock. It was hard to see anything."

"And you expect me to do a detailed examination of a man frozen hard as stone?" Waldo shot him an incredulous stare. "You may as well ask if I can bring the dead back to life."

Butler sighed. "He should thaw quickly enough out of the elements and close to a fire. I will make sure there's a fire where he is. There's a fireplace there."

Waldo rose to his feet. "Do that. I'll look at this bottle in the light and see if I can spot anything." He watched the dark liquid move as he tilted the bottle back and forth. "It would be a crime if someone contaminated a good bottle of whiskey when we all suffer from so many shortages."

"I don't know that it is," Butler admitted. "But I cannot imagine why someone would be lying frozen on the ground. It makes no reasonable sense."

"And since when was anything reasonable here?" Waldo asked him as they walked together out the door.

Butler had no answer to give him. Life in the encampment at Valley Forge had long since gone beyond his ability to fathom.

Chapter Four

Faith completed rolling a length of clean linen for bandages. That morning, she and Lucy Knox had gone down to one of the camp laundresses to retrieve the material. It was her first sojourn to this part of the encampment, and she was relieved not to have to go alone. Although nearly the same height as Faith, Lucy was stouter and possessed a powerful personality. Despite their differing demeanors, the two women had hit it off. Lucy's little girl was often with them when they worked, although the energetic toddler did not join them on this journey. Lucy had left her napping with another of the officers' wives to watch over her.

A handful of children played in the open areas around the mixture of cabins and canvas tents that made up the area occupied by camp followers. A myriad of fires blazed as women cooked, boiled laundry, and endeavored to stay warm and occupied. Faith didn't know how they survived, although she knew Washington paid for laundry services and other necessary tasks. She watched as a woman sat on a log near a fire, mending a pair of breeches. Lucy tapped her arm and pointed to a tent pitched near a fire where a large iron pot hung. The scent of lye and ash permeated the area. They had found the laundress. After folding the lengths of cloth into transportable bundles, the women returned to the farmhouse. They cut, rolled, and distributed bundles to regular hospitals and what Washington called the "Flying Hospitals."

These were places for the less seriously ill, each one built at least 100 yards away from each brigade's headquarters. Construction of these had only slightly eased the crowding at the already established hospitals, where disease ran rampant.

Cutting and rolling bandages took most of the morning. When they were done, Faith was eager to stretch her aching back and get some fresh air. Wrapping a shawl around herself, she offered to deliver bandages in order to escape the confines of the farm. Arms full, she headed down the path to the nearest facility. She soon saw the flying hospital, with smoke rising from the cabin's chimney, a structure finished only days after her arrival.

The day was mild, heralding that spring would arrive shortly. Faith relished the heat of the bright sun on her back. In the distance, Faith spotted a small herd of cattle that had been driven in the day before. She knew, without asking, that they had already butchered some cattle to feed the perpetually hungry men. They would tan the hides into leather for moccasins. Nothing went to waste in camp. They would boil down the bones for soup and broth. For the next few days, there would be something besides fire cakes for the men to eat.

A faint breeze carried the scents of urine and blood over to her as she approached the building that housed the sick. Faith bit her tongue to tamp down the rising nausea she felt when approaching the place. A woman stood outside the doorway, leaning against the wall. Faith wondered why the woman wasn't helping the men inside; she could hear some of them moaning. As she approached, the woman slipped something into her pocket and straightened up.

"I've brought fresh bandages," Faith said, offering them to her.

The woman stared at her without moving. Her eyes moved over Faith before turning back to look out at the camp. A wool blanket lay over her shoulders. This blanket, unlike the others in camp, was well-preserved. It resembled some that Lady Washington had distributed to the sick upon her arrival.

Faith didn't bother to keep the sarcasm out of her voice. "Perhaps you could take them inside for the injured to use."

The woman stared at her with unfriendly eyes. "You're one of those women who came with the Commander's wife, aren't you?"

Faith kept her tone even. "Lady Washington brought many ladies and staff with her to help." She looked at the woman at the entryway. "I presume someone hired you to help nurse the sick?"

The woman didn't answer. She looked at Faith's plain wool dress and white cap. She wore a white cap herself, although it had become somewhat gray. Her dress stretched tightly across her bosom, although the rest of her body seemed composed of hard angles, including her face. "The general pays a little for our work. You can lay the linen on the table just inside the door. The others know to look there first." With that, she strode off, heading toward the nearby cabins.

Faith thought about calling after her but realized it would do little good. That woman looked to be nothing but trouble. She entered the building, cradling linen with one hand and pushing open the door with the other. Inside were rough bunks, half of which were filled with men. An older woman with kind gray eyes approached.

"Fresh linen. Good. We need it. You can leave it there." She pointed to a short table by the door, which also contained a mortar and pestle, some plants, and an almost empty bottle. She smiled at Faith. "I am Mary Porter." Puzzled, she looked down at the table. "I had a bottle of rum for our men in pain here. Where has it gone?"

"I suspect with the woman I saw standing outside," Faith said tartly. "She didn't seem too eager to come in."

The other woman made a face. "Louisa Barrett has her mind on other things than tending the sick, although she will take the money readily enough." She shot Faith a wry look. "We must make do with the material we have to work with."

Faith bit her tongue. She knew she would not put up with someone like that for long. It wasn't her business, although it angered her that someone would take one of the few things available to treat the sick. She stacked the linen on top of the table against the wall, where it wouldn't fall on the floor. "I'm glad we can supply you with this. Would you like me to check about getting you another bottle for the men?"

Mary Porter smiled at her. "I would be grateful. I have to measure it out carefully so that we don't run out." She shook her head. "I didn't realize I would have to guard it from some of our nurses. I will be here until nightfall.

If you could give it to me, I will find a place to secure it." Her lips thinned, revealing her anger for a moment before her expression smoothed out. In the back, a man's voice cried out. She turned toward the sound.

Another woman went over to the bed. "Mary, I will need help. His bandages are loose, and he can't stay still."

Mary Porter picked up the nearly empty bottle. "I'm coming, Nellie." With a nod at Faith, she moved swiftly to the back of the room.

Faith watched her for a moment before ducking back out. She walked swiftly away, taking in gulps of fresh air to clear her lungs of the scents of suffering and despair. Throttling the errant Louisa seemed like an excellent idea, even if unlikely to happen. The best she could do was find another bottle of rum to replace the one she was certain the other woman had taken.

Thinking about it outraged her. Faith scanned the camp, but Louisa Barrett was nowhere to be seen. She intended to have a talk with her later. Someone had to set the thieving witch straight. In the distance, she could hear Schuylkill murmuring as it raced toward Philadelphia. Her eyes blurred for a moment as her thoughts turned to Hannah. It had been weeks since anyone had heard from her older sister. Philadelphia had fallen to the British in late September. Now, it was nearly March. At first, Hannah had tried to stay, but once the enemy had established themselves, they'd lost no time in seeking those homes and businesses loyal to the patriot cause. Hannah had fled to their father's farm, a day's journey outside the city. Communication had stopped as the British patrols made it impossible to get messages out.

Faith was terrified for her. She worried Jeremy would do something foolish to reach her. Washington had forbidden him to go look for her. It was far too dangerous. Yet the agony of knowing nothing plagued them both. She knew the silence was driving him mad. She'd seen him meeting the foraging parties that had gone out toward the city, asking for news. Overwhelmed by the camp noise, Faith sought the river trees, ignoring the men drilling.

Voices carried across the large swath of meadow, one bellowing in a mixture of German and French, the other in English, translating commands and curses. Faith grinned as she recognized Will's voice among them.

Looking over, she thought she could spot him alongside the colorfully dressed von Steuben. Lieutenant Colonel Laurens had to be the other man interpreting for the Baron. Washington had permitted him to gather a group of one hundred officers to train, and the stout Prussian had wasted no time getting to work.

The snow was melting under the warmth of the sun. Yellowed grass emerged in patches on the ground, giving Faith hope that spring would arrive before long. She was tired of the bitter cold. When she had arrived, she had thought there was no place more desolate on earth. It was only the hope that she could provide help and comfort to the men that kept her going. Now that she could see Will alive and unharmed, much of her anxiety had dissipated. They were surviving as well as anyone could in these circumstances.

Overhead, a flurry of birds took wings, their cries echoing across the sky. They were too small for anyone to shoot. Faith didn't like it much, but she knew some men with long rifles hunted for birds to help feed the people at camp. Faith missed the sound of birds flying overhead. In the trees surrounding her tavern back home, there were always some birds greeting the day.

As she drew closer, the river's voice became louder, dominating its surroundings. Faith walked to within a few feet of its banks, taking care not to get too close. The brownish waters roared as they traveled down toward the sea, foaming where it encountered rock along the banks. Light from the clear sky reflected on the restless waters, giving the surface a bluish cast only broken by its movement.

How long? She wondered. How long would this war last, and when would it end? Faith was tired. She longed to go home and engage in the everyday tasks involved with running her tavern. She wondered how Olivia and Titus were doing in managing Clarke Tavern in her absence. Admittedly, there had been few guests when she had left with Martha Washington's group to go north. Faith fretted about her son. She had sent a letter a few days ago, but there was no telling when, or even if, he would receive it. Though Wythe assured her of her son's progress, she yearned to see him. One of her greatest comforts after his father's passing was to go into his room and watch him sleep. Faith longed for the day they would all be together again. She drew in a shuddering breath. There was no use in fretting. It did no good. No matter how busy she kept, her worries came out in restless dreams that kept her from resting.

Moving back from the riverbank, Faith headed to a stand of trees nearby. In this valley, the forest grew in thick patches along the river and on the edges of the fields. Come spring, their branches would fill out in glorious green leaves that would shade the ground and provide relief from the sun. A sudden rustling along the ground caught her attention. At first, she saw nothing before spotting a chipmunk moving across the ground. It paused and watched her with dark eyes that gleamed in the sunlight. After a moment, it sprinted off into bushes at the base of a tree.

Smart animal, Faith thought. If anyone else had spotted it, it could have become part of a stew pot. She decided not to tell anyone about its presence. She would prefer not to eat every living thing in the valley. The poor thing would barely make a mouthful, anyway. Pausing at the base of the tree, Faith examined the smooth gray trunk along with its stout limbs. Buds were forming on some branches. Winter would break soon. It couldn't happen soon enough for her. She was tired of the cold.

The snapping of twigs made her whirl around. "Who's there?" Her eyes darted around, seeing no one in the trees or along the riverbank. The isolation, earlier so peaceful, now felt eerie. "It's probably another chipmunk." Her voice sounded hollow in the isolated copse of trees. It made her feel even more uneasy. Some intangible instinct told her she was not alone. She looked around for any signs of life. Surely no one had followed her out here. They would have been visible. This time of year, the bushes and trees were bare. There was nowhere to hide.

Troubled, Faith stepped out from the trees into the open. The sunlight made her feel less vulnerable. The encampment, teeming with people, was not far away. Feeling in her pockets, she drew out the knife that Olivia had given her. The cook had spoken softly just before she had gotten into the carriage with the other women heading north. "You are a woman alone, no matter how many are in that carriage. You always need to have a means to defend yourself. There is no telling who you will meet out there. Nothing guarantees your safety. Keep your eyes open wherever you are." Faith had taken the knife. She knew Olivia treasured her knives and kept them razor sharp.

Holding it in her hand, Faith was grateful for the other woman's caution. She wondered what could be out there. If it was another chipmunk, she would feel like a fool. Overhead, a crow let out a raucous cry before winging it over the river and out of sight. Faith let out a breath. She was being ridiculous. Surrounded by Washington's troops, who could bother her?

Anyone, a voice whispered in her head. Anyone could be a soldier. There was no guarantee that they were all honorable men. There were those in uniform who had their own interpretation of right and wrong. She had witnessed that back in Williamsburg. Three young women had died because of one man's determination to keep a secret.

As the wind stirred, an odd thumping sound caught her attention. Faith moved cautiously toward the noise, wondering what it could be. Dead leaves crunched under her feet as she went deeper into the copse of trees. Out of the corner of her eye, she caught movement on the ground. A hare burst out from the base of a trunk and raced over to the tall grasses that lined the banks of the river. Faith laughed and took in a deep breath. Feeling silly, she turned to go around the large tree.

She froze. Something hung from a stout branch of a tree. At first, she couldn't figure out what it was. It was an oblong shape, covered in cloth. Drawing closer, she gasped as her brain struggled to accept what her eyes saw.

Deep in the shadows of the encircling trees, a figure waved back and forth. When its boots hit the trunk, a faint thump echoed through the wood. Swallowing the scream that rose in her throat, Faith walked toward the nightmare dangling before her eyes.

The man wore an officer's plain blue coat, but she didn't recognize him. Valley Forge contained thousands of men, hundreds of them officers of the assorted regiments. A long red scarf encircled his neck. Her eyes tracked the other end, knotted to a rope attached to the stout limb above. His hat rested on the ground beneath him. He bobbed back and forth in the breeze; his arms waving slightly as if he were a rag doll.

When Faith heard the snap of limbs off to one side, she bolted. Running like the devil was in pursuit, she raced back to the camp, screaming for help, even though the hanging man was far past needing it.

Chapter Five

Will helped bring the body into camp. He and the other men drilling with von Steuben had been the first to respond to Faith's screams. The drummer, a skinny youth, shimmied up the tree to cut the man down. Will helped lower the man to the ground. He stared at the body on the ground, recognizing the insignia of a captain. Behind him, he heard Faith explain how she had come upon the body. Lieutenant Colonel Laurens translated her words into French for von Steuben, who, despite being technically a volunteer, held the authority of a senior officer.

Will wanted to comfort her, but realized he needed to deal with the situation at hand. From what he could hear, Faith had recovered enough to tell her story. He looked over to see von Steuben watching Faith's face intently as she spoke, nodding as Laurens put her words into a language he could understand. He took her hand in both of his before addressing her.

Laurens translated. "I'm sorry, dear lady, that you found him. Let one of my men escort you back to the care of Lady Washington while I and my men deal with this."

Will watched Faith leave. He knew both of them from his regiment. They would deliver her safely back to headquarters. Jeremy Butler's arrival to join their discussion did not surprise Will.

"Who is the poor devil?" Butler asked. He looked at the body before glancing away. "Is it a suicide?"

"Captain Lombard," Will replied. The 6th Pennsylvania is his regiment." He didn't add that the man had been a pain in the rear to most everyone and himself recently. He hadn't recognized the dark purple face. An officer from Lombard's Pennsylvania regiment had identified him before getting violently ill.

"No one knows how he ended up this way."

Laurens interrupted them. "Von Steuben wants to know who the man is."

"Tell him," Butler said as he studied the tree. "It would be a challenge to reach that limb."

Will looked and realized he was correct. The limb he had hung from was a good eight feet above the ground. "Maybe he tossed the scarf up there." His tone was doubtful. "Tying it around his own neck would be impossible."

Will studied the trunk, looking for footholds. "I suppose he could have shimmed up and jumped."

"Maybe," Butler frowned. "Surely there are easier ways to kill yourself."

Von Steuben spoke again. Laurens translated. "His uniform is too clean for him to have climbed the tree."

Will looked down. Lombard's uniform was immaculate except for a missing button. He nodded to von Steuben. Speaking in German, he said. "He could have thrown the rope up there and found a stump to stand upon." There was a scattering of them about from where men had cut trees to build cabins and keep fires going.

"Ja," von Steuben replied, although his expression showed his doubts. He spoke to Laurens. "Get him back to camp."

No one wanted to touch the corpse. Butler went with a couple of men to find a litter that they rolled the body onto. Von Steuben's face turned grim as he ordered men to carry the body back into the camp and into the empty shed where the other dead man lay. He looked over at Will and said in German. "Not good. Men should die in battle."

Will nodded. They had lost too many men to injury and disease. Once word got out, it would only darken the mood throughout the camp.

Von Steuben nodded. "You go. Tell the men to return to the parade ground. We have no time to waste. His commanding officer can inform his family." He turned to Laurens and said in French. "Tell the men to return to the parade ground and form ranks."

Will heard the pounding of feet as they went back to drill. No one wanted to linger in the shed. As the weather warmed, the other body would thaw, along with the ground. They will bury Private Jonah in the next day or two, along with those who died in the hospitals, far from the water supply and the cabins.

Seeing the farmhouse, Will spotted Butler questioning scouts. He knew what he was doing. Butler was worried sick about Hannah. Will knew the Payne farm's proximity to the city made patrols impossible without a fight, but understood Butler's need for news.

Butler spotted him and waited for him to draw near. "I take it you drew the short straw?"

Will made a face. "The baron sent me to inform Washington. He and Laurens returned to drilling the troops." He didn't need to add that he found the job distasteful. There was no good way to tell Washington or the man's commanding officer that a man had hanged himself.

Washington looked up from where he was composing a letter. He stood as they walked across the room. "What is it? What has happened?'

Will told him as succinctly as possible.

Washington's face turned grim. "We are losing too many men to disease and battle. Having an officer commit suicide is an untenable thought. Does anyone know what led him to do this?"

Will shook his head. "Not that I know of, sir."

Butler was more forthright. "People didn't like him. I've heard men in his regiment complain about his highhandedness."

"Men complain about a variety of things. Officers get the brunt of it. It comes with rank." Washington stepped from behind his desk. "I'll speak to General Conway. Maybe he knows something."

He looked at Butler. "The ground has thawed to a degree. See about getting a burial detail formed. We need to bury the dead quickly. I've received word that another man died of pox in the night."

Butler nodded. He didn't look surprised. "May I borrow Captain McKay briefly? I want to take one last look at Jonah before they bury him tomorrow."

Washington nodded his assent before turning back to his correspondence.

"Silver," he called. "Make sure these letters go out today."

Jack Silver stood up from the small table in the corner where he had been working. He looked over at Butler and McKay. "Good luck," he whispered as they turned to go.

Once they had exited the building, Will looked over at Butler. "What do you need me for?"

"To watch my back," Butler replied. "You're the one man in camp I trust. It may be a coincidence, but these two deaths don't feel right."

Butler stopped to pick up a lantern from the barn where Washington's horses, Nelson and Blueskin, lived. There were few animals in camp not intended for food, and the general kept his beloved steeds guarded.

Sharp, chilly air bit into his skin, yet his boots squelched through the ground wet with melting snow. Will knew it would freeze back overnight. He hoped the slush was a sign that winter was loosening its stranglehold. He would be glad for its end, even if it meant an eventual return to battle. The combination of cold and deprivation sapped his soul as much as it exhausted his strength.

Set away from any of the barracks, the shed had a desolate feel. As he approached, his nose picked up the faint scent of decay. Washington was right. It was time to bury the men. With a quick snap of his flint, Butler lit the lantern and went inside. Will followed close behind. The men lay on the ground, each on one side of the building. Thawing had not improved Jonah's appearance. Butler knelt by the body. He handed the lantern to Will. "Hold this so I can get a look at him."

Will complied, averting his head. The man's skin looked gray and muddy. It sickened him to see a human turned into so much clay. He'd feel relieved once they were both in the ground.

Butler said nothing as his fingers ran over the ragged clothes. "Poor devil." He turned and rose to go to Lombard, wrinkling his nose in distaste. The man's head leaned on one side at an odd angle. "Neck's definitely broken. I wonder if Waldo has had time to look him over."

Will shot him a startled look. "You asked one of our physicians to examine a suicide?"

Butler nodded. "I wanted to make sure we missed nothing." He shot Will a look. "Even suicides have a story to tell." He pointed to a gap in the uniform. "I want to know what happened to this button. Lombard was fastidious about his uniform. He wouldn't have worn a coat like this. Perhaps it came off in the struggle."

"What makes you so sure he struggled?" Will said.

Butler held up the man's hand. "Look at the broken nails. They match the scratches around his neck. He spent his last moments trying to claw loose." He sighed as he put the hand back down. "It had to have been an agonizing death."

Butler rose to his feet. "Jonah's unit wanted to bury him and say a few words. I will see if they will do likewise for Lombard." Taking the lantern from Will, he walked back to the door. Once he put some distance between himself and the shed, he took a few deep breaths.

Will did likewise. "I have no fondness for the stink of death." He shuddered. "My duty lies among the living. I must return to von Steuben. He's putting his drills on paper for Laurens and Hamilton to translate and share with other units. It's keeping everyone busy."

Butler nodded. "Let's hope his plans work. Right now, it will take a miracle for us to win this war."

Will looked at him. "If you believe that, why are you on this side of the conflict?"

Butler smiled. "We all have to have something to believe in, a dream, a prayer, a belief in a better tomorrow. I made liberty my mistress long before I met Hannah. I am fortunate that she understands. Even if we do not win, I am glad I stood with this cause and fought for a country that believes in a higher power and a common good."

Will stared at Butler for a long moment before replying. "That's how I feel, too."

Butler slapped him on the back. "Then we are brothers, bound in this cause and by the women we love. May God choose to let us come out whole on the other side."

"May He indeed," Will said as he turned to head back across the fields,

where he could already hear the bellows of the German officer he now
served.

Chapter Six

Butler strode down to the cabins that housed the unit of freedmen. The isolation of this set of cabins had never struck him before now. Why was this unit on the other side of the enormous field where the men drilled? The River Road stretched east past the rifle pit and the Brigades of Huntington and Sullivan. General Varnum's headquarters and the 1st Rhode Island Brigade (formed from persons of color, Native Americans, Freedmen, and the enslaved) were located here. Like the other regiments, there were two rows of two, with a rough roadway separating them. Snow covered the roof, lightly dusting the door frame and the edges of each hut's log. He knew from his previous visit which one to go to. Inside, he could hear a fife playing a plaintive tune. He dreaded this task. Even though he knew death was part of being in a war, he never enjoyed dealing with the dead. He had dug his share of graves in the French and Indian Conflict when he had been little more than a boy. Then Colonel Washington had assigned him, along with some of the other remaining uninjured men, to dig graves after a skirmish with the French and their native allies. The task had left him retching. Even now, he avoided dealing with death whenever he could.

He hoped the men in Jonah's unit could tell him more about him. Butler still could not wrap his head around the notion that the man had gotten so drunk he'd fallen in the semi-frozen creek, hauled himself out, and died. Many men drank to ease the boredom and depression that permeated the encampment. Besides drills, men had little to do unless assigned to chop wood, dig latrines, or bury the dead.

Many of the men played cards or dice to pass the time. A few were fortunate enough to have the skill of music on harmonica or fife. Butler heard the mournful sound when he moved about camp evenings. He felt for the poor devils far away from all they held dear. Butler's multiple duties as an officer and a spy kept him moving. If he kept still, his mind would go places it did not need to dwell. His eyes swept southeast where Philadelphia lay. Hannah's face rose before him, her bright blue eyes deep as the sea. "Where are you?" The stillness of the surrounding air only increased his anxiety. Picking up his pace, he went to the cabin that had once housed Private Jonah. Gathering his thoughts, he prayed he would find the right words to get them to trust him enough to speak with honesty.

Raising his hand, he knocked. His gloves muffled the sound, but someone inside told him to enter. Glad to exit the cold, Butler entered. Five men sat close to the fire, which roared from a recent feeding. Rising from the logs, the smell of pine rosin filled the room with its heady scent. While waiting for him to speak, the men eyed him. The fife continued its sorrowful tune. The musician was little more than a boy, not much taller than Butler, and slight of frame. After the last note faded, the young man put his instrument inside his coat pocket.

Butler squatted by the fire. "Greetings," He stretched his gloved hands out, enjoying the warmth. "I'm glad to see you are keeping warm."

"Blankets would help," one man said.

Butler nodded. "It would. Washington has been trying to get them. General Greene is now the quartermaster. He aims to fix the supply chain. None of us enjoys the cold."

He heard a derisive snort behind him. He let it pass. Life was more brutal for these freedmen. They had fewer resources to draw upon, and some of the other regiments treated them badly. Butler had nothing but respect for them. He'd seen them fight. Butler paused before turning toward them. "It's time to bury Jonah. The ground is warming up, and he needs to be laid to rest."

One man stood and gestured to the others. He was apparently their leader. "You heard the major. Let's bury our comrade. He would have done it for us."

Butler nodded to him. "Thanks." He paused, embarrassed because he didn't know the man's name.

"Sergeant Maples, sir. Jonathan Maples of the 1st Rhode Island Regiment."

"General Varnum is your commander."

"Yes, sir. He is." Maples was at least six inches taller than Butler. He bent down to get out of the narrow door to the cabin. In the light of day, it was easier to see his coppery skin and strong features.

Butler suspected he had Native American blood in him. His high cheekbones and silky hair gave him a distinct look. As they walked down to the shed, he studied the other men. He knew Varnum had pressed for the right of men of color to enlist. These men were the fruit of his labor. They gathered more of their regiment to help carry the dead to the burying ground. General Varnum met them there.

Despite the warming weather, the ground remained hard to penetrate. The men grunted as they dug down into it, removing outer garments as the task continued. Working in shifts, they dug the graves deep enough to keep any animals out. One man covered Jonah's face with part of his torn blanket before putting him in the ground. They followed a similar procedure with the second man.

Butler felt bad that there was not even a spare blanket to wrap them. It was a sad testament to the state of the encampment. He removed his hat in respect for the fallen as Varnum offered a prayer. Once they began filling in the grave, Butler left them to it.

"Major Butler," Maples called out softly. Butler waited for the sergeant to join him. "Sir, I need to say something." They walked together until they were out of earshot of the other men. Distant sunlight glinted off the Schuylkill, flowing east towards Philadelphia.

"You didn't know Jonah, but I did. He was terrified of water. I just don't see him getting close enough to the creek to fall in. He avoided water. Crossing the creek at Brandywine put him in a panic. He didn't go in until the bullets started getting close."

"Then why was he at the creek?"

"I don't know, sir. It makes absolutely no sense." Maples' face showed his frustration. "It doesn't fit with anything I know. His duties were halfway on the other side of camp."

"Did he have any friends in any regiments nearby?" Butler asked.

Maples shot him a look. "We're different from the other regiments, sir. Most of them don't care to mix with us."

Butler felt like an idiot. "I didn't mean- "

Maples interrupted. "You didn't think about it. But then there is no reason you would."

Butler said dryly. "Catholics are not terribly popular either."

Maples grinned. "You're one of those, huh? I thought all the papists were from Maryland."

"You'd be surprised." Butler didn't advertise his beliefs. He had left his mother's rosary with Hannah, although she was Quaker. They had not sorted that out yet. There was a lot they hadn't discussed. He feared they never would. As they passed a stand of trees only partially decimated by the need for wood, Butler remembered something. "Did Jonah like to drink?"

"You asked me that earlier," Maples said. "I didn't want to say it, but yeah, he could be partial to a quick nip here and there." The sergeant stood at ease, but his eyes moved constantly, watching the grounds.

"I found a partially drunk bottle of whiskey in the crotch of a tree near where we found him." Butler kept his tone neutral as he waited for what the other man would say.

It didn't take long. "Jonah didn't even have shoes! Where in the hell do you think he would have gotten something like that?" He paused and laughed. "That sneaky bastard. I bet he won it gambling. He had a good hand with dice."

"Really," Butler said, intrigued. "Who did he like to gamble with?"

Maples shrugged. "Anyone. Nobody has any money, so we use what we have." He grinned. "It had to be an officer he got that bottle from. Who else would have one?"

"Who indeed?" Butler wondered. Everyone was tight with their comforts. If Jonah had won the bottle gambling, the loser would have been upset. But would he have been upset enough to kill him?

"I bet he hid it so nobody would take it while he was on duty," Maples said. "Stuff goes missing all the time."

Butler knew that. He kept everything on his person. The one time he had found someone rifling through his bedding, he had beaten the snot out of him. After that, no one touched his bedroll. Washington found a place for him in the farmhouse's attic soon afterward. It was far more comfortable than the rough bunks of the enlisted.

Maples parted ways with Butler as they drew close to the inner earthworks. Butler continued toward the farmhouse, wondering what news there was, if any. To his surprise, he found a horse tied to the fence near the house.

"Who does that belong to?" He wondered aloud. So few horses remained. He knew them by sight. Butler scratched its nose. She was a pretty little mare. "You don't belong here," He told her. "You are way too pretty to be eaten."

"That's good to know," a familiar voice spoke from behind him.

Butler whirled around. His wife stood in the yard, looking as if she had just come from a stroll.

Hannah jumped as Butler picked her up in a tight hug, whirling her around. "How?" he marveled. "How did you get here?"

Once she caught her breath, Hannah gestured to the horse. "I walked until I got to Aunt Deborah's, then I rode the rest of the way on Gracie." She looked about. "It would be easier to speak out of the cold."

Butler nodded and took her arm. He saw one of the enlisted men tasked with tending the stock. "Take care of my wife's mare. Put her in the stable with General Washington's horses and give her the same care."

"Yes, sir." He led the mare to the barn. Hopefully, there she would be safe from anyone desiring to add more meat to the menu.

Hannah's eyes took in the encampment. Her blue eyes were bright against the paleness of her face. Butler thought she looked thinner. Dark shadows lined her eyes as if sleep had been rare. Despite the cold, she displayed a keen curiosity regarding her surroundings. She looked at the stone farmhouse. "Whose home is this?"

"I believe the man's name was Potts," Butler said. "He graciously agreed to rent it to Washington for the duration of the encampment." He didn't add that Washington insisted on paying the man rather than just taking his property. It was a model that the officers under his command followed as well.

She took the arm he offered and let him lead her inside. Her eyes danced with amusement as men stopped to stare at them. He looked in vain for Lady Washington. She was nowhere to be seen.

Lieutenant Colonel Silver came out of a room and froze for a moment before coming over. "Major Butler, who is this vision of beauty on your arm?" He bowed over her free hand, placing a kiss on the palm before releasing it.

"My wife, Hannah," Butler said, giving him a quelling look. "She has arrived recently from Philadelphia, so I am sure General Washington will wish to speak with her."

Silver smiled. "I am certain he will. Come with me, fair lady, and I will introduce you to our commander-in-chief." He reached for her hand.

Butler stepped between them, neatly cutting the other man off. "I will do that; just tell me where General Washington is at present."

Silver shot him an unrepentant look before offering Hannah a teasing smile. "It's rare to see my friend Major Butler ruffled. Seeing you, I understand why." He turned to Butler playfully, backing away as he raised his hands in mock surrender. "He's in his office. Ask him nicely, and he might find a place where you two can stay together." He bowed to Hannah before returning to the room that served as an office for the aides-de-camp when it wasn't a dining room. Butler gestured to the room next to it. The door was closed.

Butler knocked firmly. "Enter," a man's voice intoned. Opening the door, he let Hannah precede him into the room.

Washington rose from the table he used as a desk. His dark blue eyes took in both of them before coming to rest on Hannah. "Major Butler, who is this?"

Hannah smiled at him nervously before answering for herself. "I am Hannah Butler, his wife."

A brief smile crossed Washington's face before it returned to its normal solemnness. "You were in Philadelphia, I believe."

Hannah nodded. "I had a business there before the British took the city. Afterwards, I left." She paused, swallowing hard.

Washington walked over and took her hand. "We have heard that it has been difficult for our friends who remain there."

She nodded, blinking back tears. "Once they claimed the town, they began rooting out real or perceived rebel sympathizers. Since Dr. Franklin had visited my home at one time, they made their way there, destroying my wares and tossing my belongings into the street." She took a deep sigh. "My former home now houses British soldiers. I went to stay with family outside the city, but British Patrols have come there too, foraging for stock, weapons, whatever they can find." She shook her head. "I could not stay. Because my family is Quaker and has not taken sides in the war, my presence there would have caused problems. I can't let my family suffer for my choices."

Washington's voice became gentle. "I commend your courage. Although I will note that at some point we will all have to make that choice, whether or not we wish to."

Hannah nodded. "But it is not for me to make it for them." She sniffled. Washington handed her a handkerchief.

Turning to Butler, Washington said. "Take some time to get your wife settled. I imagine you will wish to stay together." He smiled. "Go to Lafayette's lodging. He will not return for some months and will not mind." He turned to Hannah. "Welcome to Valley Forge, Mistress Butler." He turned back to his desk. "I have other business to attend to." He leaned over and picked up a stick figure, a tiny cord hanging from its neck.

Butler's blood ran cold. "When did that get here?" He noted the scraps of wool forming a uniform. The figure even sported a tiny saber made of a sharpened twig. Wool covered its head. Someone had sewn scraps of wool into a militia uniform. Somehow, the artist had found a large enough piece of fabric to make a cape.

Washington's face was grim. "It was here when I returned from riding around camp. I'm assuming it is supposed to be Captain Lombard." He handed it to Butler. "What do you make of it?"

Butler took it in his hand, aware that Hannah was watching as well. He turned it over in his hand, examining the work. "Considering the man just died, there's a lot of detail here."

"I concur," Washington said. He took it out of Butler's hand and laid it back on his desk. "Is it some sort of macabre humor or a warning?"

"I don't know," Butler said. "I believe it could be a message. This isn't the first one you have received."

Washington nodded. "Someone froze the first one in ice. When it melted, it covered my papers in water. I was angry. I did not consider its meaning." He rubbed his head.

"None of us did." Butler's voice softened. "It may be sick humor. In this camp, the men find many ways to pass the time and forget their fears."

Washington shot him a glance. "I don't find this amusing. Let's pray whoever created this moves on to some other sort of entertainment." He looked at Hannah. "Welcome to Valley Forge, Mistress Butler. I hope you find your stay as pleasant as possible."

Butler took Hannah's hand and led her back into the hallway. Upstairs, they could hear the chatter of the women in Martha Washington's parlor as they worked and stitched. The door to the office of the aides de camp stood ajar, as the men were in and out, performing a variety of tasks for their commander.

Butler turned toward Hannah. "Let's get your things."

She laughed sharply. "Other than my rucksack, I have nothing. What the British didn't take, they destroyed."

Butler struggled to contain his outrage. "You did nothing wrong, Hannah. I'm sorry my actions caused this."

Hannah squeezed his hand. "It would have been done, regardless. They were looking for scapegoats. They went after my business because it was a convenient place to house their men, and they knew I wasn't powerful enough to stop them."

Butler's smile was grim. "I look forward to retaking the city."

"Stay alive," Hannah said, taking his hand. "That is all I ask."

Stepping out into the yard, Butler looked about, recalling the location of the small farmhouse where Lafayette stayed. He missed him. The young marquis was charming and generous to his men. The Frenchman had used his own funds to provide for the men under his command. He hoped he was doing well, even if he considered invading Canada a fool's errand.

"Lafayette's quarters lay south of here. We can take the Valley Road. It won't take long. You can get settled and rest until dinner. Your horse is probably safer here with Washington's. No one in his right mind will disturb his animals."

Hannah shot him a look. "If I spend my time lying around waiting for you, I will go mad. I need to do something. Surely the women in this camp have responsibilities as well."

Butler shrugged. "Lady Washington would know the most about that. You can speak to her after dinner if you like," he said, picking up the rucksack left in the breezeway. "Let's get settled first." He turned toward the dirt road, glad it had not rained recently. "The house is a little over a mile away." Butler was amid turning when a concussive boom rent the air, followed in seconds by another.

Chapter Seven

Familiar with the sound of cannon, he spun around to where General Knox had located the artillery. A haze of smoke rose and spread across the ground. As the echo died away, screams came from the parade ground. Butler dropped Hannah's pack to the ground. "Stay here," he ordered as he ran toward the parade ground.

"Let it not be Will," Butler prayed. The Scotsman had gone with von Steuben to drill the troops, translating the Inspector General's commands into English. Butler felt as if he could not reach the parade ground fast enough. Other men joined him as they raced from Washington's headquarters. Men spilled out from their quarters, some with guns, as they searched for signs of attack.

The smell of blood filled the air as Butler and the others drew near. The acrid scent of gunpowder drifted close by. Shouts in German and English filled the air as he drew close. Von Steuben and Laurens fought to bring control to the panicked men. Butler pushed his way through the crowd of men to where Will McKay kneeled by a soldier.

Butler crouched nearby, ignoring the blood that drenched the scene. The man screamed and jerked as Will endeavored to help. The sight of the man's nearly ripped-off arm made Butler's stomach lurch. His screams filled the air. Blood poured out of the torn limb in a torrent. Within seconds, the man fell unconscious.

"Where's the surgeon!" Will yelled as he put pressure on his arm. Blood soaked through his fingers as he used his wadded-up jacket to stop the flow. Nearby lay another soldier, still in the grass.

Butler leaned over to examine the other man before realizing he had no head. He sat back on his heels as a wave of dizziness washed over him. "I'm sure someone is coming."

Laurens and von Steuben moved the other men off the field and to the sides. Butler remained with McKay and the bodies of the two soldiers. He took off his belt and, with Will's help, fixed a tourniquet on what remained of the man's arm. His extreme pallor made Butler fear he would not last long.

Waldo appeared with a couple of other surgeons. He crouched by them, his hands gently examining the man. Butler moved aside to let the physician work. He rose and looked about the parade ground. A thin haze of smoke drifted across from the artillery. The surgeon was muttering under his breath. He caught Butler's gaze. "What in the hell happened?"

Butler shook his head. "I don't know, but I intend to find out." He watched as men brought litters and placed the injured on them, taking them back to the surgeon's cabin.

Waldo touched his arm. "Find that poor man's head so we can bury it with him. We'll need to know who he is so his commander can write to his mother." He strode off across the field close behind the litters.

Will MacKay was conversing with von Steuben. The Prussian looked shaken. He looked at Will.

"Die ihr eigenes Volk angreifen? Das ist Wahnsinn"

"What's he saying?" Butler asked.

Mackay responded. "He said who attacks their own people–it's madness."

"I agree," Butler said. "Tell him I intend to find out what happened."

Will translated his words. The German nodded and walked back to his troops. MacKay turned to follow. He looked back at Butler. "What do you intend to do?"

"Find out who fired those cannons." Butler looked across the field where General Knox had set the cannons months ago. The battery had remained quiet until today. From his position on the parade ground, he could see figures around the cannons too far away to be identified.

He headed that way, running across the field, hoping to catch someone who could tell him why cannon had fired on their own men. One ball sat smoking on the ground a short distance away. Butler shuddered. He had become too familiar with the noise and destructive force of artillery. Sometimes the roar of cannon and screams of the fallen filled his dreams. He wondered if the memories would ever fade away.

As he neared the artillery brigade, the position of the weaponry became clearer. A pair of cannons sat slightly askew from the rest, faint wisps of smoke rising from their barrels. The scent of burned powder filled the air. Butler spotted a group of Knox's artillerymen inspecting the guns. He trotted up to them. "Why are you shooting cannons?"

A sergeant replied. "We didn't. When we received word from General Knox to convene the unit in front of his quarters, we left immediately. We were halfway there when the blasts began."

Butler looked at the men. Grim looks covered their faces. "None of you shot the cannons."

"None of this brigade, sir," the sergeant looked across the field where men were moving around. "How bad is it?"

"At least one man is dead, another may die. I don't know about other injuries." Butler said. He looked at the men. More crowded around the guns.

General Knox's arrival did not surprise Butler. The guns were his responsibility.

His voice rang out. "Who ordered the cannon to fire?" Silence greeted him as his men looked away. Knox growled under his breath before raising his voice to a shout. "I said, who ordered the cannon fire?" No one answered. The general was a large man, tall and stout. Filled with anger, Knox presented a formidable presence. He turned to a man. "Sergeant Ross, you handle the guns. Who gave the order to fire?"

The man's face looked like paper. He looked at the general before looking down. "I do not know, sir."

Knox's voice dropped. "You do not know. These cannons sent balls into our own troops. They do not load and fire themselves. Someone had to have done it." He looked out over the men gathered. "I want to hear from all the captains. Check with your men. I want to know who fired those guns. Immediately!"

Ross looked at him. "We were inside, sir, playing cards. None of my men knew anything was amiss until it fired."

Knox looked dumbfounded. "Was no one watching over our cannons?"

The man shook his head. "Not that I know of, sir. You would need to ask Captain Brown, sir."

Knox looked at the men gathered, each with their guns. The gunnery crew assigned to the cannons that fired looked sick and angry. Knox called out. "Captains, assign watch over all artillery from this moment forward. Everyone dismissed but the crew responsible for these weapons."

Butler went with Knox to the men gathered around the fired guns. The master gunner spoke first. "Sir, these men know nothing about why these guns were fired. Nor do I. I accept responsibility for my crew."

Knox looked at him. "You realize all of you could face the lash."

The man's face whitened before he nodded. "Sir, we have accounted for all our cannonballs. Whoever fired brought his own powder and balls."

Knox was about to reply when Lieutenant Colonel Silver jogged up from the direction of headquarters. "Washington wants to know who fired the cannons." Silver huffed from running. His cloak billowed behind him before falling into place. His gloves were missing.

Another man joined them. "General Knox, sir. Three balls are missing from our supplies, along with powder and fuses."

Butler spoke to Knox. "I don't think these men had anything to do with the cannon going off, sir. We need to investigate to see who did."

Knox looked at him. "We have few men trained in artillery as it is. Investigate and let me know what you find." He went to speak with his men, leaving Butler and Silver with the gunnery crew.

Butler looked at the gunnery sergeant. "Did anyone hear or notice anything unusual?"

The man shook his head. "We were happy to get out of the cold for a bit."

Butler nodded. "Can you look at your cannon and tell me if anything is amiss?"

The gunner nodded before calling out to his men. "Gunners, matrosses, examine the guns. Tell me what you see."

The men looked at the weapons, careful not to lay hands on the cooling weapon. Ross called out, "Worm!" A man grabbed a hooked pole and ran it down the barrel, turning it as he went. As he retracted it, a bit of wadding and other material fell out. Ross looked down. "It looks like one of our rounds. Sponge." Another man ran down the sponge. He backed it out of the cannon's mouth slowly. Nothing more came out. The second cannon yielded similar results.

"Sir," one man said. "Someone found a rammer on the ground nearby, along with another cannonball."

Butler walked over to Knox, who stared at the tools. "Someone left these behind."

"A cannonball would have been too awkward to carry or conceal quickly," Butler noted. "Our man needed to get away."

Knox nodded. "It leaves the question, who would do such a thing?"

Butler nodded. "Yes, it does." There was nothing more to be gained by examining the gun. Knox was already preparing to question everyone in his unit, hoping to find the culprit. Butler wished him well, but suspected whoever had fired the cannon into the drilling troops was not part of the artillery regiment.

He walked with Silver up the road northwest toward Washington's headquarters. Silver looked back at the cannons lined up neatly between the camp's two lines of defense.

"Who do you think did this?" He asked.

Butler shook his head. "There's no use speculating. It could be anyone."

"Do you think there is an enemy sympathizer in camp?" Silver wondered.

Butler shot him a sideways look before replying. "A spy would try to stay hidden. As for these men's allegiance–I would say given how many are starving and freezing to serve, I doubt it's for the enemy." He paused. "It has to be someone who can go just about anywhere without being questioned."

Silver shot him a look. "Are you suggesting an officer did this?" His eyes widened in shock. "We've received some basic training in artillery, but no one would run out and fire on our own men."

Butler looked over at the younger man. "I'm suggesting nothing at this point. Right now, we need to gather information and see who has the ability, time, and motivation to do it. Knox has ordered the cannon guarded. That should prevent future incidents."

Sliver nodded. "There have been many people in and out of the encampment. Hostlers, camp followers, and people from the community. It is possible someone slipped up there to cause mischief and rode out during the excitement."

"That doesn't give much time for an escape," Butler noted. "Our man would have had to have a horse waiting for him nearby." Changing the subject, he said. "It's cold to be out without gloves."

Silver shrugged. "I was in too much of a hurry to pick them up. I left them in our office after all the noise." He rubbed his hands together absently before changing the subject.

"There are still stands of trees nearby, and a road runs behind Knox's artillery. For all we know, our enemy could be hiding among us. No one's going to question a man in the woods; the assumption is he's gone to relieve himself." Silver looked thoughtful. "Perhaps we need patrols inside camp."

"To guard against the enemy within?" Butler said. "You may be right. I will discuss it with Washington."

They walked in silence back to Washington's headquarters. There was no sign of Hannah at the entrance. When he entered, Laurens was waiting outside the office of the aides de camp. "Your wife is upstairs with Lady Washington."

"I'm not surprised," Butler said. "Hannah's not one to stay idle." He looked over at the door to Washington's command center.

Silver paused. "I need to complete a letter to Congress. Washington expects it to go out today." He left Butler and went into the office he shared with the other aides de camp. At a table, Hamilton read a message, using light from the window.

Laurens stood in the hallway, looking hesitant. He turned to the closed door to Washington's personal office. "He will want a report," As he turned, his officer's coat swung open, revealing a smudge.

"Wait a minute," Butler said. "You know how he values appearances." He took out his handkerchief and whisked the substance away. "How did you do this?" he said as he worked on the mark.

Laurens shrugged. "I was checking a set of dueling pistols the Baron owns. I guess there was still some powder on one of them."

Butler nodded. "A little powder can get everywhere, even when you're careful." He handed the handkerchief to Laurens, who continued to dab at the spot, unaware of the speculation brewing in the back of Butler's mind.

The door opened as they spoke. Washington stared at them. "Please come in, gentlemen. I've been waiting for news."

Laurens and Butler looked at each other before quietly filing in. Laurens handed back the handkerchief which Butler stuck in his jacket pocket. They stood next to each other, facing their commander.

Washington stood with his back to the fire. His face revealed nothing. After a brief silence, he spoke. "I heard a cannon fire from within the camp. I assume General Knox is on his way here, but I want to know what happened now."

Butler spoke. "No one seems to know, sir. Neither Knox nor his officers gave the order to fire."

Washington's face turned grim. "Someone fired that weapon. I want to know who." He turned toward the fire. "Someone will have to tell the poor man's family that he is no more. I do not want it said he died at the hands of his fellow soldiers in an act of complete incompetence." He turned to glare at the men. "Do you know anything about this?"

"I might," Lieutenant-Colonel Hamilton stood in the doorway. "I had thought it foolishness when I first came across it a few days ago, in the light of recent events, I have reconsidered." He held a piece of paper in his hand. "This arrived in a mail packet from York a few days ago. I apologize for not bringing it to your attention, but I thought it was a sick joke. I fear now that it is more than that."

Washington gestured to him. "Please read it."

Hamilton hesitated, looking at Butler and Laurens. "I'm not sure that giving this a voice is a good idea, sir. I-”

Washington's voice turned sharp. “Read it.”

Hamilton took a deep breath and held the letter out where the light from the window illuminated the page.

“Ten patriots all in a row
Ten faithful followers. Where did they go?

To wash his head, one arose.
Slipped into a creek, and so he froze.

Nine officers walking without care
One caught a branch, now he's dancing on air.

Eight recruits marching straight from bed
One little misfire took off a man's head.

Seven camp followers nursing the sick,
Until a fine horse delivered a kick.

Six at the ovens baking bread.
One played with fire, now he's dead

Five soldiers out on a drill
One found a rock useful to kill.

Four men drinking rum.
One had too much. Now he's numb.

Three young officers in their cloaks
One's scarf got caught, now he's choked.

Two fine physicians treating the ill,

One cut too deep and blood was spilled.

So many dead and the killings not done.
   How many must die before Washington's undone?"

"What in the hell is that?" Laurens exclaimed.

Washington stood still, taking it in. "Read it again, slowly."

Hamilton complied. His voice shook as he got to the end. "What does this mean?" he asked. He laid the letter on Washington's desk and backed away, as if it were toxic. The paper refused to lie flat. Creases in the pale ivory paper lifted the folded ends. Red wax from the seal resembled a bloody thumbprint on the edges.

Washington's voice was quiet. "I'm not sure. Did you say it came from York?"

Hamilton nodded. "Along with other correspondence from the congress. Silver helped me sort through it. It was heavy with messages from many places. There is even a letter from Lafayette in it. There is a small package I have not had time to open. It has a rank odor to it."

Butler's voice was sharp. "Bring it in here."

Hamilton looked at Washington, who nodded. He returned within a few moments with a bundle wrapped in cloth stained rusty red.

"It looks like it's wrapped in bandages," Laurens said. "This came in the mail?" He sounded surprised.

Hamilton nodded. "It was all in a sack delivered from York this morning. Our Congress has been busy."

Washington stared at the bundle that Hamilton had placed on an empty table. "Open it up."

Hamilton and Laurens stared at each other. Neither desired the task. Butler brushed them aside. "I'll take care of it." Pulling out a knife from a scabbard at his side, he cut through the rope that tied the bundle shut. He recognized the coppery scent of blood and dreaded what he would find. The linen cloth stuck together, unwilling to reveal its contents. Butler continued to cut until the tiny figure emerged. He backed away so the others could see the headless figure covered in blood.

Lauren's nose wrinkled in disgust. "This is madness. What does it mean?"

Silver looked like he might retch. "I assume this represents the man who died in the cannon incident this morning."

Butler's voice was sharp. "If that is so, how did this come to arrive from York at this precise time?" No one had an answer. The room was deadly quiet as the men stared at the crudely carved figure before them.

Washington's face was grim. "I need to know who sent it and what their purpose was. These figures and the poem mean something."

"The purpose is clear," Butler interrupted. "It's both a threat and a warning. Each stanza describes a death. We've already witnessed three in the past few days. Someone is killing members of the Continental Army one by one, and whoever it is wants you to know it." He picked up the figure and its wrappings and threw it into the hearth. Flames flared as they fed on the fabric. The fire briefly outlined the figure as if it had just entered the gates of Hell.

Chapter Eight

Faith walked with Hannah to a hospital. She wasn't sure having Hannah help nurse soldiers was a good idea, but her older sister had a mind of her own. They carried a fresh load of bandages with them. Regardless of the reason, it was wonderful to be outside in the chilly spring air. The early morning frost had melted under the sun and left the slowly emerging grass soft underfoot. A pale sun emerged from the clouds gathered overhead to light the sky. Across the meadow, von Steuben's corp of officers drilled under his direction. Although she couldn't distinguish the words, she saw that von Steuben had the men lined up and following commands without disruption. They were acting more like an army than a mob of armed backwoodsmen. While Faith had grown accustomed to the routine of living in a military camp, she knew it was new to Hannah. She looked over at her sister. Other than a murmured good morning, Hannah had said little to her over their morning meal, which seemed odd. Other than being thinner, she couldn't see much change since they had last spoken. But she had noticed how much quieter her normally forthright sister had become. It worried her.

Hannah walked swiftly toward the cabin. It was as if she couldn't wait to get away from Faith and the group of women at Washington's headquarters. A faint breeze blew in from the west, bringing with it the faint scent of rain. It played with the tiny strands of hair that had escaped pins and lay on her sister's vulnerable neck. Her eyes had grown watchful in the intervening months.

"There's no need to run," Faith huffed as she quickened her steps. "I'm certain the cabin is not going anywhere." The path was a narrow strip of worn earth in the ground, the grass worn away by the continual passage of feet. Over the course of the winter, it had developed washed-out areas that were difficult to walk over. She stumbled over a rough spot as she hurried to keep pace.

"I'm tired of feeling useless," Hannah said. "I need to stay busy." Her eyes stayed focused on the building down the road. When at last she paused, it was to scan the area, taking in the stand of cabins, along with the stable that stood behind them. Her breath came in and out as she paused. Her eyes scanned the breadth of the camp, watching the drilling soldiers and others engaged in various tasks such as chopping wood and cleaning the camp. Chopping wood echoed across the meadow as they fired up the earthen bake ovens. A woman gathered water from the creek in buckets. Her thin voice carried across the distance as she sang. Faith watched as she lifted her load and headed back to the camp followers' living area. A group of supply wagons proceeded on the River Road into the camp. The teamsters' voices carried over the distance as they coaxed their mules to complete the short distance to where they could unload and rest at last.

Faith shot her an anxious glance. "There is plenty to do here. If you ever want to take a few minutes to talk."

"I'm fine," Hannah cut her off. "There is nothing to discuss." She sped up so that she reached the cabin ahead of Faith. Without waiting, she went inside. Faith followed, wondering what her sister had endured in Philadelphia.

The interior was dim despite light coming in from the cabin's lone window. A fire burned in the fireplace built into the end of the building. It had not changed since Faith's last visit. Rough board beds, softened with straw pallets, filled the room's length. Worn and torn blankets were all that were available. She watched Hannah take it all in without a word. Her eyes scanned the interior, going from bed to bed. There were the faint scents of urine, soap, blood, and sweat. In the back, one woman mopped a section of the floor. A dark-skinned woman stripped a bed, piling the blanket into a basket as she plumped the mattress tick and shook the pillow before examining it for bugs. Another woman of color bandaged a man's arm as another helped him sit upright.

Within moments, a nurse greeted them. Faith recognized her from her last delivery of bandages. She smiled as the middle-aged woman came toward them. She had liked the calm efficiency of Mary Porter from the moment they had met.

"Faith Clarke, I see you have brought more bandages. Thank you for your diligence. I was most grateful for the rum you found for us. The men need all the comfort available to them as little as there is in these circumstances. I keep hoping some medicines will come in with the other supplies, but Dr. Waldo has seen none." Her dark brown eyes gazed at Hannah, noting how she didn't meet her eyes and the constant tension in her body.

"I see you have someone with you this time. I have not seen you in camp." Her warm smile showed they both were welcome. "We are women, and the battles we fight are different. I hope that whatever circumstances brought you here, you have found comfort."

Faith smiled. "Mary Porter, this is my sister, Hannah Butler. She has most recently arrived from Philadelphia to join her husband. She would like to help care for our sick and injured men."

Mary Porter spoke to Hannah. "I am grateful for another set of hands, but you should know it is not pleasant work. The men who come here are too ill to tend their own hurts. Fevers run through camp with regularity, and we have little to ease their discomfort. Some of the native women have been kind enough to share their knowledge of local herbs and have shown me and a few of the others where to find them. Frequently, what we do is provide comfort to the dying."

Hannah looked at her. "I'm aware of what nursing entails. I tended to the injuries of people caught in the middle of the siege when Philadelphia fell—women, children, and men. During summer outbreaks in the city, I've also helped care for the sick."

Mary Porter looked at her again with respect in her eyes. "Then you know what this will be like. Get an apron, and I will show you around." She pointed to a hook on the wall where muslin aprons hung. Hannah walked over and took one down, wrapping it around her and tying the strings to hold it on.

Faith watched them walk away, feeling faintly guilty that she didn't join them. She had nursed her own family, but didn't have the stomach to do it day after day. She would do what she could to support the men in other ways. Wanting to do something of use, she volunteered to go down to where the camp followers lived to check on the laundry. The hospitals went through a great deal of it, and she would be happy to deliver clean shirts and bandages if they were ready.

She had spent little time in this area of camp. It lay behind a large group of cabins housing soldiers and close to the Gulph Road that led to Philadelphia. Nearby streams provided easy access to water while the surrounding trees fueled their campfires. Sometimes at night, Faith could see the faint glow of them on the other side of the camp, looking like a swarm of fireflies in the distance.

Hastily erected tents and shanties filled this section of the encampment. It was a community filled with people who followed the army for reasons known only to them. Faith knew she would not want a life of constant movement with little shelter from the elements or ruffians. Smoke from the constant fires scattered throughout the campsite burned her eyes. Many muslin tents poked up their heads like enormous mushrooms across the clearing. It took a moment to orient herself. She had only been to the laundress once before and had not been paying a great deal of attention to where that tent lay.

A few moments later, she spotted some laundry blowing in the wind. Relieved at receiving a clue, she headed toward the tent, which stood out from the others. A large copper pot hung by a chain over a smoldering fire. Use had long since darkened it, so only the faintest hint of its original color remained. In it, pieces of cloth floated in a cloudy liquid. A woman stood over a tub nearby, a wooden batten board covering part of the opening. A large stone raised the tub off the ground. Other stones lay scattered out from the banks of the creek that flowed at a distance behind the line of entrenchments near the Commissary General's headquarters. Shirts, caps, and neckerchiefs lay on the grass, being bleached by the sun. Their stark whiteness contrasted with the dull grass beneath.

Faith kept to the narrow track that led to the tent. She had no desire to disturb the tub and tools of the trade that were scattered around the entrance. "Hello," she called out. "Are you the washerwoman?"

"You don't see anyone else here, do you?" The woman replied. Her hands worked a piece of fabric on the board, squeezing water from it as she kneaded it over the board. "Now, if you are looking for who is cleaning the blankets or a heavy coat, that's Maggie. She's further down near General Weedon's headquarters. Agnes' husband is in Varnum's brigade, so she does their wash close to Sullivan's bridge, though I personally would not want to mess with getting into the river. It's got a current to it that could pull you under in a heartbeat."

Faith nodded. "What is your name?"

The woman offered a humorless smile. "I've been called a few different things. My momma named me Rose." She lifted the shirt she'd been kneading and examined it before giving it a last squeeze and tossing it into a smaller tub on the ground. The water in this one had a faint blue cast.

"Rose, it is," Faith replied. "I'm Faith. I came to see if there were clean bandages for the hospital."

"Which one? There's more than one here."

Faith smiled ruefully. "You are right. I'm referring to the one between Washington's headquarters and McIntosh's brigade. Mary Porter sent me here."

"Oh, Mary," Rose smiled. "She's a gracious lady. You can tell her I will have her caps and aprons ready by tomorrow. Those bandages took some work. Blood needs a lot of cold water to come out. I've been soaking them with some chamber lye over there." She pointed to a pot on the side. Faith went over to look. As she approached, the potent smell took her aback.

"Oh, you haven't been around chamber lye–have you?" Rose laughed. "I collect that from the chamber pots at the farms or the men who will provide it. Ferment it a while, and it will whiten clothes real pretty. You learn to accept the scent of piss."

Faith nodded weakly. Her eyes were watering from the powerful scents of lye and urine. She didn't see how the young woman tolerated it. She looked over at the laundress.

Rose couldn't be over eighteen or nineteen, although her work-worn hands looked like an old woman's. She was about the same height as Faith, which made her taller than most other women. A dull brown cloth covered her hair, but some auburn strands escaped at the sides and front. Her skin was the color of coffee with a dash of cream. The sprinkling of freckles on her arms and face reminded her of the twins, Paul and Silas, back home. Steam rose from the pot on the fire, making sweat rise in beads on the laundress's face. Whitish streaks from soap stood out on her skin, although her knuckles looked red and rough from constant exposure to the soap and lye used in laundry.

"You're staring at me," Rose said. A child's voice echoed from the woods. In response, she turned her head in that direction. "Anna, you watch yourself! There's no telling what's out there." Leaves crunched underfoot as a tiny figure raced out and toward the tent.

"Yes, mama," a voice floated back. A little girl ran up, her face flushed from exertion. She looked to be about four with her mother's freckles and dark eyes. Neatly braided hair rolled down her shoulders. Though faded, her clothes were spotless and in good shape. Tiny curls framed her heart-shaped face. A Cupid's bow mouth was open, revealing pearly white teeth. Adorable dimples framed the smile she gave her mother.

Faith feared she might fall into the fire, but the small child skirted the laundry area with the expertise of long practice. "Your daughter is lovely," Faith said. It surprised her that such a young woman had a child this old. She wondered if the child's father was in the army or if Rose and her daughter were on their own.

"Thank you," Rose said. "Anna, can you get me more soap?"

"Yes, Mama," the little one said obediently as she trotted into the tent.

When she moved through the flap, Faith could see a pallet on the ground, along with a few scattered blankets. "Is this where you sleep?"

"Since we arrived," Rose said. "We've been traveling with the 8th North Carolina for most of the year. I contracted to do their laundry. The hospital provides a little extra, and Mistress Porter shares food supplies with us when she can." She picked up another piece of clothing from the tub below the batten. "If you will excuse me, I have a great deal of laundry left to do before nightfall."

Faith nodded. "I will leave you to your work, Mistress Rose." She walked back to camp, wondering why something about her seemed familiar. She walked back toward Washington's headquarters. After discovering a man hanging, she had no desire to go walking through the woods. Out on the parade ground, men practiced drilling under von Steuben. Will was with him, she was sure. Across the distance, she could hear words in German being shouted, followed by a translation into English. Some days, the shouting was in French. It just depended on whether John Laurens or Will were helping their drill master on that day.

Before reentering the farmhouse, she looked back across the fields at the encampment. Now that the misery of winter was passing, she could appreciate the emerging beauty of the meadows and nearby trees. She would be glad when it was time to return home.

After dinner, she went for a walk with Will. The sun had settled on the horizon, but a few hours of light remained. For once, they had a few moments to be alone.

When questioned about the baron's remarks, he flushed. "I dinna use that sort of language around ladies."

Faith shot him a puzzled look.

"The Baron uses a lot of rough language. He's a soldier. Rough language is common, although he's more creative than most. What matters is that he is an excellent teacher. There is no task too small for him to model. We've gone over how to stand, how to turn. His demonstration of proper musket care surprised me. Taking a man's gun, he cleaned and reassembled it. He's also been teaching us how to fight with the bayonets lashed to the guns." He shook his head. "These men have never had training on these sorts of things. Most have only used their bayonets for roasting meat over a fire."

He looked over at her. "Von Steuben has also been urging a cleanup of the camp. Latrines have to be in certain places downstream from camp. All dead carcasses had to be moved far from the living quarters. He insists it will cut down on disease in the camp."

"I've noticed that the smell has lessened," Faith admitted. They had paused by the fence that encircled the farmhouse where Washington stayed. Long shadows fell over the ground as the daylight waned. Up in the sky, the moon made its presence known as the sky turned a deeper shade of blue. The evening star sparkled faintly below the pale crescent. Embers glowed from the camp ovens in the distance. Large ovens had been dug into the earth on the side of nearby hills. Cooks continually used them to bake anything that could become bread to feed the men.

Will's gaze was earnest as he looked at her. "Von Steuben understands war better than anyone at camp except Washington. He has taught us more than anyone in the few weeks he has been here. If we are to win, we need him." He sighed. "We need General Greene as well. Since he became quartermaster, we have actually started getting in the food and supplies we need. I will be glad when all the men have shoes on their feet."

Faith reached out and took his hand. "I will be glad when this war is over.'

"Aye," he answered, squeezing her hand. "Whenever that may be."

Her mind returned to the present. The weather had warmed with the onset of spring. But spring had its own problems. Faith watched the clouds gather overhead, promising rain. It wouldn't take much to turn the roadways into mud. They needed clear days to let the supply wagons come in and restock the camp. In the distance, clouds rumbled a warning. Despite her wishes, stormy weather was coming.

Chapter Nine

A few days later, Faith, along with Will, joined Hannah and Jeremy for dinner at the farmhouse where the couple was staying until Lafayette returned. Already used to the unusual conditions of the encampment, they walked together down the road to the farmhouse Lafayette had rented for his men before being called on another mission. As they drew close to the small farmhouse, they heard voices in French calling out to each other as they conversed. Faith had spent little time with these men, so she watched with interest their gestures as they spoke in rapid French. She didn't know what they were saying. When the men spotted her, they came over and made her welcome in their broken English. Their mannerisms startled her at first before she relaxed and accepted that this was normal for them. They dined with the other officers under Lafayette's command in the large room downstairs that served as office and dining room.

The men pushed the tables together while the women worked on serving the simple meal of boiled cabbage and salt pork, along with some sort of biscuit. Both Hannah and Faith had stared at the bread briefly before eating it. Somewhat blackened by fire, it resembled an edible substance. By this time, everyone knew not to complain about whatever food they were served. Its remarkable chewiness surprised no one. With close to a dozen officers present, it was a crowded space, but the company was friendly, and the fire was warm. Not surprisingly, most of the men spoke French, which Jeremy was happy to translate. Those who spoke English were happy to charm the ladies. They shared a few bottles of wine someone had brought. Once that was gone, Jeremy brought out a fine jug of cider to end the meal. One of the French asked Jeremy where he had gotten it. Her brother-in-law smiled mysteriously. Following the translation of the conversation, Faith rolled her eyes. She had learned long ago not to inquire into his sources.

As the evening drew late, the party broke up. A group of men carried the tub of dishes to the outdoor kitchen to wash them. Afterwards, they pushed the tables together to clear the space for sleeping pallets. Butler took Hannah's hand and invited Faith and Will upstairs to sit around the fire and talk before the evening drew to a close.

When they entered the room, a fire crackled in the hearth, bathing the room in a warm glow. Jeremy went over to check it before grabbing a handful of cushions stacked nearby and scattering them on the floor. "It's warmer this way," he said before claiming one. Hannah sat next to him before the other two joined. For a few moments, no one spoke as they relaxed in rare privacy.

Light bounced off the exposed beams of the ceiling. A lone window stood on one end, covered by a muslin curtain that kept the night at bay. Besides the sturdy wooden bed, there was a narrow chest at the foot and a straight-backed chair. There was barely enough room for the four of them, but they made it work. Hannah leaned against Jeremy, looking relaxed for the first time since Faith had seen her at the encampment. He smoothed her hair, tucking away loose strands.

Will reached out an arm and wrapped it about Faith's shoulders. She sighed happily and leaned against his side. His heart beat steadily against her, a steady reassurance of his presence. There was no need for words right now; it was enough to feel warm and safe with those she loved.

Eventually, tongues loosened. Hannah told Faith how their father fared on the farm. "He spends his extra hours with Caleb and Bess's children. They bring him much happiness." Her face darkened when she added the British were frequently out patrolling the countryside and sometimes stopping at nearby farms, checking for forage and other supplies. Faith knew the constant incursions had everyone uneasy.

"How is Charity?" Faith asked. A shadow passed over Hannah's face at the mention of their younger sister's name. Her body stiffened as she gathered her words.

"She has been receiving visits from a British officer," Hannah said at last. "He's the reason our farm has avoided as many raids as others. He's also the reason I left." She sighed. "He doesn't seem a bad sort. He treats everyone cordially and has been a perfect gentleman to her. Unfortunately, he has colored her feelings regarding the war for independence. Charity says the war is foolish and the colonies should make peace with Great Britain." She bit her lip. "I was afraid of what she might tell him about me." She looked over at Jeremy. "And you."

"What have you told her?" Jeremy asked gently. His hand paused briefly on the top of her head before continuing down to the nape, where her bun rested. His fingers kneaded her neck, working on the tightness that lay just below the surface.

Hannah shook her head. "Nothing. I have never shared that with any of my family. It would be too dangerous for them to know. My father and older brothers have vowed to remain neutral. But she knows Benjamin Franklin stayed at my home. As far as I know, she could be why the British found out and ousted me." She shook her head in disbelief. "Charity wasn't sorry I lost my home and business. She told me," Hannah's voice choked. "That was the cost of war."

Jeremy gathered her in his arms. "You are here now, with me." He cupped her head as she rested it on his shoulder, turning away from the others.

Shock washed over Faith like a bucket of cold water. She didn't know what to say. Whether Charity was guilty or innocent was impossible to know. That Hannah considered her capable of betrayal horrified Faith. Pain washed over her at the realization of the distance between them. Her little sister had always been the quiet one, hiding away with her weaving whenever she could. "Charity is twenty-two now, isn't she? I don't think she's ever been away from home. Has she had any prospects before this soldier?"

Hannah spoke in a muffled voice. "There was a young man a few years ago. He was from a good Quaker family. He got typhoid and perished. After that, she quit going out anywhere. She refused to visit me in Philadelphia and avoided going to the market." She shook her head. "I don't know what goes on in her head anymore."

Will's voice was soft. "This war has torn many families apart. Perhaps when the war ends that we can heal. I am sorry for your troubles, Hannah. I truly am." He leaned over to poke the fire. Sparks shot up when a log shifted. Flames exploded when they found a spot of pitch from a piece of pine. Quiet fell over them as the fire's warmth chased away icy fingers of fear and doubt. As he sat back, he said. "I see we are getting more supply wagons."

Jeremy nodded. "General Greene has done an excellent job as quarter-master. I'm relieved to see more food and blankets arriving. Yesterday, a shipment of shoes came in. I will be happy if I never see another naked foot in the snow. If the rains hold off, we should be in good stead soon. Now, if we can just stop this madman in camp."

Faith looked up. "What madman are you talking about?"

Will and Jeremy looked at each other. Will said. "You may as well tell them. No one is safe here anymore."

Jeremy paused, gathered his thoughts, and then discussed the strange poem sent to Washington. "It came from the Congress in York, which makes no sense. Even after a delegation visited, they still have little knowledge of this camp. It's obviously the work of someone here. Then there are the dolls."

"Dolls?" Hannah and Faith spoke together.

Jeremy sighed. "After each death, someone delivers a doll to Washington. They are crude, carved from sticks. Each one has mimicked one death."

"What does Washington do with them?" Faith asked.

Jeremy smiled without humor. "He burns them almost immediately. I'm not sure if it's out of anger or fear."

Will scoffed. "You think our commander is afraid of dolls?"

Jeremy shook his head. "I think he fears what they mean. It takes time to create a figure like that. Despite their crudeness, they have faces. They wear clothes. They have the same injuries as the victims." He shivered. "That takes planning and thought. How does he get them to Washington with no one seeing him?"

"It sounds like whoever is doing this plans on a lot of deaths." Will looked worried. He had spoken little about the incident with the cannon, although Hannah had mentioned the man who had lost an arm had died from blood loss.

Jeremy frowned. "How could he have planned the last one? Cannons are not a precision instrument, especially at that distance."

Will's expression turned grim. "Someone aimed them at us. Whoever it was knew what would happen when that fuse was lit. He didn't care how many people got hurt along with his target."

Jeremy looked thoughtful. "Firing cannons takes a certain amount of skill. Whoever fired it knew how to load and fire it. Not everyone does. So either he has artillery training or has spent some time observing the artillery train. Do you think he meant to kill Baker?"

Will was blunt. "He killed two of Washington's Life Guards. That was not an accident. Whether he intended to kill one, two, or a dozen, we will never know. But someone turned, loaded, and fired that cannon directly at a closely packed group of men. None of Knox's artillerymen fired that shot. They have alibis."

"Then who?" Butler pondered. "Who has that ability and can move freely in this camp? He's no ghost."

"No," Will admitted. "Most of these poor men barely know how to march, much less load and fire something that big. But unless they have duty, the men could be anywhere in camp. It's not a prison, after all."

Jeremy poked the fire. "No, it's not a prison, but I don't want it to become a hunting ground, either. There has to be a way to track this person down. This could cause panic throughout the ranks. Washington hasn't even informed his generals. He's afraid of how it will affect the men."

Will met his eyes. "These deaths don't go unnoticed, mate. These men aren't fools, and people talk. He should make a statement so people can keep an eye out."

Butler shot him a look. "What would he say? That we have someone in camp who is working for the enemy, or we have a complete madman, or he is both? It wouldn't help."

Will frowned. "Is that what you believe? That someone in camp is a spy or has gone mad?"

"That poem makes me think of the latter," Butler admitted. "Who sends that sort of thing in the mail? It reeks of insanity."

Faith interrupted. "Whether he's a British Spy or a madman is not the point right now. If we are to believe his note, he is not done. What comes after the cannon?"

Jeremy paused, then recited from memory.

Seven camp followers nursing the sick,
Until a fine horse delivered a kick.

"So a nurse?" Everyone's eyes turned to Hannah, who had remained silent as the men spoke. Light from the fire reflected in her eyes.

"I'm not quitting. I rarely leave the hospital. No matter what the rumors may be, we don't treat livestock." A few chuckles greeted her response.

"You have been visiting your horse. I've seen you going to the barn," Jeremy faced the flames as he spoke, although he watched her out of the corner of his eye.

"I'm responsible for Gracie, and she wouldn't hurt anyone."

"This isn't about the horse. It's a part of the camp that is not closely watched. The only people going in and out of there besides you are Washington and the stable hands. It's not safe to go there." One of his hands balled into a fist that he dug into his leg.

"As you say," Hannah said. "The only people going in there are General Washington, his trusted stable hands, and me. Unless Washington is a suspect. I believe the occasional visit to my horse is not dangerous."

Jeremy's tone sharpened. "You need to take this seriously, Hannah. Anyone could go in there."

Hannah rose. "I will be careful. I'm not living my life ruled by fear. Besides, the person I see most is the General. He brings treats to his horse every day."

"Can you at least time your visits for when Washington is about?" He pleaded. "I worry about you."

Hannah bit her lip. "I can do that."

'Good." He looked at the other two. "It's getting late."

Will and Faith rose as well and headed toward the door. Downstairs, a board creaked as the officers settled for the night.

Faith looked at the other three gathered around her. "Everyone needs to be careful."

Jeremy nodded. "You three are the only ones I trust, although I doubt Washington has anything to do with this." He looked at the darkening sky. "You two need to get back before it gets too late. I will walk with you to be safe."

Will glanced over at him. "And walk about a mile back in the dark by yourself? No, you stay here with your wife. I can walk Faith home. There are nearly always some of von Steuben's men hanging about for a drink and a talk. I can join them for the short walk back." He smiled grimly at the other man. "I still have the knife you gave me if there's any trouble."

Butler cocked an eyebrow at him. "Just keep your eyes and ears open. A knife only works if you have time to use it." He nodded at Faith. "Do you still have that pistol?"

She nodded. "It's in my pack in my room. I have powder and shot for it as well."

"Do me a favor and keep it where you can use it," he said. "Your sister will hold me accountable if you get into trouble."

Faith glanced at Hannah, who did not contradict him. "I will."

Once they went downstairs, the conversation ceased. Butler held a finger to his lips to remind them not to disturb the soldiers occupying the other room. Already, a few snores drifted through the closed doors of what had been the dining room. Soft voices conversed in French in front of the fire, visible through the cracked door. Jeremy returned a wave as they went to the door. After saying goodbye, he walked onto the porch with Faith and Will. Hannah remained inside.

Will lifted the tin lantern he had lit before exiting. It exuded a dim light that would help them see the road, which was just a dark line in the distance. The moon rose high in the sapphire sky, surrounded by a host of stars that gleamed in the darkness. The bare silhouettes of trees stood outlined by the light of the stars. No breeze disturbed their branches. There was little noise beyond their footfalls on the porch and the moan of a step as it accepted their weight.

Faith held her shawl close around her body. "It's not as cold as I would have thought." Her breath was a faint vapor in the night. She turned to Jeremy. "You truly believe that someone is causing these deaths? How do we know that someone is not using deaths that have already occurred to pull some sort of sick joke?"

Butler contemplated her face. "It's possible that someone wants to frighten us. I intend to find out who sent that hideous doll from Congress. Lauren's father is there. He might know something."

"Do you think John had something to do with this?"

Butler shrugged. "I don't discount anyone. He seems to be an honorable young man. His language skills have certainly been a blessing to Washington and von Steuben. If anyone could send from York, he could. But that's not enough to condemn anyone. I will talk to him tomorrow. As to whether there is a killer, the actions of the poem are not complete. Keep that in mind." With that, he bid them goodnight and reentered the house.

Will gave Faith the lantern to keep his hands free. "I don't think anyone will attack us on such a well-traveled route, but I don't want to take any chances," Will said as "Hoo-hoo-ha-hoo" echoed through the darkness. A barred owl sounded its distinctive call in the distance. Before they had gone far, a dark shape crossed overhead, swooping down in the bare field before rising again and heading into the trees. "He found something to eat."

Faith nodded. "So it seems." Although she couldn't imagine what would be creeping about on a cold, dark night.

The ground crunched underneath their feet as they continued down the road to where Washington's headquarters lay. The silent darkness enveloped them like a blanket. "What's it like to work for Baron von Steuben?" Faith asked.

Will said nothing at first. He kept his eyes moving, checking out skeletal groups of trees and thick clumps of grass as they walked along the packed earth of the road.

"Not bad," he said at last. "Except for Laurens and me, most have been with him since he was in Germany and France. They all seem quite fond of him." He paused thoughtfully. "Von Steuben has traveled throughout Europe. Battlefields have occupied most of his adult life. He has a lot to teach us." He chuckled wryly. "I'm not sure how much to believe of his stories. I think if he had gathered that much glory, there would be no reason for him to be here."

Faith nodded. "So you like being one of his aides?"

Will nodded. "It's a suitable position, far better than when I was one of many of General Muhlenberg's troops. He is fair to a fault. When I'm not translating, I help Laurens and Hamilton translate his notes for the field manual he is writing for the troops. Washington hopes to share it with all the commanders under him."

Faith listened to him. There had not been a lot of time to talk at Valley Forge. They both stayed busy with their duties. The darkness made it difficult to see much more than his outline in the darkness. She had watched him over dinner and afterwards. Even though it had been a little over a year since she had seen him in Williamsburg, he seemed older and grimmer. She worried she might not recognize him by the time the war ended.

Once they climbed a brief rise, the farmhouse where Washington lived came into view. White smoke rose from the chimney from the fires that burned inside. The moon highlighted the remaining snow on the rooftop. As they approached, they heard a hello from a soldier on patrol. Will acknowledged him, and when asked, told them about their business.

"We're headed home after dinner with some of Lafayette's men." He nodded at Faith. "She bunks with some of Lady Washington's women. I'm expected at Baron von Steuben's house." Will paused at the bottom of the short set of steps that led to the main entrance. Light glowed faintly through the front windows. Darkness lay over the outside like a shroud. Faith handed him the lantern as she ascended the steps. She paused on the stoop, looking out into the night, amazed at how quickly the darkness had overtaken them. Only a faint rim of burgundy lit the western horizon behind the farmhouse. "Are you coming in?"

Will shook his head. "Tomorrow will be here soon enough. I'd best head down the road."

"Alone?" Fear made her voice sound shakier than she wished.

"It's not far." Will turned to go, lifting the light to illuminate the path. Just then, a few men came out from the breezeway. From their enthusiastic greetings in German, it was clear they were von Steuben's men. He looked at Faith. "I can walk back with these men. We all know each other. I don't think I am in much danger."

Faith went in and watched them from a window. Faint singing drifted in from the distance. As she watched him disappear down the road, she realized he was right. He was not in much danger. The poem had made that clear. The target was not a soldier this time, but a nurse. Faith prayed that her headstrong sister was not in the killer's sights.

Chapter Ten

Faith awoke tired and achy. She had spent the night in and out of restless dreams where death stalked her loved ones. Next to her, the woman with whom she shared a cot snored softly before turning on her side away from her. Relieved that the other woman continued to sleep, Faith stared at the ceiling in relative privacy.

The attic room she occupied remained dark, as did the outside. The roof slanted down on either side, making it a challenge to stand up without bumping one's head. Her nose was cold. She sniffed, trying to keep it from dripping. Any warmth to be had would be downstairs in one of the main rooms. Her thoughts turned wistfully to visions of a roaring fire and a hot cup of coffee. Washington and his wife were early risers, so coffee was available long before breakfast. With that thought, her stomach grumbled.

She listened carefully for signs anyone else was awake. The attic remained quiet except for the sounds of the other women sleeping. In a room on the other side of the attic steps, a bed creaked as someone turned. Another coughed. A faint rustle from the rafters made her stiffen. The last thing she wanted to discover was some creature had taken residence up here with them. The sound ceased, making her relax slightly.

Sleep was not returning. "Brrrr." She gasped as bare feet hit the cold floor. Faith grabbed her stockings from where she had squirreled them on her side of the bed and pulled them on swiftly. Faith rose and hurried to throw on clothes in the icy air. Once she had put on enough to be decent, she descended the stairs, deciding to put on the rest in a place where her breath was not a vapor.

Martha Washington met her on the landing of the second floor. Her gaze went to Faith's gaping bodice. Noting the pins in her hand, she said. "You may want to fix that before you go downstairs." Lady Washington was immaculate in a wool dress of deep blue. A ribbon on her starched white cap matched the hue perfectly. Her maid followed, helping her keep the folds of her dress from catching on the bannister as she descended.

Faith sighed and stared down at her jacket. It was still cold. She could smell coffee down below. Its seductive fumes reminded her she had not eaten in several hours. The front door slammed, announcing someone's arrival. Voices went up the stairwell before the door to Washington's study opened and shut. Her nose and fingers were still cold, but she couldn't appear undressed before strangers.

Faith sucked in her breath and began pinning the opening, trying not to yelp when she stuck a finger. She sucked on it for a moment to ease the sting. When she arrived downstairs, she looked like a lady even though her fingers hurt, and her stomach was empty enough to eat a bear.

Lady Washington said nothing as she joined the others for breakfast. The pushed-together tables made a long expanse around which everyone gathered, the general at the head and his lady at the foot. After saying a brief grace, Washington signaled for the meal to begin. Staff passed around bread, cheese, leftover salt pork, and mush. Faith gratefully drank her first mug of coffee. When Hannah Till refilled it, she wanted to declare the woman an angel.

After breakfast, the men and ladies separated. Washington met with his officers and aides while Lady Washington gathered the ladies to assign them different tasks. Some women went to help nurse the sick and injured, others gathered their material to knit stockings or mend clothing. A few wrote letters either for themselves or for men unable to do so without help. Some kept the farmhouse neat.

Faith was not one of the gentry, like Lady Washington, Lady Sterling, Caty Greene, or Ann Knox. Nor was she one of the serving staff. She fell somewhere in between, which meant sometimes Lady Washington seemed uncertain what to do with her. Today, she was inventorying the farmhouse's supplies. Given her background with running a tavern, it was a logical choice. Faith was happy to go out to the kitchen and cellars to check on their stores of foodstuffs and other necessities.

Exiting the breezeway, she caught her breath. The sun had crept over the horizon, illuminating the landscape with its pale glow. A faint coating of frost coated the meadow's grass in silver. Ghostly fog rolled in from the banks of the Schuylkill River to the north. Its waters murmured restlessly in the distance. Across the meadow, she spotted a scattering of dark shapes of cattle left from the last herd driven in a few days previous. They grazed, lowing softly. They didn't care for the morning chill either.

Faith inhaled the cool air, glad for a few moments to herself. Her dark wool shawl kept most of the cold away. It was lovely not to smell another person for a few moments. The crisp air was redolent with the faint scents of hay and manure, along with a hint of rain.

Faith searched the sky. Clouds were gathering in the west. She would have to complete her task before the weather rolled in. Walking in pouring rain and mud was decidedly unpleasant. Before she went to check the cellars and sheds where they stored food for the General's headquarters, she knocked on the door to the kitchen and entered.

Hannah Till kneaded bread on a wooden table in the center of the room. She looked mildly surprised to see Faith. Her arms bore a dusting of flour up to her elbows.

Faith nodded to her. "I'm sorry to disturb you, Hannah. Lady Washington has me checking food supplies to see if we are desperately in need of anything. She knows General Greene will meet with General Washington sometime today." She looked at the woman. "I don't want to interrupt your work, but if there is something you need, let me know, and I will pass the information to Lady Washington."

Hannah nodded. "We need salt, Mistress. There's mighty little of it to be had. Any vegetables the general can provide are welcome as well."

Faith nodded. "I will inform her." She turned to go. "I will check the cellar and shed as well to make sure there is nothing else we need." As she left the kitchen, she shook herself. There was no reason to tell the cook where she was going, but she felt safer knowing someone knew her location.

The door to the root cellar stuck at first, unwilling to open. Faith wrestled with the latch before bracing her feet against the edge of the frame and pulling with all her strength. The hinges squealed as the door jerked open. Faith staggered, wobbling back and forth as she struggled to regain her balance. She had forgotten to bring a lantern. Letting her eyes adjust to the dimness, she stared down the stairs into the narrow confines of the cellar. Taking inventory should not take long.

Deciding the open door offered sufficient light, Faith walked down the steps and into the shadowed room. A few strands of green hung from the rafters. Her nose caught the faint scent of garlic, long since taken up into the kitchen. Long wooden shelves lined the space. Most of them were bare. Dusty outlines told the story of goods once stored, but long since used.

Three barrels sat on the earthen floor. Faith opened the nearest one and peered inside. Grayish white flour filled the lower quarter. It was too dim to see if bugs had gotten inside. But then, would knowing such information change anything? There was too little food to be picky. The other barrel contained a few remnants of salt pork. Grains of course salt lined the interior of the barrel, while what remained of the meat lay on the very bottom. Faith doubted there was enough to flavor a pot of beans well. Sighing, she closed that barrel before going to the last one. Its lid was firmly in place. Grunting, she pulled on the edges. "What could this possibly be?" She wondered as she fought to discover its contents. It lay in a corner covered by shadows. The light from the open door did not extend that far.

A scrabbling in the dark corners alerted Faith that something else inhabited the darkened storage space. "Rats," she said aloud. Faith didn't like rodents. It was one reason she had allowed Olivia to take in a stray cat at the tavern back home. It earned its keep by keeping mice, rats, and other creatures out of their supplies.

A loud creak was all the warning she had before the root cellar door slammed shut, leaving her in the dark. "Wait," Faith yelled. "I'm down here! Open the door!" No one responded. Faith felt her way to the steps and stumbled up them in the darkness. The door moved slightly but didn't budge. It was heavy and unwilling to move. She pounded on the door, yelling and screaming for a few moments, but no one responded.

The cold, dark space felt like a tomb. Faith took a few deep breaths and sat down on the steps to take stock of her situation. Outside, thunder rumbled in the distance. Rain would come soon, which meant people would seek shelter. She didn't know how long it would take before someone noticed her absence. Only Hannah Till knew where she had gone.

A few glimmers of light shone through cracks in the door frame. Faith was grateful, even if there was not enough to illuminate the room. She rose and pushed against the door again. It rose a few inches but did not open. Faith grunted and pushed with all her strength, but the door refused to give.

The roaring wind warned of the storm's imminent arrival. She did not want to spend hours trapped in the cellar. Faith screamed in frustration, pounding on the hardwood until her hands throbbed. A sob tore in her throat. Outside, the thunder rumbled close by, warning everyone that a storm was imminent.

Men's voices carried across the yard, their boots thumping as they ran by. Faith shrieked again. There was a pause. "Did you hear that?" A voice said.

"Help! I'm stuck inside." She pounded on the door.

The door groaned as it opened. Two men stared down at her. They wore the long hunting shirts and breeches of the enlisted. One offered her a hand up out of the cellar. "How did you get in there?" The man asked. A few drops fell from the sky before lightning flashed in the distance, followed by a threatening rumble of thunder.

The other man looked at the sky. "Let's get inside before it gets worse."

They ran around the side to the breezeway of the farmhouse. Faith thanked them. "I guess the wind blew the door shut as I was checking supplies."

The two men looked at each other and back at her. "Ma'am, that door wasn't just shut; someone latched it closed. You wouldn't have gotten out if we hadn't been coming by."

Faith stared at them. "Why would someone do that?"

No one answered. Rain poured down from the sky, covering the landscape in a veil of gray mist. One of her rescuers looked at her. "We'd best all get inside. We need to report to Washington, and you are better off out of this weather."

Faith went in glad to be around people, even as she wondered who could have shut her in the cellar, and more importantly, why? She went up to her attic room to tidy herself before seeking Lady Washington. A small tin mirror hung on the wall next to the door. With the pouring rain, the room was dim and shadowed. Faith decided not to waste a candle and used the faint light from the small window opposite the door. She wiped smudges of dirt off her face and hands. Brushing off a cobweb, she went downstairs to Lady Washington's parlor/bedroom.

No one commented when she opened the door. Only a half-dozen women populated the room. Faith suspected some were at the various hospitals caring for the sick or working elsewhere on tasks assigned to them.

Lady Washington was speaking to one of her servants, a slender, dark-skinned woman with huge dark eyes and a faintly crooked nose. When she saw Faith, she said. "There is Mistress Clarke." She looked at Faith. "Have you finished checking our food supplies?"

"Not exactly," Faith said. She told her about getting trapped in the storehouse. "I can tell you we are almost out of salt pork and flour, and Hannah needs more salt. But I did not get to the Commissary General to inquire about when to expect more supplies."

Martha Washington did not comment on her getting locked in the cellar. Instead, she looked at the rain streaming down the windows. "I don't think today would be a good day to walk out to the commissary." She looked Faith up and down. "You need to tend your appearance, Mistress Clarke. Cobwebs do not belong in your hair." Her tone was dry. "Perhaps after that, you would like to help Mistress Knox complete more socks for our men? When the rain ceases, I hope to have some delivered to the hospital to comfort those who are convalescing there."

Faith nodded and headed upstairs. She changed into her spare apron before washing her face with the cold water in the basin. A quick touch of the comb neatened her hair. Shivering, she hurried back down. Faith was happy to sit by the fire and knit. There was security in being in the farmhouse surrounded by the other women. Helping deliver socks later that day could give her some time to see Hannah. She was relieved that her sister was safe and out of Philadelphia. Lucy Knox smiled as she sat beside her. Her little girl slept on a small pallet in front of the fire. Her dark curls spread out around her head like a halo. Light from the fire highlighted a few auburn strands amidst the mass of dark brown. Her chubby fist held a bunched-up mound of the pillow. Her cap had fallen off and lay next to her. Someone, probably her mother, had spread a shawl over her sleeping form.

Lucy's eyes met Faith's. "She didn't want to leave me."

"There is no reason she should have to," Faith replied. "She is doing no harm."

Lucy nodded and went back to work. She finished a stocking leg and focused on turning the heel. Her plump fingers were nimble as they worked the short rows necessary for the heel flap. It spoke of long practice.

"I find heels the hardest part," Faith commented as she picked up her needles. Her stocking was only halfway down the calf. She had many rows to complete before dealing with the heel.

"I don't mind the heel, doing the toes, so there is no bump to irritate, takes the most time for me. Henry is particular about his feet." Lucy smiled as she worked. It was obvious she loved him. Lucy was a large, plump woman, almost equal in size to her own husband. Rich, dark brown strands of hair tried to escape her cap as she looked down at her work.

Faith found it easy to relax in the other woman's presence. They worked together in peace as rain pattered on the roof. Footsteps ascended and descended the stairs outside the door. Men's and women's voices murmured, although the words were indistinct. Will's whereabouts in the pouring rain were a mystery to her. They couldn't possibly be drilling in the deluge. She suspected he was sheltering with von Steuben's men. He could be busy planning for the next day or translating the German's words for the field manual he was writing for the troops.

Will didn't enjoy writing, but he was proficient. Although Hamilton and Laurens excelled and did most of the work, Will, with his German skills, helped ensure accurate interpretation of the baron's words.

By dinner, the rain had ceased, and the sun had come out. Water dripped off the edges of the roof into muddy puddles that surrounded the house. Faith was just coming down the stairs for dinner when the front door opened, and a group of men came in. The mixture of languages in their speech led her to conclude that the men were von Steuben's.

Hurrying the rest of the way down, she looked around, hoping to see Will. She was not disappointed. Water dripped off his hat as he stepped inside. He wiped his feet before entering. A smile lit up his face as he saw her coming toward him.

"You are a welcome sight." He allowed one of Lady Washington's servants to take his coat to dry by the fire. Will paused and then said with a sigh, "I don't think I'm fit for the company of ladies yet." He followed a group of men out to the breezeway, where they had set up some basins. When he returned, his face and hands were clean, and he was shivering. When he entered the dining room, he sat with his back to the blazing fire, soaking in the heat.

Faith sat next to him. To her delight, Hannah and Jeremy joined them at the table along with a man she had seen before, but did not know. He was slender, with dark hair and eyes that looked older than he likely was. Jeremy nodded to him. "Let me introduce you to Dr. Albigence Waldo, one of our camp surgeons."

Faith smiled as introductions went around. The surgeon said little but dug into his meal with eagerness that showed that he, like so many others, had suffered from the deprivations of the winter camp. "I'm glad that we're getting more regular supplies in camp," she said after they finished their meal of stew. She wasn't sure what was in it and decided it was prudent not to guess. Dessert was a cobbler made with dried apples she had seen Hannah Till soaking overnight in the kitchen. Not very sweet or with any spices to be had, it was still a welcome treat.

As they finished, Waldo looked over at Jeremy Butler. "I have finished examining that man you brought to me, along with his companion." He rose as servants cleared the table. They all moved the tables and chairs, restoring the room to its use as the aides-de-camp's office.

Butler spoke. "Let's find a more private place to speak." He, along with Waldo and the others, walked out into the hallway. He looked about, taking in the closed door of Washington's office, and the people going in and out of the room they had just left.

Faith spoke. "There's a small room upstairs, just off from Lady Washington's parlor and the other bedroom. There should be no one there now." Butler nodded and gestured for her to lead. She took them up the stairs to the small room that was part storage and partly for sleeping, although no fireplace graced the space. A window provided light, although the rain gave it a grayish cast.

Waldo looked faintly amused. "Have we taken to hiding in closets now? I'm not a spy, you know. I report to Washington like anyone else."

Butler shot him a look. "I'm aware, but I prefer not to stir up the camp if I can avoid it."

Waldo shrugged. "It really doesn't take much to stir things, that is true. Your bottle of whiskey is fine, by the way. I could find no hint of poison or any other substance other than liquor. Marvelous stuff too." He ignored Butler's stare. "Your first man drowned. As soon as he thawed, water started coming out of his lungs and belly. The rope may have been a belt, but it wasn't frayed like his clothes. I think someone used it to drag him back after the water had done its work. After he thawed, I saw a knot over his left ear, so I think someone knocked him out and tossed him in the water. The man wouldn't have had a chance with the wet and cold. He probably succumbed pretty swiftly."

Butler's face looked grim. "No chance of an accident, then."

Waldo shot him an exasperated look. "If he fell in the water and drowned, how did his body get back on land? I've heard that someone laid him out on the ground near the water after pulling him out. I suspect that's why the rope looked freshly cut."

"Why do that?" Will asked hoarsely. "Jonah wasn't a threat to anyone. He played cards a little, but we all do to pass the time. He did nothing to deserve this."

"What about the other man?" Butler said.

Waldo rubbed his arms. Even with the press of people, the air was still chilly. "He strangled to death. I found a piece of rope embedded in his neck under the scarf. Whoever strung him up knew little about hanging. The poor devil struggled a while before he died."

Faith's voice was quiet. "Two murders then, just like the poem. That, along with the other mischief happening."

Will turned to Faith. "What mischief are you referring to?"

Faith shared about being locked in the cellar."

Will's face turned dark. "That was a nasty thing to do. Any idea who would want to pull such a trick?""

Faith shook her head. "It could have been a warning, but against what, I do not know."

Butler frowned. "You haven't been stirring things up, asking questions about the dead man by the river – have you?"

Faith shook her head. "Until now, I thought the poor man's death an accident. There are plenty here who have died from disease and misfortune."

"Perhaps it was a poor attempt at humor," Waldo said. "The lads are restless and long to have something useful to do. I can see some of these idiots pulling pranks without considering the consequences."

Will sighed, not happy at the notion. "Make sure you don't go off alone again."

Faith nodded. "I have no intention of doing so." Thinking of being shut in the dark cellar, even briefly, made her skin crawl.

Conversation turned back to the death by the river. "What reason could there be for killing Jonah?" Will asked. "He was a threat to no one, and why would someone make him part of a poem?"

"What poem?" Waldo's eyes bore into Butler's.

"Someone sent a poem to Washington describing a series of murders." Butler recited it swiftly.

Waldo whistled softly. "So the killings are not done. That's a lot of death someone has planned. Any idea who sent it?"" The others shook their head.

The question echoed through the small room, unanswered. Even within the confines of the encampment, thousands of people went about their business. Among them, a killer walked, watching and waiting for his next opportunity.

Chapter Eleven

Once the rains started, they continued for days. Water poured from the sky, covering the ground and turning the roads into a soupy mess. Wagons of supplies slowed to a crawl as drovers struggled to make any progress on the waterlogged roads.

Faith longed for the sun. The press of bodies and endless chatter in the house were driving her mad. The dampness seemed to penetrate her bones, causing her to shiver as her body longed for warmth. Mud, tracked in by scores of feet, covered the floor, despite being constantly cleaned by staff.

In the parlor, the fire crackled. A faint haze of smoke rose from the still-damp wood, filling the room with its acrid scent. Faith's head throbbed from the constant chatter of the women gossiping as they knitted and sewed. There was always mending to be done. The light from the fire was poor, and the dimness of the rainy skies made it difficult to see well enough to thread needles or mend holes with delicate stitches. She sighed as she lay down the shirt she was reattaching buttons to. Her eyes blurred with the effort.

Outside, the patter of rain slowed before ceasing. The light outside brightened as clouds moved to allow the sun to reveal itself. Faith sighed in relief. Maybe it would stay bright for a while. She was ready for warmth and light and the fresh scent of flowers in the air.

"Perhaps the clouds will continue to clear away," Lucy Knox said as she continued to knit a stocking. Her large, capable hands could turn out stockings in record time. She barely looked at her work, relying on touch to tell her where she was.

Faith looked at the window. "I hope so. I was wondering if it would last forty days and nights."

"Let us hope not," Lucy chuckled. "I doubt this house floats, and if Washington has requested an ark from Congress, it will not arrive until after the flood, I am sure."

Faith laughed. Lucy was easy to be around and had a wonderful, warm humor that lacked the sharp edges of some of the other women. At their feet, her daughter played with a doll that Lucy had made with scraps of fabric and yarn. It reminded Faith of the dolls Jeremy had described being sent to Washington. The little one whispered to her toy and hummed as she rocked it gently in her arms. Lucy's eyes were soft as she looked down at her. The little one looked up at her mother and laughed before using her mother's skirt to pull herself up.

"I hungry." She shot her mother a piercing stare.

Lucy Knox looked down at her chubby-cheeked child. "It hasn't been all that long since your breakfast, Lucy."

"I hungry now," little Lucy replied. Her chin wobbled. A meltdown would soon follow if she didn't get what she wanted. Despite her slight frame, the child's piercing cries echoed throughout the house when upset.

Faith put down her mending. "Let me go down to the kitchen. I'm sure the cook may have something that can keep her until dinner."

Lucy Knox shot her a grateful glance. "Thank you." She looked down at her daughter. "John insisted on naming her for me. She is the first of our children and the apple of his eye." Her eyes looked away. "I experienced two miscarriages before we had her."

A knot rose in Faith's throat at her words. She was fortunate to have a healthy son, but she knew the aching loss of miscarriage. It was a pain that might fade, but never really left. She rose from her seat. "I will return shortly."

Lucy nodded and went back to her determined child, trying to distract her until Faith could return.

Faith knew that little ones had no patience, so she hurried down the steps, eager to prevent earth-shattering shrieks. Surely there was something that could assuage the child's hunger and keep the peace for a few more hours.

The hallway was empty as she crossed it to the door to the breezeway. Only the door to the office of the aides de camp stood open. No one was inside at the moment. Faith suspected they must be meeting with Washington if they were not busy in the encampment.

Once out in the breezeway, she took a deep breath. A gentle breeze brought the scent of damp earth and grass. The meadows were already turning from yellow to green. A flock of robins worked their way across the ground in the main yard, seeking to make a meal of the worms all the rain had brought up. The trees near the house were developing buds that would shortly turn into leaves.

Mindful of the short waiting ability of the very young, Faith knocked and entered the kitchen as soon as Hannah acknowledged her. Hannah Till was busy rinsing the salt pork she had set out to soak the night before. It was the only way to make the preserved meat edible. Steam rose from a large black pot that hung from a hook over the fire. Once Hannah finished preparing the pork, she chopped it up and added it to one of her pots.

She looked up at Faith. "A little pork can really flavor a pot of beans." She washed off her hands and dried them on her apron.

Faith nodded. "Yes, it can. I have done that many times myself." Outside, the steady chop of an axe told her someone, probably Hannah's husband, Isaac, was chopping wood to restock the always hungry fires.

Hannah looked at her. "Can I help you?"

Faith smiled. "Yes, I have a starving toddler upstairs who will not wait until dinner. Is there anything I can give her to hold her over until then?"

Hannah smiled. "Young ones are often hungry. Young Miss Lucy is a growing child." They both heard a wail from upstairs. "Let me get you some bread and butter for her, along with a cup of milk. Isaac just brought in a pail, so it's fresh."

Faith smiled gratefully. "That would be wonderful." Once the cook gave her the food and drink, she hurried back up the stairs and into the parlor, where Lucy Knox tried to calm her fussing daughter.

The crying stopped when the little one spotted the food. "Mine," she snuffled, reaching for it with eager hands.

"What do you say, Lucy?" her mother whispered.

"Thank you," the tot said obediently before snatching the bread and stuffing a piece in her mouth.

Faith set the plate and cup on a table by her mother and went to her chair to pick up her knitting. She opened the window to let in some fresh air and ease the scent of bodies and damp diapers. Taking a deep breath, she welcomed the scents of earth and grass. A light breeze swirled the curtain into an undulating pattern.

Across the lawn, she saw the stone barn where Washington kept his horses. It also housed Hannah's mare, Gracie, there, protecting her from the weather. A woman in a dark cloak came down the path. Faith watched as the figure looked around before entering the building. Given the distance, she could not identify the woman, but she knew there was no reason for her to be there. Washington had men assigned to care for the animals. The memory of the dinner she and Will had shared with her sister and her husband flooded back. Hannah had promised to be careful, but she was also stubborn. If she thought her mare needed tending, she would go regardless of the lack of escort. Faith might hope she wouldn't be so foolish, but she had a feeling that her sister would do as she pleased.

Faith turned back to the room and looked at her knitting, waiting for her in a chair. Lucy Knox was helping her child wipe her mouth and hands after her snack. Lady Stirling and a few other wives were also in the room. Downstairs, she could hear a woman's voice in measured tones. Undoubtedly, it was Lady Washington making sure the house ran smoothly.

There was no reason she had to stay in the parlor with the other women. Faith picked up the empty cup and plate. "I will return these to Mistress Till," she said and walked out the door before anyone could object. She would drop off the dishes and then find out who was in the barn.

Hannah Till kept a washtub for dishes underneath the overhang on the outside of the kitchen. It took a few minutes to walk around to it and deposit them into the soapy water. Wiping her hands on her apron, Faith rose and walked out into the yard.

The mild air cleared her head. The ground squelched under her feet, still wet from all the rain. Her foot slid on the wet grass before she recovered her balance. Even with its slickness, it was preferable to the slimy mud of the path. Faith slowed down to better watch her steps as she walked to the barn.

Out on the training ground, she could hear the strong bellow of von Steuben, although she could not distinguish his words. She watched the company of men moving across the field, their lines much clearer than they had been a few weeks prior. They had recovered from the shock of being under fire within the camp. It was an issue, unlikely to reoccur now that the artillery remained under constant guard. Faith knew that John Laurens and Will McKay were present among the men to translate and instruct them in the art of war.

As she approached the barn, she saw horses in the corral, enjoying the fresh grass. Sunlight caught water drops on the grass as the horses moved about. Gracie nickered as she came closer. The little mare knew her from her visit to Philadelphia a few years ago. She had been her aunt's primary mode of transportation. Loaning her had been a generous act and a practical one. Having Hannah out of Philadelphia undoubtedly made everyone breathe easier.

Faith stroked a velvety muzzle and rubbed between her ears. Washington's large bay, Nelson, watched from a distance with liquid eyes. Gracie's ears perked up as Faith spoke to her, telling her about what she had seen in camp and how much she longed to go home. She leaned into Faith's hand, silently promising that today's frustrations would not last, and she would listen anytime. Despite the damp seeping into her shoes, Faith enjoyed the little mare's company. Blueskin, Washington's regal white mount, stood back, eyeing her cautiously as he nibbled on the early grass. She chuckled as Nelson trotted over for attention. She rubbed his nose as well. "Hello, handsome. I take it you are not used to being ignored?" Her nose caught an unwelcome odor. Looking down, she could see something dark splattered on the horse's legs and feet. "What have you been into?" she murmured. Kneeling down, she reached an arm through the space between the fence rails and ran it up Nelson's leg. He shivered but did not retreat. Faith looked at the reddish smear of blood on her hand. Gray fog came over her eyes as her heart pounded in her chest. She took a deep breath. "Don't panic, don't panic," she whispered as she hurried to the barn.

The barn door creaked as she swung it open. "Hannah?" No one answered. Up in the loft, rodents scuttled. Shuddering, she continued inside. Tiny fingers of light shone through cracks where the door met the frame. Dust motes danced in the golden rays. The barn appeared empty, but something didn't feel right. Strands of hay crunched underneath her feet as she continued her journey deeper inside. Perhaps she had imagined seeing the figure of a woman enter earlier? Anything was possible. But if that was so, why were the horses out in the rain-soaked corral?

A faint squelch made her look down. Dark liquid stained the ground. Her nose caught the unmistakable scent of blood. Stopping abruptly, Faith caught her breath. Now that her eyes had adjusted to the light, she could see the dark red hue puddled on the ground. Her heart thudded in her chest, along with an instinctive sense of dread. "Hannah!" The sound of her voice echoed against the walls of the empty stalls.

There was too much blood to have come from a minor accident. Fear filled her heart as she looked for any signs of life. A creaking door down the rows of stalls warned her she was not alone. Following the trail, she continued deeper into the barn, frightened at what she would find. Seeing a long stick leaning against a stall door, she picked it up just in case she needed a weapon.

Hair rose on the back of Faith's neck as she watched a stall door swing back and forth. It had been closed just moments earlier. She gripped the stick she had picked up earlier and raised it above her head. Whoever was hiding back there was going to regret troubling her.

"I know you're back there," she called. "I'm armed, and others are not far behind me."

Sobs broke the silence, followed by sharply drawn breaths. Thoroughly confused, Faith walked toward the open stall before her courage failed her. As she drew close, part of a dark skirt became visible, falling out from the doorway. She stopped just short of the entry, where she could see a woman kneeling next to a prone figure. Leaning forward, Faith bumped into the door, causing it to swing open. The woman whirled around to stare at her with wild eyes.

"Hannah." Stunned, the two sisters stared at each other for a space of seconds before Faith took in the scene. A woman lay sprawled in the straw. Her cap rested beside her. Dark stains marred her neck and shoulders, as well as the apron Hannah wore. "What happened?"

"I swear I didn't lay a hand on her." Hannah's face was pale in the shadows of the stall. It was quiet, except for their breathing. "I wanted to check on Gracie, but when I arrived, I found the horses agitated, especially Nelson." I found her lying in his stall. Initially, I believed her injured, but she's dead." As she stood, Faith saw her hands stained with blood.

"What are you doing here?" Faith stared inside, trying to figure out what had happened. "You promised Jeremy you would only come when Washington's staff was here. Shouldn't you be at the hospital?"

Hannah slid past her onto the walkway. "I wanted to speak to Louisa Barrett. I caught her rifling through our supplies at the hospital. We got into a loud argument. I intended to take her to Washington, but she shoved past me. Despite my best efforts, she lost me in the camp. Since I was out anyway, I came to see Gracie." She looked down at the floor. "I wasn't expecting this."

"Who is it?" The figure was face down in the hay, making it impossible to see much. She faced away from them; blood soaked her dark hair. She wore a dark dress and white apron, like most of the nurses in camp.

"Louisa," Hannah said, looking down at the body. "I saw her headed this way and wondered what she was up to." She looked down, then quickly away. "I wasn't expecting this. Something caved in the back of her head."

"Perhaps that?" Faith pointed to a dark object next to the woman's head.

Hannah reached for it. "A horseshoe?" She said incredulously. "Is Nelson missing one? I didn't notice."

"I didn't look." Faith bit her lip. "What in the world was she doing here?"

Hannah stood up. "There is no way to know. Louisa was always sneaking around, avoiding work, and stealing. We all suspected, but no one caught her before today. She could have been meeting a lover, getting paid for what she took-God only knows what happened."

Faith spoke the words dancing in her head.

"Seven camp followers nursing the sick,
Until a fine horse delivered a kick."

Hannah shot her sister a look. "I seriously doubt Nelson committed a murder."

"It seems like an incredibly convenient accident." Faith shivered. "Let's get out of here. It stinks of death. Someone will have to inform Washington that his horse may be responsible. It's just like the verses said."

Hannah stared at her. "That poem again. Who wrote it? It sounds like madness to me."

Faith shook her head. "I don't think the writer is mad. I think he is bored, and killing doesn't bother him anymore. It's like a savage game where no one wins. He's toying with us, and we have been able to do nothing to prevent him from killing."

Hannah looked around nervously. "I have no intention of playing. I'm leaving." She turned toward the door. Before she took more than a few steps, someone opened the door, letting in the sun and kicking up dust where it dragged on the ground.

Faith blinked in the light, blinded for a moment. Silhouettes were all she could see at first, followed by the thud of boots over the floor.

A man's voice spoke. "Who are you, and what is your business here?"

Faith spoke first. "I am Faith Clarke, and this is my sister, Hannah Butler. You need to get Major Butler and a surgeon here immediately. There is a dead woman in that stall." She pointed to where the door still stood open.

Two men came over. Faith remembered hearing that some of Washington's guards cared for his animals. One look in the stall and the man backed away, looking as if he might be sick.

"What happened here?" The other demanded. His face turned pale after a glance inside.

Faith answered. "We're not sure. My sister came to check on her mount and found the body. She put the horses out in the corral and came to see if she could assist. Unfortunately, the woman was already dead."

"That stall is for one of General Washington's horses. The little mare stays in the stall next door." He pointed to a slightly smaller stall that Faith had not noticed. "It's too wet for the horses to be out." He motioned to a man who had just walked in. "Bring them in, put them in a stall, and dry them off. We can't have the general's mounts take a chill."

Hannah said nothing. Her eyes faced the ground as her fingers pleated her skirt. As the surgeon threw open the barn door, she shivered.

Faith stood beside her. "My sister has had a terrible shock. I would like to take her back to Washington's headquarters, where the other women can tend to her." She put an arm around Hannah's shoulder. Her sister leaned against her.

The groomsman nodded. "Make sure you inform Washington's aides de camp. They will need to inform the commander."

Faith nodded. Taking her sister's arm, she led her out of the barn and back toward the farmhouse. Once they exited the barn, she saw Hannah more clearly. Blood stained her apron and skirt in broad patches. Her hands were also bloody.

"I need to clean up," Hannah said. "I can't go inside covered in blood."

Faith took her to the breezeway where Lady Washington kept a bucket and basin for the men to use before coming in for meals. Hannah's teeth chattered as she plunged her hands into the basin of water.

"Lord, this is cold," she hissed. The water turned brown as she scrubbed her hands with soap and let Faith pour clean water over them.

"Hand me your apron," Faith said. Hannah needed help to untie it. Her numb fingers wouldn't cooperate. Faith spread the apron on the grass in the yard. Taking the basin of rusty water, Faith poured it over the bloody stains. They faded but did not disappear. "I have a spare apron you can use for now," she said. "I can put this in the laundry."

"No," Hannah said. "Let me take it back to the hospital. Bloody aprons are not unusual down there. It can go with the next batch of items for the laundress."

Faith nodded. Slipping upstairs to her room, she found her other apron and took it to where Hannah waited. As she helped her sister into it, she wondered why her sister had so much blood on her clothes.

A group of men entered the barn carrying a stretcher. An aide de camp stuck his head out the door. Faith recognized Alexander Hamilton. "What is happening down at the barn?" He inquired as he walked over to them.

Faith hesitated before answering. "Someone found a dead woman in a stall."

Hamilton whistled. "Washington will want to know." He turned toward them. "Do you know who it was or what happened to her?"

Faith's voice was soft. "She was a nurse. It looks like a horse kicked her."

Hamilton was quiet for a moment. "Tell me it wasn't one of his mounts."

At her silence, his face paled. "I will tell the general." He turned and went back to the house. The door closed behind him.

Faith looked over at her sister. A few bloodstains were visible on the hem of her skirt, as was the brownish water dripping from the apron in her hands. Hamilton couldn't have missed it.

Chapter Twelve

"What in hell were you doing in the barn?" Jeremy Butler's outrage poured out. He still felt the shock of hearing that there was a dead woman in the barn where Washington kept his horse.

"I told you," Hannah's voice was tight. "I went to check on my horse."

"You were supposed to go when there was someone else present, such as General Washington or one of the staff he has assigned stable duty."

"I'm not informed of his schedule," she spat back. "It is the middle of the day. The barn is in clear view of the house, where there are many soldiers, including the general, present. It seemed safe." She stood with her arms around herself as if she were chilled.

Butler added a log to the fire, although he suspected the shivers were more from shock than cold. He looked at her.

Hannah glared back. Her eyes were bright, as if they held back tears.

"A woman died there," Butler dropped his voice before he resumed pacing back and forth, unable to be still. Fear coursed through his body at the idea that it could have been her lying dead in the stall. He took a deep breath, exhaled, and tried to calm the sheer terror he felt when they summoned him to headquarters.

Hannah hadn't yet explained her presence kneeling over the other woman's body. Waldo had checked on her before leaving with the corpse of the other woman.

He had spoken to Butler in private before he left. "Get her to drink a little whiskey for shock," he advised. "She has no injury to her body that I see, but she's shaking. None of that blood is hers. I think it got on her from kneeling over the body."

Butler nodded. Finding out what happened would not occur as long as he vented his fears. His heart turned as he watched her. A few wings of hair fell over her face, concealing it. She raised a hand to rub her eyes. A sniffle came from her nose.

He sighed and crouched beside her. "I'm sorry, Hannah," He reached up and wiped tears off her cheek. "When I heard there was a dead woman in the barn, it terrified me. I don't know what I would do if anything happened to you."

She sniffled. "Then why are you yelling at me? I did nothing wrong." Jeremy gathered her in his arms, rubbing her back until they both calmed down.

He was glad that no one else was currently in the farmhouse Lafayette had rented. The soldiers under his command were out in the field. Coming here allowed for a few moments of privacy before the world intruded. Butler knew Washington expected a report, and he would get it once he was sure Hannah was alright.

As her breathing steadied, Butler led her over to a chair near the fire. After she sat, he went over and stirred the logs, adding a new one to feed the fire. Having ensured the fire was well-fed, he fetched the bottle of brandy he kept hidden for emergencies. He brought it down and poured her a modest amount. "Drink," he said. "You need it to steady your nerves."

"You could use one yourself," she remarked before taking a sip.

Hannah wasn't wrong. Butler poured himself a small measure. It burned down his throat and warmed his belly. He corked the bottle before the temptation to empty it overcame him. "I need you to tell me what happened," he said. "How did you end up in a stall with a dead woman?"

Hannah set down the glass. Her gaze turned to the fire. Her breathing slowed as she contemplated the flames. Finally, she faced him. "I try to visit Gracie every day or two. It does me good to get out of the hospital and get some fresh air, and she's good company. I also intended to confront Louisa Barrett about her thieving. She is- was," she amended, "pretty blatant, and I had had enough of it. Her greed had no place here. The soldiers need the supplies we receive for them. There is little enough to go around as it is without someone helping herself regularly. Mary Porter should have spoken to her long ago, but didn't want to stir up a fuss." Hannah rolled her eyes. "Someone had to step in. This morning, I found a rucksack of our supplies underneath her cloak. I reclaimed them when she went out to the privy. She didn't see me, but I think she knew I had done it. Her temper was something to behold when she discovered her stash had gone. We had words until Mary stepped in and bid us to tend to our duties. Those poor men must have felt they were being nursed by a hornet. Later, when she stepped out, I followed her."

Hannah's gaze was rueful. "Following through camp without being discovered is tougher than one might think. This place is like a city but without as much organization. There are cabins and fortifications all over the place. And the tents! Louisa knows her way around far better than I do. She lost me within moments with whatever she had purloined before she left." Hannah paused and scooted closer to the fire. Her color had returned, but she still looked vulnerable.

Jeremy knelt next to her and took her hand. She placed her other hand over his. Hannah drew in a deep breath.

"Because I was already out. I went to see Gracie. It had been a few days since my last visit. Stable hands are always nearby, so it seemed safe. I had never seen Louisa at the barn before today. I wondered why." She caught Butler's eyes. "There's not a lot to do in a barn, unless it's time to tend the stock, which it was not."

"Well," he acknowledged. "There are a few things, but you would need a partner to engage in them."

Caught by surprise, she giggled. Tension eased from her body. "I didn't see anyone else go inside."

"So whoever she met had to have been already there."

Hannah nodded. "I guess so. I went in when the horses started whinnying. Something was wrong. I found her in Nelson's stall. He was dancing about, agitated, and his legs had blood on them." She drew in a breath. "I put the horses out so they could calm down. Nelson nearly ran me over in his eagerness to escape. I'm fortunate he is a well-trained animal."

Butler rose and stood near a window. "Does anyone know if Louisa had a man here at camp?"

Hannah shook her head. "I don't know. I can ask the other nurses. I don't even know where she stayed at night." She sighed. "I'm sorry, I am so little help."

"You had no reason to know her well," Butler said. In the distance, he saw Lafayette's men heading toward them. It was nearly time for the midday meal; their private interlude was ending.

"I have to go to Washington after dinner," he said. "He expects a full report. Will you be alright here? There will be some staff around, and I will assign a few soldiers to patrol close by."

Hannah looked at him. "I can return to the hospital. I'm not injured."

Butler shook his head. "Washington ordered you to remain here until the situation resolves." He omitted telling her that the general placed guards outside.

Hannah shot him a look that told him she knew what he wasn't saying. There were times her stubbornness was remarkably inconvenient. Before she could say any more, the first group of soldiers burst through the door. They greeted each other in French, then moved to the main room, arranging tables for dinner.

Butler was grateful for the interruption. He needed time to think about how to proceed. Washington would never blame his horse. Perhaps it was just a tragic accident. He didn't really believe that. Nor did he believe his wife was responsible. There had to be another explanation. Despite the mysterious poem, Hannah was the most obvious suspect. First, she had argued with the woman, then Faith found her kneeling over her body, a potential weapon beside her. He would have to be careful with what he said to Washington.

Lafayette's men lightened the mood with their chatter. From them, Butler learned Lafayette was still waiting for orders to invade Canada. The idling was becoming frustrating to the young Frenchmen. His letters showed his rising irritation.

"Who knows?" one man said. "One day, we may see him ride back into camp."

Butler nodded. "That could be so." He reached for the salt cellar to sprinkle some on some green peas that had come into camp. There was no telling when Lafayette would return. He had his doubts that an invasion of Canada was going to happen. Like many, he suspected it was a ploy to weaken Washington. His eyes flicked over to Hannah. She had said little beyond basic pleasantries. He knew she was unhappy, but he had no choice; her safety was his priority.

The meal ended with cheese, wine, and pieces of pound cake. He could smell the rum that flavored it. The tender, buttery slice melted in his mouth. He was glad to see that Hannah enjoyed some as well. He hoped she would use her time at the farmhouse to get some rest. She hadn't sat still for more than a few moments since her arrival, and he knew her sleep was restless.

After the meal, he helped the other men rearrange the room and take dishes back to the kitchen. Within moments, the small group of men returned to camp. Butler looked over at his wife. "There is a soldier outside if you need help."

"With what?" Hannah's voice was tired. "He likely cannot knit. I may write a letter to my father so he knows I am safe."

Butler nodded. "He would appreciate that. There is paper and ink on the desk." He walked her to the smaller of the two downstairs rooms, where a desk faced one of the two windows. An ink pot sat in one corner. He opened a drawer and found a selection of goose quills along with a small, sharp knife. He reached in to grasp one until Hannah touched his arm.

"I can do this," She selected a feather to sharpen into a quill. Underneath the feathers were a seal and some wax. She put that on top as well. On the far corner of the desk was a stack of paper. "Someone must write quite a few letters. It's hard to find paper these days."

"I imagine this was Lafayette's," Butler answered. "He has a wife and daughter back in France. He won't mind you using it. I always found him both gracious and generous."

"I hope he still feels that way when he finds we've been sleeping in his bed and using his stationery," Hannah noted wryly as she sat down.

"I will be glad when he returns," Butler replied. "He's one of the few totally loyal to Washington. I would not hesitate to trust him."

Hannah blinked. "Is trust so rare a thing here?"

"It can be," Butler was blunt. "Ambition is a nasty beast, and many of the generals under Washington dream of replacing him. They don't seem to realize that most of these men put their faith in Washington more than our government."

Hannah said nothing as she took in what he had said. But then she had experienced the bitterness of betrayal in her own family, so perhaps the knowledge that their commander-in-chief suffered like struggles didn't surprise her.

Butler leaned over and kissed her cheek. "I have to go." He departed, leaving her sharpening a quill as the light from the window spilled onto the desk, illuminating her face and hands.

The road back to Washington's headquarters had little traffic. He nodded to a group of men headed out to patrol the perimeter of the camp. Across the meadow, he saw smoke rising from the camp ovens as the cooks worked on the next meal. Soldiers drilled on the large meadow that formed the grand parade ground. They were tiny figures in the distance. The orders of their drill chief drifted over in a dull roar of sound. His words were indistinct in the distance. Butler wondered if it was von Steuben or another group.

The rain of the past few days had settled the dust that typically rose from the road if anyone passed. Butler kept an eye out to avoid any lingering mud holes or animal waste. With supply wagons coming in every few days, the roads were receiving a lot of wear. He preferred to walk on the edges where patches of fresh grass had sprung up.

Overhead, a V of geese called out as they flew past, seeking a place to land. They would settle on any nearby lake or pond they could find on their journey north. A meadowlark in the grass called out a warning, letting him know he was too close to her nest. Butler picked up his speed, having no desire to be attacked by an angry mother bird.

I'm going," he called out as he trotted past. "I've no interest in your brood."

He had no intention of sharing her location either. Too many men would try to capture her for food. Butler would prefer to leave the avian family alone.

The simple stone farmhouse where Washington headquartered appeared in the distance. It was about a mile from Lafayette's place, so the walk was not long. No one hung about the entrance or in the breezeway. Butler entered without knocking, wiping his feet on the grass before ascending the steps into the main hall.

The door to Washington's office stood ajar. Butler rapped gently on the wood.

"Enter," a voice called out.

Washington rose from the table where he had been looking at maps. He walked over to meet Butler. "What can you tell me?"

Butler told him what Hannah had shared. Washington's expression revealed nothing.

"Is there anyone who can verify her story?" He asked.

Butler shook his head. "Someone may have seen her in camp, but I don't know if any of the stable hands were around when she entered the barn.'

"I sent Hamilton and Silver to talk to them. No one admits to being near." Washington shrugged. They mucked out the stalls and fed the animals early that morning. They would have been drilling with their units." He shot a glance at Butler. "Your wife should have been at the hospital, as should Mistress Barrett. It appears there are some people who are prone to wander from their positions, no matter what I say."

Butler bit his tongue. There was nothing he could say to defend Hannah. It wouldn't help. She had no experience with the discipline required of the military, and she was used to being her own boss. He respected her independence and was glad she could manage when he was not around. Yet in a situation like this, she needed to exercise more caution.

Washington was looking at him. Butler realized he had been saying something, but didn't know what. "Pardon, sir. I didn't hear you."

His commander shot him an icy glare before repeating. "Did you share the poem with your wife?"

Butler nodded, not sure why this was important. Someone knocked on the door. Washington told them to enter. Both Hamilton and Silver came inside. He looked at them. "What have you found out about the two women?"

"People at the hospital heard Mistress Barrett shouting at Mistress Butler," Silver said. "She tried to slap her, but Mistress Butler grabbed her hand and told her she would regret her actions. Mistress Porter intervened, and both women went back to tending the men. Later that day, Mistress Barrett vanished. Within a few minutes, Mistress Butler left as well. The other nurses were not pleased to be shorthanded."

"No one recalls seeing either Mistress Barrett or Mistress Butler once they left the hospital. Neither returned." Silver looked apologetically at Butler. "They could have been anywhere."

Washington looked at Hamilton. "Does Dr. Waldo know what killed Mistress Barrett?"

"A sharp blow to the head, sir. She would have died instantly."

Washington paused. "Like from a horse?"

Hamilton paused. "There was some blood on the hooves of all the horses, sir. It's hard to say where they got it. Nelson had the most. There's a trail down the middle of the barn."

Washington scowled. "Are Nelson, Blueskin, and the mare unharmed?"

Hamilton nodded. "Both animals are fine. The grooms are washing them down as we speak. Despite the horseshoe in the stall, neither is missing one. Nelson refuses to enter the large box stall, so someone placed him in another. There are plenty of empty ones to choose from."

Washington's face cleared. "I will check on him later. See if the grooms can find some oats for the animals. I'm sure this has been hard for them as well. Let me make this clear. I will not blame Nelson. That woman had no business in the barn. Any animal will react when faced with a threat, if that is truly what happened. It seems far too convenient to blame the horse." His face turned grim. "Did Mistress Barrett have any family or close companions here?"

Silver answered. "I believe she was keeping company with an officer from a Massachusetts regiment, sir. I have asked his commanding officer to send him here when he gets in. He was part of a patrol sent out to forage at first light." He shrugged. "Many of the men find comfort with a woman from the camp. They don't consider the consequences of such behavior."

Washington nodded. "Very well." He shot a look at the men. "Whether either of the horses took part, we have another death on our hands that follows the poem. The question is, was this death a terrible accident or a murder?"

He looked at Butler. "Keep your wife confined to your quarters until we know the truth."

"You cannot believe Hannah has anything to do with these killings. She wasn't even here when they began." Butler protested. Shock and anger raced through his blood. Hannah was headstrong, but she was no killer. Although he knew she had a hot temper, he had never seen her lose control of it. He prayed the privations she had suffered had not changed that.

Washington's tone was even. "I don't believe she did, but I cannot show any favoritism. She will remain at Lafayette's farmhouse for the time being. Sentries will guard the house to ensure her protection."

Butler nodded. The sentries would not only keep her safe, but they would prevent any escape as well.

Chapter Thirteen

Bad dreams peppered Will McKay's sleep. A cannon roared in the distance. He felt the burning heat as the ball whizzed past him before hitting someone a short distance away. When he ran to help, he stumbled over something. Looking down, he saw Faith's decapitated head, her hair red with blood from the wound, her open mouth still screaming. In his dream, he ran away terrified. It was as if he were a child again, trying to escape his father's drunken rages. No matter how far or how fast he ran, the nightmare continued. Butler appeared with bloody stumps for arms, waving them around as he attacked faceless redcoats. Blood splashed on the ground, forming a current of deep red that flowed into a river, staining it red as well.

He awoke in a cold sweat. The fire popped from across the room. It was mostly ash, but sections still burned dark red. It made him think of hell. He shivered. Such thoughts would not help him sleep. Downstairs, the snores of von Steuben and some of his men drifted up, reminding him he was not alone. It was oddly comforting.

Will lay still as his heart rate returned to normal. Outside, rain fell, promising a soggy day for drilling. He hoped it would stop before morning. Slippery grass would be bad enough, but he hated icy fingers of rain running down inside his collar. His breathing slowly returned to normal. He was grateful he hadn't pissed in his sleep. It cost him endless beatings as a child. Will shuddered. British prison had damaged his father beyond repair, unleashing a monster on his family. His ghost had no place in Will's life and was unwelcome.

Will knew he wasn't the only restless sleeper. Sometimes he heard whispered lullabies or the sound of someone pacing the floor. A few times, he had found men spooned near the fire. He refused to question any of it. Many of the men were young. This was probably the furthest they had been from home. In this time of war, men found comfort where they could. Will refused to judge or make any effort to confirm rumors that ran around camp. Will was determined to survive and go back to making a life of his own choosing. He focused on his job. Helping translate Von Steuben's notes kept him busy after he completed the morning drills. The other officers tasked with working on the field manual spoke excellent French. They needed Will to translate the occasional German phrase that appeared. He was learning a lot about how an army was supposed to work.

Will rolled on his side, wondering how close it was to dawn. With the rain coming down, it would be difficult to tell. His body was tired, but his mind remained restless. Finally, he began counting marching steps in his head. He could picture the men moving in sequence before the baron ordered them to turn. Before he knew it, exhaustion claimed him. This time, no dreams intruded. He slumbered until someone shook him. Will stared at the other man blearily.

"Will, Raus aus dem Bett." One of his roommates looked down at him. When he saw Will was awake, he went back to completing his morning toilet.

Will sat up and began pulling on his stockings. "Save some water for me to wash up." He muttered as he pulled on his breeches and grabbed his boots from where he stowed them close at hand. Thunderous sounds on the steps informed him that his other roommates were heading down. He would have to hurry to make breakfast. He'd seen them eat.

After a quick splash of ice-cold water, Will finger-combed his hair and braided it into a neat plait before heading downstairs. The men had already pushed tables together. Someone handed him a huge mug of coffee. He slipped into an available seat. Breakfast was fairly quiet. A good number of the men stayed up late drinking and playing cards. Although immaculately dressed as usual, Von Steuben had bags under his eyes. His morning shave had missed a few places under his chin. Dark eyes studied him from beneath enormous dark brows. "Wir reden nach dem Frühstück."

Will nodded and responded in the same language. "Ja, we can talk then." He wondered what was on his mind. He didn't have long to wait. After the meal, the baron left his staff to clear the table and rearrange the room. Gesturing to Will, he went out the door.

The rain had stopped, although the sky remained overcast. A pale sun peered out from the edges of the clouds, promising to clear the sky at some point. Tiny droplets fell off the edges of the roof, glittering as the sun's rays caught them. Von Steuben walked out from the house, avoiding the puddles that littered the walkway. He waited for Will. His voice, for once, was soft. He spoke in his native tongue, which meant it took Will a few moments to translate.

"I have heard nothing regarding your appointment. General Washington is working on it, I am certain. He is a man of his word." In truth, von Steuben had done far more than the man who held the title of Drillmaster General, and everyone knew it. Now that Washington had found the man he needed to train his army, he would move mountains to keep him.

The other man nodded, then said something else. Will paused before asking him to repeat it. He was hoping he had misheard. He hadn't. "No one knows who fired the cannons on your men. Major Butler and I are investigating the incident. General Knox is keeping the artillery under guard to prevent another incident."

The baron nodded. His face looked troubled. "Too many have died here," he said at last.

Will agreed. Although his German was not perfect, he had little trouble interpreting von Steuben. "Spring is coming. We will march out in a few months' time."

The baron nodded. "I hope you find the madman committing these crimes," He pulled out a piece of paper he had tucked into his jacket. "du Ponceau translated it for me."

Will recognized it. Someone had shared the dreadful poem with the baron. He reached for it, but the baron waved his hand away and stuck it back into his jacket. "General Washington has received a copy as well."

The baron's eyes glittered. "A madman hunts here. We must find him and deal with him."

Will nodded. "Yes."

The baron looked back at his men, who were exiting the house. "We will speak more of this later." He went over to his men, who were waiting. With a signal from the baron, they went down the road toward Washington's headquarters to receive orders for the day.

Will kept to the back of the group. He needed to think, and the baron's men were a boisterous group who liked to talk. Usually, he enjoyed the camaraderie, but the baron's words rattled him. He wondered who else had received a copy of the poem. Surely it was the product of a dark and tormented soul. But no one he knew fit that description. There was plenty of drinking and dicing to pass the time and dispel the memories of battles fought and comrades lost. The problem was he was looking for a man like his father had become. The type of man Will had sworn never to become.

A faint drizzle fell from the sky. Will pulled up the collar of his jacket to keep the chilly drops out. He looked out across the already sodden field. It was shaping up to be a lousy day all around. As he entered the farmhouse, his spirits lifted at the sound of women's voices and the smell of coffee.

Jeremy Butler stood near the entrance to Washington's office with two mugs in his hands, steam rising from them. He offered one to Will, who was grateful for its warmth. "The General wants to speak with us." He turned to go inside with Will at his heels.

Washington's generals and aides-de-camp filled the room. Washington stood near the fire, watching as they entered. Once they had cleared the entryway, Hamilton closed the door behind them. Voices ceased as everyone waited for their commander to speak.

Washington glanced around the room to ensure everyone's attention was on him. "I know that all of you have received copies of a poem detailing deaths, some of which have already occurred in this camp. If you know the author or have any suspicions, you need to let me or one of my aides de camp know immediately. This behavior cannot continue."

Voices broke out in a tumult at his words. General Conway demanded, "Why didn't you tell us? We are leaders in this camp. Something like this is far too dangerous to be kept a secret."

General Greene interrupted. "Saying too much would cause widespread panic. Already, soldiers desert to go home almost daily. There must be order in how we proceed."

Will wondered how anyone could keep anything secret once all these generals learned about it. The noise of all the men arguing and interrupting each other was deafening. Washington's face remained impassive, although his cheeks flushed as the barrage continued.

Finally, he held up a hand. Within moments, voices ceased. "We have an enemy within, far more dangerous than those we have fought on the field of battle. This one feeds off fear and plays on our deepest nightmares. He is like a disease that, if left unattended, will spread through camp like wildfire, infecting it with fear and doubt until men turn on each other. We cannot ignore the danger, for in losing this battle, we lose all hope of winning the greater war."

As his words ended, General Greene spoke; his deep voice resonated in every corner of the room. "What do we do then? Each of us holds the lives of many in our hands. We handle the safety and well-being of all those who choose to serve our noble cause."

Washington spoke again. "I entrusted you with your units. That's why you are here. We need to know of those who seem angry, disenchanted, or perhaps are no longer fit for duty. I will send my aides de camp to check those who have followed us here, regardless of their attachments to members of the army. Major Butler and Captain McKay will focus on this investigation while we prepare for when we leave this encampment. Von Steuben will take a group to search for any hidden encampments and see if we have someone sneaking into camp to commit these crimes."

"What about the native camp?" a voice enquired. "Could they be involved in it?"

Washington stared at the man. "Many tribes have passed through and traded with us. They provided food and skins for our people before leaving.

If you are referring to the Oneida, they came at my request. They have led our scouting parties and fought in some skirmishes with the enemy. I trust them implicitly, perhaps more than some of you." He turned sarcastic. "This problem began before their arrival, unless you are suggesting they sneaked in a few months ago unnoticed by an entire army to kill a select few?"

Under the weight of Washington's withering tone, the man hushed. No one else spoke. After a few minutes of silence, Washington dismissed them. The generals left, murmuring among themselves. Greene stayed, as did the aides-de-camp, along with Butler and McKay. Will was relieved to see them go. He disliked crowds and the acrimony among those who should have been united against the British.

Washington turned to them. "Other than the spread of that bloody poem, what else has happened?"

Hamilton answered. "We've increased patrols within the camp so far there have been no more acts of violence. I sent an inquiry to York regarding the mail. They deny putting any bloody packages in the bag. No one seems to know where it came from."

Butler interrupted. "Have you gotten any more dolls?"

Washington was shaking his head when a knock came at the door. "Enter"

Albigence Waldo entered. Ignoring the others in the room, he walked straight to Washington. "I found this on top of the corpse of the woman that came in this morning, addressed to you." He laid the small package on the table. It was a small sack, made of homespun and tied with a narrow band of blue ribbon.

Washington stared at it for a moment before taking it in his hands and examining it. It was plain, with no markings on it other than a tiny scroll of paper, that, when unrolled, said Washington in a flowing script Will did not recognize. The General put it back on the table. "There is something inside," he said, "But I cannot fathom what."

Butler removed a knife from the sheath at his side. "Let's find out." At Washington's nod of assent, he cut the ribbon holding the bag shut. Taking it by the bottom, he shook the contents until they slid from the cloth and landed on the desk.

Another doll-like figure lay on the desk. Its dark, painted eyes stared back at them. The doll's red lips curved into a smile against the whittled branch, exposing the white wood inside. A white scrap, used to make a cap, exposed a smidgeon of dark hair. Over its stick body was an apron and skirt neatly stitched. Someone wrapped and tied a minute shawl around her torso and arms. Two small branches peeked out from the bottom of the skirt, darkened with what looked like wood ash. It would have been a lovely toy if it weren't for the blood spotting the clothes. Washington turned it over. The back of the cap was dark with dried blood that stained the entire back and matted the hair.

"That's disturbing," General Greene spoke at last. His face had paled. Will recalled that he had young children of his own. He wondered if one of them had a doll similar.

Washington picked it up to throw into the fire. "Wait," Butler said. "Don't destroy it. It could tell us something about the killer."

Washington stared at him and put it down. "How?" he demanded softly.

Will replied. "Someone made it. Whether the killer or someone he enlisted, it took time to craft. I think the hair came from a horse. Its clothes are of good-quality fabric and sewn with tiny stitches. I might inquire if someone's child is missing a doll."

The general raised an eyebrow. "You think our killer stole a doll? I suppose nothing is impossible." He sighed before nodding. "Very well, then. Take it with you. It has no place here."

Butler slid it back in its bag. "Is there anyone who has shared a grievance with you or harbors a grudge?" He pointed to the doll. "Someone addressed to you. The poem mentions you by name. It would seem someone wants your attention."

Washington's face remained expressionless. "I have no time for such games. There is a war to fight and men to prepare for battle." His voice was grim. "Find who is doing this, and then I will deal with him. There is no place in this camp for a cold-blooded killer who preys on the innocent." He turned to this desk filled with papers and maps. "Deal with these gentlemen while I deal with the Congress. Without their support, our army will not survive." He sighed and sat at the table. It was as if the weight of the world had settled on his shoulders.

Will followed Butler out of the room. The other man exited the house and continued toward the barn. "Wait," he huffed. "Where are you going?"

Butler paused. "Let's go somewhere where nobody can hear us. There are very few people I trust here." He looked at Will. "Washington and his generals can search this camp all they wish. I do not believe anyone is hiding on the outskirts, sneaking in to do harm. I think our enemy is here in camp."

Will nodded. He listened to Washington make his plans for a search and had kept his doubts to himself. "What do you intend to do?"

Butler pulled out the small bag containing the doll. "Find who made this. There cannot be too many people making dolls with such attention to detail. I've seen quite a few whittling, but these are meticulous from the nose to the modeling of the hands. They have faces painted on them. They wore clothes, and their injuries match the victims. The question is, does our adversary make them or is he paying someone?"

"I would find it peculiar if someone asked me to smash the head of a doll and cover it in blood," Will said bluntly.

Butler nodded. "I would surmise he does that bit himself, but there are children here. Some of them may have dolls their mothers make for them. If our killer doesn't create his own, perhaps he pays someone to do it for him. I'll check the tents for doll makers." He continued down the path to one of the main roads. This one led to the camp that housed so many of the women and children who followed the army into Valley Forge. Canvas tents and a few log shelters filled the small clearing.

Will spent little time here, although Faith had told him she had gone back and forth to a laundress for bandages. Butler seemed familiar with the area. As they approached, a dog darted out and back into camp, running on long skinny legs. The dog's survival amazed him despite the harsh winter.

Butler walked toward a series of small tents set up apart from the others. The end facing the camp had its flaps closed. As they approached, a soldier exited one, buttoning his breeches as he left, whistling a cheery tune. He looked startled when he saw the two other men. Butler nodded at him and said nothing as the other man hurried past, heading back to camp.

Within a few minutes, a woman with tousled gold curls emerged. She finger-combed it and twisted it back behind her head, securing it with a few pins. Her gaze sharpened as she spotted them. A smile covered her face.

"Can I help you, gentlemen?"

Will's skin crawled as embarrassment flushed his face. The woman seemed amused by his discomfiture.

Butler seemed unfazed. "Do you know anyone here at camp that makes dolls?"

The woman placed her hands on her hips. "You would be better off asking a woman with children. I don't have any."

"I see that," Butler replied. "But you know quite a bit about what goes on in this camp."

She shrugged. "I hear things. It's hard for these boys being far from home." She shot Butler a knowing glance. "Everyone needs a little comfort now and then. I'm Magdalena Ross, but most of the men call me Lena."

Butler nodded and turned to Will. "Let's continue on then. This woman knows nothing."

"I wouldn't say that," Lena said. "I can find out most anything for a price." Her pale eyes glittered as the harsh sunlight revealed lines at the corners of her eyes and lips.

Butler turned back to her. "I wouldn't advise anyone to keep information from Washington. He can be generous to those who are loyal, but he never forgives a betrayal."

Lena snorted. When her mouth opened, Will saw a gap where a tooth had once been. "I may be a whore, but I'm a patriot whore. Why else would I be in this wretched place?" Her eyes narrowed. "I'm doing my best to survive just like anyone else. Even that native woman, Polly Cooper, has a job. She cooks all that corn."

"Corn?" Will asked.

"Corn, maize, whatever you choose to call it," Lena replied. "The Oneida brought baskets of it, but she was the only one who knew how to cook it. Every day, she's got soldiers coming to her to learn how to cook it. People have been starving here. They will eat anything, and she feeds them all from that huge kettle of hers." She smiled knowingly. "Huge iron pots like that don't come cheap. Somebody gave it to her. I would love to know what she did for it."

Butler's eyes narrowed. "She's feeding hungry men. That's worth far more than an iron cook pot."

Lena shrugged. "I bet she's met most everyone in camp in the brief time she's been here. She may even know who your doll maker is."

Butler nodded. "She may, indeed. Thank you for your time." He gave the woman a coin, which she checked before sticking it in her pocket. "You can contact me at headquarters if you have any other useful information."

She nodded before smiling wickedly at Will. "You can drop by anytime. I will be here."

Will let out a sigh of relief when they were out of sight of that tent. "I'm not returning. I've heard men talk about her. She's probably serviced half the camp."

"Don't be so quick to judge," Butler said. "These men seek what relief they can find. Women like Lena help stave off the loneliness and despair so many feel. I've seen her nurse the sick and dying as well. She's like all of us. She has a purpose to serve."

Will shook his head. "If you say so." They walked a little further before turning to a path that led through the woods. "Where are we going now?"

"The Oneida Camp," Butler replied. "That's where we will find Polly Cooper."

"Have you heard of this woman before?" Will asked. He had seen natives in camp but hadn't realized a native woman was in camp, much less one who cooked for the camp.

Butler turned to look at him. "I've worked among the Oneida for many years now and spent time in their camps. They are an honorable people, and loyal to our cause. Having them here is a blessing. They are excellent scouts and hunters. Their wives farm the land and know how to survive the cold winters." He paused on the outside of a clearing.

Will looked around him and saw the camp. Smoke rose from a fire over which hung an enormous iron pot. A native woman stirred it with a long-handled stick, all while talking to a group of three men who watched her closely. She spoke English to the men, gesturing as she spoke. "You must stir the pot so nothing burns. Like this." She pushed the stick down to the bottom and stirred slowly in broad circles. The contents looked pale and granular. She sprinkled salt over the mixture and then ladled some into small wooden bowls. "Eat."

The men took the bowls of steaming corn mush. Lacking spoons, they sipped from the edge. The native woman studied Will and Butler with bright, dark eyes. "You come for corn?"

Butler shook his head. "I have questions." He took the bowl she offered him and gestured for Will to do likewise.

Will carefully took a small swallow. It was hot and burned his tongue, but the flavor wasn't bad. He blew on it for a few minutes before trying again. The mild, buttery flavor reminded him of Olivia's corn cakes. He flushed. Of course it did. The difference was that Olivia traded the natives in Williamsburg for ground corn. This was full of round kernels. It also surpassed much of the camp's food he had eaten. "Very good," he said to her. "Thank you."

Polly Cooper nodded. "Corn is good for everyone."

Butler nodded. "We are grateful for what you and your people have done for our camp. It has been a rough year." He finished his bowl before setting it down on the stump that served as a table. He took out the sack that held the doll. "Do you know who made this?" He shook it out so that the doll lay on the stump.

Polly Cooper looked at it curiously before picking it up. Her face turned serious as she studied the blood-stained back. "This is evil." She said. "The Oneida did not make it."

Butler nodded. "Have you seen anyone making dolls like this?"

Polly shook her head. "Many men whittle, but those are white women's clothes." She stroked the cloth. "Your laundress handles many clothes. I've seen her drawing water from the creek and spreading clothes on the grass. She has dark skin and red hair. Her child plays with things like this."

Butler nodded. "Thank you. We will speak with her." He turned and walked out of the clearing, followed by Will. They walked halfway through the woods before Butler slowed down. Will nearly walked into him.

"What?" he asked.

"Shhh." Butler hissed. "We're not alone."

Will looked around. He could hear the rustle of dead leaves and the call of a bird in the distance, but nothing that sounded human.

Butler cocked his head, standing so still he didn't appear to breathe. "Over there," he hissed before he took off into the woods. Will fell behind as the other man outdistanced him. When Will caught up, Butler was kneeling on the path, looking at something.

"He got away."

"Who was it?" Will asked.

Butler shook his head. "I'm not sure. A flash of blue in the trees caught my eye." He stood, holding a stick with one end peeled, exposing the white. The peeling of one end exposed the white. "He must have been whittling, either that or he idled here while we were with the Oneida." Butler frowned. "He bolted when he spotted me. If it weren't for this tree root, I might have caught him. Whoever it was is probably back in camp now."

Will looked at it. "Do you think he was getting ready for his next kill?"

"I don't know," Butler replied. "It could have been someone just cutting through the woods. We have no way of knowing."

"If he was wearing a blue coat, it was an officer," Will said. "Why would an officer be wandering through the woods by himself? And why would he run from you?"

"I don't know," Butler said, tucking the stick into a pocket. "But I want to find out."

Chapter Fourteen

Will joined Faith to collect clean bandages from the laundress, which surprised her. "I've been doing this for a few weeks now. Nothing has happened."

"I know," he said. The brilliant midday sun made his eyes squint. "But I see you very little these days, and it is a lovely day for a stroll – don't you think?" He fell in step beside her, a welcome presence despite her protest.

Faith shot him a look. "I think you would not be apart from Baron von Steuben without a good reason."

"Laurens is with him. He's taking his troops to search the outskirts of camp. Our commander has units combing through every barn and patch of woods. He wants to know if any of the enemy is hiding nearby."

"Wouldn't it be just about impossible to hide with all the people here?"

Will shrugged. "Hard, but not impossible. Some of the British Ranger Units are stealthy little buggers. Don't underestimate them." He scanned the fields and trees along the pathway, noting the birds flying overhead. A faint trail of smoke rose from a nearby fire. The faint scent of burning wood drifted through the air. Damp leaves had gotten caught in the blaze, leaving a bitter, moldy scent.

Faith bit her lip. She respected General Washington, but she doubted the British were killing people in camp, which left her wondering who was.

The rain of the past few days had cleared away, leaving the sun to dry the earth. A train of supply wagons traveled down the Gulph Road. A herd of bawling cattle went before them, announcing their presence. There was plenty of fresh grass in the meadows to feed them and keep them content after their long journey.

Faith was glad to be moving away from the chaos. The path to where the laundress did her work was far from the road and away from the primary group of tents. She stayed close to the creek upstream from the others, where she had a ready source of clear water.

"What do you know about the laundress?" Will's voice was casual, as if he were discussing the weather.

"Her name is Rose. She has a little girl named Anna. Just by observation, she does laundry for most of the hospitals. I think she's a freedwoman." Faith shot him a sideways look as she spoke. Everyone was a suspect these days. Regardless, she was not comfortable discussing people as if they were pieces on a chessboard.

"Why do you think that?" Will stopped to help her over a limb that had fallen over the path.

Faith paused. "She's not mentioned a master or mistress. She said she had come up with a regiment from one of the Carolinas. I don't remember if it was north or south."

Will nodded. "So she's been here a while."

"I guess." She shot Will a look. "Shifting a dead body demands substantial strength. She's not a large woman." An image ran through Faith's mind of sinewy arms hauling laundry out of an enormous pot. Was she strong enough to move a dead body? She did not know.

"I want to speak to her. Laundresses talk to many people, and they see a lot."

As they walked, Will's eyes swept either side of the path. He had a knife scabbard at his belt, which Faith had not seen before.

Faith took a few moments to gather her thoughts. "If no one finds signs of the enemy, someone here is doing the killing."

"Yes,"

"How do we find out who it is?" Faith said. "It could be anyone. Some people have been here for months. Some for weeks. These killings are recent. We don't have any new arrivals, except for the hostlers, who come and go as they deliver their goods."

"It's not a hostler." His voice turned grim. " It's someone who's been here all along suffering alongside us."

"If that's so, why kill people now? These people, his victims, are comrades in arms. They all came to serve General Washington, to fight our common enemy. Why murder them in such a gruesome manner?"

"I don't know. I've taken no pleasure in freezing or starving these past months. The suffering has been appalling, but we have survived. The men have food now, as well as blankets and shoes. It's an odd time to snap." He sighed. "There's something we're missing. What made this person snap? Something changed, but for the life of me, I don't know what."

Faith didn't know how to respond, so she kept her silence as they walked together. Before long, the canvas tents and small cabins of those who followed the Continental Army came into view. Unlike the orderly rows of the regimental cabins, these spread out over the area like the limbs of a tree. A path worn into the ground led to the center, but other narrow walkways snaked to other areas tucked away from the casual eye.

Faith led him to where the path turned north. Here, the ruts of a small cart had dug into the ground, leaving indentations in the ground. As they moved farther from camp, the creek's gurgle grew louder. The muslin of the laundress's tent was soon visible in the distance.

"She's far away from the others," Will noted as they approached the huge fire burning in a large earthen circle outside the tent. His nose wrinkled as he realized why. "What is that horrible smell?"

Faith tried not to smile, but failed. His expression was priceless. Her eyes burned from the powerful scent of ammonia. The laundress stood over a huge copper pot that she stirred briskly with a long paddle. The rising steam created a dense cloud of humidity.

"Are ye sure we're not entering a level of purgatory?" Will muttered as they approached.

"Which one?" Faith repressed a snicker as he rolled his eyes and continued into the campsite with no further remarks.

Faith resisted the temptation to cover her nose with her sleeve. She opted to breathe through her mouth as much as possible.

Sweat ran down the woman's face. A turban covered her hair, although damp strands straggled down the side of her neck and at the edges of her brow. Her rolled-up sleeves revealed well-muscled forearms. "Can I help you? You've caught me in the middle of my grand wash, so I've little time to spare."

"I won't take much time." She reminded Will of someone, although he could not place who. He was certain he had never met her before. Her café au lait skin, with its sprinkling of freckles, was distinctive, as were her green eyes. A memory teased at the edges of his mind, refusing to come into view. "I was wondering if you knew anyone who made dolls here for the children in camp."

"I thought I had seen your daughter playing with one the other day," Faith said. She looked around. The little girl was nowhere to be seen.

"Anna is with a woman who watches her for me in exchange for clean clothes. Her daughter is the same age, so it works well for both of us." Her eyes glanced at Faith. "You've been here before to pick up bandages for the hospital. There's a stack on the table ready to go."

Faith nodded. "Thank you. I will take them back with me."

"She turned to Will. "Quite a few people make toys for their children when they have a moment. My mother used to make them for me and my brothers when we were small. I've made a few for Anna myself. I made a doll for her with sticks fallen from trees and scraps of fabric. She likes to pretend it's her baby."

Faith looked at Rose. "Is any of your family nearby? I know there is a regiment with free men in it."

Rose shook her head. "Just Anna. I haven't seen my family in years." Her expression turned bitter. "Property isn't supposed to care if it gets sold."

Faith winced. She could not imagine having Andrew taken away. "I'm sorry."

Rose shrugged. "It was a long time ago."

Will asked. "Have you made dolls for anyone else?"

"Why do you want to know?" A bubble popped loudly in the kettle. Picking up her paddle, she stirred it before using a crank to haul the chain holding the laundry higher, huffing with effort.

"Let me help," Will said as he turned the crank to raise the pot. "Where do you want this?" he grunted. His eyes watered as steam rose up to his face. "What's in this water? It smells like piss!"

Rose chuckled. "That would be chamber lye. Turn the handle so it's off the fire. I'll get the fabric out so I can soap it real good once it's cooled."

Will did as he was told. Once he finished, he stepped back to get some breaths of fresh air. Sweat trickled down his back, making his shirt stick. He didn't know how Rose could withstand doing this day in and day out. The constant smells and heat, not to mention the intensive labor, exhausted him just to think about it.

Faith walked over to the table where the bandages lay. She noted a few clothing items folded next to them. A neatly mended skirt lay next to a spool of thread with a needle threaded into it. "Do you mend?" She asked curiously.

"Sometimes, when it's required and not too complicated," Rose answered. "A ladies' maid taught me in a household where I worked."

Faith wondered what sort of past this woman had lived. The only time she had seen her smile was when her little girl was present. As she began gathering the bandages, she looked inside the tent. She could see a pallet on one side with blankets spread over it. A small square chest rested beside it. On top was a flask and a powder horn. Lying across the pallet was a stick figure dressed in a brightly colored dress. Faith froze as she took in the sight.

Will joined her. Without hesitation, he entered the tent and took the doll in his hands. In the bright light of day, they both could see it more clearly. A thick branch formed its head, torso, and legs. Carved feet peeped out from the end. Charcoal darkened them so that the doll appeared shod. Underneath a dainty white cap, dark hair flowed down its back. Covering the bright blue dress was a tidy white apron. Someone peeled back the bark to create a flat surface for painting two dark eyes, a nose dot, and red lips. If Faith hadn't seen the dolls sent to Washington, this one would have beguiled her.

Will's voice was hoarse. "Did you make this?"

Rose had put down the shirt she had been scrubbing. "That belongs to my daughter. I made it for her to play with. What business is this of yours?"

"That depends," Will said. "How many have you made?"

The laundress shrugged. "A handful. I have little time between loads of laundry. A few of the women requested them for their children. It seemed a small thing."

"Not when a murder is involved."

Rose stiffened. "I have been involved in no crime. I work to support the Continental Army and provide for my child."

Faith interrupted. "No one doubts you." She put a hand on Will's arm to settle him. "We're hoping you can help us find someone who has killed people here. The killer leaves a doll with each of the victims. A doll that looks a lot like this one."

Rose snorted. "I know nothing about that." She returned to soaping clothes.

"We need to know who you made dolls for," Will said.

Rose shook her head. "I'm staying out of this. When white folk come sniffing around, they are looking for someone to blame. That will not happen to me."

Will pressed. "How many have you made?" As he approached, she grasped her wooden paddle, raising it. He backed away, lowering his arms in a placating motion. "I need help if I'm to stop the man who is doing this."

"I haven't made dolls for any man," Rose said. "Only women."

Faith asked her softly. "Could you tell us who? We just want to talk to them."

"That's how it starts," Rose said grimly. "But action always follows talk. I'm not getting into any trouble."

"Agreed," Will said. "Tell us what we need to know, and we will leave you to your work."

Rose sighed and wiped the sweat from her forehead. "You are costing me time and money by hanging around. I made dolls for three women; two I know had small children. The other, I haven't seen with a child, but she paid with British coins. I don't see many of those, though I imagine she sees them more often in her line of work."

"Who was she?" Faith asked.

"I've heard the men call her Lena." Rose jerked her head back toward camp. "You'll find her tent over close to the path from the soldiers' quarters. She's nearly always there."

"Thank you. I appreciate your help." Will picked up a stack of clean bandages and left, followed by Faith.

The laundress's eyes burned into Faith's back as they left. Once they entered the outer edges of the forest, Faith looked back. The laundress bent over her work, scrubbing away filth.

Will didn't speak as they walked back. He took long strides that ate up the ground as they traveled.

"Slow down," Faith huffed. "I can't keep up with you." She was grateful when he stopped and let her catch up. Unsure of what had gotten into him, she stood and worked on catching her breath. As her heart slowed and she could breathe once more, she asked, "Why are you in such a hurry?"

"I need to find that woman," he answered. "She could be the key to finding the maniac who's been terrorizing us. I need to speak with her."

Faith looked at him. "Do you know where to find her?"

Will nodded. "Jeremy and I spoke with her a few days ago. Lena Ross is a whore who does a steady stream of business here. She lied to us when we asked her about the dolls. She claimed to know nothing about them. I want to know why."

Faith stilled. "You know a camp whore by name and where to find her?"

Will's response was quick. "I went there with Jeremy when we were searching for strangers or anyone who knew something of the dolls. I promise you I have not gone there to seek her charms."

Faith looked into his eyes and saw only his straightforward gaze. Her body relaxed. If there was one thing she knew, he was a man of his word. Will was stubborn and sometimes difficult to understand, but he had never lied to her. "Let's find out why she lied to you."

"I'm not sure this is an appropriate place for you to be," Will said. "The men that go there-"

"Are likely the same men I see going in and out of General Washington's headquarters, to the hospitals and on the roads and paths here," Faith said. "This is a camp, not a city with its layers of civilization. Given how antsy you are, I bet it is close by. Is it on the way back?"

"Pretty close." Will's face was unhappy, but he ceased protesting. Dead leaves and small branches crunched under their feet. Before long, Will turned down a path that led to a tiny clearing populated by a series of small tents. As they approached, he noticed that the fire outside the tents had dwindled down to where it barely smoked. The tent flaps were all closed. "Hello, the camp," he called. "Lena Ross–are you here?" No one answered. Will called out again. Faith hung behind him with watchful eyes. "Stay here. Something's not right." He left her at the entry of the clearing while he went to investigate.

He continued to call as he went from tent to tent, pulling the flaps up to see inside. The first two held nothing but rumpled bedding on top of straw pallets. When he opened the third tent, he found a man sleeping inside, his breathing a soft hiss of air going back and forth. "Wake up." Will shook him hard.

"Whahhh," the man groaned. "Go away. I'm not on duty until later tonight." He tried to burrow back into the blankets, but Will snatched them away.

"Where's Lena?" he demanded.

The man rubbed a hand over his face. "She went out to take a leak."

"When was this?"

"How would I know? I fell asleep after she finished with me." The man sat up and glared at Will. "You're an officer–aren't you? A fellow enlisted man would have a little sympathy."

"My sympathy lies with your wife. I haven't seen Lena around camp, and the fire's gone out. Are you sure you know nothing?"

The man shivered and pulled on his long hunting shirt before standing up. He shivered as he pulled on his breeches, followed by his boots. "Why did she let the fire go out? I fed it before we went inside." He combed his hair with his fingers. "I heard her talking to someone outside before I fell asleep.

It was a man. I thought she was sending him away since I was already here."

"What did they say?" Will hoped Faith was not seeing what he was. He didn't dare turn around and look for her. He kept his focus on his unwilling witness.

"I don't know," the man said. "I'd had a lot to drink, and we'd just completed our transaction. All I heard was the sound of their voices whispering, then I went to sleep." He looked about forlornly. "You don't think she left, do you?"

"I don't know," Will said. When he stepped back, the man bolted, disappearing into the woods away from where they had entered the clearing. Will continued to search the tents. They were much the same, each with a pallet and blankets. The largest tent contained a leather chest with two dresses, a shift, and some stockings. One stocking concealed a cache of coins in the toe. Will poured them into his hand, whistling softly as he identified a few guineas. One large piece of silver caught his eye. "I'll be," he muttered. "A whole Spanish reale, uncut." He'd dealt with pieces of eight at the print shop, but until now had not seen a whole one. He poured it back in the stocking before placing it back and continuing his search. Dried lavender lay in a mesh bag in one corner, perfuming the air with its sweet scent. The smaller tents contained nothing of interest, only pallets and a few blankets. They were for business only.

While it might be Lena's camp, he bet she let others rent space for their work. The tents all stood empty, although he was certain they would be full later in the day. Her disappearance troubled him. Lena Ross knew something. He hoped it hadn't gotten her killed.

As he walked back to where he had left Faith, she emerged from behind a stout tree. He shook his head as he met her gaze. "Lena is gone. I don't know where."

"Do you think she will return?" Faith looked at the large tent with the three smaller ones lined up alongside. Now that the flaps were open, it was easy to see the pallets and blankets lying on the ground. A few pieces of clothing lay on top of some blankets, left either by the women or their clients. No one had picked up. It was as if everyone had vanished.

"I don't know. I'll see if Butler has heard anything." Will turned away from the small clearing. "Let's get back to camp."

The woods thinned as they drew closer to the main camp. They passed many bare stumps, testimony to the frantic drive to build shelter before the ferocity of winter had unleashed itself. A few had sprouted recent growth. He hoped that once they left, the forest regrew itself and healed from the scars the war had inflicted upon it.

He was glad when they entered a small meadow where he could see all around the camp. Off to the west was the Gulph Road, upon which many of their supply wagons had come. Ahead was the first line of entrenchment, an enormous earthwork put in place to defend against invaders. A lot of work had gone into it, as Will well knew. He had spent hours digging into the cold-resistant earth, piling up dirt and nursing his blisters late at night.

In the distance, he spotted the rooftops of the cabins that housed Weedon's Brigade. Next to them would be Muhlenberg's men. They had already passed the Commissary General's quarters. More fortifications gradually became visible as they walked toward the heart of the camp. Men resembled ants, indistinguishable in the distance. Will knew some were coming and going from their duties, others went to play dice or visit friends, finding various ways to pass the time away from home. He drew in a breath, glad for a few stolen moments with Faith. When they left this valley, it could be months before they saw one another again.

The bright wings of a cardinal flared as it went through the trees. As he turned to share it with her, an explosion rent the air, deafening in its concussive force as it shook the ground. Leaves and pine needles rained down on them as both struggled to stay upright. The rumble continued like a mythological beast, bellowing fury and destruction as it struck.

Faith's eyes widened in terror. She grasped a tree limb to keep from falling. Her gaze never left the burgeoning cloud rising over the trees ahead.

Will struggled to catch his breath as a cloud of dust rose from the disturbed ground. For a few moments, they stood in the clearing waiting for the shaking to disappear. "We have to go," Will said at last. "There's no telling what lies ahead."

Chapter Fifteen

Erie silence fell over the encampment, uninterrupted by the cries of birds or the movement of animals. Within moments, they heard shouts of men from within the camp, their voices indistinguishable amidst the roaring and rumbling a stone's throw away. Another explosion filled the air, followed by the unmistakable cracks and pops from a fire. Their noses filled with the acrid scent of burning.

Taking Faith's hand, Will hurried toward the outer line of defense for the camp. The solid earthworks had sheltered them from the brunt of the blast. It also blocked the view.

As they passed the cabins of Glover's Brigade, Faith stopped. "Look," she said, as black smoke billowed, forming a massive cloud that obscured the sky in a menacing gray shroud.

"What in hell?" Will said. His heart pounded in his chest as fear dropped over him like an icy rain. As much as he dreaded it, Will knew he had to go toward the source. He dropped Faith's hand and ran. Behind them, he could see a wagon stopped in the distance. Its driver paused, as if trying to see what was happening. Smoke continued to spread over the encampment. "That's near Muhlenberg's Brigade."

"Let's go," Faith said, keeping pace with him. "People will need our help." Strands of hair escaped from her cap and hat as she ran. Streams of the bandages she had clutched to her chest blew over her shoulders and out like the tail of a kite. An acrid scent filled the air, along with the shouts of men and cries of the injured.

Another boom rent the air. They fell to the ground, covering their heads as ash rained down. Will stumbled to his feet and offered a hand to Faith. She grabbed up the pile of bandages and piled them into her apron. They continued at a slower pace, trying to determine what lay ahead.

A huge fire, red and orange, quickly became visible in the distance. Timber and bricks lay scattered on the ground. Flames fully engulfed one cabin, while men struggled to smother another's burning roof with dirt. Sparks rained down on nearby cabins, causing panic as men ran out to escape the blaze. "Balls of fire are coming down the chimney," someone yelled. "The bunks are burning."

Will swore at the chaos. Seeing no one of higher rank, he took charge. "Get some shovels from the shed," he yelled at a sergeant. "Take some men with you." He looked about wildly. "Is anyone hurt?" He hoped Faith had enough sense to stay out of harm's way. He could no longer see her in the smoke.

He couldn't approach the blazing mound. Too much heat poured out of it. Smoke made it difficult to see. Someone was screaming nearby. He crouched and circled around, trying to see where the injured man lay. Two mounds belched flames and smoke along with sputters of debris. In the smoke, he spotted someone dragging a body away. Will ran to help.

"Get the other one," It was Jeremy Butler. His face and hair were dark with ash, but there was no mistaking the authoritative voice with the hint of Irish. "He's not far back." Coughing ended the conversation.

Will stumbled behind him. Others were there in the smoke and debris, hunting for the injured. He spotted an arm on the ground and reached down to drag the man to safety. Two other men joined him. One got the other arm while the other grabbed the feet. Together, they got him away and onto a patch of grass where Albigence Waldo had arrived and was setting up a triage. Will lay the man where Waldo directed. On the man's arms and chest, he saw blisters. Red scorch marks marred the man's nose.

"Here." Faith handed him her neckerchief. "Cover your nose and mouth to help keep the ash out." She waited until he took it before turning to assist the doctor with the next patient. It didn't surprise him. Faith was a remarkable woman.

"Thanks," he rasped. His lungs already burned from the smoke. It was only slightly better further out in the meadow. He spotted Butler nearby. The man he had rescued was moaning on the grass. The fire had seared most of his hair, leaving a raw scalp. Will turned away, sickened at the sight.

Butler walked with him back toward the burning mound. "Someone blew up the ovens," he said bleakly. "I don't even know who is alive or dead." He watched men running back and forth, dragging out bodies or throwing buckets of dirt on the fire. Others lined up to a branch of a nearby stream using chamber pots and buckets to hold water to throw on the blazes on the nearby cabins. They watched as men from Varner's brigade used shovels to throw dirt on patches of burning grass.

Sergeant Maples directed men to dig a fire line around the damaged ovens to keep the flames from spreading into the camp. Others joined them, pulling up the grass with whatever tools they could find.

"It's a good thing it rained a few days ago," Will said. "Otherwise, there would be no stopping this."

Butler nodded as he walked forward. "I think our enemy was counting on that. He wanted a show, not an apocalypse." Spotting a man with shovels, he grabbed one and joined in, throwing dirt on any burning patch. Will joined him, digging into the ground and tossing shovelfuls where any spark fell. They dug until all remaining fires were extinguished, covering the ground with holes and mounds of dirt. When he looked up, he realized the camp's commander had joined the fray.

General Washington rode around on Nelson, his eyes taking in the disaster as he spoke to his men and checked in on Dr. Waldo's work. Will did not know how long he'd been there. He had been checking the ground for wayward sparks. The caved-in ovens continued to burn. Their roar drowned out any surrounding noises.

Men got as close as they could to throw dirt on the blaze, making it smoke as the flames sought air to burn. The fire collapsed the closest cabin. The sun ran its course over the sky as they fought the flames.

Will helped throw dirt on hot spots until the smoke made it virtually impossible for him to breathe. When dizziness caused him to stumble,

Butler dragged him out. "We need no more casualties," he said. "Go help Waldo." Will went over to where women from the nearest hospital had joined Faith and Hannah, tending the half-dozen men caught near the explosion. His lungs burned as he struggled to draw breath. Plopping on the ground, he focused on breathing, aware that his previous experience with arsenic poisoning had probably damaged his lungs. Will mentally cursed his weakness. There were things that needed to be done and people who needed help. He heard Faith's voice in his ear.

"Take slow breaths. It will help. You need to go to the hospital, where we can get you something that will help that cough." Squeezing his shoulder, she moved away. He could hear her voice in the distance. Something hard pressed into his hip. Bending his arm, he got his hand underneath his body. Something warm and metal touched his palm. Curling his fingers about it, he pulled it out, intent on examining it. His vision grew gray and foggy as consciousness left.

When he awoke, he saw above him the rafters of a cabin, but it wasn't one he had been in before. His throat burned, but he could draw his breath without strain. Raising his head, he looked about, seeing other men in bunks nearby. Catching the scent of alcohol and herbs along with the muted scent of blood, he knew he must be in a hospital.

When he opened his eyes again, a woman of middle years smiled down at him. "I'm glad to see you are awake, Captain McKay. How are you feeling?" Will sat up, relieved that he could do so without feeling dizzy. His head throbbed dully, but the pain was tolerable.

"I'm well enough," he answered. "I don't think I know you." He looked up into her eyes. "How did I get here?"

The woman sat in a chair near his bed. "I'm Mary Porter. I manage this hospital for General Washington. Someone brought you in with other men injured in the oven fire."

"Were many people hurt?" He looked about the room. Bandages covered the patients nearby, leaving only an impression of a white swathed figure. He pitied the poor devils badly injured, far from home.

Mary Porter's smile remained, although a sad look came into her eyes.

"Regrettably, two men died from their injuries. There are some men here with various burns. Some succumbed to the smoke. You felt its impact upon yourself. The smell covers the camp, although the blaze no longer burns. You have had a few visitors since your arrival last evening. Baron von Steuben dropped by last night, inquiring after your well-being. I didn't really understand his words, but he sat by your bed for a time before he left. Major Butler has also been here. He wanted to know when you awakened." She smiled sweetly. "A lady from Lady Washington's group has looked after you. Mistress Clarke bathed the smoke and ash off you and gave you honey for your cough and your burns."

"Burns?" Will said. Looking down, he saw someone had wrapped one hand and wrist. When he lifted it for a better look, it throbbed.

"Nothing serious," Mistress Porter assured him. "I imagine sparks hit you as you fought the blaze." She felt his cheek. "You have no fever. I think it will be safe to send you back to your regiment today. I will see if we have some breeches for you to wear."

Will looked under the blanket and realized he wore nothing beyond his nightshirt. His cheeks flushed when he realized someone had bathed him and changed his clothes while he slept. That had not happened since he was quite small. He hoped it hadn't been Faith. The idea of her bathing him like an infant was mortifying.

He looked around, hoping to find his boots. To his relief, they rested next to his bed. Mary Porter soon returned with a pair of breeches. "I'm afraid your other pair is with the laundress. They were quite a mess. But I'm sure Rose can sort them out. She's quite good at what she does." She handed them to him and left. He looked around. The nurses were in various parts of the open building, tending to patients. None were close by at the moment. Grabbing the breeches, he slid them under the blanket, put his feet on the floor, and pulled them on. He tried to jump up quickly to pull them up, but he wobbled and had to put a hand on the bed to correct his balance. He hauled the breeches up with one hand and buttoned them as best he could one-handed.

A cough alerted him he was no longer alone. He looked up to see Jeremy

Butler with his eyes averted and a smile on his face. He held a pair of stockings in his hands.

"Hannah thought you might appreciate these. She's been quite industrious during her confinement."

"I thought I saw her at the fire."

"You did." Butler handed him the stockings. "She came out to help when she heard the first blast. Washington has let her return to nursing. We need her help." He waited as Will pulled them on, followed by his boots wincing as he used the injured hand.

Butler reached into his vest. "I found this in your pocket. I was wondering what it was."

Will took the bent piece of metal and looked at it in confusion. "I don't know." His memory cleared. "I found it on the ground out from the ovens."

Butler nodded. "It looks like a buckle." He frowned as he inspected it. "Not from a belt, maybe from a saddlebag?"

Will shot a look at him. "Why would a saddle bag be in an oven?"

Jeremy Butler shot him a grim smile. "I think someone filled it full of gunpowder, shut it tight, and stuck it in the back of a cold oven underneath a load of kindling."

Will stared at him. "Like a bomb."

"Someone put a load of powder in two ovens so that whoever lit it would cause an explosion." Butler's face grew thoughtful. "I've found some scraps of leather around the oven. It was a well-made bag. It took time for the heat to penetrate through it." He looked at Will. "It takes money to have one bag like that, much less two. I wonder who they belonged to."

"I think we need to find out."

"Yes, we do," Butler said. "Come with me. I'm hoping Washington or one of his aides de camp has seen it. If they have, we may discover who is terrorizing this encampment."

Chapter Sixteen

Will stared at the collection of bits and pieces of charred leather on the table in Washington's office. The buckle he found lay next to a strap, burned at one end. It was scorched down its length; a few flat pieces burned almost into charcoal, and a curved section still held together by stitching. He didn't see how any of it survived the blast.

Butler walked around, arranging pieces in an order seen only in his mind. Washington turned his head to watch from time to time before returning to the letters he was writing to families of the deceased. It was a task Will was glad he did not have to do.

Alexander Hamilton came in with a tray of charred bits. "Some of the enlisted men dropped off these. I was told to bring them here." His distaste was apparent. "I don't see why we are bringing debris inside. The smell is terrible." He wrinkled his nose.

Will took the tray. Hamilton was not wrong. The odor of burned hide inundated the room. Small bits of ash drifted up, tickling his nose. He sneezed.

"Careful!" Butler exclaimed. "We don't want to lose anything!"

Will set down the tray and looked at him. "What is there to lose? There is nothing of value here. I only see blackened scraps of leather. It may have been a satchel once, or a saddlebag, or God knows what. It's been burned beyond recognition."

"Not completely." Butler gestured to the table. "These are the remains of a bomb. Someone filled a leather bag with black powder and sealed it, probably with wax. Then the devil put it under a load of kindling, where the poor soul who lit the oven wouldn't see it. He did likewise in another oven, making a death trap for those with kitchen duty on that side of camp." Butler poked around the pieces, picking up various bits and arranging them until a skeletal semblance emerged. "I cannot say what belonged to which bag. The pieces lay scattered on the ground like leaves."

Will moved to the table. "Are you thinking these belonged to the bomber?"

"I can only hope." He tapped a charred bit of braid still attached to a flat strip of leather, burned black. "It takes a lot to burn heavy leather. When I saw these few inches of braid, it stirred a memory. For the life of me, I cannot tell you where I saw it."

Will frowned and took a deeper look. He could see where straps once hung on the blackened metal rings, even though one was badly warped. The curved strip could have been from a flap, maybe. Try as he might, he could not picture how it had looked before the blast had ravaged it.

Washington rose from his desk and joined them at the table. He scanned the scraps of leather intently. "We use bags like that for carrying messages between our camp to the congress, among other places." He frowned thoughtfully. "Most of them do not have this sort of trim. I've seen this recently. Braided-trim leather bags—I can't recall the owner." He opened the door and shouted. "Hamilton, Silver, Laurens— Come here, please."

Boots clattered on the hardwood floor as the aides de camp entered their commander's office. Silver wrinkled his nose as he came in. "What is that smell?"

Hamilton curled his lip. "It is a foul odor indeed. Why are we gathering these putrid scraps into the office of our commander?" He cast his eyes on the table, then at Butler. "What are you doing?"

Laurens looked at the burned leather bits. "Does this have to do with the explosion at the ovens?" His tone was curious.

"Possibly." Butler looked at the men. "This used to be a leather bag. A pair of them was used to fill the bake ovens with gunpowder with predictable results. Do any of you recognize it?"

Laurens shook his head. "I see nothing but burned scraps. It would be hard to tell what it once looked like."

Silver and Hamilton approached the table and examined what remained of the bag. Hamilton spoke first. "It's hard to say, but if I were to speculate, I would say it was a messenger or saddle bag. It would have been heavy leather for even this little of it to remain."

Silver nodded. "Good quality goods. Not every man could afford one, much less two." His eyes went to Laurens. "Don't you have something like this?"

Laurens shifted his feet. "My father sent me a set for my luggage since I will travel with General Washington when we leave this place. They are upstairs under my bunk."

"Can you bring them down here?" Butler asked. "I would like to compare them with what remains of these. It will help us get an idea of what we are looking at."

Laurens hesitated. "Is that really necessary? I cannot see how looking at mine would be of any help in this endeavor." He gestured at the charred remains on the table. "There is not enough remaining here to compare it with anything."

Washington replied. "I would appreciate anything that leads us to the culprit. It will at least help us determine how the bomb was built. If you would, go upstairs and get your bags."

Laurens looked like he wanted to protest further, then shrugged and headed to the door. "It may take a moment to pull them out," he said before exiting. His feet thudded as he went up into the garret two floors above them. Muted thuds, along with the scrap of wooden legs across the floor, floated down. After a few moments of scuffling and muted swearing, he walked down the stairs.

Laurens reentered. Anger flushed his face and flashed in his eyes. "They're gone! Some foul scoundrel has made off with them. I had them tucked well underneath my bunk for safekeeping. I saw them just a few days ago. This is outrageous! Do men here have no honor than to pilfer what little another has?"

Silence greeted his outburst. Butler gestured to the scraps on the table. "Could these be your bags?" No one else said a word as John Laurens walked slowly to the table.

"Surely not. Who burns good leather? They were a gift and appreciated. I lost my previous bags in the debacle at Brandywine. I was looking forward to having something more stable than a potato sack." He eyed the bits before coming to rest on the small strand of braid resting among the fragments. "My bags had braid stitched across the top flap. It was beautiful workmanship." He turned back to the others gathered there. "Who has done this? Why destroy my things? I have offended no one that I know of."

Butler's voice was soft. "They were used to make a bomb, John. The explosions killed three men and injured many more. Some may not last the night."

Laurens bit his lip and nodded. "You are right, of course. The assault on our men is the more serious issue. The person who did this has much to answer for."

"Yes," Butler said. "He does indeed. Whoever committed these acts will face the consequences of his actions once convicted." He looked over at Laurens. "I'm sure you wouldn't mind if I searched your room to see if I can find any evidence of the thief?"

Laurens nodded quietly. "I suppose so. Keep in mind I share the space with Hamilton and Silver, so all our things are there."

"I will be most careful with everything there." He gestured to Silver. "Come with me, Jack, you can show me where each man sleeps so I do not create too much of a mess."

Silver looked over at Washington for permission before following Butler upstairs. Their feet echoed on the wooden steps as they went up to where the aides de camp slept.

Will went over to poke the fire in order to escape the heavy silence. Like everyone else, he liked John Laurens. He had always seemed an honorable young man, eager to serve his country and lend a hand to all. That his bags had been used to blow up the ovens was disturbing.

Laurens walked around the room restlessly. "Why won't any of you look at me? I had nothing to do with this." His voice rose in frustration. "You know me–all of you know my character. I have served alongside you." He shot a beseeching gaze at Washington.

The General responded. "John, nobody has made any accusations. We have to look at all avenues to find this man, and none of us is above suspicion. My horse was used to cover a crime. Don't be angry with Major Butler. He is doing what I have asked him to do."

Laurens sighed. "So be it." He went to the fire and stared morosely into the flames as they crackled. Their flames danced across the logs as they fed on the dry wood.

The minutes went by like hours as everyone waited for the two men to reappear. Will tried to ignore the muted sounds above as he stared down at the table at the darkened pieces that had once been a fine piece of luggage. It was very little upon which to condemn a man.

Washington returned to his letters, writing with the same efficiency that he commanded his men. He wrote, signed, and dried the letters before sealing them for the next messenger. He didn't rise until he heard boots rumbling like thunder on the stairs as they approached.

The two men said nothing as they returned to the room. Silver paused to wipe the sweat off his face with a handkerchief while Butler walked to the table and laid a small object on it. The other men crowded around to see what he had brought. Dread filled Will's heart as he joined the others. Only one thing that size would put such a grim expression on Butler's face.

A figure made of carved sticks stared up at them from the table. Filthy, charred clothes covered the body while ashes covered its hair. Its muslin shirt was gray, and its breeches sported burned spots, as if sparks had tried to ignite the cloth.

Washington's face was grim. "Where did you find this?"

"Someone rolled it up inside some of Lieutenant Colonel Laurens's bedding."

"I've never seen that thing before." Laurens shot Butler a horrified look. "You cannot believe I had anything to do with this. These killings are the work of a deranged monster." He shot a pleading glance at his commander.

General Washington was silent for a moment. Pallor washed over his face even as his expression did not change. He gestured to Butler. "Take him into custody."

"I am an innocent man," Laurens protested.

Butler put a hand on his shoulder. "Come with me, John."

He shook off Butler and stood up straight. "I will go because General Washington requests it, but I swear on my honor I have raised a hand to no man." Laurens's voice choked. His face flushed as tears filled his eyes. His comrades avoided his gaze as Butler placed a restraining hand on his shoulder. Swallowing hard, he walked out stiffly, followed by Jeremy Butler and two of Washington's guards.

"Where are they taking him?" Will asked as they went out the front door.

"To a cabin we use as a brig," Washington answered wearily. "I will have to tell his father. If this is true, it will break Henry's heart."

Jack Silver spoke. "Surely there is a reasonable explanation. John has been with us for months, fought in the battles, eaten with us." He shook his head. "I cannot believe he would do anything like this."

"Someone is committing these crimes who knows how to hide in plain sight. I pray it is not John Laurens, but the evidence is damning." Hamilton's face was tight with frustration.

Washington nodded. "He can prove his innocence at his Court Martial. Let us hope for now that these mad killings have ceased."

Will hoped so as well. He watched as Butler collected the charred figure before exiting Washington's office. He followed, unsure of what else to do. Butler said nothing as Will joined him. He seemed distracted.

Will broke the silence. "Do you believe this is the end of it?"

Butler shook his head. "I'm not sure. All the evidence was there as if someone tied it up in a bow and handed it to Washington." Butler shook his head. "John Laurens is young, but he's not stupid. If he were committing these murders, he'd leave no evidence where we would find it."

"Everyone makes mistakes," Will noted. "Maybe he grew careless."

"Maybe." Butler sounded doubtful. He looked down at the charred doll. "I want to find out more about these. I doubt the killer made them. He's found someone to make them for him, outside of the barracks. I've never seen Laurens go down into the camps. Perhaps someone can tell us if he did."

"Perhaps someone delivered it to him," Will suggested. The doll looked even worse in the harsh daylight. The charred wood coated Butler's hands with soot. "I'm surprised the blast didn't consume it."

"It was nowhere near it," Butler said. Holding it up to catch the sun's rays, he turned it over in his hand. Tiny flecks of ash fell to the ground. "This one is inferior in craftsmanship to the others. You see how ragged the edges of the cloth are? No one bothered to hem the sleeves or the bottom. The breeches have just been stuck on with glue. I don't see a stitch in them. If this had been in the oven, it would have turned to ash almost instantly." He laid it on the fence rail. "Someone singed this over a smaller fire and then rubbed ash into it. He taunts Washington with them." Butler looked thoughtful. "This one's purpose appears to be incriminating John Laurens."

"How long until the court-martial?' Will asked.

Butler shrugged. "It could be days, maybe weeks. It depends on whether he waits for Lafayette to return. I hope he does. Lafayette is a fair man."

"What happens if they don't, and he's found guilty?"

Butler waited so long that Will wondered if he hadn't heard him. When he spoke, his voice was rough with weariness. "They will execute him. There is no middle ground. If he's found to be both a traitor and a murderer, they will end him as swiftly as possible."

Will inhaled sharply. "So if we do not find evidence to the contrary, he will die."

"Yes," Butler said, staring down at the macabre figure in his hand. "It's up to us to find the truth because no one else will look until it's too late."

Chapter Seventeen

aith spent the next few days at the hospital, caring for men injured in the explosion. She took turns changing bandages and applying ointments to ease their pain. In truth, there was very little they could do to comfort those most severely injured. Faith generously poured liquor and helped clean and dress wounds. When grief overwhelmed her, Faith stepped outside where her tears would not distress her patients.

Desperate for distraction, she listened as news drifted in. With each shift, nurses and patients gossiped. Word of Lieutenant Colonel John Lauren's arrest spread quickly. She wondered if it was true. It didn't fit with the friendly young man she had known over the past few months. There seemed no reason for him to have committed such terrible acts. Yet the evidence was damming. She tried to engage her sister in conversation, but Hannah had nothing to share. When Butler came in to question the men recovering from the explosion, Faith stopped him before he exited. His response was curt when she tried to ask him for news.

"Stay out of it." He shot her a hard glance. "Neither of you need to meddle in this."

Faith wanted to speak to Will, but he didn't put in an appearance either at the hospital or Washington's headquarters later that day. She supposed he was with the baron, especially since Laurens had been one of von Steuben's chief interpreters before his arrest.

She noticed at mealtime that Lieutenant Colonel Hamilton hurried through his meal at midday and was back at work almost before they had completed putting the room back together. The casual chatter of previous gatherings had vanished. People didn't look at one another as each consumed their food. It was as if a wall had come down, separating each person. Faith watched him for a few moments. Overnight, the young Lieutenant Colonel had aged. Dark circles rimmed his eyes, while lines had carved themselves into either side of his mouth. Silver looked no better. His casual banter had ceased. He chewed his food as if eating were an act of will.

As the day drew to a close, she spotted Will as he entered for supper with the baron's men. He looked exhausted. With Lauren's incarceration, the burden of translating von Steuben's orders to the troops had fallen upon him with a few breaks from Hamilton. The hours of drills, plus the responsibility of conveying the drillmaster's commands correctly, occupied most of his time.

"How goes it?" she asked as they sat down to eat a meal of boiled corn, cold beef, and cabbage left from dinner.

Will did not answer at first. He focused on eating the food placed before him and taking long drinks of cider. Once he had eaten a few bites, he turned to look at her. His voice was soft, but carried over the clinking of cutlery on plates. A few eyes rose to watch as he spoke. "It goes well enough. The men have gotten to where they understand a good many of the Baron's commands even before I translate them. They can complete many drills from memory. Most importantly, they keep their muskets clean and ready to go." He smiled grimly. "The majority have finally figured out that the bayonet is good for more than roasting something over a fire."

Faith nodded. She didn't want to imagine what it could do to a human body. She struggled with the idea that Will and Jeremy would head into battle, along with the other men. He didn't tell her, but she knew he had faced combat many times since he left Williamsburg last winter.

Finished with his meal, Will accepted a hot cup of coffee from Hannah Tills after her husband cleared away all the plates. The table was quiet as they drank coffee over dessert and relaxed from the day's work. He looked over at Faith. "What have you been up to?"

She paused. "Nothing as exciting as preparing to fight the British."

He shook his head. "Fighting isn't exciting, it's terrifying. The drills are boring, but necessary. I want to hear about your day. Nothing is as pleasurable as hearing about normal life. I miss the routine of the press and seeing people plant their fields. When I get home, I want to visit the market and watch you haggle with the vendors over the cost of beans or carrots." He shot her a rueful look. "Remembering the past helps me endure those long nights when all we can see is the faint glimmer of enemy campfires in the distance."

Faith bit her lip and forced a smile. "Then let me tell you about my day." She left out her visit to the hospital. He didn't need to hear about that. He did laugh as she described chasing down an obstinate ball of yarn that had rolled across the floor and out the door. It would have continued down the stairs if she had not stepped on the sock she had begun before the rogue ball yanked it out of her hands.

As the meal ended, they helped the others finish clearing the table. Some men began moving the chairs back to where they needed to be for the aides-de-camp to conduct their business. Will went to pick up the latest round of notes from von Steuben to translate, but Hamilton waved him off. "He's been writing pretty consistently in French, except for the curses for which I need no translation. Go spend some time with your lady. I can manage this."

"You are sure?" Will hesitated.

"Washington's horses understand French better than you, my friend," Hamilton said dryly. "Let me transcribe his notes while you help him in the field until this situation with Laurens clears up."

"You don't believe he did this."

Hamilton shook his head. "I've shared a room and broken bread with John and Jack for months. While I might argue listening to him sing is torture, I have not seen that kind of madness." His face turned dark. "I pray we find out who our enemy is within this encampment. We're running out of time. Now I need to get this done. John is laid up with one of his headaches, so there's twice the work tonight." He turned to the stack of notes left on the table. Pulling over a seat to take advantage of the fire's light, he began reading Baron von Steuben's latest notes before dipping a quill in ink to write them in English.

Faith walked with Will out to the breezeway. The sun was well on its way west, hanging above the horizon as the clouds turned shades of pink and orange. They watched in silence as the evening stars emerged above them.

"What did he mean about running out of time?" Faith turned to him.

Will's face remained turned toward the sky. "He means until we march out of this place. Now that spring is coming, Washington will plan his next move. The enemy will break winter camp in a matter of weeks. I suspect he hopes Lafayette will return in time to join us. He is fierce in combat, and the men respect him."

Faith nodded. "Are the men ready to face the British?"

Will turned to look at her. "We're ready. We've trained day in and day out for weeks, absorbing what the baron has to teach us. Our next meeting will surprise the British. These aren't boys anymore. They are soldiers. They can fight, and they know what to do when the enemy engages them. Let's hope it's enough to drive the enemy across the Atlantic, far away from us."

Faith nodded. It was what they all hoped, although a small, quiet part wondered what would happen to Charity when her soldier left the colonies. She had chosen the opposing side, and Faith didn't know what to make of it. Over time, the little girl she knew with the faintly crooked teeth had turned into a woman with a mind of her own. There was no telling where her choices would take her. In all fairness, Faith knew the same applied to herself. The war had changed all of them.

As the sky darkened, Will took her back inside. "I prefer to walk back before it gets pitch black," he said. "There are still a few of my bunk mates about, so it's good timing."

Faith wished him good night. She watched as he called out to a small group as they headed out the door. She didn't understand German, but the exchange seemed friendly. They disappeared down the path in the twilight, the sound of their voices carrying across the field long after they disappeared from sight.

As she went upstairs to bed, she thought about his words. Will didn't talk about the battles he'd been in or the places he had seen. He talked about home, the small everyday things that no one really considered until it was no longer a part of one's life. The suffering of war was far more than the trauma of battle or the grief felt for fallen comrades. It was the intense loneliness caused by separation from all that was familiar and held dear. As Faith lay in her bed, she thought about her son Andrew, safe in Williamsburg with his teacher, George Wythe. Her mind turned to her tavern, being run by Olivia and Titus, far more than servants, now dear friends. She prayed for their safety and well-being. She hoped no British Warships had sailed up either the James or York Rivers. Most of all, she prayed the war ended soon so they all could go home.

Her head barely touched the pillow when the other ladies in the loft woke her. "What is happening?" She muttered, still half asleep.

"Lafayette has returned," someone called out as they headed down the stairs.

Faith sat up to realize she was the only one left in bed. She jumped up and rushed through her toilet before going down to join the others. From the stairwell, she could hear voices speaking rapidly in French downstairs. Although she did not know what they were saying, the jubilant tone was obvious.

Upon reaching the main floor, someone offered her a glass of wine as everyone present saluted the popular Frenchman's return. She swallowed and felt the alcohol burn down her throat. It was an interesting way to begin the day. The celebrations continued well into breakfast. Faith was relieved when she could claim coffee and food in place of all the wine. She was certain some of those present were going to be tipsy from all the toasts.

The Marquis de Lafayette was a slender man who looked barely out of his youth. He sat next to Washington, where they could converse easily. The Marquis spoke English with a light accent. He thanked Hannah Till as she filled his mug with coffee. "Madame Till. I missed your skills. There was no one who could compare with you at our encampment. Many are the nights I considered deserting just so I could sit at your table once again."

The cook blushed. Her warm smile remained on her face as she went back and forth carrying platters of meat, eggs, and bread into the main house. The return of the Frenchman lifted the mood of everyone present. People lingered over the breakfast table as he recounted his adventures in the north.

"There was never a chance to invade Canada," he said dismissively. "No matter what the Congress said, we didn't have the men, the weapons, or the supplies. I do not know whose idea this was, but it was ill-planned." He raised a dark eyebrow at Washington, who acknowledged it with a nod. It was no secret they believed the war department was out of touch with the realities the army faced.

"Now that you have returned to us, we can plan for the coming season," Washington said. The table grew silent at this statement, wondering if the Commander-in-Chief planned to announce something. Instead, Washington raised a cup and took a sip before placing it down and delicately wiping his lips with a napkin.

Conversation returned to a steady hum until the meal was complete. As Hannah and Isaac Till worked to clear the table, Washington signaled to the men to lend a hand. As he stood, the rest of those gathered did likewise. Quickly, they cleared the table and rearranged the room for the day's tasks.

Washington walked toward his office with Lafayette at his side. Jeremy Butler, who had come in with Hannah, watched his back. "I guess we will need to pack up," he murmured.

Lafayette turned at the sound of his voice. "No, Major Butler. Stay with your wife in my bed. I will lodge downstairs with my men. Having your heart's joy at your side is a blessing. Enjoy the time you have before the drumbeat of war draws you out." He offered a quick bow to Hannah. "Now I see why his temperament has so much improved in the last year. I am glad he has found happiness with you."

Hannah smiled. "You are most kind."

Lafayette's eyes twinkled. "Somehow I think that the men under my command would not say that, particularly after a day's march in the rain!" He turned and followed Washington into his office. The door shut behind them.

Will eyed the closed door. "I imagine they have a great deal to catch up on."

"Such as what Lafayette saw and heard while he was away," Butler responded. "Make no mistake, Lafayette is loyal to Washington. He observes his surroundings. That Frenchman would have made a great spy, had he not been so hungry for combat."

Faith looked at him in surprise. "He looks little more than a boy."

Will McKay snorted. "He's lethal with any sort of blade and fearless in battle. I've watched him lead a charge. It's terrifying."

Faith didn't answer. The details of war made little sense to her, and she didn't care to learn. She simply wanted it to end. The sooner the better. As they stood together in the hallway, General Gates and Baron von Steuben passed them before knocking and entering Washington's office.

"That will take up a good bit of the morning," Butler commented.

Faith shot him a look. "Why do you say that?"

Will answered. "Because they are planning the spring campaign. Now that Lafayette has returned, there is nothing to keep them here once the weather stabilizes." He gestured to the door. "Let's go outside. The hallway is far too narrow for people to stand around." The door protested as he opened it. Humidity from recent rain had swollen the boards, making it a tight fit in its frame. Once they were out, he pushed it shut. A light breeze brought scents of fresh grass and pine from nearby trees. The training ground stood empty for once.

Faith shivered. Although she was tired of life at Valley Forge, she wasn't eager for either Will or Jeremy to return to the fray. They had been fortunate to escape injury, but there was no guarantee either man would return home unscathed. Working in the hospital had educated her on the dangers of the battlefield. She tried not to dwell on what she had seen. How Hannah bore it was something Faith could not comprehend. The hospital gave her nightmares, but her older sister went every day.

The fields across the meadow had turned a tender shade of green. Sprinklings of flowers dotted the grass with stretches of yellow and white blossoms. The sky was a vast expanse of blue, undiluted by haze. Faint haze drifted up from a nearby creek whose gurgles murmured in the distance. Sun glinted off dew that peppered blades of grass in the meadow. Cattle lowed as they fed, watched by a small crew of men who were silhouettes in the distance.

"It looks so peaceful," Hannah said as her eyes looked into the distance. "It's almost like being back home."

Faith nodded. "Pa's cattle were black and white, but otherwise, everything else is much the same." She wondered how they fared. Her father was firmly nonpartisan. Despite the leanings of his children, he refused to become involved in the ongoing conflict. Unfailingly courteous, he refused to aid either side. The result was both confiscated his livestock and raided his pantry, and neither defended him from the other. It was infuriating and totally like him. Faith feared what might happen to him.

Will squeezed her hand. As her eyes met his, he smiled. "I wasn't sure where you were. I called your name, and you seemed deep in your own thoughts."

Faith offered an apologetic smile. "I'm sorry. What troubles thee?"

His eyes softened. "You must be thinking of your Pa. It brings out the Quaker in you. There's many like him surrounding Philadelphia. I doubt the British are going to trouble him. Outraging the populace is the last thing they want."

Faith nodded. She hoped he was right. Her suspicion was he was trying to ease her fears. Will knew about as much as she did about the current situation in Philadelphia and the surrounding area, which meant virtually nothing. If Jeremy had heard anything, he didn't enlighten them.

Will spoke. "Jeremy and I are going to gather von Steuben's men and complete a few drills while he meets with Washington. They need to make the most efficient use of their time now that the warm weather is here."

Faith nodded. Will kissed her cheek. "I will see you tonight."

As the men took off across the field, Hannah looked over at her. "Would you like to join me for an errand?"

"I can. Where are we going?"

"To the Oneida encampment." At Faith's startled look, Hannah added. "I hope that native woman with the corn will share what she knows about her people's remedies for ailments." She bit her lip. "There is little to offer our sick and injured here besides liquor or laudanum, of which there is little.

These people have lived on these lands for untold generations. I'm sure they know the uses of many plants to treat their own people. I hope she will share her knowledge so we can help ours."

"She's been pretty generous with her knowledge of cooking," Faith acknowledged. "Although I'm not sure how wise it is for two women to enter an Oneida Camp without an escort."

"They are here at the invitation of Washington. I doubt there will be any trouble. Besides, we are going to speak to Mary Cooper. Many in the camp have visited her fire with no trouble."

"That's true," Faith said. "They are not much different from the natives who come into Williamsburg to trade." She met her sister's gaze. "I don't know many native remedies. Who knows? We may learn something useful. It cannot hurt to ask."

Hannah smiled. "That is what I am hoping."

They fell in step as they went down the abandoned road that led past the burying ground. Last year's weeds stood up in patches that brushed their skirts as they passed. Their yellowed stems bowed down, some broken by the weather, others bending down from the weight of their long since dead seed heads. A few dew drops sparkled as they passed, reflecting the brilliance of the sun. A bird cried as it flew overhead, speeding as it flew over the field and into a copse of trees.

Faith listened to the crunch of the earth underneath her feet, glad that the ground had dried since the last rain, although damp from the taller grass penetrated her skirts. As they entered the forest that separated the army camp from the native one, the trees overhead filled the ground with shadow. The narrow path surrounded by trees increased the sense of isolation. It made Faith uneasy. Her ears caught the whisper of branches and the crackle of leaves. Yet the shadows revealed nothing. No one would notice if they disappeared in this thick patch of woods. The men stayed busy preparing for war. No one would miss them until the next meal. Will would suppose she was at the hospital. He would have no reason to worry until nightfall.

Faith shoved the troublesome thoughts aside. "Don't be a ninny."

"Did you say something?" Hannah asked.

Flushing, Faith shook her head.

Hannah showed no such unease. With confidence, she walked ahead, each step suggesting familiarity with the path. Either she had been this way before or listened carefully when Jeremy had told her the way. She turned back to look at Faith.

"It's not much further now."

Faith nodded. Hannah turned back to the trail before she could respond. Her speed showed strong interest in speaking with the Oneida woman. Before long, they entered a wide clearing, filled with shelters made of hide and bark. A large campfire roared with life close by. A middle-aged woman stirred a huge dark pot. Sun fell on the top of her head, turning the raven black strands reddish where the light struck.

The woman continued her work, although she had seen them approach. Her eyes focused on her task. Hannah waited for her to finish stirring before she spoke. "I am Hannah Butler. I work with the sick and injured at General Washington's encampment. Many have said you have been a tremendous help in teaching my people about corn. Could you share your knowledge of native plants that your people use as medicines?"

Polly Cooper didn't speak at first. Her eyes, dark as pitch, regarded both women. She was a handsome woman of medium height with dark hair parted in the middle and put into braids that streamed down her shoulders to her waist. She wore a dress of printed fabric with deerskin leggings and moccasins. Steam from her pit made small tendrils of hair stick to the sides of her broad forehead. Her voice was deep for a woman, but melodic. "You wish to know of the medicines of my people. Why? Don't you have medicines of your own?"

"Normally, that would be true," Hannah replied. "But we have very little to treat the sick, to clean their wounds, or treat their fevers. Our people suffer. My father traded with the Oneida in the past and said you were intelligent and honorable people who know this land better than anyone. I would like to learn what I can so that I can help those who are ill and injured at Valley Forge."

Polly Cooper contemplated her. "The Oneida have agreed to help

Washington. I will give you red cedar, which is good for aches and fevers when boiled in water. Come back tomorrow early, and I will show you how to find bloodroot, sweet grass, and sage. Tobacco you already have in the camp."

Hannah smiled. "Thank you. I am grateful."

They left with their pockets full of bark and some leaves from a plant that the Oneida woman called bloodroot, which she said was good for infections. Hannah seemed pleased with the interaction. Faith looked over at her. "You enjoy working with the sick."

"Enjoy is not the term I would use," Hannah said wryly. "I hate the suffering. But if I can ease some of the suffering in this camp, it gives me a purpose. We don't need to lose soldiers to illness. They need proper care and good food. Hopefully, now that the supply chain has improved, we can get more of them well so that they can complete the work they came here to do."

"I hope so, too," Faith said. As the encampment came into view, the sound of soldiers drilling drifted across the fields. They moved in neat lines across the ground. When ordered, they fired as one. "They have come a long way from the boys who entered this camp."

"Yes, they have," Hannah replied. "Let's pray they return home."

Chapter Eighteen

Faith slapped a mosquito as it bit into her neck. It buzzed away, unharmed. Neither of her companions seemed to notice. Hannah focused on the forest floor, looking at the latest plant that Polly Cooper identified. The Oneida woman glided through the forest effortlessly, never stumbling over a root or stone.

Faith had no such luck. She seemed to find every root and hollow in the ground as she followed the other two. Being the tallest by several inches meant she had to be careful of low branches that the others could easily duck under.

"Hurry," Hannah called back to her. "Polly doesn't have all day."

Faith scratched the itchy spot on her neck. "Give me a moment. I need to finish sketching this cedar." Both women had brought paper and pencil to record images of the plants Polly Cooper showed them. Her fingers flew as she wrote brief notes on each plant and its uses.

Moisture soaked through her shoes, making her feet wet. Low spots in the meadow kept moisture from the last rain. When she caught up, Hannah was already sketching the tall stand of weeds that Polly Cooper called sweet grass. "What is this good for?" Faith asked.

The native woman's dark eyes studied Faith before moving to Hannah. "It is said that sweet grass cleanses the spirit. Smell." She handed each woman a few stems.

The scent was sweet and heady. "It's sort of familiar," Hannah admitted. "I'm not sure from where."

"Perhaps native traders in Philadelphia?" Faith said. She had smelled nothing like it before.

Hannah shook her head. "I think it was when a group of Spanish came with spices and chocolate. They intermingled this with their other goods. It was the best-smelling table at the market."

Faith shrugged. "If you say so." She found the market in Philadelphia overwhelming. She preferred the familiarity of Williamsburg. She took a few stems to add to her collection and followed the two women.

"I know that plant," Faith said, staring at the pale lavender leaves. "This is tobacco, although not what we grow in Virginia."

Polly Cooper's voice was solemn. "My people have used it for medicine and for ceremonies for years. It is the white man that burns it for no reason."

Faith had no answer for that. She disliked the smell of it burning in her tavern. It lingered and made the air stale and foul. She was happy when they moved across a field where the land showed signs of past cultivation.

"Sage," Hannah said as she squatted down to examine a plant poking through the ground. "I have some in my garden in Philadelphia." Her lips twisted. "If the current occupants haven't destroyed it, along with the rest of my possessions."

. Hannah had taken pride in owning her own business and being independent. It was unfortunate that someone had mentioned that Benjamin Franklin had stayed at her home, if only briefly. The enemy had gleefully made examples of all those who had supported the Patriot cause. She was lucky they hadn't done worse.

Nearby lay the scarred remains of a dwelling. Faith felt a wave of sadness wash over her. "What was this place?"

Hannah answered. "Someone's home. The British came through here a few months before Washington arrived. According to Jeremy, it was a nasty sweeping raid. They stole supplies, destroyed forges, and burned down a lot of homes." She looked at the ruins. "I guess this family fled rather than face losing everything all over again." Biting her lip, she turned away. "Let's finish up and get away from this wretched place."

Faith agreed. She made a quick sketch before gathering a few small handfuls to put in her pockets. They should have brought baskets, but neither of them had thought to do so. It was unfortunate since she wasn't sure if she could find her way back to the places Polly Cooper had shown them. She had tried to pay attention to direction and check for landmarks, but keeping up with the agile Oneida woman proved to be a challenge.

When she stood up from where she had squatted to sketch, the other women were nowhere in sight. The isolation spooked her. "Hannah? Mistress Cooper?" Silence greeted her. Surely, they wouldn't leave her? Faith looked around, trying to see if they were exploring the ruins.

From the collapsed roof of the burned cabin, damaged logs lay scattered. Scattered belongings lay in the yard, bearing testament to tragedy. Faith bit her lip as she identified the remains of a spinning wheel, broken except for the telltale wheel. The spindle lay cracked into pieces beside it. It was a tool no one would willingly leave behind. As she drew closer, she could see the remains of a stone hearth, mostly whole. Once it had warmed a home and cooked meals. Now it stood as a lonely testament to life interrupted, an unacknowledged victim of the forces of war.

Seeing movement, Faith walked toward the barn, hoping to spot the other women. Once it had held the family's livestock. All that remained were charred ruins of an upended life. Fire-blackened walls stood upright, except for where a large tree had crashed down, taking the roof and most of the facing wall. The other two women stood near what had been the main door. The door sagged halfway to the ground, partially blocking the entrance. As she opened her mouth to speak, a putrid smell overtook her.

Decay polluted the air, drowning out the underlying scents of moldy hay and earth. Hannah's face was pale while Polly Cooper looked impassive. A fly buzzed past Faith as she joined them.

"What is it?" She asked.

"Death," Polly Cooper said. "It was not here when last I came."

Faith and Hannah looked at each other. "Could an animal have wandered in?" Faith said at last. She didn't want to say what they both were wondering. There had been too many strange deaths of late. With John Lauren's arrest, she had hoped it had ended.

"No animals come around here," Polly Cooper said. "The British took all the food and burned the hay. Nothing comes here of its own accord." She gestured to the tumbled-down barn. "Something bad has happened. Whatever lies within has not been there long." She wrinkled her nose. "The smell is too bad for it to be old."

Faith started breathing through her mouth. The odor was beginning to make her nauseous. The Oneida woman wasn't wrong. Something was rotting in there, and the carrion eaters had not had time to do their job.

"We need to see what is in there," Faith said, looking at the other two.

"Why does it have to be us?" Hannah protested. "Can't someone else find out what died?"

Polly Cooper watched them for a few moments before shaking her head. "There is evil here. It is not the business of the Oneida. I have shown you what I know. I will return to my people." With that, she turned and walked back the way they had come. Within moments, she disappeared into the woods they had come out of.

Hannah and Faith stared after the way she had gone before turning to face each other. The deserted homestead was quiet. Not even a breeze stirred.

"We could go for help," Hannah suggested, looking back toward where the encampment lay. "It's not too far away."

Faith shook her head. "What if someone moves the body once we leave?"

Hannah shot her a look. "How do you know there is a body in there? It could be a dead squirrel or a rat. We cannot assume a person died in there."

"That's why we have to look." Faith glanced past the sagging door to the shadows inside. There was nothing to attract anyone to it. "I'm not summoning Will and Jeremy out here for a dead rat."

"Jeremy would appreciate that." They both knew he hated rodents, dead or alive.

Faith stared at her sister. "You keep watch. I will go." She walked to where the door leaned over the opening, the remaining hinge holding it halfway up.

"Wait." Hannah handed her a stout branch as long as her arm. "Better go armed just in case there is something alive in there that's unfriendly."

Faith nodded, thanking her for the weapon. Ducking under the space formed by the door, she stepped inside. The contrast between the sunlit yard and shadowed barn blinded her. She let her eyes adjust. Dust motes danced in the faint fingers of light provided by cracks in the walls and along the roofline. The moldy straw evidenced rain from the damaged roof on the ground. She wondered what had happened to the people who once lived here. The people left so much behind, as if they had fled suddenly. She stumbled. As she righted herself, she spotted a broken hay fork lying across the ground. Faith picked it up and set it aside. Looking around the darkened space, she longed for a candle, or better yet, a lantern, to dispel the gloom. The darkness unsettled her. It felt as if she were entering a long-abandoned tomb bereft of life. She contemplated going out for a torch, but thought better of it. The last thing she wanted was to set the barn afire. The idea made her shudder.

"Let's get this done with," she muttered, creeping down the center, peering into stalls as she went.

"Is everything all right in there?" Hannah called.

"Fine," Faith snapped. "It's like a garden party."

"There's no need to be snippy. I was worried." Anxiety sharpened her tone.

Faith sighed. "It's just dark," she called back. Although Hannah irritated her, she was glad for her presence. The darkness amplified every little creak and crackle. The putrid smell made her stomach roll. Even as her nose adjusted, her stomach continued to heave. More than anything, she wanted to turn and run back to the safety of Washington's headquarters, or better yet, her tavern in Williamsburg. She longed to be anywhere else. Yet stubbornness propelled her forward.

Near the back of the building, sun poured in through a hole in the roof. A large tree branch had fallen in and covered the floor. The only way past would be to climb over it. Faith really did not want to do that, even with the pool of sunlight to illuminate the way. Dread made her heart beat faster. The musty straw itched her nose. She couldn't restrain the fierce sneezes that exploded from her face. Faith inhaled through her mouth, hoping to ease the irritation. Branches like enormous fingers perched precariously on the edges of the stalls. Some had collapsed under the weight. Broken stall boards lay beneath branches, holding onto their green leaves. The last rain must have brought it down. A long, high-pitched creak warned her the barn was not terribly stable. She needed to hurry and get out before it collapsed.

Faith scanned the next few stalls and found nothing. The barn shifted slightly as the wind picked up.

Hannah called from the entrance. "You need to hurry. I don't trust this building."

Faith agreed. Just a few more places to check. She was not risking climbing over or under the tangle of limbs from the fallen tree branches. The dying leaves covered the ground like a shroud. She almost missed the puddle of liquid underneath a bunch of limbs that overlay a stall whose sides had caved in. What remained formed a small cavern, covered in torn cobwebs and shadows. Faith recognized the metallic scent of blood. It made her gag.

Biting her tongue, she forced herself forward, hoping to find a dead squirrel or opossum. It would be so much easier to deal with. Faith had almost convinced herself that was what it was until she saw the hand.

"Oh Lord," she moaned. A dark cuff surrounded a pale arm outstretched along the ground. The fingers were small and pale and dusted with dirt. "Who are you?" she asked, knowing there was no one who could answer.

Using her stick, she lifted a few branches, enough to see the pale outline of an apron. Levering up the limbs with her branch, she could see a head covered in what had been a straw hat. A bedraggled bow trailed across the squashed brim. Underneath, a mass of dark hair straggled out of a bun. Swallowing hard, Faith reached in to confirm what she already knew. The skin was cold to the touch. As she drew back, something slimy rolled across her hand; the maggot plopped on the ground gray and lumpy. Faith recoiled as if it were a snake. Backing out, she ran toward the door, stumbling in her hurry.

Once out, she shoved past Hannah and bent over the nearest bush, vomiting violently into the shrub. Her stomach heaved as she struggled to unsee the horror in the broken barn. Faith gasped and began heaving again; her stomach emptied itself. After several moments of retching, she leaned back and wiped her nose with her sleeve. The smell of vomit made her feel even more ill.

"Here," her sister said, handing her a wet handkerchief. "Wipe off your face while I get you some water."

Faith watched as her sister stepped over to a small well and raised a bucket, which she then brought over. She cupped her hand into it and held it out. "Rinse out your mouth first and then drink. You've had a shock."

Meekly, she followed her older sister's directions, not unlike when they were younger, and Hannah watched over her, except the bossy tone was missing.

Faith took a few deep breaths. "There's a dead woman inside."

Hannah nodded. "We need to tell someone. Do you know who it was?"

Faith shook her head. "Hair covered her face. When I touched her-" Faith swallowed hard, trying not to heave.

"Don't tell me," Hannah said quickly. "Let's get back to camp and let someone else figure this out. You've done enough for one day."

Faith let Hannah take her arm and lead her back to the road that led to camp. They came out close to Lafayette's headquarters, where Hannah and Jeremy had been staying. A few soldiers met them on the road and led them inside.

"I need brandy," Hannah said. "My sister has had a shock. Then we need to speak to someone in charge."

"That would be me, Madame Butler." Lafayette strode into the room. His dark eyes filled with concern. "What has happened?"

Faith let Hannah tell him. She focused on breathing and sipping the powerful cognac that Lafayette insisted she drink. Her body shook as the fiery liquid burned its way down her throat. A wave of dizziness overcame her, and she felt herself sliding forward. She heard the Frenchman exclaim something as her vision grayed and consciousness slid away.

Chapter Nineteen

Faith awoke in bed in an unfamiliar room. Will sat on one side, Hannah on another. They both looked worried. As she stirred, they both leaned over the bed.

"Faith," Hannah's voice was soft. "Can you hear me?"

"Of course, I can hear you. I'm not deaf," Faith struggled to throw off the heavy blankets that covered her. "Where am I?" Her mouth felt full of cotton, and her head throbbed. She shook her head to dispel the faint dizziness that made her head spin.

Will put a restraining hand on her shoulder. "Take it easy. You've had a shock. Give yourself a moment."

"I'm not an invalid." Faith looked around. "Whose bedroom is this?" The fireplace looked familiar. She caught Hannah's gaze. "This is your room, isn't it?"

"Technically, it belongs to the Marquis de Lafayette," Hannah said. "But he lent it to Jeremy and me since his wife is still in France."

Faith swung her legs over the side. The floor felt cool to her stockinged feet. "How long have I been out?"

"You roused for a few minutes after you fainted, then drifted off to sleep," Will answered. "Dr. Waldo said to let you rest as long as you needed. He checked on you before going with some of Lafayette's men down to the ruined barn you two found." He frowned at both of them. "Neither of you had any business there. It's too dangerous to be wandering about without an escort. That barn could collapse at any time." He glared at Faith. "How could you be so stupid as to go inside? It could have fallen in while you were there."

Faith didn't answer him. She turned to her sister. "Does anyone know who she was?" Her throat rasped. She coughed. The violent motion made it hurt more.

Will stood. "Now that I know you are recovering, I must return to the baron. Our days in this encampment will end soon." He looked over at Hannah. "Monitor her and please, no more adventures out of camp without an escort."

Hannah didn't reply and kept her gaze focused on her sister.

Will huffed as he rose. "At least let Lafayette or another officer, such as your husband, know when you go out."

"I can do that," Hannah answered. "Jeremy knew we were going to see Polly Cooper today. I told him early this morning."

"That's something," Will growled. He looked over at Faith. "Have you been carrying your pistol?"

"It's in a drawer by my bed upstairs," she answered. "I didn't need it when I was knitting socks with Lady Washington. I don't believe anyone would dare bother her."

"I wouldn't count on anything," Will answered. "When you get back, keep it on you no matter where you are."

"I will," Faith promised. Getting back to Washington's headquarters and knitting was her most fervent desire. She was sick and tired of death and destruction. She intended to grab what peace she could find for however long it lasted.

The door closed with a sharp thud behind Will as he left. His boots thudded on the steps, indicative of his upset. The outside door opened and shut with a sharp bang that echoed in Faith's head. She leaned down to find her shoes. A faint wave of dizziness overcame her, and she sat back.

Hannah looked at her. "You need to take it easy." She reached over for a mug that was sitting on the table nearby. "Try some mint tea. It helps with both the head and stomach. I've been drinking it myself lately."

Faith looked at her. Hannah was a trifle thinner, but there was a glow about her. "Have you been ill?"

"Just a little nausea that comes and goes, usually in the morning or if I'm exhausted, which seems to be a lot these days." Hannah didn't seem upset. A slight smile curved her lips. "My breasts have become tender, too. The cold air makes them ache."

Faith caught her breath. "Are you pregnant?"

"Possibly," Hannah said. "It's been a few months since my courses. At first, I thought it was stress from all that's happened, and then I started getting ill. Mary Porter sent me home the other day after I got ill after changing a bandage. She asked me a few questions and suggested I could be with child."

"Does Jeremy know?"

Hannah shook her head. "Not yet. I want to be sure. He has so much on his mind. I don't want to add to his worries."

"A child is a blessing," Faith said as she felt the wonder of it wash over her. "Something to look forward to and rejoice. You are definitely coming home with me to Williamsburg when camp breaks. It is no time to be by yourself, and the farm is too dangerous right now."

Hannah nodded. "Jeremy has already said as much, and even if the British leave, there is nothing left in Philadelphia for me to return to."

Faith stepped into her shoes and went to the door. "I'm going back to Washington's house. I really have no business here, and I do not need to lie abed."

Hannah followed her out and down the steps to the main rooms. Only a few soldiers remained. "Lafayette took a group to the barn to retrieve the body and look for any evidence of who could have left her there."

Faith grimaced. "She's been there long enough for insects to find her."

"That doesn't take long. The warm weather brought them out."

The door opened, letting in Jeremy Butler. He went over to his wife and kissed her cheek before looking over at Faith. "I hear you two made a discovery."

Hannah grimaced. "That's one way of putting it. Does anyone know who she is?"

Butler nodded. "Once Lafayette's men got her out of the barn, they recognized her. It's Magdalena Ross. Someone strangled her and hid the body in the abandoned barn. She hadn't been there long. She only went missing a few days ago. I doubt anyone would have found her if you two hadn't gone poking around." He shot them both a look. "You're fortunate that the killer was not around. We might never have found you."

Faith shivered. He wasn't wrong. Whoever the killer was, he had done a good job of concealing his identity. A thought struck her. "How does this fit in with the poem?"

"It doesn't," Butler responded. "I believe that is why he hid the body. The others have been on display where his work would draw attention. I think she knew something and tried to blackmail the wrong person." He looked over at Faith. "I'm glad to see you have recovered. Will was quite worried about you." He glanced over at Hannah. "You seem better than you were earlier. Stomach doing better?"

"Much," she replied, meeting his gaze.

Faith looked at the two of them, gazing into each other's eyes. Never would she have guessed they would make a couple, yet here they were. "I need to get back," she said, heading to the door.

"I'll walk you back," Butler said. As Hannah went to join them, he stopped her. "You need to take care of yourself. You work too hard." His gaze was tender as he looked at her. "I couldn't bear it if anything were to cause you harm."

Hannah nodded and stepped back. "I am going to sort through the herbs Polly Cooper shared with us. I want to make notes on all she said." She looked over at Faith. "I'll come down later to see how you are. I will bring more mint. There is plenty growing in the garden out back."

Faith watched Jeremy squeeze his wife's hand before they left. Realization struck her. He knew, or at least suspected, that his wife was pregnant. It showed in every loving gaze and the protectiveness he showed. Hannah needed to talk to him soon.

Jeremy walked her back along the road that connected Lafayette's headquarters to Washington. Neither spoke as they walked along. They remained deep within their own thoughts. Across the meadow, they saw a group of men bearing a litter.

Faith swallowed hard.

"Try not to think of it," Jeremy said. "There is nothing you can do. At least now we can give her a decent burial."

"Are you any closer to finding out who is doing this?" Faith looked away and down the road toward Washington's. "John Laurens remains under guard. It's been a week. He couldn't have gone out to kill anyone."

Butler shrugged. "It depends on how long she's been dead, but it doesn't look likely. She only went missing a few days ago. We cannot say for sure her death has anything to do with this. Lena Ross served a variety of clients. It could be someone didn't want to pay or wanted something she was unwilling to provide."

"Is that what you believe?" Faith didn't look over at him but kept her gaze on the road.

Butler was silent for a few minutes. "Not really," he said at last. "Lena Ross knew more than she said when I spoke with her last. Our discussion enlightened her regarding the purpose of the dolls. I think she pressed whoever she was buying them for, and that individual decided it was easier to end her than to pay her."

Faith shuddered. "That seems so cold."

Jeremy Butler nodded. "It does, but then I have seen nothing that shows this lunatic respects life. He kills people as if it is an elaborate game."

"That is madness. Life is a gift. It shouldn't take it so needlessly."

His voice was matter-of-fact. "Men and women have died every day as this war has dragged on. Who's to say who lives or dies?" His eyes glittered. "That said. I don't agree with a needless waste of life. Too many good people have passed. We have to find this monster, and quickly. Else wise, there will not be many left to march out of this valley."

"It's not long until we break camp," Faith said. "What if the killer is not found by then?"

"Then we will fight a war on two fronts. The British will meet us on the battlefield. While within our own camp, a hidden enemy waits to strike on whomever he pleases."

Chapter Twenty

Will squinted as he gazed across the meadow. He recognized the formation that the men were in. It was one of several they had learned to execute. He felt a brief stirring of pride. Baron von Steuben had done well with these troops. The group looked nothing like the bedraggled bunch that had limped into the valley of the forges months before. They moved as a professional unit, listening for the signals that told them what to do, staying in formation and using both muskets and blades with lethal efficiency. They would be ready when the order came to break camp.

He missed John Laurens. The lieutenant colonel had been a steadying presence. Laurens had helped him feel a part of the cause in those awkward early days when he struggled to translate the baron's German swiftly and accurately. While von Steuben would curse loudly at the delays, Laurens knew how to smooth ruffled feathers and keep the chain of communication open. He spoke fluent French and was not afraid to share a joke or quick repost. He could make the baron roar with laughter, along with the men. Will hoped they would release him now that they had found another body.

Washington urged caution. There was no clear evidence that the death of the prostitute was in any way related to the gruesome killings that went along with the poem. Everyone was aware of those gruesome verses. Will heard them whispered over campfires as people eyed each other in suspicion and fear. Some of the men had taken to laying bets on who the next victim would be based on the verses. Will thought it tasteless even though he comprehended the need to fend off fear by belittling it. Then there were those who struck out, replacing terror with rage. He had helped break up a few fights among men who were sure they had found the killer, usually someone with whom the individual held a grudge.

He watched men scurry across the field carrying baskets of bread. After the destruction of one set of ovens, the remaining ones had to take on the extra load, guarded to avoid any more explosions. There were more guards in the camp than there were sentries on the perimeter. At Washington's request, Native scouts watched the camp's outskirts. If an enemy was sneaking into camp, the Oneida would find him.

As it was, he gave the side eye to junior officers when he came into contact with them. Whoever the killer was, he had to be an officer. No enlisted man could go to so many places unquestioned. And if Laurens was not guilty, it raised the question of how someone had gotten into his gear upstairs. It was as if a ghost hunted them, its deadly presence wandering among them unseen. He shook himself mentally. There was no point in harboring such foolishness. Fear, left unchecked, could drive a person mad. Will had no intention of letting that happen to him or anyone else if he could help it.

Von Steuben watched his troops execute their maneuvers. He observed every move, shouting if something was out of line. Will now knew most of the commands and the accompanying profanity. To everyone's amusement, he translated all of it.

Out of the corner of his eye, he spotted someone trotting across the field to join them. He recognized that pale blonde head anywhere. Jeremy Butler slowed to a walk and took a moment to watch the troops.

Baron von Steuben flicked a glance at him before returning his attention to his men. When he yelled at them to dismiss, they did so before Will had time to translate.

"They've learned a lot by now," he said to Butler as the men scattered back to their cabins.

"I see that," Butler said. "The sound of 'dismiss' is the same in every language. Let's hope they are as eager to follow orders in battle." Butler's tone was mild. Dark shadows lined his eyes. Despite that, his gaze remained watchful.

"They're ready," Will said. "They've worked hard at it. I think Washington will find he has an entirely different army under his command."

Von Steuben looked over at Will. "Werden Sie sich uns anschließen?" He shot Butler a curious gaze before looking over to where Washington's headquarters lay.

Will shook his head. "Nein, Wir sehen uns später, Kommandant."

Jeremy glanced at him. "What did you say?"

Will watched the German walk across the field, headed toward the farmhouse that housed the center of command. "I said I would see him later. He's going to report to Washington now." Catching Butler's raised eyebrow, he added, "Hamilton can translate for him. He's fluent in French."

"It seems all the aides-de-camp are,"

"Well," Will said. "I don't think Jack's French is quite on a par with the others. He understands it and can speak it well enough, but the pauses when he translates make it clear he's not fluent. John Laurens used to help him." He looked over at Butler. "Surely you know him better than I. You've been involved with Washington for a while."

Butler shrugged. "I know a bit. Jack Silver's father was a minister in Massachusetts. He was largely taught at home until he got a scholarship to King's College. That's where he met Hamilton. He left school after his mother died. I think his father passed recently, just after the fighting started. He still has an older sister back in Cambridge. He writes to her now and then."

Will nodded. "He seems pretty sharp."

Butler nodded. "He reads constantly. His father taught him Greek and Latin. Since his parents passed, I believe he considers the army his home."

Will thought about his home in Williamsburg, the print shop where he had worked for years, and the many friends he had. Most of all, he thought of Faith and her tavern. He could not imagine replacing that with the army. A sharp pang of homesickness struck him. For all the revolution might bring, part of him longed for the life he had left behind. Although he knew he had enlisted in order to gain his freedom from indenture. Taking a deep breath, Will changed the topic. "What do you know of Hamilton? Isn't he pretty much self-taught?"

Butler shot him a look. "He's had to be. Alexander was born a bastard, out in the Caribbean. He didn't have a father or patron to help him along. Like Jack, he got a scholarship to King's College. He left before he completed his degree, but it doesn't seem to have hurt him any. He has one of the sharpest minds I've seen. Washington regards him as a son. I have little doubt he will be successful no matter what he gets into after this war ends." His gaze turned contemplative. "It can't have been easy coming from such a background. I imagine he's had to fight for everything he has."

"I'm sure he has," Will said. "He seems devoted to the cause." What neither man said was whether something lay beneath the layers of loyalty and devotion that Hamilton expressed. Will walked with Butler back toward headquarters. Dandelions had popped out of the grass across the field. The fields had become lush in recent weeks, reminding them that the winter interlude had ended. "Do you think either of them is capable of this?"

"I wonder that about everyone," Butler acknowledged. Seeing Will's startled look, he amended. "Not you or the women. But no one is hiding in the woods waiting to pick one of us off. We and the native scouts have searched the hills and valleys surrounding the camp. Whoever is doing this is within the camp, someone we encounter regularly."

Will agreed. It was what kept him from sleeping well, wondering if he would wake to someone wanting to end him. As he traversed the training ground, his eyes searched the trees and shadows.

Butler paused. "What is that?"

Will looked where Butler pointed. They had passed Huntington's Brigade's quarters and were nearing the rifle pit. The dugout area served several purposes, depending on what types of drills were being held. Today it was quiet. But something lay in there motionless, but familiar. Will wasn't sure what. After the explosions at the ovens, he was leery of running up to things.

Butler drew his saber as they veered toward the pit. "Someone's in there." His tone was grim. "Look at the uniform."

Will spotted the blue coat with its lighter colored lapels. As they approached, a flash of green became visible. "It's an aide-de-camp." He broke into a run, terrified he would find a friend had joined the dead.

Butler jumped into the pit just ahead of Will. The man was face down in the dirt. The back of his head was a dark mass of dried blood and dirt. His hands were pale against the darkness of the disturbed soil.

"Is he dead?" Will looked down at the still figure. Just then, the man groaned as he struggled to roll over.

The moans continued as the men worked to roll him to his back. Dark hair partially obscured his face, along with streaks of blood. The man tried to sit up, failing halfway. "Easy mate, we're here." Butler leaned over the man, checking for injuries.

Will went to the other side. The man's head was a mess, blood and dirt mixed into his hair, which covered his face. The man attempted to push it away, but it flopped back. He half sat up, but waved back and forth like a leaf in the wind. "Take it easy." Will sat behind him and let him lean back.

"Ohhh. My head." His voice held the faint nasal tone of the Northern colonies. He took a few deep breaths.

Will winced as blood dripped onto his jacket. He was certain he knew this man. There was something familiar about it.

"Jack," said Butler. "Can you hear me?"

The man nodded and then moaned again. "My head." He reached up a hand and drew back a bloody hand. "What happened to me?"

"I'm guessing someone tried to bash your skull in," Will said as he looked at the ground behind him. Hand size stones lay scattered on the floor of the pit. Some were splattered with blood. One was covered in it.

Butler removed a flask from the chest pocket of his jacket. "Take a drink. It might help."

Jack Silver took a sip and coughed. He took another swallow and shuddered. "No more," he gasped. His face appeared waxy. Streaks of dried blood darkened his cheeks and forehead. A shudder went through his body. "I was on my way back to headquarters. Someone called out to me from the woods. I remember going toward the trees to check it out." He shook his head, then stopped looking sick. "That's all I remember."

"That's no wonder," Will said. "You've got a nasty lump on your head."

"Do I?" Sliver's voice was faint. "That explains why it feels so bad." He looked at the other two men. "Did someone try to kill me?"

"Let's get you to the hospital. You need care."

Together, Will McKay and Butler helped Silver to his feet and wrapped an arm around to steady him. Silver closed his eyes and took a few deep breaths. "I feel faint."

"Keep moving," Butler said. "Focus on putting one foot in front of the other. We'll need you conscious to get out of the pit."

Silver nodded. He stumbled against the rough ground. Will let go of him to leap out of the pit and lean over the edge to help pull the injured man up. Butler pushed from behind until the injured man was out and on the leaf-strewn ground.

He lay there for a moment, gathering his strength. The sun glinted through the trees, dappling the ground. "Lord, that light is bright," he turned his head aside to avoid the stabbing rays.

Butler squatted beside him. "Let's get going. The sooner you're at the hospital, the sooner you can get proper care and a soft bed."

"Very well," Silver said. "Maybe you can find a pretty nurse to tend to me." He smiled weakly before rolling to his hands and knees. He glanced up at Butler. "You look amazingly tall from this vantage, Major Butler."

Butler smiled. "Everything looks tall from the ground." He offered a hand. "Let's get going."

It took a few tries to get Sliver off the ground. Will and Butler supported him on either side as they walked toward the hospital. Heavy supply wagons and rain had damaged the road. It made for rough going with an injured man. They stumbled along until they heard the quick sound of a horse's hooves trotting down the road.

Soon, the rider came into view, slowing to a stop. A man hopped out of the saddle. "What has happened?" Alexander Hamilton looked at them, his eyes bright with concern. "Jack! What the hell is wrong with you?"

Silver looked up at him with a faint smile. "I apparently have riled someone unawares."

Hamilton harrumphed. "You need to be more careful around the ladies.

Their husbands have tempers."

Silver snickered, then it faded to a moan. "Personal experience speaking, old friend? One of these days, Washington won't be there to rescue you." He paused to catch his breath, wheezing slightly. "I fear it may be more serious than that. I think someone meant to end me."

Butler interrupted. "We need to get him to a hospital. Can you help us?"

Hamilton nodded. "My horse can carry him. Let's get him up."

Together, they got the man astride. Hamilton held the reins. After seating Silver, they proceeded to the hospital. Silver's lips set in a tight line as he fought to stay conscious and mounted. Hunched over the saddle, the man looked ready to pass out. Only the tight knuckles of his hands on the saddle horn showed he was alert enough to hang on.

Will stayed close to his side, worried that he would not make it far. Butler took the other side, likely thinking the same thing. Hamilton kept glancing back, monitoring Silver as well.

"What happened?" He repeated as he kept the horse walking steadily up the road. Overhead, a hawk shot across the sky, capturing a smaller bird. It disappeared with a triumphant cry, leaving the sky clear.

Butler answered. "We found him in the rifle pit. It looks like someone tried to smash his head in. McKay and I must have arrived before the killer could finish the job." He quoted from memory.

"One found a rock useful to kill."

"Ah, that wretched poem again," Hamilton exclaimed. "When will this madness end? We do not need to lose anyone else. Fear grips everyone. It is like a sickness that has spread throughout the camp. We must stop this killer."

Butler shot him an irritated look. "If you have any suggestions on how to do that, please share them."

Hamilton continued looking down the road, trying to avoid the rougher places. "I meant no offense." He looked up at the cloudless sky. "A devil runs rampant here, filling our people with fear. It cannot continue, or everything we have worked for will fall apart. I hope and pray it ends soon. It must. We are only weeks away from rejoining our battle with the British. We cannot hope to defeat them when we battle this enemy within our ranks."

"I agree," Butler said wearily. "I would like nothing more than to put an end to this evil game. We all need to focus on preparing for the spring campaign."

"Agreed," Hamilton said nothing more. The cabins of McIntosh's Brigade appeared in the distance. No one was visible. The men were out either on patrol or drilling for coming battles. Beyond the cabins lay the cabin built to house the sick and injured. Smoke rose from the chimney despite the mild weather.

Will sighed in relief. He didn't like how pale Silver looked. Whoever had walloped him on the head had done a nasty job. He hoped his injuries were not serious. The young man swayed in the saddle before leaning over the saddle. "Are you doing alright, Jack?"

"I'm alive," he cracked with a weak smile. "That's one that didn't end up dead." Silver closed his eyes. "Although my head feels like it might explode."

"We're almost to the hospital," Butler said. "I'm sure the ladies will have something to help with the pain."

Silver huddled in the saddle. His head drooped forward. A drop of blood splatted on Will's sleeve as he reached to steady the injured man.

Will looked up at him. They should have taken a moment to wrap Silver's head, but neither of them had thought to do so in their hurry to get him to the hospital. It was hard to see the injury through his tangled hair. Silver was lucky to be alive. Had they not come upon him, the killer might have taken time to make sure of his kill. As it was, the killer had attacked one of Washington's aides-de-camp. The message could not have been clearer. No one was safe.

Chapter Twenty-One

Hannah had just finished splinting a man's arm when she spotted Alexander Hamilton enter, asking for help with an injured man. He exited to return with Will and Jeremy, who supported a man on either side. Jeremy's eyes met her across the room, saying things he did not verbalize. She knew he worried about her being around the sick and injured. It was a conversation frequently repeated when they were alone. Her time at the hospital was nearly over. Her own body told her that. But nursing gave her the sense of purpose she'd lost after the destruction of her business. Getting up early was becoming increasingly difficult between nausea and exhaustion. Even now her body longed for rest, which was why she worked far fewer hours than she had. Faith had taken on many of Hannah's responsibilities at the hospital, despite her squeamishness. Hannah rose; her task completed and moved to see where she could assist next. The room fell silent as Dr. Waldo ordered the man placed on a clean table he kept for examinations.

He gestured for Mary Porter to assist him. The chief nurse walked swiftly to the surgeon's side. Jeremy and Will lowered the man to the table gently. The patient groaned as he lay down. "Lieutenant Colonel Silver, I believe," Waldo said. "The last time I saw you was over dinner."

Silver cracked open an eye. "It was a far more pleasant time than the present."

"I imagine so," Waldo ran his hands over Silver's head, moving aside bloody hair as he sought to see injuries.

"Ouch!" Silver jerked.

"Sorry, I need to see the wound." Waldo looked over at Mary Porter. "I need a basin of hot water and some clothes. I'm going to need to clean away the blood and dirt before I can see anything." He looked over at Silver. "I'll have to cut some hair away, Jack. I'm sure the ladies won't mind."

Silver winced. "Just don't leave me bald, old man. The weather is still chilly at night."

Waldo snorted. "Old man, is it? I'm not among the ancients yet, young stripling. Were my wife here, she would assure you of that!"

"No offense," Silver offered a weak smile. He stifled a cry as Waldo prodded further.

"You've got a nasty lump, and something took a slice out of your scalp."

Silver hissed as Waldo moved the hair sticky with dried blood aside. When a basin of steaming water appeared, the doctor dipped in a cloth, wrung it out, and placed it on Silver's head. In a few moments, he lifted it and began rubbing his patient's head with it. The cloth came back rusty with blood. He continued for several minutes before taking scissors and trimming away hair. Damp strands fell on the floor. "Don't worry, the rest of your hair will easily hide it. The lump is pretty far down. This scrape bled all over your head, but it seems pretty shallow. I'll clean it, and it should heal without stitches."

"So I will not have you sewing up my head," Silver muttered. "That's something."

He cursed loudly as Waldo took a bottle of alcohol and poured it over the wound. "What the hell?"

"Alcohol will remove any foul humors that have found their way into the wound." Waldo patted it dry with a clean cloth. "That should do it. I'll wrap it for now, but it will have scabbed over by morning."

"Thank God." Silver shuddered. He sat still while the doctor continued to work, shuddering when he touched a tender spot.

The doctor stood back. "I've done what I can. From what I can tell, you took a nasty blow, but I do not see signs of deeper injury." He looked Silver in the eyes and studied him. "Your eyes look normal."

"Thank you." Silver's tone was dry.

"Mismatched pupils are a sign of brain injury," Waldo explained. "I will check on you later. Right now, I suggest you get some rest and don't wander this encampment alone anymore. Stay here for now and let the nurses look after you. Tomorrow you can go to your own bed."

"I won't be going anywhere soon." Silver let Butler and Will lead him to a cot. He stretched out carefully, placing his head where the injury would not press against the pillow.

As he closed his eyes, Butler asked. "What were you doing out there?"

Silver cracked his eyes. "I received a message that General Varnum needed me at his headquarters. When I arrived, no one knew anything about it, so I turned around to head back. On my way to Washington's headquarters, someone called me from the trees near the rifle pit. I went over there to see who it was." He shook his head. "From that, I remember nothing until I heard your voices."

Butler's voice was soft. "Get some rest, Jack. You should be safe here."

A nurse came by and spread a blanket over Silver. He sighed. "I don't know why this is happening. I've offended no one I know."

Will's tone was blunt. "Insanity requires no reason. You are lucky to be alive."

Silver did not answer. Within minutes, the slow, even tones of his breathing told everyone he had fallen asleep.

Will stared at the resting man for a moment before he left with Butler. As he stepped out into the cool spring air, he wondered when the madness would end.

Hamilton nodded to them as he mounted his horse. "I am overdue for a meeting with some of my fellow officers. I must be off. What did the surgeon say?" Hamilton's voice was soft as he waited for an answer.

Butler replied. "He has a nasty knot on his head, but the doctor seems to think he will be alright."

Hamilton nodded. "I am glad to hear that. When I am done, I will report back to General Washington. I will share this news if he has not heard by then." He headed back toward the road from where they had come. His horse's hooves made a steady drumbeat against the ground.

Butler and Will watched groups practice maneuvers across the vast meadow that served as their training ground. Will knew he would need to report to von Steuben soon, even though his unit had trained earlier in the day. The drill master would be restless and itching to involve himself in something. "What do you make of this?" he asked.

Butler sighed. "The killer is getting bolder. Attacking one of Washington's aides-de-camp is a daring act." Anger laced his tone. "People are frightened and with good reason. We've had to increase patrols to turn back would-be deserters. No one feels safe here."

"Can you blame them?" Will's tone was bleak. "They expect to face death in combat, not in camp. No one knows who the killer is—it's enough to drive one mad." They walked in silence. Smoke from a nearby cook fire drifted past, bringing with it the smell of wood and roasting meat. In the distance, they could see the figures of men posted about ovens and the nearby cook fires. "At least no one will blow up any more ovens."

"I doubt he would repeat that anyway," Butler said. "He's already shown that he can." He scanned the area. Most of the troops were training or on patrol. Few remained in camp. Figures moved about the camps; some on duty, others recuperating.

Will watched with him, wondering what was on the other man's mind. A light breeze stirred the young leaves on the trees, causing the sun's light to flicker where it shone through the branches. In the distance, he could hear the hoarse cry of a crow intent on finding a meal in nearby fields. He had watched life emerging from the barrenness of the winter. When the heavy rains stopped, the roads would become passable. Soon thereafter, Washington would give the order to leave.

Washington met with his generals daily with the door closed. Sometimes the murmur of voices broke into shouts, other times it remained a low rumble, like the thunder of an approaching storm. Yesterday, a rider came in from York. Congress wanted to know the General's plans. As far as Will knew, he had shared his thoughts with no one, eliminating the chance of information escaping to the enemy.

"Hannah is pregnant," Butler said quietly. "We want to keep the information close right now."

Will's face lit up. "That's wonderful news, man." He enveloped the other man in a bear hug. Butler grunted and returned the hug before stepping aside and taking a few deep breaths.

"You're stronger than you look. For a moment, I thought I heard my ribs crack."

"Sorry about that." Will couldn't stop grinning. "Does Faith know?"

Butler nodded. "I don't imagine there are many secrets they keep from one another. I'm hoping she can persuade Hannah to leave the hospital. She doesn't need to take that risk."

"Surely, the threat of disease-" Will began.

Butler shook his head. "She stays away from that area. She continues to help with the injured, although she's doing that less and less. Faith has been going in her stead." He shook his head. "Hannah doesn't like to be idle, but she needs her rest. These past months have been difficult for her. She lost all she had worked for in Philadelphia. She came with little more than the clothes on her back. In truth, there is no reason for her to return there. When the camp breaks, she will join Faith in Williamsburg. It's safer than Pennsylvania right now." He sighed. "If I cannot be there for her, I would like her to be with family and trusted friends."

Will turned to look at him. "You won't be there?"

Butler's face turned sad. "I don't see this war ending soon–do you?"

Will paused before shaking his head. "I wish it would, but I don't think the British have any plans to surrender. They still believe they can defeat us." What he didn't add was he worried that they might, unless something changed soon.

He didn't like to think about rejoining the fighting. It was a brutal business. The British knew their way around a battlefield. He had quickly learned that one never knew when a group of lobster backs would pop up in the dip of a meadow or in a hidden pocket of woods. They were sneaky devils, for sure. Will sometimes woke hours before dawn from dreams where British regulars appeared through the fog to engage Washington's troops, he among them.

It was Brandywine at its worst. The battle raged–gunfire, screams, charges–he fought back, reloading, dodging, and disarming. If not for Washington galloping over to take command personally, he knew the enemy would have overrun them. As it was, it had been a challenging withdrawal. Will had seen too many young men fall to the better-trained British regulars. It was one reason he worked so hard with von Steuben, hoping that the German's strict training would increase their success on the battlefield.

As the stone farmhouse where Washington stayed came into view, they saw men running in and out of the door. Faint shouts reached them across the clearing, but distance distorted the words. Butler glanced at Will. "Could word have come so quickly?"

"I don't know. Unless something else has occurred." At that thought, both men broke into a run.

Chaos ruled the yard as men ran in and out of both the front and side doors. Will called out to a soldier rushing by, but the man continued down the road past him. "What the devil is going on?"

A man answered. "There's been another attack. Someone found one of Washington's aides-de-camp with his skull bashed in. We're all going to die here. It's every man for himself!" He ran off before Will could reply.

Butler exchanged glances with him. "Word travels faster than I had reckoned. I guess we'd better make sure our general has facts rather than wild rumors."

Will nodded. The yard cleared out as they made for the front door. They found the hallway deserted. When he knocked on Washington's door, a familiar voice told him to enter.

Washington stood alone, holding a green sash, the ribbon of office for his aides. Will realized it had dark stains scattered across it. The general appeared not to notice them as he looked out the window at the fields outside.

Butler wasted no time. "General Washington. Someone attacked one of your aides-de-camp." Silence greeted him as the commander turned and regarded him thoughtfully. Light from the window cast a harsh light on Washington's features, revealing shadows and exhaustion imprinted on his face from years of war.

"I'm aware." The General held out the sash. "The man who found the body brought this to me. It belongs to the Marquis de Lafayette. I fear a dear friend and ally has joined the fallen." Despite his stoic expression, grief resonated in his voice. His hands gripped the fabric before he eased his grip, letting the folds fall through his fingers.

Stunned silence greeted this statement as the two men stared at their commander in disbelief. Butler shook his head. "Someone attacked Jack Silver. We found him in the rifle pit off the River Road. He's alive, although he has a nasty lump on his head."

Washington froze, his gaze intent on Butler. "You are certain of this."

"Captain McKay and I delivered him to the hospital with the help of Lieutenant Colonel Hamilton. We were fortunate he came riding by when he did. Having a horse made transporting him far simpler than it could have been. He was barely conscious."

Washington looked confused before schooling his features into his normal, calm façade. "Hamilton was on the road on horseback. I had wondered where he was." He laid the sash before continuing. His expression turned thoughtful. "I have no reason to doubt you, Major Butler. But I fear we are discussing two separate events. I had not heard of the attack on Lieutenant Commander Silver. Unfortunately, I just received word that someone discovered an officer's body on the Gulph Road, less than half a mile away." He let the information sink in before elaborating. "This fiend has attacked two men within the space of a day. One lives." His eyes glittered. "This has gone on long enough. I want this monster found."

Butler nodded at the sash Washington held. "Was that found with the body?"

Washington nodded. "It was. Something crushed the man's head; the soldier who found him couldn't identify him." He sighed. "Several men are bringing the body into the barn that serves as our mortuary. I am preparing to go there to see if I can verify who the man is." He stared down at the sash. "This is Lafayette's. I had his initials embroidered on it for him. There is none other like it."

Outside, the front door slammed, followed by heavy steps running until they stopped outside the door. A knock echoed against the wood. "Enter." An enlisted man came in. Flushed and panting, he took a moment to catch his breath before speaking.

"We've found the marquis' horse. Scouts found it wandering around Fort Huntington. It's being taken to the stable to be tended."

Washington's eyes sharpened. "He had gone to check the outer line of entrenchments. He was going to report to me later today. Are there any signs of injury to the animal?"

"None that I have heard," the man answered. "My sergeant sent me to inform you. May I return to my duties?"

Washington dismissed him before turning to look at Butler. "How did the horse get so far away from the body?" He stared at the men.

Butler said. "We cannot be sure it is Lafayette, sir. As you noted, the damage to the head prevented identification. We need to be sure."

Washington looked at the green sash and then back at Butler. "You have doubts?"

Butler looked at his commander, meeting his gaze squarely. "Lafayette is not a man easily taken by surprise. I'm not sure whether it is him. I would want more evidence than a sash before writing to his wife in France. If he is not dead, he has to be somewhere in this encampment."

"Search the encampment. Find him if you can," Washington ordered. "I will not rest until I know his fate." His face turned grim. "I will go look at the body. Seeing the man may reveal the truth, however bitter it may be. Report back to me."

Will looked at Butler. "We will, sir."

They walked out the door. Butler went to the stable. "We'll cover ground more quickly on horseback, and I want to look at his mount."

Will followed him into the barn. Both of Washington's horses were in their stalls. Hannah's mare nickered softly as Butler approached. He scratched between her ears. "You could use a run, couldn't you?" he whispered. "Give me a moment or two, and we'll go out."

Lafayette's horse Ajax stood nearby, flicking his tail. A stable hand had already removed the saddle and was busy brushing his side. The animal had a rich brown coat and black stockings. Its ebony mane and tail cascaded down in silky lengths.

Will admired it. "That is a magnificent beast."

Butler agreed. "Lafayette treats it as if it were his own child." The horse cast him a curious gaze out of dark liquid eyes. "I wish you could tell us where your master is," he murmured. He turned to the stable hand. "What shape was he in when he arrived?"

"He was fine." The stable hand replied. "He'd had a fine run, but no signs of stress. There was some mud and blood on the saddle, but not an excessive amount."

Butler walked over to where a saddle rested. "Is this it?"

The hand nodded. "I haven't had time to clean it."

Butler nodded and went over to it, walking around to examine all sides. "I see what he means."

"That could be from anything. There's not a lot," Will pointed out.

Dried rusty spots of blood or mud speckled the saddle. It was hard to tell what was what. "You're right." He sighed. "There is little to be found here. Let's mount up and see what we find."

While Butler saddled Gracie, Will found a gray he had ridden in the past. Together, they set off down the Gulph Road at a steady clip. The trees had leafed out in recent weeks, making it difficult to see what lay off the road. They slowed when they spotted a group of soldiers carrying a blanket-covered litter.

"Where are you headed?" Butler called out.

"To the barn where the dead go," one replied.

Butler recognized Sergeant Maples. "Where did you find him?"

Maples gestured further down the road. "There's a washout alongside the road about a quarter mile down. One of my men spotted him face down in it. He went to turn him, but it wasn't a pretty sight." He met Butler's glance. "There have been too many men murdered in this camp, sir."

"Yes, there have," Butler agreed. "I will want to speak with you later about what you may have seen."

Maples nodded. "I need to get this man to the barn." He gestured for the men to continue.

Butler nodded and turned his horse back down the Gulph Road. As they continued, the sound of the men faded into the distance. Small groupings of trees edged the road, interspersed with vistas of rolling meadow. Groups of cattle dotted the land. Any other time, he would have stopped to appreciate the beauty of the pastoral scene.

"I think we should head toward Knox's place," Will said. "He would have had to have gone that way if he was heading to his residence."

"I agree." Butler put the mare into a gallop and took off down the road. Will followed. The trees blurred as they passed. As they drew closer, Butler slowed to a trot. "There's little point in exhausting our mounts," he said. "It's a good place to look for clues. We're a stone's throw away from Knox. You can see smoke from the chimney."

Will looked at where Butler gestured. A wisp of gray smoke spiraled up into the sky. "His cook must be at work. It's not that cold out."

"Cooks are always at work," Butler responded. "It's a hard job."

Will nodded his agreement as they approached the house. Not surprisingly, Knox was not present. This time of day, generals were out with their troops practicing or patrolling, preparing for when they would leave the encampment. An enlisted man hailed them from the porch.

"What brings you here?" he called. "General Knox is inspecting the artillery. He's not expected back until tonight. Lady Knox is with Lady Washington."

Butler leaned down. "We're not looking for Knox. Have you seen the Marquis de Lafayette?"

The enlisted man looked puzzled. "The tall Frenchman? No, he's not been here. His quarters are further down the road. Since his return, he's been spending most of his time with Washington, or so I've heard."

Butler didn't answer the implied question. "Thank you. We will head there." He turned his horse and headed back toward the road.

"He didn't seem to know what has happened," Will commented when they were well out of earshot.

"Good. There's one less to jump to conclusions," Butler said. "This camp is in enough of a panic as it is. I've no intention of adding to it." He looked on either side of the road. The nearby trees cast shadows over the roadway. A pair of squirrels chittered as they passed, running out on a tree branch that stretched over the road to stare down with bright, curious eyes.

"Inquisitive creatures," Will noted. "They don't seem to fear us much."

"They don't need to anymore," Butler replied. "There's enough meat in camp for the men. No one is hunting them. The meat's pretty stringy, anyway."

Will stared at him for a moment. He'd gone hunting a few times in the winter but seen no squirrels, or much of anything else either. There had been times he'd halfway considered eating his boots, but decided the risk of frostbite was not worth it.

A flash of red in the forest caught his eye. As he turned, Butler shook his head. "It's a bird." He continued down the road. His eyes moved back and forth, checking for signs of activity. Suddenly, he stopped. "Did you hear that?"

Will stopped as well, straining his ears to catch what had caught the other man's attention. In the distance, a voice called out.

"Hello!" Butler called out. "Who are you? Do you need help?" His voice echoed against the trees. They didn't have to wait long.

"Further down the road," Will said, signaling his horse to walk.

The men edged down the road, listening as the voice became louder as they drew closer. A man stepped out onto the road, waving his arms.

"What the hell?" Butler squinted into the shadows. "He's in uniform, whoever he is."

Will gripped the knife he kept at the ready, a trick he'd learned from Butler when he'd first enlisted.

"Hello!" the man called. "Quel soulagement! I am relieved to see you, mon amies!"

Will looked at Butler. "I think we've found Lafayette."

"So we have," Butler replied. "Maybe he can tell us what is going on."

Chapter Twenty-Two

Lafayette had plenty to say. "Someone took my horse! Quel imbécile! I stopped to relieve myself, and when I return, my Ajax was gone! Now I must find him before harm comes to such a noble animal."

"Ajax is well," Will said. "Someone found him wandering through the forest. He is being cared for at the stable where Washington's horses live."

Lafayette paused. "That is good. I feared I would never see him again." He paused. "I do not understand how he came to be abandoned. Excellent horses are tough to find. It makes no sense to take such a fine animal and leave it."

"I agree," Butler said. "Someone found Ajax near Fort Huntington," Butler said. "The men who found him feared you were dead."

Lafayette looked startled. "Why would anyone think that?"

"Someone found a soldier's body with your sash. They assumed it was you. Washington has gone to try to confirm that."

"Plainly it is not! Here I am, alive and well. As for my mark of office, I gave it to Toussaint to take to the laundress. I had carelessly spilled red wine on it during the celebration of my return. I hoped she could clean it so I could wear it with pride once again." He paused. "Why would anyone mistake Toussaint for me? He and I are the same height, but we look nothing alike." He searched the faces of the two men.

"His head was smashed beyond recognition." Butler's tone was bleak. "Apparently, the killer realized pretty quickly that his first victim survived, so he found another. Maybe in the shadows of the forest, he thought it was you until it was too late."

"Another man is dead." Lafayette's voice trailed off. "Who else did they attack?"

"Lieutenant Commander Jack Silver," Will said. "He should recover."

Lafayette shook his head. "It is too much, all this killing. It has to stop." He cocked a look at them. "People believe the dead man is me?"

Butler nodded. "Washington sent us to look for you. He's quite worried."

"Mon Dieu!" Lafayette looked at the two men. "I must go to him immediately. Can I beg a ride from one of you?"

In the end, Will shared his saddle with the Marquis since he had the larger horse. Lafayette returned to headquarters, where people greeted him with cries of relief.

Washington came out to find out what caused such a clamor. At the sight of the Frenchman, his face lit up. "Major General Lafayette, I am glad to see you alive!"

Lafayette smiled. "Commander-in-Chief. I am glad to be alive."

Cheers went up as the news traveled. After returning their animals to Washington's stable hands, Will and Butler went to Washington to hear what Lafayette had to say.

Washington listened as Lafayette repeated what he had told the others. "So someone took your horse in the few moments you left him tied up along the road?"

"I did not leave Ajax on the road," Lafayette corrected. "I tied him to a sapling just off it, where he could enjoy some spring grass while he waited for me. When I returned, he was gone!"

"You heard no voices, no sound of horse hooves?" Will asked.

Lafayette shot him a look. "It is a busy road. Hearing horses' hooves is not unusual. Someone is always riding down the Gulph Road."

"He has a point," Butler admitted. "No one would think twice about seeing a man on a horse, especially if he wore an officer's uniform."

Lafayette raised his eyebrows. "You believe an officer did this? Who?"

"I do not know," Butler admitted. "But an officer can go many places an enlisted man cannot. No one would question an officer unless he had a higher rank. There are many officers in this camp."

"I have ordered John Laurens released," Washington said. "These crimes were impossible for him to commit. He's been under guard. Tomorrow he resumes his duties. We need him now more than ever with Silver laid low."

Butler nodded. "I am glad to hear that."

Chapter Twenty-Three

Word of Lafayette's return from the dead spread like wildfire throughout the encampment. Faith heard it from three different people who had come into the hospital to share the news. She had come down to check on her sister. Hannah didn't argue when Faith suggested relieving her. Pregnancy sapped her energy even if she didn't want to admit it. She went escorted by a couple of enlisted men who promised to see her to the doorstep of Lafayette's headquarters. Looking at the exhaustion on her face, Faith was pretty sure she would nap. She hoped so. Hannah needed to take care of herself.

Faith went to check on Jack Silver. A white bandage encircled his head. Only the top showed his hair. His hair spilled untidily over the top. He had slept for most of the day since he had arrived at the hospital. As she looked down on him, she thought he looked quite young, too young for the many responsibilities thrust upon him. He opened his eyes when she leaned over him.

He smiled up at her. "I must be in heaven. I see an angel."

Faith snorted. "You must have a bigger lump on your head than I had heard if you believe that." She put a hand to his cheek. No fever. His pulse appeared steady despite his harrowing brush with death. "You look better than when you arrived." She was glad he showed no signs of fever. Too often, men had come in with a minor injury only to contract an illness from one of the other men. It was a sad fact that more men had died of illness than anything else at camp.

"Tell my head that." He looked over at her. "Is there any chance you would bring a sick man a bottle of rum? I have one stashed upstairs in my room." His face was hopeful.

Faith shook her head. "Dr. Waldo said no hard liquor for the next day and night. It will muddle your head and slow your recovery."

He glared, then smoothed out his expression. "Dear Dr. Waldo. I bet he's got a flask hidden somewhere."

"No one hit him in the head with a large rock."

"Lucky him," Silver said. "Can I at least have something for my head?"

"I can get you some willow bark tea," Faith said. "It will ease the pain. You need to rest." She rose and walked away. Silver appeared to have suffered no long-lasting damage, given his flirtatious manner. She rolled her eyes. Why did men think all women wanted flattery? Going over to the hearth, she spotted the kettle on a spider over some graying coals. She smiled. The water should still be hot. Nearby, some earthenware mugs hung from a rack along the wall. Picking one up, she added some willow bark from a nearby basket and poured steaming water over it. Setting it to the side to steep, she went to check on some of the other patients until it was ready.

The warming weather allowed them to prop open doors, letting fresh air into the building. Faith was grateful. Normally, the hospital carried the scents of sweat and alcohol, along with faint hints of waste and blood. They had hired some women from the camp to clean, which helped. A middle-aged woman with a bucket worked on mopping the floor. Earlier, she had emptied the chamber pots and cleaned them with lye soap, so they no longer stank.

When Faith returned with Silver's tea, he had fallen asleep. Hopefully, he would return to his own bunk tomorrow. It would be better for him to be away from all the sickness that permeated the hospital. She left the mug at a table next to the bed and left him to rest. He remembered nothing of the attack, but the trauma would likely not leave him for some time. Faith shuddered. Not even Washington's aides were safe.

Mary Porter put her to straightening the shelves where they kept herbs and medicines for the sick. "So many people come in and out to help with the sick," she said. "We need to make sure our medicines do not become confused. You recognize the herbs and know their uses. I need your help to put everything here to rights."

Faith pointed to the dried remains of a plant that she could not identify. "What is this?"

Mary made a face. "People use henbane for stomach ailments and calming mad fits, but it's best to treat it with caution. Too much can be deadly." She swept it into her hand. "I will put this where someone will not carelessly grab it. That's a problem we don't need."

Faith nodded. She had learned to be cautious when administering herbs and decoctions she was unfamiliar with. Patent medicines made her suspicious. Her mother had taught her how to use herbs and treat ailments. She didn't believe in using unfamiliar medicines.

Sorting the herbs took a little while. Some were so dry she couldn't identify the leaves. She had to use her nose. Mint was easy; milder ones like hyssop were more challenging. Bottles of preparations such as ipecac, she recognized. Toward the end of her task, she realized something was missing that she had seen before. The bottle that contained the laudanum they used to ease the pain of their most injured patients was gone. Concerned, Faith went to find Mary Porter.

"That can't be right," Mary said, walking over. "You must have mislaid it. It's an amber bottle, slightly smaller than the ipecac. I saw it here just this morning."

Faith shook her head. "I've looked all through the drawers."

Mary Porter sounded exasperated. "Check and see if someone left it at a bedside. Such carelessness! We have so few medicines as it is." A man cried out from the back. Mary bit her lip. "Keep searching. We have to have it."

Faith nodded. She spotted the sandy head of a physician, Isaac Walters. He had arrived a few weeks earlier with a group of men from the Congress at York. Despite his youth, he was skillful in stitching wounds and treating ailments.

Walters smiled as she came by. "Greetings, Mistress Clarke. It is nice to see your smiling face." He looked across the room. "Mistress Porter is busy with a patient. Perhaps you can help me. Are there any new patients I should see?"

Faith nodded. "I can take you to them. We've had a man come in with fever and chills, and then there is Lieutenant Commander Silver, who has a lump on his head."

Walters raised an eyebrow. "How did that come about?"

She explained what she had heard. Walters was silent for a moment. "He's fortunate it's not worse," he said at last. "It sounds like he is stable. I will check on him later. Where is the other man?" Faith led him to the section of the room reserved for those with fevers. As they approached, she could hear coughing from a nearby bed.

One nurse was dosing a patient with honey. The man swallowed before lying back down on the cot. "Rest. The doctor will come by shortly to check on you."

Walters stepped to meet her. "I'm Doctor Walters; please tell me about this patient."

Faith left him conversing with the other nurse. She wanted to continue searching for the laudanum. Although she knew she had nothing to do with its disappearance, Mary Porter's scolding stung. She was determined to discover what had happened to the bottle.

After circling the perimeter, Faith focused on checking every table and bedside within the cabin, hoping it would appear. While she found an assortment of preparations and a small hipflask of cheap liquor, no laudanum appeared. It bothered her. Laudanum was the strongest painkiller they had for the severely injured. The liquid opiate could also be deadly if not handled properly. Mary Porter warned all the nurses about it when they started treating the sick.

"In small, managed doses, it numbs pain better than anything, but too much will end life." She had told Faith when she began taking over for Hannah. "Only give it if a surgeon directs you, and only the prescribed amount. If you are not careful, it can become an addiction or worse, end life."

Faith treated it with extreme caution. She trusted her knowledge of herbs, but medicines like this frightened her. She left them to the doctor to dispense.

One of the other women called her over to the sick section to help sponge down a man with a raging fever. Making sure she had a clean apron on over her dress, Faith went to help. Afterwards, she helped feed men broths and soups to help build up their strength, along with coffee and bread. Some men ate well, others turned away, too weak for more than a spoon or two. After washing up and changing her apron, she went to tell Mary Porter that she could not find the laudanum.

The older woman was busy organizing a load of bandages that had come from the laundress. The whiteness of the bandages stood in sharp contrast with the dark wood of the medicine cabinet. She organized the linen by size for easy access and to prevent waste on minor wounds. She looked up as Faith stood before her.

"I cannot find the laudanum," Faith confessed. "It's not in the cabinet, nor anywhere else I have looked. I do not know what has happened to it."

Mary Porter blinked. "It's right here." She pointed to a small amber bottle in a recess of the cabinet. "You must have overlooked it. I spotted it just a few moments ago when I came to fold the fresh linen."

Faith looked at the bottle, dumbfounded. "It wasn't there earlier." She had gone through every inch of the cabinet looking for it. It had not been there earlier.

Mary Porter smiled patiently. "I know it's been difficult taking over for your sister. Hannah has a talent for nursing. Not everyone does. Adjusting to our routines and finding things will take you some time."

"I know where to find it, along with the other medicines and items we use," Faith said, trying to keep her temper in check. "I checked thoroughly when I completed the inventory."

Porter nodded. "I'm sure you did, Mistress Clarke, but keeping track of medicines is not like keeping track of foodstuffs at a tavern. Someone was probably dosing a patient and returned it after you finished your inventory. In fact, I'm almost certain of it. The liquid has gone down over an inch. I cannot imagine who would need that much." She shook her head. "These doctors. They come in. They take over and tell us nothing. We need to know how they are treating the patients so we can provide proper care."

Faith nodded, although she wasn't sure she agreed. She saw a handful of Valley Forge's surgeons come in and out every day she was present. Most took time to speak to the staff regarding the care of their patients. Isaac Walters walked up to where they were speaking. His shy smile warmed her heart.

Mary Porter wasn't immune either. "Dr. Walters, can I help you?"

His face flushed. "Yes, ma'am. I need to set a broken bone. If you ladies could help while I put it in place."

Both ladies went to help. The man lay quietly on a table. Two other enlisted men stood beside him. Faith went by the man's head. His face was pale, his breathing quick and shallow.

Dr. Walter's voice was kind. "Tell me again what happened, Tom."

The man started, then cried out as he tried to sit up straighter.

"I'll tell it," one man said. "We were wrestling around. We'd been playing cards, and I thought Tom had slipped a few up his sleeve, so I was trying to shake them loose."

Another man interrupted. "Sam found the cards and tried to punch Tom, and knocked him into the side of our cabin. By the time I broke it up, Tom was on the ground moaning, and Sam was trying to help him up."

Walters shot Tom a look. "It's not a good idea to cheat your friends."

Tom nodded weakly.

"I think you may have broken a rib or two. Let me look at you." Lifting his shirt, he felt along the man's ribs until he yelped. "I don't feel a break, but it could be a minor crack or bad bruising. Either way, let's wrap you up to keep your bones stable until they heal. You should be right as rain in a few weeks." He looked Tom in the eye. "No more cheating."

Mary Porter helped hold him still while Faith went and got a long roll of linen and held it while Dr. Walters rolled it around the man's ribs. Once finished, he split an end and used it to tie off his work. After settling the man onto a cot, he walked back to the cabinet with the two women. "You can give him willow bark tea for pain. Now that I have wrapped his ribs, he should feel better." He sighed. "It's a good thing we're still in camp. Marching with a broken rib would be painful."

Faith nodded. She looked over to where the man rested. His friends had left. Here, he had time to rest and heal. There would be little time for that once the army marched out. She was glad when her shift was over, and she could return to the farmhouse.

The sun was beginning its progress to the western horizon. Faith's stomach grumbled. She realized she had not eaten in a while. Had she missed dinner? As she approached Washington's headquarters, she smelled meat roasting. Smoke drifted in a pale stream out from the chimney. As she entered the hallway, she could hear the scrape of tables being pushed together.

Martha Washington supervised the rearrangement of the furniture for the meal. She acknowledged Faith's arrival. "I see you have completed your day at the hospital. Wash up and join us for dinner."

Faith nodded and complied. Within moments, the men drifted inside, drawn by the promise of hot food and good company. Lady Washington directed them all to the basins outside as she supervised the setting of the tables. Faith sat with her back to the wall, facing the door, as instructed. As the men joined the ladies, Lady Washington directed them as well. No one questioned her. After they sat, General Washington offered a short grace for them all.

Will sat across from her next to Jeremy Butler. Faith looked at him. "Is Hannah not joining us?"

He shook his head. "She's sound asleep. I tried to wake her, but she said she wasn't hungry. I'll take her something later." He shrugged, but Faith could see the worry in his eyes.

"Being tired early in a pregnancy is normal," she said. "It will get better as time passes."

"You know this?" he asked, shooting her a direct look.

"I'm familiar with the experience," she said dryly.

He nodded before taking a deep drink of wine. Jeremy Butler wasn't fooling anyone. He was terrified.

Faith hoped he would adjust as the months passed. Hannah was happy, even with all that the pregnancy took out of her. Within weeks, they would be in Williamsburg, where she could rest far away from this troublesome war.

Toward the end of the meal, Lafayette entered. Washington excused himself and went with the Frenchman into his office. Lady Washington looked annoyed for a moment before returning to her normal, polite expression. She signaled for dessert to be served, a cake made with nuts and honey. Her conversation mainly focused on the weather and when to plant certain crops in Virginia.

Faith listened with half an ear. Despite the façade of a normal meal, tension filled the air. They all wondered if they sat next to a killer who plotted death in between courses served on Lady Washington's china. Faith shivered. This was the first time in a while that John Laurens had been at the table. He looked pale but otherwise much himself. A few of the women shot him sideways glances from where they sat with their husbands.

Laurens ignored them and ate his meal in relative silence, taking a moment to compliment Lady Washington. "A most excellent meal," he said. "It is good to enjoy good food among excellent company."

Lady Washington smiled at him. "I am glad to see you as well, John. How is your father?"

Laurens smiled. "Much relieved, I imagine. He has told me of the many prayers he and my mother have sent regarding my safety and well-being. In my last letter, I told him there is no more honorable position than to be in the service of your husband."

Jack Silver looked over his wine glass. "I imagine confinement such as yours would inspire much prayer." He took a sip. "You certainly had mine." He looked over at Lady Washington. "Did your dear husband pray as well?"

Lady Washington ignored him before smiling at Laurens. "He is most glad of your return. He sent a letter to your father as soon as you were released."

Laurens nodded. "I'm sure that made him glad. It was most kind of him to reach out directly. There is much work to be done before we leave this camp. I pray we can all work together to see this noble endeavor to the end."

"Hear, hear," General Greene said, his voice resonating within the room. The other officers joined him as they saluted the return of one of their own.

What no one mentioned, but no doubt wondered, was when death would once again strike their ranks, robbing them of another friend or ally when least expected.

Chapter Twenty-Four

The next few days remained quiet. Hannah quit going to the hospital, so Faith went every day in her stead. She rose early and walked down the road to the hospital as the last vestiges of pink faded from the sky. Troops filled the parade ground, practicing drills as they prepared for battles to come. Steady influxes of visitors from the Continental Congress came to view the army. General Washington and Baron von Steuben showed the army's newfound prowess to them. Even to Faith's untrained eye, there was a sense of professionalism in the men that had not been there a few months before. As the weather warmed, restlessness permeated the troops. Everyone was waiting for what would happen next. Uneasiness gripped her as she watched and waited. She didn't need anyone to tell her why they were there. Everyone wanted to know when Washington would break camp. What remained unsaid was the longing to escape the string of violent deaths in the camp.

Fear was the enemy that sapped strength and sharpened tempers. Faith watched people go in and out of the hospital, whether for treatment or to drop off supplies, or visit a friend. Watchful eyes kept friends and acquaintances at arm's length. Patients cast fearful eyes on the surgeons and nurses who tended them, wondering if they brought healing or death. Faith struggled with the tension as she made rounds to check on the sick and injured.

She smiled as she approached Tom. Despite the pain in his ribs, he sat up and played cards with two friends. Dr. Walters intended to release him later today after he had examined him.

Faith helped apply poultices to ease the soreness before wrapping his ribs back up the evening before. She also prepared willow bark tea to help ease his pain so he could sleep. The doctors forbade giving him anything stronger. Dr. Waldo had seized a contraband liquor bottle from him earlier, despite Tom's protests.

"Hard liquor is the last thing you need at present," He had said when he found it next to his bed.

"What harm can it do?" Tom protested. "Can't a man have just a nip to help him rest?"

"You don't take just a nip," Waldo said. "That's how you ended up here. Stay sober and stay safe. You will need a clear head when you return to your unit. You know that."

Tom glared at him for a moment before shrugging. "We all drink. You know that. After a battle, it numbs us to what we have seen."

Waldo's face softened slightly. "Be careful, Tom. I want you to live to go home to your family."

The injured man nodded before turning in to sleep. Waldo watched him for a few moments before sending Faith home for the night. "You need your rest, too, mistress. There is no point exhausting yourself before the battles begin."

Faith let him send her home with a few soldiers. Once her head had hit the pillow, she had slept like the dead, only rousing to the relentless rooster's cry. Now she was back, and it felt as if she had never gone.

Tom smiled when he saw her approach. His shirt was clean, and he had shaved. The young soldier looked far better than he had when he had arrived a few days past. "Greetings, Mistress," he said, saluting her with a mug. The smell of strong coffee wafted over, providing a welcoming scent against the usual aromas of vinegar and alcohol.

"How do you feel?" His friend's eyes remained on their cards, but Faith could see a faint smile on his face.

"Seeing a pretty face does much to ease any ill humors that remain," Tom replied. "The only thing that would make it better would be a swallow of rum. I don't suppose you could find any–for medicinal purposes."

He looked so earnest, Faith wanted to laugh. "I'm afraid we have no rum right now. I would be glad to get you some mint tea. We have plenty of it." One woman had found a large supply of mint growing behind a barn. They frequently harvested it for tea.

Tom made a face. "Mint tea. I've drunk enough of that to fill a washtub since I've been here. Surely you have something stronger? Even General Washington supplies us with alcohol."

"When you return to active duty, you can ask about your ration of drink," she said. "Until then, you can drink your tea and be glad your injuries are not worse."

Faith heard one of the other men snicker. "I'll tell the sergeant you're looking forward to returning to sentry duty. I'm sure he'll be glad to hear it."

"Bastard," Tom grumbled. "You're the reason I'm here."

"You were cheating, I caught you," Sam looked him over his cards. "For all I know, you're cheating now."

Tom held out his bare arms. He had pushed his sleeves above his elbows. "Where would I put them? You are a suspicious man, Sam. You shouldn't be accusing a helpless man."

Sam snorted. "You're as helpless as a rattlesnake."

Tom smiled, breaking the tension. "You're a suspicious old bear, always have been. Let's get back to cards before you go on duty."

Faith left them to their game. They were enjoying themselves. Restlessness was the undoing of more than one soldier. They were tired of waiting and ready to engage the enemy. She was not so eager. As much as she longed to return to Williamsburg, Faith dreaded sending Will back into battle. There were no guarantees he would return in one piece or at all. It was a thought that kept her up nights as she prayed for his safety.

Mary Porter entered the hospital just before noon. After putting on a fresh apron, she checked the medicine cabinet before relocking it and walking around to check on the patients. Before long, she came upon Faith. "I see you are here early," she said with approval. "Have there been any changes in our patients?"

"I believe Tom Frakes will be returning to his unit later today. Dr. Walters wanted to check his ribs one last time before releasing him. More men have come in with fever and chills. They are with the others with similar maladies. I've sent someone for more blankets. Dr. Walters thinks it may be grippe."

Porter frowned. "We already have five with that. One's fever has broken, and he seems on the mend. The others are still fighting the disease. I will request that someone air their cabin, since the weather is warm," she said, heading toward the sickroom and tucking stray ends of hair into her cap.

Faith nodded. She knew the importance of keeping contagion from spreading. They wiped down beds with vinegar and boiled water. In the back, she heard the coughing of the sick. It worried her. She was glad the doctors were planning on sending the men with the mildest injuries back to their cabins and away from disease.

Jack Silver sat up in his bed. His eyes took in everything in the room. When she walked toward him, he smiled. "I did not know how busy it was here." His eyes swept the room. "It seems there is always something happening."

Faith nodded wearily. "The warm weather brings on disease."

He shot her a shrewd gaze. "That must be frightening to a nurse."

"The sick need care." She looked at the open windows. "Maybe the fresh air will dispel the ill humors and allow these men to heal."

Silver nodded. "It helps dispel the scent of all the vinegar." His eye looked sad as they swept the room. "It's a shame that a touch of sun and spring breeze can't cure all illnesses."

"We do what we can. It's better to clean than risk the spread of illness." Faith was sick of the smell, too, but it was better than the fetid scents of disease. She was glad she would leave in a few hours. She would have time to bathe and grab a bite to eat before bed. If she were fortunate, she would see Will.

Before long, afternoon shadows stretched out from the walls. Faith stepped out for a moment. Both Doctors Waldo and Walters had gone outside and stood underneath the shade of a broad tree. She didn't blame them for taking a moment away from the sick. Walters had arrived earlier than she; Waldo took the night shift. The battle against disease never ended. Nor did the deaths. She had seen a wagon leave with blankets covering the bodies. She was becoming numb to it. Only the strange series of murders still had the power to frighten her.

General Greene rode past. She wondered if he was checking the camp's sanitation. He and von Steuben had been vigilant regarding the placement of latrines and the management of camp sanitation. In truth, their orders had made camp far more tolerable.

Faith watched as he met another rider. She squinted to get a better look. Faith suspected it was Hamilton. She had seen him on that horse. They were too far away for her to catch their words, but they were not friendly. Greene pointed the way back to headquarters. Hamilton protested before turning his animal and heading back to whence he came.

Later, she mentioned the incident to Will as they sat down to enjoy a bite of supper. He looked surprised. Butler did not. "Rumor has it he's been visiting a woman outside of camp. Greene would not appreciate that. He prefers to keep the peace with the people who live in this valley."

Will raised his eyebrows. "I wouldn't think there was time for that sort of foolishness. Washington keeps his aides busy with all the correspondence going out. They also have to complete the Baron's drill book."

"Laurens is back. He may feel he deserves a break from all his hard work during John's incarceration. Neither Jack nor Will is as fluent in languages as the other two." Butler's tone was mild. He bit into a young potato and chewed thoughtfully.

Down at the far end of the table was the man himself. Hamilton sat between Lady Sterling and Caty Greene. The conversation flowed. Hamilton smiled widely at something Caty Greene said. She laughed, the sound like tinkling glass. General Greene sat across from her, his face lost in thought. He ate slowly, as if unaware of what he put into his mouth.

Faith watched them with puzzlement. They seemed so different, the young, vivacious Caty and the solemn older man who was her husband. Faith noticed they spoke often, her dark head close to his as they shared a private moment. They seemed to share a love of books. General Greene did not mind that his wife spoke her mind, voicing opinions on a variety of subjects. She wondered what had drawn them together. Was it enough to survive all the time apart?

"Hey," Will chided. "Where did you go? I've asked you twice to pass the salt."

Faith flushed. "I'm sorry. It's been a long day." She slid the salt cellar down where he could reach it. Tiredness dragged at her. She longed for her pillow and the silence of the night when all she had to do was close her eyes after saying her prayers. It was where she felt most secure, curled up in bed, far from the dangers that roamed the camp.

After the meal, she helped put the room to order so that it would be ready for the morning. The abundance of people facilitated the swift gathering of dishes and repositioning of tables. After the meal, Washington and Greene returned to the Commander's office, shutting the door behind them. A variety of emotions passed over Caty Greene's face as she watched him go: fear, anger, and then finally heartbreaking sadness. He had taken her aside moments earlier and told her he was sending her back to their cabin with a group of soldiers. He ignored her protests. "I will be along later, dear," Greene said firmly before following Washington.

Lady Washington wasted little time in wishing her guests good night and standing at the door to encourage their exit. After all had left, she went upstairs to the room she shared with the general, no doubt already used to the long separations that came with marrying a soldier.

Faith stood in the breezeway with Will for a few moments. The sun balanced just above the western horizon, offering a faint glow of light that burnished the sky. The nearby trees were cast in shadow, too dark to see within their depths. An owl hooted, its cry resonating through the night as it searched for prey. She shivered, wondering what had ended up in its powerful claws.

Will wrapped an arm around her shoulders. She sighed and rested her head on his chest. Her heart was at peace for a few brief moments. In the distance, they could see the faint glimmer of white on apple trees that some enterprising farmer had planted in years past. They would be long gone before they turned into fruit.

Faith's mind turned to Williamsburg. As the weather warmed, Olivia would plant seeds in the garden behind their tavern. Her husband, Titus, would have turned the soil over not long after the last frost. A wave of homesickness swept her. She longed to see her son, studying law under George Wythe, and to sleep in her own bed. It had been months since she had greeted guests to her tavern and watched the barkeeper Malachi pour drinks and monitor everyone who entered the tap house. She sighed. "When do you think we will be home again?"

Will drew her against his chest. "I don't know," He admitted. "You ladies will leave before long. We will be with our general, back to war. All I can do is pray it will end before too long. Not a one of us has forgotten what we've left behind." He looked off over the shadowed meadows and trees. "I pray it will all be as it was when we return."

Faith felt him shudder beneath her head. He had seen towns the British had burned and ransacked. She prayed that never happened to Williamsburg. "Let them stay north," she prayed silently. She didn't know what she would do if she lost all she had. Hannah didn't speak of it, but she knew fleeing Philadelphia had been painful.

Reluctantly, she stepped away from Will. "You had best get back to your cabin before full dark," Faith said. "It's not safe to be alone."

Will nodded. "Good night then. I will head out once you are inside."

She shot him a look. "I'm just outside the door."

He smiled. "Then go inside where it's safe."

Rolling her eyes, she complied. As the door swung shut, she heard him call out to someone. The reply was faint. The last she heard was the sound of his feet running toward whoever it was so that they could walk back together in the twilight.

Chapter Twenty-Five

Butler despised roosters. They destroyed a peaceful morning with their dreadful crowing. The demonic avian outside didn't seem to care that people inside were trying to sleep. It continued its morning reveille without end. The unearthly noise echoed against the side of the house, multiplying the noise. He tried pulling his pillow over his head, but it did nothing to ease the din of the relentless bird. He groaned.

Next to him, Hannah giggled. "It's not going to stop soon." Her amused glance met his. Her dark hair spread out over the pillows in a dark wave. The ends brushed his shoulders, smelling of the soap she used to wash it. Her deep blue eyes gazed into his, humor crinkling the edges. She had gotten thinner in the past few weeks. This morning, however, she looked rested.

"How do you feel?" Jeremy rolled on his side to see her better. He reached out to cup her cheek, stroking the soft skin with his thumb. He hadn't woken to the sound of her retching into the chamber pot for the past two days, which made him hopeful she had gotten some rest. The pregnancy filled him with worries he didn't voice.

Hannah smiled lazily. "Better than I have in a while." She sat up and combed her hair with her fingers. It fell down her back in a deep mass. A few shadows lined her eyes, but her expression was peaceful. She looked at the curtain-covered window. "It's still dark outside."

The rooster crowed again, eliciting a scowl from Jeremy along with the desire to swear. He changed his mind when his gaze returned to Hannah. Her skin glowed like a pearl. Her beauty took his breath away.

She leaned over, placing her hands on either side of his head. "We have a few hours before you have to leave.'

Jeremy nodded. "I suppose I do if you want to rest." He oomphed as she rolled on top of him. His eyebrows shot up in surprise as he struggled to catch his breath. Hannah was a solid weight, albeit a welcome one. "Are you sure about this?" He squeaked. She silenced him with a kiss. The movement of her body over his took away all rational thought. The rooster continued his cries unnoticed as the first streaks of dawn shot across the sky.

Sometime later, Butler hurried into his clothes, well aware he was late for the morning drill. Hannah watched him unrepentantly from beneath the covers. Her satisfied smirk said what she did not express.

"Washington will have my head," he warned. "He is a firm believer in promptness."

"I could write you a note," she offered. "Telling him you were taking care of your wife."

Butler rolled his eyes. "Thanks a lot. I don't need my wife to protect me from my commander."

Hannah laughed before sitting up herself and grabbing her shift from where it had fallen. "I'd best get downstairs myself. I thought I smelled bacon a few minutes ago."

Butler was glad to see her acting more like her normal self. "I believe you're right. I'll ask the cook to save you some."

"It won't take me that long to get ready," Hannah shot him a sideways look as she pulled on her stockings. "At least I don't have to worry about my breeches being misbuttoned."

Jeremy looked down. She was right. He hurried to fix his clothes as she snickered. Hannah adjusted her stays and pulled on her petticoats before he had both boots on. She was reaching for her skirt as Jeremy hurried down. The meal was still being served as he entered the room, to the good-natured ribbing of the French.

Within minutes, he had secured two mugs and two plates containing eggs, corncakes, and bacon. Hannah came down just as coffee was being poured. The men greeted her cheerfully.

"Madame Butler, it is good to see you again. I trust you are feeling well."

Lafayette, always the gentleman, inquired as he stood to greet her.

Hannah smiled. "Well, thank you–and yourself?"

Lafayette nodded before sitting and returning to his meal. He had been very thoughtful when he realized Hannah's condition. Fresh fruit and cheese had appeared in the house, along with light ales and delicate pastries designed to tempt her appetite.

Hannah had noticed that, along with the small bouquets of wildflowers that graced the tables. The men found many small ways to share their happiness at her pregnancy.

Jeremy was glad that Hannah had people who cared for her. Her presence in a military camp, where disease and a killer were at large, was a source of worry for him. It relieved him when she quit going to the hospital. His prayers for her good health continued.

As they finished the meal and cleaned up, a messenger arrived. At the sound of horse hooves, Lafayette and a few of his men went out to greet the rider. Butler heard the murmur of voices, although he could not fathom their words.

A man entered, followed by the Marquis. "Major Butler, your presence is required at headquarters. General Washington sent me to get you."

Butler nodded. "I'm on my way." Washington apparently had no patience for a tardy officer. He'd best submit to the scolding he undoubtedly deserved. Hannah shot him a concerned look. He smiled at her. "Don't worry, he's a fair man." He leaned over to kiss her cheek before grabbing his hat. The rider followed him out. The sight of two saddled horses in the yard surprised him.

"Washington was clear. He needs your presence as quickly as possible."

Butler mounted the animal. "Let's go." He urged the animal into first a trot and then a full gallop. The messenger stayed with him on his dappled gray. Although he had never ridden the black gelding before, its responsiveness to his touch and smooth gait pleased him. "You like to run, don't you?" He said as it carried him. Strands of its silky mane drifted over his wrists and arms as they raced up the road.

He hated for the ride to end. As the farmhouse drew into sight, he slowed to allow both of them time to cool down. Washington didn't believe in wasting men or mounts. Butler could not imagine how angered he was to send a rider and horse after him. Regardless, Butler didn't regret the time with Hannah, even if it got him into trouble with his commander. She had been deathly ill. Seeing her act like her normal self relieved him. That she had regained some appetite eased the tight knot that had formed around his heart as he had watched her struggle.

A stable hand met him in the yard. "I'll take Henry for you."

"Henry?" Butler said as he stroked the horse's ebony coat.

The stable hand nodded. "A stud on Patrick Henry's farm sired him. Washington owned the mare, so when this fellow was born, he named him Henry."

Butler grinned. "Does Virginia's governor know someone named a horse after him?"

"I do not know, sir." The man answered. He ran gentle hands down the horse's neck. His skin was nearly as dark as the horse's. The horse nickered and nuzzled the man's neck affectionately. The man smiled and rubbed between its ears. "He's a fine animal. He only needs a gentle nudge, and he will give whatever you ask."

"Take good care of him," Butler said. "He's an excellent mount."

"I surely will," the man replied as he led the animal to the stable.

Butler entered the front door. The hallway was quiet for once. Lady Washington was not present. He guessed she was upstairs in her makeshift parlor with her ladies. One soldier stood outside the door of Washington's office. When he saw Butler, he came to attention and rapped on the door before opening it and announcing him.

Butler entered the room from which Washington commanded the Colonial Army. For once, no fire burned in the fireplace. Instead, a cracked window let in a gentle breeze. Washington stood looking out over the fields that ran out from the stone farmhouse where he had spent the winter. "Major Butler."

"General Washington," he replied. Unease filled him. There was no one else in the room. He was alone with the Commander-in-Chief. He wondered how much trouble he was in.

Washington turned and studied him. His expression revealed nothing. "Have you come any closer to solving these troublesome murders?"

Butler started. This was something far more serious than tardiness. "No, sir. Evidence cleared Laurens. He returned to work yesterday. I still feel certain this is an officer, but I have not narrowed it much further."

Washington frowned. "At one point, you were investigating my aides de camp."

"I still am." Butler walked until he stood in the middle of the room. "Along with other officers."

"I jailed Henry Laurens' son based on your suspicions," Washington said grimly. "He's been a friend for years. I wrote yesterday to reassure him his son's name was clear. I feared he would never forgive me for incarcerating his only son."

"They held Lieutenant Colonel Laurens based on the evidence found in his room," Butler noted. "His luggage made the bombs that destroyed those ovens. Someone concealed a bloody doll in his bedding." Washington frowned. "Laurens was in custody during the discovery of that woman's body and Silver's attack. He could not have done either." He shot Butler a narrow glance. "I haven't seen any more figures of late."

Butler nodded. "Nor have I. I think Lena Ross supplied them. I suspect someone killed her to keep her quiet." He chose his words carefully. "Someone wanted him to look guilty. It had to be someone with access to his room. A room he shares with two other men. People would have seen a stranger going up into the attic."

"Not necessarily," Washington countered. "People go in and out all day: messengers from the colonies, members of Congress, and officers from within camp. Can anyone say they know every face in camp? I cannot."

"Nor can I," Butler acknowledged. "But a stranger would not have known about Lauren's new luggage. Then, there are the women." At Washington's startled look, he smiled. "They miss nothing. Your wife runs this house. She would have noticed a stranger going up the stairs." He didn't add that boots would have echoed on the bare wooden steps, alerting everyone that someone was there.

Washington sighed. "Lieutenant Commander Silver lies injured in a hospital bed. He's fortunate he didn't end up with his skull crushed. Staff Sergeant Toussaint was less fortunate. Silver barely escaped death. Hamilton and Laurens have gone to bring him back here."

"I am glad he is well enough to return. I hear there is camp fever there."

Washington nodded. "When you group men together for this length of time, the chance of fevers and plagues increases. It's one reason we will break camp in a few weeks."

Butler drew in a breath. "That soon?"

Washington nodded wearily. "It is time to rejoin the battle. Our men are ready." He shot a keen glance at Butler. "I need this killer stopped. We're out of time. You've investigated some of my most trusted men and found nothing to prove their guilt."

"I haven't investigated everyone," Butler said slowly.

Washington stilled. "Who do you mean?" His face tightened. "Hamilton."

"Hamilton," Butler agreed. "I never stopped to question why he was on the road when we found Silver. His arrival appeared fortuitous, and God knows we needed his help to get Silver to the hospital. He could barely stand."

Washington bit his lip before speaking. "He has yet to explain why he was on the road that day. I had not sent him on any errands." He shook his head. "Hamilton has served me loyally since his enlistment. I have no reason to suspect him of any misdeeds." The general paced restlessly. "I cannot accept it. Why would he do such a thing? He's one of the most brilliant men on my staff. He's well-liked and successful in all his endeavors. Despite his humble beginnings, he has done well for himself."

Butler nodded. He knew little about Alexander Hamilton, other than he was a protégé of Washington, along with the other men. The General treated his aides like surrogate sons. He trusted them implicitly. "I'm not sure he has done anything. But I need to rule him out, so that I know where to proceed."

Washington nodded. "He is working with Laurens on translating Baron von Steuben's field manual. Our plan is to send copies to other units so that they can learn the drills as well. I will tell him he needs to speak with you and hold nothing back."

"Thank you," Butler said. He turned to go.

"Major Butler," Washington said.

Butler turned back to look at the General.

"Give my regards to your wife." Washington's eyes twinkled briefly before turning to his desk, back to the maps and notes accumulated as he planned his army's return to battle.

As Butler moved toward the door, it sprang open without warning. "Sir, you need to see this!" An enlisted man stumbled in with his eyes wide. "Out in the breezeway, Isaac found them as he was bringing in more wood."

Washington exchanged a glance with Butler before taking long strides out the door. Butler followed him, wondering what had frightened the soldier. He didn't have to wait long. Men gathered around the table where a basin of water sat untouched.

The men cleared a pathway for the General. Butler followed in his wake. As he approached the table, he saw what caused such a stir. Two dolls rested on the tabletop. One lay spread-eagled, its limbs widespread. A rock, rusty with blood, crushed its head. A doll-sized blanket covered its unmarked body. The faint scent of whiskey wafted through the air.

"Two?" Washington said in puzzlement. "Why are there two?"

Butler's voice was rough. "Because he's struck again, and we haven't found the second body."

Chapter Twenty-Six

Faith enjoyed sending men back to their cabins. It meant they had recovered and would soon be whole. She liked to think that in a few months, they would return to their families. It was a naïve wish, but it sustained her through the hours of aiding surgeons and treating seriously ill men.

She saw John Laurens and Alexander Hamilton enter the hospital, which surprised her. "Hello. What brings two of Washington's aides here? Neither of you appears ill." Both looked well, albeit somewhat tired. She knew from Will that both had been putting in long hours, completing von Steuben's field manual. They would send it to a printer soon, then distribute copies to other units for implementation.

Laurens smiled. "We are well, Mistress Clarke. We wish to retrieve our friend. I've heard John has a bump on his noggin, but has recovered."

Faith nodded. She was glad to see him out and about. "He's ready to go." She gestured to where Silver was already sitting up, getting his head freshly bandaged. "Let Dr. Walters finish with him, and then he's free to go back to his duties."

Walters overheard her. "No riding and no military drills for another week," he admonished. "You took a hard rap on the head. I've done all I can, but you need to take care. This camp can fell the vulnerable."

Silver nodded. "Don't worry. I have no intention of doing anything that makes my head hurt worse." He grinned over at his mates. "John! It's great to see you out and about. We've sorely missed your talents."

Laurens chuckled. "You've not been sneaking curses into the drill manual, have you? Washington would not appreciate it even if the Baron would."

Silver shook his head. "It's all I can do to translate the orders correctly. I'll leave the embellishments for you and Alexander. I'm fortunate that he is far more skilled in French, or the project would be in peril."

"I wouldn't say that," Hamilton said. "Your French is more than adequate for the task, and I cannot match your fluency in Latin and Greek."

Silver shrugged. "Papa excelled in ancient languages. He spent many an hour with me learning them. He believed in a well-educated mind. There was not much time wasted on frivolity." His expression turned ironic. "Regrettably, his knowledge of tongues still being spoken was far less skilled."

Hamilton replied. "You had a father to teach you. Being a pastor's son afforded you a better education than many."

Laurens smiled. "Don't underestimate your skills, Jack. I've never seen a faster learner. You are a tremendous asset to Washington. He appreciates your hard work."

Silver smiled. "Thanks, friend. That means a lot." After pulling on his boots, he stood gingerly before joining the other two. "Shall we return to headquarters?"

Faith watched them go before turning to check on the remaining patients in her assigned area. Once she had made sure everyone was as comfortable as possible, she stepped outside. Away from the scents of sickness and vinegar, the air outside was fresh with the scents of pine and grass. Out in the pasture, cattle from the last shipment grazed, their tails switching as they warded off flies. Their moos carried over, their sound mournful as the animals enjoyed their respite from being driven down the road to the camp, innocent of their eventual end. It was still early. The sun had turned the sky bright cerulean as it shone down on the rich green fields that surrounded the hospital. Off in the distance, Mount Joy was visible, its green expanse hazy as it rose toward the sky. Behind it lay Mount Misery, which looked no different but reflected the conflicting feelings that ran through the camp.

Faith longed for the faintly salty scent of the York River from where it met the ocean. Back home, people were going to market, eager to buy spring produce from farmers who had arrived before dawn to set up their tables.

In Virginia, the weather warmed weeks ago, allowing plants to grow and thrive. Gardeners planted the gardens as soon as the ground thawed, so plants were already sprouting and producing food. At the tavern, Olivia would already have picked early peas and onions from the kitchen garden to cook for dinner. Her husband Titus would be busy chopping wood for the cook fire, the sound of his axe echoing in the yard.

As she turned to go back inside, Faith heard voices in the distance, calling men to drill. Within minutes, a volley of gunfire resonated across the field, followed shortly by another volley. They had gotten much faster at reloading. Will had told her as much. Now her ears confirmed his words. She wondered if he was with the group in the field. He spent most of his time there with the army's drillmaster. She wondered if that would continue when they broke camp. It would make sense. The Baron understood some English, but he needed help to communicate. At his side was Will, Laurens, or Hamilton, if not his own man, who spoke English but didn't always have the best words to translate von Steuben's commands.

Mary Porter was busy checking their medical supplies when Faith came back in. Mary nodded to her before finishing her inventory. "We need more clean linen. Can you see if the laundress has some for us? Rose was working on it yesterday. I'm hoping she finished cleaning it and it's had time to dry."

Faith nodded. She would rather be outside than in the confines of the hospital. The moans of men battling fever echoed throughout the enclosure. There was little they could do to ease their distress. Faith considered bleeding patients barbaric, even if it was standard medical practice to release foul humors. It was far better to ease misery than compound it. She had helped wipe down fevered heads and pour broth and medicines down throats inflamed with illness. The scent of the vinegar they used to clean burned her nose, but she used it to help keep down the threat of contagion. She noticed two empty beds in the fever section. Someone had occupied them when she left the night before. She knew without asking that the men had succumbed to disease.

Once outside, she took in a few deep breaths to clear her lungs. Dew from the grass dampened the edges of her skirt, but she preferred walking on the grass to the dirt and muck of the road. By now, she knew the way to the laundress by heart. In very little time, she passed the cabins of McDowell's and Conway's brigades. As she continued her journey, the small school and Knox's artillery came into view. A faint mist rising from the grass enveloped the cannons in fog. She could see the outlines of the soldiers guarding them. Following the shooting incident, someone always guarded the artillery guns.

Faith shivered at the memory. As fog rose from low places in the ground, fed by the distant creek, she wondered if she should have requested an escort. It had seemed a silly thing in the bright sunlight around the hospital, but here amongst the silent stands of trees and rising mist, she felt vulnerable.

She strained her ears but heard nothing but the faint cries of birds overhead. She picked up her steps. The sooner this task was complete, the better. The vinegary scent of the hospital didn't seem so bad anymore. At least it was secure. The presence of so many people prevented harm to anyone there. Someone would notice a stranger.

Her feet crunched on gravel and dirt clods as she moved further into the road, away from the dark shadows cast by the trees. Faith gazed up at the glowing orb of the sun and wished it would hurry to burn away the lingering mist. Anything could hide out here. She felt underneath her apron in the large pocket attached to her skirt. The weight of the pistol dragged at the side, but she didn't care. Cleaning and loading it the night before comforted her. She kept a hand resting on the barrel in case she needed to draw it out quickly.

In the distance, she heard the faint sound of voices. Someone laughed, and then another broke into song. Faith recognized the tune, sung by young soldiers who peppered the streets back home. She supposed many of them took it as a point of pride to be considered a Yankee Doodle Dandy. A group of men became visible in the mist. They hushed when they saw her. A couple of them looked embarrassed. She smiled as they drew close. They passed one another without a word. They nodded to her before continuing toward the field where units were already at work. Once they had gotten a stone's throw away, they began talking once more.

Faith waited until she was sure no one was doubling back through the woods before continuing her journey. Once she had passed the outer line of entrenchment, the fog had mostly melted away, although it lingered in low places along the ground. The small village of camp followers hummed with activity. A pair of boys ran through, passing close in front of Faith. Their laughter floated back as they chased one another. A goat bleated in the distance. She had seen a few just outside of camp, tied up where they could eat fresh grass and not someone's belongings. Somewhere, someone was cutting wood. A group of women met her on the path, their aprons full of limbs. Faith stepped to the side. She wondered if it was kindling or for some other enterprise. Her eyes darted back and forth as she strode through the pathway that snaked through the canvas tents and wooden shelters people had erected. A woman stood outside over a large pot, stirring something. Although she could smell meat, Faith could not identify what else was cooking. People lined up with mugs, which she filled, after taking payment. Some had coins, others offered goods such as a lace handkerchief or a metal utensil. She carefully threaded her way around them. The path meandered through the tents until it entered a stand of pine trees.

Shadows enveloped Faith as she stepped into the forest. Overhead was a canopy formed of pines and deciduous trees. Light trickled in through breaks in the branches that spread out from tall trunks that spiraled up toward the sky. A mixture of pine needles and fallen leaves covered the ground, muffling the sound of her feet. After the noise of the camp, the hush of the woods felt strange. She quickened her steps.

Ahead, she heard the rush of water from the creek nearby. Rose stayed near the creek so that she had ready access to water for her business. Being further away from the camp also meant no one remained close enough to complain about the smell of some of her cleaning agents.

Faith knew she was drawing close when her nose picked up the scents of ripe urine and soap, among other things. She was glad her sister was not with her. Hannah could not handle the odors emanating from the laundress's campsite.

Rose didn't see her at first. She was busy stirring a boiling pot that dangled over a large fire. Using a long pole, she fished a shirt out of the water and laid it over a tree limb behind her. It steamed as water dripped off the edges to run down into the grass. Using her pole, she took a skirt off the limb and placed it on a board that rested on a stump. Grabbing a container, she took out a handful of something foamy and rubbed it briskly into the fabric.

As she turned to speak, Faith spotted a strand of beads around her throat. Tiny and white, they were difficult to spot under the collar of her shirt. She looked up at Faith. "Good morning, mistress, pardon me while I soap this up. It just got cool enough for me to handle."

"Keep working," Faith replied. "I came to see if you had any bandages ready for the hospital. If they are ready, you can just tell me where to get them, and I will be on my way."

Rose didn't reply as she worked on the waistband. After a few moments, she examined it. Taking a gourd, she dipped it into a bucket of water and poured it over the fabric. Soap ran down the sides of the stump and into the ground. Over time, soap had turned the grass yellow. Satisfied, she dipped it into a washtub of water, immersed it, lifted it, and wrung out the excess water. Once this was done, she put it into a cart with others. She nodded at Faith. "I'll take this over to lie on the grass once I have finished my wash."

Wiping her hands on her apron, Rose strode over to a tent with a large overhanging cover at the entrance. On a bench, a stack of light-colored cloths rested. "Here is the next load of clean linen," she said. "It took some work to get the blood out, but I did it." Triumph laced her tone.

Faith hated to think about what it took to remove some of those stains. She had noticed how rough the laundress's hands were. Laundry was a brutal job. She was glad she didn't have to do it.

"Thank you for your hard work," Faith said. "I will let Mistress Porter know."

"Let her know I still need to be paid," Rose said bluntly. "I can't buy food on promises."

Faith nodded. "I will tell her."

Rose paused. "Does that man of yours still want to know who has been buying dolls?"

Faith nodded. Will hadn't mentioned it, but she was sure he did.

"No one has asked me lately, but I saw Mabel, the lady who makes baskets from tree bark, making some. She wouldn't tell me anything, but someone said she's gotten some British coins from somewhere. We all like those."

Faith nodded. Who didn't like British coins? They were worth far more than continental dollars, which lost value nearly every day. She couldn't think of anyone who had British coins, especially to pay for a doll. It was strange. It was a mystery for Jeremy Butler to sort through. She would tell him the next time he appeared.

Faith walked back slowly, not wanting to trip and drop her load. Tree roots snaked across the ground, any of which could catch an unwary foot. Skirting the village, she headed straight for the road. It was her most direct route to the hospital. She hoped to encounter Jeremy or Will at the hospital after delivering the linens.

Dolls stayed in her mind. Faith had not heard of any new information about them. She had thought they had stopped after Lena Ross's death, but if Rose were to be believed, someone still wanted them.

Once she returned to the hospital, she sorted the bandages by size so that the staff could grab what they needed without wasting precious materials. Faith completed her task. Behind her, someone cleared his throat.

Faith startled and turned around. She recognized the homely face of the soldier who had come in the previous day to visit his friend with the broken ribs. "Sam?"

He nodded. "Yes, mistress. I came to get Tom and take him back to our cabin. Doc said he would be ready to go come morning."

Faith nodded. "I'm sure he will be happy to return there." It surprised her he remained in the hospital, but Dr. Waldo had wanted to watch him for another day.

"Sometimes broken ribs can puncture something inside," he had explained. "You can't always see it at first. He looks fine, but I want to make sure no ill humors erupt once he has left the hospital."

Faith had nodded. She understood little of medicine, only what she knew to treat with the herbs grown in her garden. Tom was one of the most engaging patients in the hospital. He noticed everything that went on around him. His stories entertained patient and healer alike. She would miss him, even if she would be glad he had recovered enough to leave.

Sam looked anxious. "I can't get him to wake."

"Oh?" Faith said. "It's long past breakfast. I wouldn't have thought he would still be asleep this late."

"Me neither." Sam shifted his feet. "I've shaken him and yelled in his hear but he doesn't respond. I don't know what else to do."

"Let me see if I can help," Faith said. She hurried over to where the two men had played cards the night before. An upright wooden chair with a woven seat sat next to the cot. The small table they had commandeered the night before stood next to it, a pack of worn cards scattered over the top. Tom lay under the covers. His eyes were closed. Dark lashes fanned his cheeks, making him look far younger than he had. Her nose picked up the scent of rum. "Were you two drinking last night?"

Sam shrugged. "He had a bottle of rum. I had a sip. I was getting ready to go on sentry duty, so I only took a sip."

"I'm guessing he really enjoyed it," Faith said. "Let's hope he doesn't wake with a bad head because of his indulgence. A dark blue bottle slipped out from under the blankets. It was almost empty. The scent of rum permeated the air.

Sam's eyes widened. "He must have had most of the bottle. It was nearly full when I left."

"That may explain his lethargy," Faith commented. Her eyes darted over the man in bed. A chill went through her when she realized he was still. His chest was not rising and falling with his breathing. She pulled the blanket away. As her hand brushed his arm, she felt the unnatural coolness of his body. Life had departed in the night, leaving a corpse in its wake.

Chapter Twenty-Seven

Faith stared down at the dead man on the cot. Her throat ran dry. When Sam saw her face, his own paled.

"Is anything wrong, mistress?" His tone was anxious. "Do you need me to get the doctor?"

Faith nodded. Her heart pounded like a wild thing in her chest. "Please." She pulled the blanket back over him, covering a man beyond comfort. A knot of grief rose in her throat. He had been laughing and joking with his friends the night before. Her lip stung as she realized she was biting it hard. Faith licked away the blood and swallowed as she took a few deep breaths. Panic was not an option. She had other men who depended on her to tend their needs.

Dr. Walters came over with Sam. "What's wrong?" He asked, looking at Faith's face. He didn't wait for an answer, but reached down to check for a pulse. A stunned look crossed his face as he leaned down to examine the man further. He passed a hand over his mouth and nose to check for breath. Rising, he asked Faith. "Did anything happen during the night?"

"I don't know. I haven't been here long." Tears burned in her eyes. She swallowed hard as she looked down. "He was playing cards last night with his friends. He appeared fine."

Mary Porter walked over to them. "Please keep your voices down. Everyone can hear. It's upsetting the other patients." She looked at the doctor. "Is anything wrong?"

"This man is dead," He sighed. "Perhaps we missed something." As he stepped back, his foot struck something. A dark blue bottle rolled across the floor.

"That's his rum," Sam said. "I recognize the bottle."

Dr. Walters picked it up and pulled out the cork, sniffing it. A sweet smell drifted out. "Did you say this was rum?"

Sam nodded. "That's what Tom said. Someone gave it to him before I got here. He offered me some, but I was leaving for duty, so I only took a sip. It had a bitter aftertaste, but he said he didn't care; it was liquor. I didn't like it."

Faith looked at the bottle. She had seen similar bottles back in Williamsburg. People used them for a variety of drinks or medicines. She looked at Walters. "Do you think someone added something?"

Walters sniffed it again. "It's hard to tell. The smell of the rum is powerful on its own."

"Let me see it." Faith had spent plenty of time tending the bar at the tavern. She knew the scents of many drinks. The bottle felt cool in her hand, its deep blue surface revealing nothing. A dark line showed how much remained. Only a few inches remained. Faith sniffed it as well, but could detect nothing beyond the molasses-sweet scent of rum. Taking a finger, she dampened it and touched it to her tongue. "There's bitterness in it that shouldn't be there." She spat into a nearby chamber pot.

Sam protested. "I had a sip, and I'm still here." His anxious gaze swept over his friend's body. Grief filled his face. "He was fine last night. All he could talk about was getting back to duty. He wanted to shoot some lobster backs. The British had come through and burned his family's barn last year. Tom was looking forward to turning the tables."

"Did you feel any different after you left for your post?" Faith asked.

Sam colored. "Don't tell Sergeant, please."

"What happened?"

"I fell asleep." Shame covered his face. "I swear I felt fine when I took my post. I kept watch like I always do. The next thing I know, someone is shaking me awake. I don't know how long I slept." He faced the ground before looking up at Faith. "I came here because I promised to take him back to our cabin. I can't believe he's dead." His face contorted in grief. "What will I tell his ma? Our families live close to each other."

Walters placed a hand on his shoulder. "Tell her he served his country faithfully until his heavenly father took him home."

Sam sniffled as Walters led him away. Mary Porter looked at Faith. "The body needs to be removed."

Faith nodded. "I will call for some men to come in." Reaching down, she pulled the blanket over his face. Looking down at him was too painful. She swallowed a knot in her throat. After all the weeks at Valley Forge, one would think she would have gotten used to death. The sense of loss still stung. As she stepped toward the door, she spotted where the surgeon had left the bottle next to the bed. Picking it up, she stuck it into her pocket. Perhaps Jeremy knew someone who could check it for poison.

She watched as Mary Porter went to the medicine cabinet to check their supplies. Once again, the laudanum was out on the table where anyone could reach it. Someone called out for help. Moving quickly, Porter went to check on the patient, leaving the bottle out. Stealing it, even for a few moments, would be all too easy.

As enlisted men came and loaded the dead man into a litter, Will McKay came in and looked about the room until he saw her. He said nothing as the litter passed. They had all become used to death. Fevers had taken a toll, more than injuries from drills. Faith wondered what had brought him to the hospital. She didn't have long to wait.

"Have there been any unusual deaths lately? Someone who died who didn't seem all that ill?"

She pointed to the blanket-covered litter. "Tom came in with bruises and a few broken ribs. He was supposed to go back to his cabin this morning."

Will's eyes went to the litter. "What happened to him?"

"I don't know. He didn't wake up. When I went to check on him, he was dead." Suddenly, it became too much, and Faith ran out. She stopped just past the door, breathing deeply of the pine-scented air. She knew Will stood behind her. "He was fine the night before. He was playing cards and talking about his girl back home." She sniffled. "It's not right. He should still be alive."

"None of this is right," Will said, placing a hand on her shoulder.

The warmth of it comforted her. "I don't know what happened to him."

"Did he have anything to drink?"

Faith shot him a puzzled look. "Yes, he did." She fished the bottle out of her pocket. "He had this." She handed it to Will. When he pulled out the cork, she cautioned him. "It has a bitter aftertaste."

He shot her an incredulous look. "You tasted it?"

"Just a little. I wondered if something contaminated it."

"Did it not occur to you that if someone poisoned the bottle, it might kill you as well?

Faith shrugged. "It was just enough to dampen my finger. It didn't hurt me."

Will glared at her. "Some poisons take very little to have an effect. Never do that again." He walked with her back inside the hospital. A few loose strands of hair fell over his face, making him look a little like a friendly dog. Will absently tucked it behind his ear. His brow wrinkled in thought. "Mistress Porter said the laudanum was low."

Faith nodded. "It disappeared for a few minutes yesterday. I could not find it."

"Long enough to doctor a bottle of rum," Will said. He looked in the bottle. There wasn't much left. His eyes scanned the room, watching all that happened.

Dr. Walters stood near the medicine cabinet, crushing some herbs in a mortar and pestle. He frowned as he stared down into the bowl, checking on his work.

Will looked over at him. "How much laudanum would it take to kill a man?"

"Not much." Walters looked at the bottle. "If that started as a full bottle, spiked with a few spoonfuls of laudanum, it would do the job."

Will asked. "Did anyone see who gave it to him?"

Sam shook his head. "He had it when I arrived. He was already drinking it."

Will looked at Faith. She shook her head. "The hospital was busy yesterday.

Some men came in, exhibiting symptoms of fever. Lieutenant Commanders Laurens and Hamilton came in to take Jack Silver home. I was completing an inventory of our medical supplies as well. I saw nothing unusual.

"But you noticed the laudanum went missing."

She nodded. "One minute it was there. The next it wasn't."

Mary Porter interrupted. "A nurse could have been administering a dose to a patient. It is the best treatment for pain."

Will looked thoughtful. "So it could have been at a bedside in the room."

"Briefly," Porter acknowledged. "The nursing staff stays busy caring for the injured and ill in this camp." Her gaze flickered over Will. "I have living patients to attend to. If you have no further questions, Captain. I have work to do." She left without waiting for a response.

Faith shivered. Mary Porter disliked the assumption that someone had poisoned a patient of hers. She didn't blame her.

After Will left, Faith stripped the bed, piling the linen to go to the laundress with the next load. It didn't take long before another man was lying on the cot. Dr. Walters attended him. Mary Porter sent her to help another nurse change a bandage. Even though she knew she had done nothing wrong, she still felt Porter blamed her for the missing laudanum.

The day felt long. By the time she left, a dull headache throbbed behind her eyes. More than anything, she wanted a few moments to herself. As she approached the farmhouse, she could see Jeremy Butler with Will waiting alongside in front of the breezeway that separated the kitchen from the main house.

They had benefited from a recent shipment of clothing. The recent clothing shipment replaced their old uniforms, so their breeches were no longer tattered, and their jackets were clean and whole. Their jackets were dark blue with crimson facings, white vests underneath. Instead of boots, both men wore buckled shoes. Leather leg stocks covered their legs to the tops of their shoes.

Faith took time to admire them. "You are both looking well." She smiled as she let her gaze drift over Will until he blushed. The sun had turned his nose pink and brought out a sprinkling of freckles across his cheeks.

"General Washington expects us to look professional. He sent us to get new uniforms, along with the other officers."

Faith nodded approvingly. "You very much look the part." She headed to the front door.

Butler stepped in front of her. She shot him a curious glance. "I want you to tell me what happened in the hospital this morning."

"I told Will."

"Now tell me." His tone was mild, but he continued to block her way.

Faith repeated what she had said earlier. Butler waited until she finished before asking questions.

"Both Hamilton and Laurens came to get Silver?"

Faith nodded. "They were happy to see him. They joked back and forth as they waited for him to get dressed. Laurens helped him with his shoes."

"Did he now? Did Hamilton help with anything?"

"Not that I remember." Faith thought. "Wait. He went and got Silver's hat. It was on a shelf. We had all forgotten about it until Jack asked for it."

Butler nodded. "That was very helpful. Thank you, Faith. I hope your afternoon is far more pleasant." He stepped aside, letting her go.

As she mounted the steps, she heard Will say to him. "Surely you don't think-."

"I think nothing, but it's past time for Hamilton to explain himself."

Chapter Twenty-Eight

lexander Hamilton was difficult to find. He knew the man had to eat, so Butler planned accordingly. He rose well before the sun or the roosters. After kissing Hannah on top of the head, he dressed and slipped downstairs. No one stirred as he went out the door. The moon stood sentinel in the dark sky. An owl hooted in the pitch-black trees. It was also using the night to seek its prey. The hard earth crunched beneath his feet as he set off down the road with the stars for company. Only Hannah knew his plans. Rather than dining with his wife and Lafayette's men early, he slipped out before dawn to go where Washington stayed with his aides. By the time he reached the stone farmhouse, a faint glimmer of light gleamed in the east. Lady Washington blinked in surprise when she saw him as she descended the stairs.

"Major Butler, you are here early. Can I offer you breakfast?" Her shrewd blue eyes assessed his presence and the fact he lingered near the outside door, preventing anyone from leaving without his notice.

"That would be most kind, Lady Washington." Butler moved to allow her to go out to the kitchen to inform the Tills that there would be an extra mouth at the table. Upstairs, the scraping of furniture and sound of feet offered clear signs the house was waking. Soon, all the inhabitants would be downstairs to start the day, including his quarry.

Butler didn't have long to wait. Hamilton came down, followed by Laurens and Silver. Jack Silver had left the bandage off his head. A faint scrape was all that was visible of the injury that had laid him low. He smiled as he saw Butler.

"I thought you would want to spend your mornings with that pretty wife of yours."

Butler smiled. "Duty calls." He followed them into their office and helped move tables together for the morning meal. As the others arrived, he got a seat across from Hamilton and near the door.

After grace, Isaac Till began bringing in platters of ham and eggs. The scent of his wife's biscuits filled the air as the group broke bread. Hannah Till came in with a tray full of mugs of steaming coffee. Butler was more than happy to take a cup. Mornings were chilly, and he enjoyed a hot drink to chase away the cold.

People eyed him curiously. Most knew he didn't join them for the morning meal, although he had been there for dinner many times over the past few months. No one questioned his presence. There was little conversation this early as people prepared for the day.

Butler was content to eat and wait for his moment. As the meal drew to an end, Hamilton excused himself, saying he needed to work on more translations. Butler excused himself as well and followed Hamilton out.

"Your office is a dining area. It's going to be hard to find a place to work while people are eating," Butler noted as Hamilton headed for the door.

Hamilton shot him an irritated look. "That is why I have had to locate an alternate workspace. There is no time to waste. The drill manual must be ready to go to the printers in York within the next few days. Washington has ordered it to be distributed to his troops so they can prepare for the spring campaign."

Butler followed him out the door. "Does your new workspace require a horse to get there?"

Hamilton turned around to answer. "No, it does not, Major Butler. Although I don't see why this is your business. I have use of a section of space in a cabin of the Lifeguards. There I can work undisturbed, translating Baron von Steuben's words. I will meet with Laurens after dinner to compare notes. Now, if you do not mind, I have important work to complete." He turned and walked away at a rapid pace.

Butler picked up his pace as well until he was side by side with Hamilton, who shot him an angry look. "Our commander appreciates your diligence, I'm sure, but he didn't even know where you were when you conveniently appeared to help us with poor Silver after his attack."

Hamilton stopped. "What are you implying, Butler?" His icy tone matched his expression.

"I'm saying that you appeared right after someone attacked a man. Where did you come from, Lieutenant Commander Hamilton?"

"You do not have the authority to question me about anything, Major Butler. If you must know, I was about my commander's business."

"Washington did not know where you were," Butler repeated. He waited for a response. Soldiers passing by stared at the two men. They were attracting attention.

Hamilton noticed the stares. His face flushed. "Washington knew. He may not have remembered at the moment, but he knew I was taking care of some personal business."

Butler's eyebrows shot up as he waited for Hamilton to explain. The other man turned and walked away at a rapid pace. Butler broke into a trot to catch him. "You still haven't answered my question."

Hamilton whirled about. "Why do you need to know?"

"I'm trying to find a killer. One who's been terrorizing this encampment for weeks."

"Surely you cannot think I had anything to do with that." Hamilton stared at Butler, his outrage obvious.

"I haven't ruled out anyone. Tell me where you were." Butler stared back at the taller man, refusing to be intimidated. Overhead, a bird cried as it flew over them. They were a short distance from the cabins of the Lifeguards in a small clearing.

Across the fields, troops lined up to drill, preparing for the battles soon to come. The cried commands of their officers were indiscernible in the distance. A pale sun illuminated a clear blue sky, promising a beautiful spring day.

The two men stared at each other. Their duel of words so far had been a draw, with neither willing to yield. Hamilton glanced down. His breathing slowed as reason took over from injured pride. "I went to see a woman, a widow, who lives on the outskirts of the valley. She had been very kind and helpful, but I feared she was becoming attached. I went to speak with her to make sure she understood."

"That you had no plans to marry," Butler finished.

A frown wrinkled his brow as he looked away into the distance. "We will leave in a few weeks. I didn't want her to rest in any illusions that I planned to return."

"What's her name?"

Hamilton blinked. "You cannot mean to disturb her. She is a widow, sympathetic to our cause. Cannot you leave her in peace?"

Butler shook his head. "Once I've confirmed your whereabouts, I can move on to other officers."

"Officers? You think this killer is one of us?" He looked shocked.

"Who else can go all over this camp without being questioned?" Butler asked. "A unit and its duties bind an enlisted man. It leaves very little time to sneak about committing murder. The killer has some education. He wrote a poem detailing his plans. A good number of our men can't read. Some can barely write their own name."

Hamilton stood still, taking this in. A variety of expressions crossed his face: anger, doubt, worry, and exhaustion. "Go hunt your killer and leave me to work. There is more than enough responsibility for everyone here."

Butler didn't disagree. Once he had prized the name of his lady friend from his lips, he left him to his work. Heading over to the stables, he saddled Gracie for the brief trip to the farm where Alexander Hamilton had charmed a widow. The mare's ears perked up as they left the stable and set off at a steady trot across the green meadows toward the foothills of Mount Joy. From there, they forded Valley Forge Creek. Light dappled the water as they crossed, revealing the small current that threaded through the water, faintly muddy from the last rain. Rock peppered the edges of the stream while a few larger ones stood out from the bank.

It would have been an excellent day to fish. He could see a few trout darting in among some exposed tree roots. Unfortunately, duty called him elsewhere. Butler crossed to the other side. His was a different sort of fishing expedition. The sun was still in the eastern sky when he arrived. A calf was bawling at his mother when he rode into the yard. For a moment, he wondered why the commissary general hadn't claimed her herd. Then he realized Hamilton had undoubtedly not reported their presence. It was a sneaky move, but one he could appreciate. There were other ways to keep one's lady love happy, besides jewels.

A man exited the barn. He wore a broad-brimmed straw hat. Rolled-up shirtsleeves revealed his muscled forearms and a scattering of dark hair that matched the hair tied behind his head. Tension radiated as he walked toward Butler. Once he came close enough to see him, his posture relaxed. "Can I help you, sir?"

"I wanted to speak to the lady of the house,"

"That would be my sister Rosalyn. She's not here. She left yesterday to visit our grandparents in Berwyn. I'm not expecting her back for a while."

Butler took this in. "Did an officer come by here a few days ago? He may have visited here before."

The man's face darkened. "I know who you mean. Alexander Hamilton." He spat on the ground. "He came just long enough to upset her. I told him that if he showed his face again, I'd introduce him to my brown Bess."

Butler's eyebrows rose. "I take it there is no love lost between you."

The man looked at him. "I didn't touch him, if that's what you're implying. I told him to leave my sister alone. She lost her husband last spring. Hamilton paid her attention. But a man like that has no plans of committing to a countrywoman. His type has bigger plans. Once she realized that, she left. She's not returning until that camp has broken up and gone."

Butler nodded. He didn't disagree. "I hope her visit does her well. I'm sure as the weather continues to improve, the troops will leave. Since she is not here, I do not need to linger." Gracie turned with the lightest touch of the reins. "Let's get back, girl."

The mare circled back to the path that had brought them here. Sun filtered through the leaves just emerging from the trees, providing dappled shade on the well-worn path. Within minutes, they were heading back to camp.

The relaxing rhythm of her hooves cleared his head and provided time to think. Hamilton's story seemed to be true, but there was no way to tell how much time he took before he appeared on the road as they were aiding Silver. The ride itself took minutes. Hamilton had ample time to return, tie up his horse, and wait for Jack Silver to arrive. All he had to do afterward was ride out and return in time to discover the body. Or help take his victim to the hospital since he survived. Whether he was innocent remained to be seen.

Once he returned, Butler brushed Gracie and tended to her needs. She nickered softly as the brush stroked her sides. He smiled as he guided the comb over her neck and back, taking pleasure in her enjoyment. He took care of her legs and checked her feet, finishing up with her mane and tail, combing through the wind-blown tangles. Butler stroked her nose one last time. "I will see you later." She swished her tail as he went, seeking his quarry.

Hamilton's coming and goings had gone unnoticed by everyone in camp, including him. Butler knew little of him other than Washington trusted him implicitly. He appeared to be an elegant gentleman, well-educated, and versed in the social graces. It had startled him to discover his origins were far more humble, although Butler acknowledged that being a bastard did not automatically make one a killer as well. His past was his own business. What concerned him more was that Hamilton seemed to vanish regularly. Once he returned, he revealed nothing regarding his activities.

Butler looked into the office of the aides-de-camp. John Laurens was busy writing on a piece of parchment. Sunlight from the nearby window cast a golden light over him and his work. His quill made a steady scratching against the paper. Other than that, the only other sound was the periodic buzz of a fly. He remained focused on his task until Butler spoke.

"Where are your companions? Surely you are not working alone today?" Butler kept his tone light. His eyes swept the room, noting the absence of his compatriots.

Laurens finished his task and set his quill down before blowing on the sheet in front of him. "There is always plenty to do around here," he smiled up at Butler. "I presume you are looking for someone. Silver left a moment ago for the necessary. He should be back shortly. As for Hamilton, he was here. He dropped off a few sheets he'd translated and went to run an errand. I presume it's for General Washington. I'm not sure when he will return. As for Lafayette, he stays busy preparing his troops for the spring campaign. I imagine we will get the announcement to break camp any day now."

Butler nodded. He expected the same. He turned to go and then turned back. "Do you know if Hamilton is on horseback or on foot?"

Lauren's brow wrinkled as he thought. "Foot, I believe. I have heard no horses go by." His face bent over the parchment. "Forgive me, but I must return to this task. There is much to translate, and little time left to complete it."

Butler nodded. "Thanks." Being a suspicious man, he went to the stable anyway to see if any of the mounts were missing. He stopped to scratch Gracie's nose. She was a sweet girl, but too old to go to war. He had convinced Washington when he had shared that Hannah had told him that Gracie had been at her aunt's household for over twenty-five years. "No battles for you, girl," he whispered as he rubbed her velvety nose. She was going to Virginia with Hannah. Hopefully, both of them would be safe down south. Butler had received no information about a southern campaign by the British. He hoped Washington kept them busy enough to stay north. None of the horses was missing, which confirmed what Laurens had said. Butler left the barn and looked out across the pastures where men drilled. "Where are you?" he murmured. The killings described in the poem were not complete, which worried him. He hoped to stop whoever was committing them before it was.

Spotting the quarters of Washington's Lifeguards in the distance, Butler walked that way, wondering if Hamilton was there. It had not rained in the past few days, leaving the road dry as he walked down it. Rock and dirt crunched beneath his feet, stirring up a faint trail of dust. These cabins looked no different from those of enlisted men. Workers built all the cabins hastily to keep out the bitter cold of Pennsylvania winters. Now that spring arrived, they left the doors open to let in the breezes and freshen the rooms.

It didn't surprise Butler to find no one around. Von Steuben had spent weeks drilling the guards, and now he dispersed them throughout the camp to assist in training the other brigades at Valley Forge. He knew some were always near where Washington was to ensure no assassins came close enough to strike. The General knew full well that the British would welcome his death. He would not make it easy. Butler scanned the rows of cabins. He would have to check each one. Hamilton could be inside any of them, translating. If that was truly what he was doing.

The warmth of the sun hit his back through the wool of his coat as he emerged from a stand of trees that stood close to the line of cabins. It was good to feel warmth after all the months of cold. He rubbed the back of his neck absently. Strands were already escaping the leather strap he'd used to tie back his hair. Maybe Hannah would fix it for him after dinner. She did a far better job than he. "Hello!" he called out. No one answered. After waiting a few moments, he proceeded to the nearest one. He looked inside. Neatly made bunks lined the sides. Winter's chill hadn't ended, so logs lay ready in the unlit fireplace.

The next two cabins were much the same. The Lifeguard was at work, training troops and protecting Washington. His visit had been a waste of time. There was no point in continuing his search. Butler turned to leave when he heard a dull thump. "Hello? Who's there?" No one answered. Puzzled, he walked, listening. The clearing appeared deserted. A squirrel circled the trunk of a tree, ignoring Butler. It had other things on its mind. Its mouth was full as it darted up to wherever it was storing food, well beyond the reach of predators.

Butler turned when he heard leaves rustling in the trees, but could see nothing. A light breeze stirred them again. Satisfied that no one was sneaking up on him, he turned back toward the cabins. His ears caught a series of thumps once more. Butler did not know what it was, although the frantic noise unnerved him. He ran toward the sound, unsure of its source. "Who's there?" Butler's voice echoed against the wooden logs. No one answered.

Door to door, he ran, propelled by a sense of urgency. Something felt terribly wrong. His lungs burned from running. The last cabin stood apart from the others. A sapling leaned near one corner where the log ends extended out. When Butler went to open the door, it held fast. "Is anyone in there?"

Frantic thumps answered. Butler put his shoulder to the door, trying to force it. It didn't budge. The boards groaned and held fast. The thumping continued, followed by a drawn-out creaking as if something were being forced to bear an unexpected weight. "I'm coming!" Butler yelled. He slammed his shoulder into the door again, ignoring the jolt of pain it produced. Gathering his breath, Butler threw the full force of his weight against the door.

With an agonized shriek, it split. Butler fell inside, his knees and arm taking the brunt of the landing. Looking about wildly, he saw a figure sliding across the floor. His body dragged as he fought the force of whatever impelled him forward. The man clawed madly at his neck, which had a long red strip of cloth around it. On the other end, a rope dangled over a ceiling rafter. Attached to it, a large bag dangled too high above the floor for Butler to reach.

The man's boots thumped against the floor as he battled the weight. Butler ran past him and grabbed the rope. Grunting with the weight, he pulled back, trying to give the man on the floor enough slack to free himself.

The weight pulled against him, forcing him forward. Butler tried to find an edge to help keep him from going forward, but he continued to slide. If he could not break the rope, the man was going to die, strangled by the force of the weight on the other end.

He didn't dare let go to reach for a knife. Butler looked over at the man on the floor. Alexander Hamilton shot him an agonized look as he clawed at his neck. His face was turning purple as he struggled to breathe. Butler tried to yank the rope back, but it refused to yield. His back and shoulders ached with the strain. His mind raced to find a solution.

"Jeremy!" Will McKay's voice shouted from a distance.

"In here!" Butler bellowed. "Hurry!"

Outside, feet ran across the ground. Will came through the door. "My

God!" He ran and grabbed the rope and dug in, lending his strength to stop the rope's deadly advance.

"Hold fast while I cut it," Butler let go and grabbed for the knife he kept at his side. Will grunted as he struggled with the added force of the rope. Butler's fingers were numb from gripping the rope, making him fumble. He grasped the handle and began sawing through the rope. As he cut, the strands frayed until the last few ends ripped apart. The bag fell to the ground with a heavy thud that made the floorboard vibrate.

Butler, along with Will, ran over to where Hamilton lay. The men worked to find a loose end to release the cloth's deadly hold. Knotted tightly, the fabric refused to yield. Hamilton wheezed as he struggled to breathe.

"Hold on," Butler said. "I'm cutting the knot."

It had tightened into a tight ball, almost embedded in Hamilton's neck. Butler swore as he tried to find a place to insert his knife.

"Just cut through," Will urged.

"I don't want to cut his throat," Butler snarled as he sawed through the knot.

"You don't have time to be picky. He's dying. I'll hold him steady while you cut."

Butler nodded as he placed the blade against the base of the knot and began sawing through the thick wool scarf wrapped around Hamilton's throat. Flesh rose on either side where the fabric had embedded itself. Threads unraveled as he frantically cut through each strand of the knot.

Will unwrapped the blood-red scarf while Butler raised the man's head. Hamilton lay on the floor, taking in deep breaths. A faint whistle escaped his lips as he breathed in. His eyes remained closed as he lay still, taking in air.

"What happened?" Butler said. "How did you get this way?"

Hamilton tried to speak, but only a rasp came out. He took a deep breath and tried again. Will produced a flask and offered it to him. Hamilton took a swallow, choking as he did so. Amber liquid dribbled down his shirt and vest. He took a few more breaths. His voice was unintelligible.

"Try again," Butler leaned over him, straining to hear.

It sounded like a hiss. Agitated, Hamilton waved his arm about desperately.

Hamilton's rough breathing filled the room. The purple had faded from his face, leaving it ghostly white. He gestured again, writing with a finger in the air.

Butler focused on his movements. "Slower, man."

Hamilton shot him an irritated look and complied.

Will studied his motions. "The first letter is S. Is this about Silver?"

Hamilton nodded and turned toward Will. Again, he tried to speak.

"Are you saying you believe the same man attacked you as Jack Silver?"

Hamilton shook his head. His eyes flashed.

Realization dawned on Will's face. "That's not what he means." He looked at Hamilton. "Were you attacked by Jack Silver?"

Nodding, Hamilton lay back on the floor. His breath made a tortured sound as the air went in and out. Butler remained beside him, silent as he processed this information.

Will rose and took a few breaths himself. As he looked around, he spotted something hanging from a rafter. Curious, he left Butler to deal with Hamilton while he investigated. He first thought it a shaving mirror, then realized it wasn't. A chill went down his spine as he beheld a figure in an officer's uniform dangling in the air, a red strip of fabric wrapped tightly around its neck.

Chapter Twenty-Nine

Will's reaction was swift. Taking a knife from his sheath, Will chopped it loose, tossing the macabre figure on the floor near Hamilton.

Butler looked down at it and back at Will. "Another doll. I'm getting sick of seeing them."

Will looked down at Hamilton. "Maybe he can help us end this."

Hamilton opened his eyes and stared up at them. He rolled into a seated position and tried to rise. The first few times, he fell back. Will and Butler each grasped him under the arms and lifted him up. His chest heaved as he caught his breath. "Shhhhh."

"What? Try again," Butler urged.

"Shhibuh," Hamilton's voice was the barest whisper.

Will and Butler looked at each other before uttering the same thing. "Silver."

"Shibur," Hamilton repeated. He continued to take deep breaths, working to get air down his damaged throat. He staggered as he tried to walk. Butler caught him before he fell.

Butler looked at Hamilton. "You need to go to the hospital. You're lucky to be alive."

Will looked at him. "Then we need to find Jack Silver."

Hamilton protested. A raspy whisper emerged. "Work, I have work." He gestured at a pile of parchment scattered over the floor. An upended table lay on the floor. Next to it were candles, broken into pieces, and a shattered chair.

Butler eyed the mess thoughtfully before turning to Hamilton. "You put up a hell of a fight."

Hamilton reached for the parchment. His face whitened when he saw it smeared with ink. He tossed it aside before reaching for another. Wheezing, he struggled to gather the parchment before being stopped by Butler.

"We'll get it. Laurens can manage until you recover."

Hamilton shook his head and tried to rise. He would have fallen if not for Butler reaching out to steady him.

Will rolled his eyes. "We don't have time for this. He needs to go to the hospital, and we need to find our quarry before anyone else dies." Nervous energy consumed him. He was ready for the reign of terror to end.

Butler went to examine the mess. "Maybe there is a clue in all this." Ink puddled nearby, slowly leaking through a crack in the floorboards to the earth below. Spotting feathers, he squatted down to pick up a turkey feather, its end sharpened for writing. As he lifted it, the top half bent and fell back to the ground, the shaft broken beyond repair. Butler tossed it. Working slowly, he gathered the mass of paper. Ink splattered most of them. Some papers bore writing in Hamilton's elegant script. Other pieces were blank except for ink spots. Back against the wall, he spotted a sheaf of paper in von Steuben's cramped writing. It amazed him anyone could read it, much less translate it.

Gathering it into a pile, he took it to Hamilton. "We'll take it to headquarters after we drop you at the hospital. He stifled the other man's protests. "You can barely breathe, much less translate. Laurens can do it. You need to see a doctor now."

Hamilton wobbled so badly that Will and Butler supported him on either side as they walked to the hospital. His face was paler than paper, although his neck was a sea of rising bruises. Butler eyed him with worry. He hoped his throat wouldn't swell. He needed a poultice of some sort to ease the bruising. It wasn't his area of expertise, but he knew someone at the hospital would know. With any luck, Waldo would be there. He was the only one Butler trusted.

As they approached the hospital, shouts echoed across the clearing. "What now?" Will said as his eyes met Butler's.

The other man shook his head. Helping support Hamilton was hard work. He labored to put one foot in front of the other as they continued up the road to the hospital. As they came in sight of the sturdy log structure, they saw grim-faced sentries posted at the door.

"That's new," Will commented as they drew close.

One sentry hailed them. "What is your business?"

Butler gestured to Hamilton. "We're bringing in an injured man."

The soldier nodded. "Lieutenant Colonel Hamilton, my apologies, sir."

"Just let us in," Butler said. "We will go once we get him inside."

"What has happened?" Will said as they entered the building. Toward the back of the room, figures rushed back and forth. No one noticed their arrival.

"Look down," Butler said. Dark patches of blood stained the floor, some of it in shallow puddles and drops. A woman passed them with a bucket in hand. The water splashed as she poured it over the floor and entry before using a broom to sweep it outside. Broom straws scratched against the floor as she scrubbed the stains. The trail of blood led back to the surgery. Albigence Waldo's voice carried across the room.

"Hold him down. I need alcohol, needle, and thread. We have to stop the bleeding." Waldo bent over someone. His head turned to fire more orders at the nurses before returning to his patient.

Faith ran toward the table, bottle in one hand, strips of linen in the other. She handed them to Waldo, who continued bellowing orders as he worked. Two other men leaned over the table. Mary Porter, ghost white, assisted the doctor, handing him instruments. At the table, only the man's shoes and feet were visible.

Arms flapped before lying still. Mary Porter looked down. Tears streaked her face. Her rich contralto carried across the room as she crooned to the man on the table. The soft lullaby contrasted with the activity that surrounded her.

Butler led Hamilton to a cot and sat him down. The man's breathing was rough, as if the act of taking air in and out was a struggle. Deep red marks indented his neck, along with bloody marks from where he had clawed to free himself. Butler's eyes searched the room for a physician or nurse. Faith came over. She had swollen eyes, as if she had wept.

"What has happened?"

Faith swallowed. "Dr. Walters," she began. "He collapsed as he came inside. There was so much blood." Her hands shook as she swept stray hair from her face. "He'd been here all morning. Dr. Waldo had just arrived, so he left to eat and get some rest." Faith bit her lip, taking in a few deep breaths. "I was helping distribute a load of blankets that had just come in. We'd propped the door open for fresh air. I saw him enter. I didn't realize anything was wrong until he hit the floor." She shook her head. "Someone stabbed him all over his body."

"Dr. Waldo ran over when someone screamed. I grabbed a stack of linen to help staunch the blood. They took him to surgery immediately." She reached up to scrub tears off her face. Faith looked at Hamilton. "I can tend to these injuries. Let me gather some things."

Faith returned with a basin of steaming water. Floating in it was a plant with deep blue flowers and pointy leaves. Its sweet smell helped dissipate the scents of sweat, blood, and vinegar that permeated the air. Setting the basin down on a nearby table, she began unrolling a length of linen before laying it in the water. The bandage sank as the cloth became saturated. Faith left it there while she examined Hamilton's neck. Will helped him out of his jacket and neck cloth, freeing his throat so Faith could reach it.

"What is that?" Will asked, staring at the plant.

"Comfrey," Faith replied. "It will help with the bruising and relieve inflammation. Someone found it growing along the riverbank. I've used it before back home."

Will nodded. He was more concerned with what Jeremy Butler was doing. The man had left him with Hamilton while he roamed the room. He saw him chatting with nurses and patients. He returned after a few moments.

Hamilton lay on the bed, turning as Faith tended his wounds. Butler looked down at him before looking at Will. "We need to go."

Will nodded and walked with him to the door. He was relieved to leave.

Visiting the hospital reminded him of the cost of war. Too many young men died. He inhaled a few breaths of air as he stepped into the yard, relieved to smell the clean scents of pine and grass.

He was speechless when Butler handed him another doll, its clothing sticky with blood. Shuddering, he gave it back. "Where was this?"

"On the medicine cabinet, lying next to a scalpel."

Will shuddered. "When will this end?"

"We're ending it now," Butler said as he tucked the figure into a jacket pocket. "There is no time to waste." His walk turned into a swift trot as they hit the pathway that led to headquarters.

"Where are we going?" Will asked.

"Headquarters. It's where Silver is supposed to be."

Will raced after Butler. "How could it be him? We found him with his head bashed in. You saw it as well as me."

Butler kept moving. His words came in between breaths. "I never understood why someone attacked Silver and then killed another man nearly a mile away on the Valley Road. You would need a good horse to get from one place to another."

"Yes, you would."

Comprehension dawned. "Lafayette's horse."

Butler nodded. "He thought he'd killed Lafayette, so he took Ajax and rode to where he was within easy distance of the rifle pit. He left his horse in a discoverable location and waited for discovery.

Will whistled softly. "He hit himself with that rock? Good Lord Almighty."

"Prayer would be a good idea," Butler said. "Pray we can stop him before he encounters his next victim."

"And who might that be?" Will huffed. Butler might be shorter, but his speed was remarkable. Will was hard put to match his pace.

"Washington," Butler said as the stone house appeared in the distance.

Chapter Thirty

Nothing appeared amiss as they approached Washington's headquarters. No one lingered outside, either on the front stoop or by the breezeway that connected the kitchen to the main house. This time of day, troops were on patrol or drilling out in the fields. Everyone felt the urgent need to prepare for the battles ahead. War waited for no one. The absence of Washington's lifeguards puzzled Will. There should have been one or two around.

The steady chopping of an axe broke through the stillness. To the side of the house, Isaac Till worked to cut up wood for his wife's cooking fire. A small stack of split logs testified to his industry. Wood chips blew to either side as he worked. He acknowledged their presence with a nod before continuing his work.

Will swept the clearing with his eyes, wondering what to expect next. In the corral next to the stable, he heard the snort of a horse followed by restless hooves. Looking over his shoulder, he could see them trotting about, enjoying some freedom. He turned back to follow Butler up to the front stoop. Butler looked about; his eyes squinted against the bright morning light. He knocked on the sturdy wooden door. The sound reverberated in the empty yard. When no one answered, he twisted the knob and entered the house.

No one was in the main hallway. Upstairs, the muted sound of women's voices drifted down. Their chatter was a steady hum with no sign of distress. Butler strode down to Washington's office. No one guarded the door. He rapped the door firmly before letting himself inside. The room was unoccupied. An open window let a breeze enter. It ruffled a stack of papers on the Chippendale table in the center of the room where the Commander met with his generals. Someone had wisely weighted the papers down with a stoneware mug to prevent them from escaping.

Will noticed a map spread out beside the papers. As he leaned over it, he could see the pencil marks where someone had noted all potential crossings over the Delaware River into New Jersey. He wondered what Washington had in mind.

Butler looked out the window. "Where is he?" he growled as he paced the room.

Will looked over at him. "Why are you so sure it's Washington he's after? The General has always treated him well. He has no reason to harm him."

Butler's answer was swift. "It completes the poem.
So many dead and the killings not done.
How many must die before Washington's undone?"

Will swore. "What is it with the bloody thing? This makes little sense." He looked around the room, wondering if it held any clues to their Commander-in-Chief's location.

"None of it has ever made sense," Butler agreed. "Only in Silver's mind." He shook his head. "Washington has always treated his aides well. Some would say like sons. Why would someone betray a father figure?"

"Can I help you?" John Laurens stuck his head in from the hall. He had obviously been hard at work. Ink smudged the side of his nose and along his temple. His fingers also bore the mark of much time spent with a quill.

"Where's General Washington?" Butler asked.

Laurens blinked. "He went for a ride. Jack asked about him a short while ago, too. Has something happened?"

Butler drew in a sharp breath. "Jack Silver was here. How long ago?"

"Not half an hour," Laurens answered. "I've been hoping either he or Hamilton would return soon. There is much work to do before the drill book is ready."

"Hamilton is in the hospital. Silver tried to kill him."

Laurens looked startled. "Jack tried-"

"He's our killer," Butler said. "He's played us for fools all this time."

Laurens paled. "He was so adamant about my innocence. He visited me every day when I was under house arrest. I never dreamed it could be him. Why would he do such a thing?"

Will opened his mouth to speak, but Butler interrupted.

"Do you know where Washington went? It's important."

"I can't say for certain. Sometimes he likes to ride along the road, other times he goes along the river or through the paths in the forest." He brushed the hair back from his face, leaving another smudge. "I'm sorry. I'm not sure which way he went today."

Will followed Butler outside and to the stable.

"We'll cover ground more swiftly on horseback." Butler went to the corral and coaxed Gracie to come to him. Will grabbed the bridle of a dappled gray nearby.

"I don't know whose horse this is, but I hope he doesn't mind me borrowing him," Will said. He cinched a saddle to the animal, who regarded him with curious eyes.

He frowned as he looked at the remaining animals in the corral. "Isn't that Nelson?'

Butler nodded. "So it is. He must have taken Blueskin." Most everyone could recognize the big white horse Washington rode for reviews. He nodded at the animal Will saddled. "I think I've seen General Greene ride that one a few times." Butler finished adjusting stirrups on Gracie. "He should appreciate the effort you're making to save our general's life." He walked the little mare out into the yard. Will followed close behind.

As they mounted, one of the stable hands came running up. "Where do you think you're going?"

Butler looked down at him. "We're seeking General Washington on urgent business. Do you know where he went?"

The hand looked at him. "It must be pretty urgent to send two different messengers." He frowned at them. "I'll tell you what I told the other officer. The commander took Blueskin for a run. That big white looks pretty, but he's skittish under fire. He can really run, though. Washington went towards the river to give him a workout." The man paused. "He looked like he had a lot on his mind. I suspect he wanted some time to himself, even if one of the guards insisted on accompanying him."

Butler leaned down. "Who accompanied him?"

"I don't know everyone's name. He wore the uniform of a Lifeguard. He took Nellie, the big bay, and went with him down the road. They were talking about looking at the ford."

"Fatland Ford?"

The hand nodded. "That's the one. General Greene uses it to bring in supplies. I haven't heard about any wagons coming in. All the recent rain slowed down the supply trains."

Butler thanked him. Together, they took off down the road. They galloped, kicking up dust in their wake. Butler slowed to a trot before long. "We can't exhaust the horses. It's over a mile to the ford. I was hoping to catch up, but I think they've gone too far ahead."

"Do you think Silver has caught Washington?"

"I hope not." Butler scanned the road ahead. No other riders were visible. Every plant was leafing out, making it difficult to see through the brush.

A mosquito buzzed close to Will's neck. He slapped at it with one hand as he looked about, hoping to see signs of his commander or the man he had once considered a loyal compatriot.

Before long, they turned north toward the Schuylkill River. The road showed signs of heavy use by wagons and loads of cattle. They slowed to avoid the holes that might catch a horse's foot and cause injury. Will looked to see if there was a clear path off the road, but there were too many trees.

"They've been this way," Butler said.

"How do you know?"

"Look down."

Will's eyes dropped to the ground. Fresh horse droppings lay in the center of the road. Flies buzzed over the pile, swarming over the steaming mound. His nose wrinkled as he carefully walked his horse around it. "They can't be too far ahead."

Butler nodded. He edged his mount to the side where the road was smoother. "Let's hope so." He encouraged Gracie to pick up the pace. A clearing opened that led to the cabins of Sullivan's Brigade. A sharp whinny caught their attention. Butler stopped and looked into the clearing. Trees surrounded the entrance, casting sharp shadows left from the direction of the sun. Butler looked puzzled. "They've been on patrol across the river. They've been gone since yesterday morning," Clucking to Gracie, he turned into the clearing. Will followed.

Sun filtered through the trees, dappling the ground and the nearby rooftops. The air was fragrant with the scent of pine and other plants. Overhead, a hawk circled, making a sharp cry as it hunted.

"Hello," Butler called. No one answered. He walked his horse in, one hand drifted back to the holstered pistol he carried. No one appeared. The cabins stood empty. No smoke billowed up through the chimneys.'

"Look," Will called out. He pointed to another horse pile on the ground. A snort carried from a short distance away. Will whistled, hoping the animal would respond.

A whinny rang out, followed by the steady beat of hooves. A medium-sized bay trotted over to them, reins dragging the ground. Will dismounted and went over to the animal. "She looks like someone was riding her." He checked the saddle as the horse nickered. Her feet danced anxiously. "How did you get here?" Will stroked the mare's nose. He looked at Butler, who remained mounted.

"She's not hurt. She seems antsy, though."

Butler frowned. "She didn't get here by herself. Somewhere there's a rider missing his mount."

"It's not Washington. He took Blueskin." Everyone recognized the big white horse, even Will. They also knew his reputation. He was a magnificent animal unless there were loud noises, which was why their commander avoided taking him into battle. Nelson was far more reliable.

A shot rang out close by. Butler swore as he looked for the source.

"Look behind that cabin." Will pointed to where a faint puff of smoke drifted around the side. Picking up the reins of the stray horse, he mounted and followed Butler to the source of the sound.

Butler slowed as he spotted two men just outside the tangle of trees that sloped down toward the river; one on a splendid white horse that danced nervously over the ground. The other rider watched as Washington worked to calm his steed.

"Have a hard time controlling your beast?" Silver said. "Such a shame. He's a beautiful creature. No wonder you avoid taking him into battle."

Washington settled his mount. "Blueskin is not a war horse. He would be out of place there. Not only that, but his coat would make a target for whoever rode him."

"I can see that," Silver said, studying the two of them. "But then you are always the center of attention, aren't you–General Washington? My father likened you to Moses, leading his people to freedom. Perhaps I should say the man who called himself my father, but you already knew the truth, didn't you?" His smile didn't match the darkness in his eyes.

Washington stiffened. "I've known your father for many years. We never discussed personal matters. I know he was very proud of you. He wrote to me when you received your scholarship to King's College. I wrote to him when you joined my staff."

Silver's eyes flickered. "Was he? He had little to say when I last saw him, just before we entered the Valley of the Forge."

Washington nodded. "You had received word of your mother's illness. She died just after your arrival home. I regret I could not attend the memorial."

"She left me a letter, you know." Silver paused. "She wanted to absolve herself of any blame." He laughed sharply. "Imagine my surprise when I read she was actually my grandmother. Sarah, my older sister, gave me life." He shook his head. "She tried to deny it, but then she told me I looked just like him, a gentleman from Virginia, who she met while attending school in Baltimore."

Washington's face remained stoic. "I never knew your sister, Jack. She had gone to school when I first met your family. We never met. Your father and I exchanged letters because we held like views on the state of the colonies. I didn't meet you until you joined the Sons of Liberty."

Jack Silver shook his head. "Is that what you want me to believe? Papa's toughness with me, even as a child, made me wonder why. He spent years trying to train the stain of my birth out of me. I worked so hard learning Greek and Latin and French. I wanted my father to be proud of me." His bitter laugh ended in a sob.

Washington looked at him, over the pistol in his hand. On the ground lay another pistol, its barrel still smoking. "I'm sure he is. You have been an asset to my staff since your arrival." He gestured to the ground near a tangle of bushes. A man lay on the ground, not moving. "Henry did nothing to deserve your wrath."

"He laughed at me," Silver snapped. "He saw I had misbuttoned my vest and made fun of it. I outrank him! He had no right!"

Washington nodded, never taking his eyes off the pistol. "You must have been furious."

Silver shrugged. "It doesn't matter anymore. It's all about to end." He lifted the pistol.

"What about the others?" Butler asked. "Why kill them?"

Silver looked over at him. "You're a nosy little man, always poking around in someone else's business. It has been incredibly difficult to avoid you."

"To answer your question, they were disrespectful, so they got what they deserved." He looked sad for a moment. "Dr. Waldo confirmed what I discovered in New York. I have the Great Pox. It's going to kill me if I don't go blind and mad first." He offered a mocking grin. "The woman who bore me passed it down to me. Her lover gave it to her. At first, my family was certain I had escaped it, but when I reached adulthood, it became clear I had not." He shook his head. "I thought it was smallpox at first, when I got the first rash. Unfortunately, no." He sighed. "It keeps getting worse. I knew then I would need to seek my vengeance sooner rather than later." He looked at Washington. "All I wanted was your respect, some validation before I passed, but you were always too busy. Too busy fighting the British, too ambitious to own up to your own mistakes." He laughed. "Does Lady Washington know? I bet she doesn't. She brought you immense wealth and land. What did you bring her?"

Washington's voice was mild. "I'm sorry to hear of your troubles, Jack, but

I'm not your father." He looked at his aide-de-camp. "You have suffered a great deal, but it is time for this to end. Put down the gun. I promise you will receive the care you need."

Silver stared at him for a long moment. "I want to believe you. You are more respected than anyone. Being your son was my dearest wish. Perhaps it's better that I am not." He raised the pistol and pointed it at Washington's heart. "Goodbye, George Washington. There has been none like you, nor will there be ever again."

A roar from a pistol rang out. Blueskin reared in panic, neighing as Washington fought to stay in the saddle. Will watched the pistol drop from Silver's hand, and he turned and looked at the other men.

Smoke billowed out from a gun in Butler's hand.

"You bastard," Silver said. Blood dripped down, covering his hand. "You'll never catch me." Kicking his horse's side, he galloped off into the woods, just missing being hit by the hooves of the panicking white horse.

"Don't sit there," Washington roared. "Get him!" He continued to fight his horse for control.

Butler took a wide berth around the agitated animal before taking the path in the woods. Within moments, they passed from sight. Dropping the reins of the riderless horse, Will followed. A murder of crows startled into the air as they raced past, shrieking their dismay. He ducked to avoid a low-hanging limb and hoped Butler had done the same. At one point, a tree split the path. Will coaxed his mount around it, taking it slow over the uneven ground. He lost sight of Jeremy Butler. Both he and their quarry were deep in the woods. A branch slapped him before he avoided it. Will slowed down as the terrain became hillier and tangled with brush. He wasn't sure his mount would make it through. He hoped those two idiots ahead of him didn't get thrown into the thick brush. Negotiating through the forest required monitoring a trail which was not made for horse traffic.

He stopped to look ahead, trying to determine which way to go. The snort of a horse told him that one of them was not far away. He hoped it was Butler. Will wasn't sure what he would do if confronted by a madman. Unlike Butler, he didn't have a pistol, and he was pretty sure that Silver's bayonet was longer than his.

Gracie's gray coat appeared through a break in the trees. Butler had lost his hat but looked otherwise intact. He startled before he recognized Will. "It's about time you showed up."

Will shot him a look. "There's a lot of undergrowth and low hanging limbs.'"

"It's not too bad," Butler noted. "I passed underneath most of them."

"That's because you're short."

Butler shot him a look. "I'm not that short."

A shot rang out, knocking down a tree branch between them. Both men ducked and looked around, trying to see through the trees. Silver's horse appeared on a rise, silhouetted by the afternoon sun. Beams of which shone on his musket barrel. As they watched, it fell from his hand down into the bushes. Maniacal laughter rang out. "You got lucky that time." More laughter rang out. Soon, the pounding of hooves replaced it.

"How did he do that with an injured arm?" Will marveled.

"He can't reload on horseback with an injured arm," Butler said. "We can catch him."

"Don't forget, he still has a blade," Will said as he followed.

"I'm not going to." Butler took the lead, following Silver's direction.

They broke out into a small clearing. Will would have gone forward, but Butler raised an arm, signaling him to hang back.

"Let's see what's out there,' He said as he scanned the area. Except for a few squirrels that raced around a tree trunk, the clearing appeared empty. As they moved ahead, Will heard a whinny in the distance.

"That way," Butler pointed north. The ground slanted downward as they approached the banks of the river. Light reflected off the water as it raced downstream.

Will heard the river churning over the sound of horses' hooves. The Schuylkill had swollen with all the recent rain. He had heard drovers complaining about it in camp. The Quarter Master, General Greene, had fretted about getting supplies across, worrying that the rising waters would cover the narrow island of land that formed the ford.

The muddy river roared as they drew close. Silver's horse danced as he rode along the bank, seeking a place to cross.

"Fatland Ford is underwater," Butler called out. "You will not make it to Sullivan's Bridge. It's well guarded, and Washington is undoubtedly already there to warn them. One thing to know about Blueskin: he's one of the fastest horses in the colonies."

Silver turned toward him. "Is that so? Interesting. I wondered why Washington kept such a high-strung beast." He urged his own horse toward the water. The animal balked, refusing to enter. Its eyes rolled as it backed away. Silver kicked its sides, trying to force it to cross. The horse reared, dumping its rider and taking off as fast as it could go.

Will let it pass, judging it would slow down once it got over its fright. Silver picked himself up and faced the two mounted men. His right arm dripped blood. Will, judging from the angle of his wrist, suspected a break.

Silver's eyes darted back and forth like a cornered animal. He drew his saber with his uninjured arm, holding it between them. He bared his teeth in a predatory smile. "You're not taking me." The blade blazed in the reflected light of the sun.

"There's nowhere to go," Butler said. "Surrender."

Silver shook his head. "I'm not hanging." He looked at them and then at the muddy waters of the Schuylkill. "I'll take my chances with fate." Backing a few steps, he ran forward and jumped into the water, swimming out until the swiftly churning current caught him and carried him away.

Butler left his horse and ran to the bank.

Will dismounted. He reached him on the edge of the bank and grabbed his arm. "Don't be a fool! You have Hannah to think of and your child." He looked at Silver's head bobbing in the water. A wave washed over it before he completely disappeared.

Butler stared after him, breathing hard. "Why would he do such a thing?"

"He knew he was going to die. At least we know he won't kill anyone else." Will looked down at the ground. Silver's saber lay in the mud where he had dropped it before leaping into the current.

Butler reached down and picked it up. "This should go to Washington. He will know what to do with it. There's no way he could survive that."

Will stared at the relentless brown waters. "We can hope." As he turned to check their horses. Silver's mount stood nearby, its reins dragging in the mud. Clicking his tongue, Will went toward the animal. It snorted but didn't move away. Grasping the reins, he spoke to it in a gentle voice. "It's alright. We'll get you back to camp and into a comfortable stall." The animal stood still as Will crooned. As he went to lead it back to the other animals, he spotted something sticking out of a saddlebag. A doll stuck out, dressed in the uniform of a Patriot general.

Butler stared at it before snatching it out of the pack. Cocking his arm back, he threw it out into the river, letting the current carry it away. "It ends here."

Will agreed. "It is over." He cast a look at Butler. "Let's get back to camp. We have people waiting for us."

"Yes, we do. Those we love and who dare to love us in return are more precious than gold." Together, they turned back to their horses. He glanced at Will. "It's time you spoke to Faith."

Will stared back at him, speechless.

"Close your mouth, take a few deep breaths, and ask her to marry you. You've known her how long, four years? Don't you think it's about time?" Jeremy Butler laughed and slapped him on the back. "Find what happiness you can before we leave this place."

"Perhaps it is time," Will said as he caught his breath. "Perhaps it is."

Chapter Thirty-One

Faith picked at her dress anxiously. It wasn't even hers originally. Someone had remade it from one of Lady Washington's gowns. She stood while Lady Sterling arranged a lace fichu over her chest. It had appeared earlier that morning as the women discussed what would be appropriate for the ceremony. Caty Greene pinned a painted enamel brooch onto the fichu to hold it in place.

"You can borrow this for the ceremony," she whispered. Her eyes sparkled. "All is ready downstairs. The men are in their places. Nathaniel has made sure their uniforms are all in order. He just brought in the minister a few moments ago."

Faith nodded. She was too nervous to speak. Being the center of so much attention was both gratifying and unnerving. Hannah shot her an understanding smile. It had not been all that long since she had been a bride. She reached out and squeezed her sister's hand.

"All will be well." Faith nodded, although her heart continued to pound. A wave of dizziness fell over her.

"Breathe," Hannah hissed. "You don't want to faint now." She squeezed her hand hard.

Faith took a few deep breaths, and the faint feeling left.

Her sister looked at her. "Everything else is under control." Her expression gentled. "All you feel right now is perfectly normal."

"Did you feel all these nerves? I didn't think I would after my first marriage."

Hannah nodded. "I did, but all my fears left once Jeremy and I were together. It will be the same for you and Will." Her face shadowed with regret. "I wish you two had more time before he leaves, but at least you will have these few days to celebrate your union."

Faith nodded. The thought of Will leaving to fight the British unnerved her. She swallowed and smiled as she said yet another silent prayer for his safety. Shivers went down her spine as Hannah slipped out to check on the preparations downstairs.

Lady Washington came over to inspect Faith's appearance. The women had pooled their resources to ensure she had all she needed for her wedding. Lucy Knox fussed with her hair. Faith winced as she felt another tug. Finally, she ceased. Faith blinked away the tears that burned in her eyes.

"I guess that will do." Lucy stood back. "You look lovely." She smiled at her. "All will be well."

Faith wanted to sigh with relief, but her stays hampered her ability to exhale. Her face flushed. "Thank you."

Lucy smiled. "It will be a memorable occasion. Lady Washington has been hard at work decorating. She found ingredients for a cake. I don't know when we last had something to celebrate. It's the best way to end our time here."

Faith nodded. Her head was spinning with all that was happening. She hadn't expected Will's proposal, much less that word of her acceptance would spread throughout the camp like a wildfire.

Once Lady Washington had heard the news, she insisted that the wedding had to take place at Valley Forge. "It is the perfect time." She looked around. "There are many preparations to be made in the next few days. I will request the pastor of the local church perform the ceremony. I'm sure we can make everything ready within the week."

Faith had been speechless. She had not expected to wed so soon. Soon, the joy of the occasion swept her away. Now they had a future to plan; one that would last far beyond the brutal realities of war. Throughout the encampment, people celebrated the news of the upcoming nuptials. Will complained that so many people slapped him on the back, he feared a cracked rib.

The seamstress measured and fitted Faith for her gown, taking all her time. The farmhouse hummed with activity as Lady Washington found food and musicians for dances. She had worried about all the frivolity when they were preparing for war, but Lady Washington stopped her.

"After all these months of deprivation, everyone needs something to celebrate. Let us share this occasion so that we can have this day of happiness to remember in the times ahead."

There was no stopping Lady Washington once she had determined a course of action. In the days before the wedding, she moved the aides-de-camp out of their office. Extra staff joined the Tills in the kitchen. The farmhouse overflowed with people and goods coming into the house. General Washington met the disruption with amused tolerance, deferring to his wife while he and his generals kept to his office to complete preparations for leaving camp. Faith became used to hearing musicians practicing outside as she went back and forth.

Faith found herself in the center of a hurricane of events. There were dances, games, and a lot of drinking. It was as if the sun had come out after a long bout of rain. She wondered how the men could drill after spending so many nights up drinking and dancing.

Henry Knox arranged for a display of cannon fire. He claimed it was to show his men's skill, but she had seen the twinkle in his eyes when he had looked at Will and Faith. All of this led up to the current day, her wedding day.

Hannah entered the room. Her smile deepened as she gazed at her younger sister.

"How are you doing?" Faith asked. They had had little time to speak in the past few days. The other ladies left the room to allow the sisters to talk.

"I'm well." Her gaze darkened. "I don't know how to feel about going to the Virginia colony. I've never been there, and Jeremy must stay with Washington."

Faith nodded. They both worried about sending their men to war. "You will like it there," she said. "It's away from the war. It will be a safe place for you and the babe."

Hannah nodded. "I will be glad to get out of this valley. Staying here doesn't do Jeremy a lot of good. He hasn't slept well in days."

No one spoke of Jack Silver. Washington had sent men to search the riverbanks along with members of the Oneida. No one had turned up a trace of him. But sometimes Faith wondered. Searchers had not found his body. Whether his corpse had traveled far beyond camp, or he had somehow survived, no one knew. She hoped he was gone. It still frightened her to think he had been among them for so long and yet no one had realized what he was doing.

Martha Washington bustled in. Her plump figure looked elegant in a blue gown that matched her eyes. A lace-covered cap fit neatly over her high combed hair, which appeared pure white, although whether it was nature or artifice, Faith was unsure. Her eyes met Faith's. "It's time, dear. Your guests await you."

Faith swallowed. Downstairs, Will waited for her. With him, she had a promise of a future that she could not have foreseen a few years ago. Hannah met her eyes. Her expression said that she understood what she did not say. She preceded her sister to the stairs. As Faith went down, she saw a sea of faces looking up at her.

The ceremony went by in a haze of nerves and excitement. Faith repeated the vows as her heart pounded in her chest. Will smiled at her. The warmth of his hand in hers grounded her. Her nerves settled as they turned as one to face the crowd of people gathered to wish them well.

The celebration continued. For three days, people danced, feasted, and gamed throughout the encampment. While the continual celebration exhausted her, Faith dreaded its end. Washington had already announced that camp was breaking up at the end of the week. The men would march out while the women would travel back to their respective homes.

Faith was not ready to leave Will. Their time together had been too short. She looked across the dinner table at him. As he turned to catch her glance, his face broke into a smile.

Butler laughed when he saw them staring at each other before being elbowed by his own wife. He cocked an eye at her. "What? Can we not jest about these two making eyes at each other? It isn't as if we don't know what they're thinking."

Hannah blushed. "I know what's on your mind. Perhaps you need to see the laundress to clean up."

"I'm not sure Rose has anything for that," Faith said. Her brow wrinkled. "I finally realize why she seems familiar. It could be the hair, but she reminds me of Athena's sons. She could be their sister."

Jeremy Butler looked at her at the mention of his sometime partner in spying, who had remained in Williamsburg. "She had a daughter. Her name was Rose."

"That's an interesting coincidence, that they bear the same name," Faith said.

Butler rose from the table and headed to the doorway. The other three stared at him in confusion. He paused as Hannah reached out to put a hand on his arm.

"Perhaps not," Butler said. "Someone sold Rosie when she was barely a teenager. Athena has never given up looking for her." He turned toward the doorway. "I have to go. If this is her daughter, I need to know. Athena deserves that."

The others joined him. Outside, the sun had just started its turn west. Bright light illuminated the lush green fields. Dandelions sprinkled spots of bright yellow in the meadows. A pair of meadowlarks danced above the waving grass.

The path of those trailing the army grew familiar around Valley Forge after months of use. News spread that the camp would soon disband. Empty spaces replaced the former tent sites. People were getting ready to leave.

Butler ducked around people, focused as a bird dog on its prey. As he cut away from the village and down to the creek, he broke away from the group, hurrying to the laundress's campsite. Faith and the others lost him in the trees. When they caught up, Jeremy Butler stood in the clearing.

The creek gurgled nearby. Butler stared at the deserted space. Holes remained from where posts had pulled up after being driven into the ground to hold up canvas. The stumps and logs used by the laundress stood surrounded by grass yellowed by the various agents she had used to clean. Wheel ruts dug into the ground. They followed the remains of an old road that led toward the Gulph Road and out of camp.

"Where did she go?" Faith asked, puzzled. "It's not yet time to break camp."

"Some units have already gone," Will replied. "They have further to go and petitioned to begin their journey as soon as the weather moderated. I'm guessing she belonged to one of them."

Faith responded. "She once told me she had come up with one of the North Carolina regiments."

Butler looked around. "Some of those regiments headed out earlier this week." He searched the horizon as if he could summon a view of the laundress in the distance. "She's gone. I don't know what to tell Athena."

Hannah took his hand. "You can't tell her what you do not know. False hope is cruel."

Butler sighed. "I wish I had taken time to speak to her. I confess I had not thought about her in some time." He looked at Faith. "I don't remember her face well, but I believe she looked like her brothers. They all had that reddish hair and Athena's eyes." He shook his head. "It would mean the world for Athena to see her daughter again."

"We know she travels with a North Carolina Regiment," Faith said. "Could you encounter her again?"

"Maybe," Butler said. "It depends where they go to fight. In this war, we travel. The regiments split and reunite. We do not know for sure if she is Athena's daughter."

Faith walked around the abandoned campsite. Very little remained. Rosie had taken all the tools of her trade. As she moved, her eyes glimpsed something on the ground. A slender object glimmered in the dust, catching the light of the sun as it filtered its way through the trees that crowded against the bank. Her fingers brushed away the dirt to reveal a strand of seed pearls. The pearls had a small wooden cross strung among them. Curious, she lifted the delicate strand to the light to see it better.

"What do you have?" Butler asked as he walked toward her.

She turned to where he could see it stretched between her fingers. "Seed pearls," she said. "I don't know where they came from."

Butler took the necklace and held it in the palm of his hand. "Ireland," he breathed. "I would know that cross anywhere. My father made it. It was my mother's last treasure sewn into the hem of her gown. She gave it to me before she died. She feared the sailors would search her body when she died."

"They didn't search you?" Will asked. He'd had his own experiences with sailors.

"They did, but not where I had it," Butler replied. He ran the string through his fingers before handing it to Hannah.

Will decided not to ask with the ladies present.

Hannah looked at him. "If this was your mother's, how did it get here?" She cupped it in her hand as she gazed at him.

"I gave it to Athena one Christmas when I was but a lad. When I was first indentured, she took me in. The man who bought me owned her. She's the only reason I survived those years." A smile crossed his face. "She must have passed it to Rose. I'm amazed she held onto it. Generosity is not a trait of slave owners."

"She said she was free," Faith interjected. "She was adamant that no one owned her."

Butler nodded. "She's her mother's child. Rose must have freed herself." He looked down the wheel rutted path as if hoping to see her wagon in the distance. "She was here all this time, and I never knew."

"We found her once. We can find her again," Hannah said. "You have contacts throughout the colonies. I have faith that it can happen."

He studied the pearls in her hand, his face unreadable. "The odds are against it. Troops will move all over the colonies. There is no telling where she went."

Will looked at him. "She was with the 1st North Carolina when she came here. We can start there." He joined the other three. "Between the four of us, we can bring her home."

"Maybe within a few short months, we all can be free to go home." Faith's voice sounded like a prayer in the clearing's stillness.

A Note from the Author

Valley Forge was a turning point in the Revolutionary War. When Washington withdrew his army there, they had endured a series of defeats at the hands of the British. When they emerged, they were a force to be reckoned with. It was a miracle that anyone survived, given the poor sanitation, lack of supplies, and cold weather. But the majority did, forged into a fighting unit by their determination to survive, and the arrival of Baron von Steuben, who used his experiences in Europe to mold the men into soldiers. Walking through the reconstructed cabins, reading the personal accounts, and taking in the diagrams of the events was illuminating. As far as I know, there were no serial killers ravaging the encampment. While my story is a work of fiction, it is rooted in a setting of historic fact.

Acknowledgments

No one writes in a vacuum. Writing a historical novel requires research in order to discover the relevant facts. I want to thank the staff and interpreters a Valley Forge National Historic Park. Being able to go there and learn about the experiences of those encamped them in 1778 made an indelible impression on me. The National Park Service does an incredible job in preserving and interpreting these monuments. I also want to express my heartfelt thanks to my husband, Bill, and Aunt Barbara, my first line of defense in editing. They keep me from repeating myself and ensure my commas and periods are where they belong.

About the Author

Julie Bates' first novel, *Cry of the Innocent*, premiered in June 2021. She lives in North Carolina with her husband, son, a pack of huskies, and a few cats. She loves a good cup of coffee and a stack of books by her side. When not sweeping up dog hair, she enjoys knitting and painting. Her family has grown tolerant of the collection of books on poisons and crime that are intermingled with the cookbooks on her bookshelf. She is a member of Sisters in Crime, Triangle Sisters in Crime, Mystery Writers of America, Southeastern Mystery Writers of America (SEMWA), and The Historical Novel Society.

Also by Julie Bates

Cry of the Innocent

A Taste of Betrayal

Rise to Rebellion

No Greater Loss